A DEFIANT DEVOTION

E.B. NEAL

Cover Art by
MYA SARACHO

ALSO BY E.B. NEAL

A Truth Universally Acknowledged

*For those who have loved
a lady pirate.*

FOREWORD

When it comes to historical accuracy in fiction, it is impossible to please everyone. However, I believe that when writing in a particular era, certain fixtures, figures, and details should be included to preserve a degree of authenticity. To this end, I have adhered to historical accuracy where it serves the story, and set it aside where it does not. These choices were made with deliberation and care, and to the end of guaranteeing a better fate for the characters of this narrative, a fate that may not have always been available to their historical counterparts.

A playlist to accompany this story can be found on my Instagram.

CHARACTERS

THE KNIGHT HOUSEHOLD
  Mr. Richard Knight
  Mrs. Edwina Knight
  Lucas Knight, their eldest son
  Thomas Knight, their second son
  Brandon Knight, their third son
  Katherine Knight, their youngest and only daughter
  Mr. Graves, the butler
  Rita, the lady's maid

THE JOHNSON HOUSEHOLD
  Maximus Johnson, the Earl of Alwyn
  Anneke Johnson, Lady Alwyn
  Sophia Johnson, their second daughter
  Rebecca Johnson, their youngest daughter

CHARACTERS

THE GENTLEMEN
    Mr. John Ransom
    Mr. August Heath
    Lord Oswalt

THE LADIES
    Lady Charlotte Prince
    Miss Rosaline Bailey
    Lady Gertrude Cawdor, eldest Johnson daughter

SPRING 1812

❧　I　❦

The clock chimed a quarter past the hour, and Katherine shot it a glare. Soft peals, cheerful as the bright morning air, echoed across the empty parlor, emphasizing the audacity of her presence. She wobbled slightly on her toes, and the intricate scrollwork of the door grazed the shell of her ear.

Eavesdropping, it seemed, was a precarious business.

Katherine put a hand to the wall, righted herself, and ignored her aching feet. A ballerina she was not, but some things were worth the sacrifice.

"—poor old Toady's got himself into quite the mess, don't you think? Caught with his hand in his—"

"You know Sal's had his number for months now." Her brother's voice was strange like this, oddly muffled and tinny. "He'll make a handsome packet off the—"

Katherine wobbled again and swallowed a curse as the keyhole slid shut. This confounded door! She took a steadying breath, wiggled her toes, and reached for the escutcheon. Her touch, light and dainty as a fairy's, gently slid the piece of metal upwards, leaving the keyhole bare. Why it had to be nearly six feet off the ground was beyond her. This was the only door in their Mayfair house with such a feature, and the inconvenience felt almost personal.

"—at least two thousand."

"But it is not enough, not for—"

Her brother and his guest turned away from the door, toward the fireplace. Most unhelpful. Katherine strained to catch their conversation, her mind churning with possibilities.

A sudden chuckle, and a slap to the shoulder. "If only his words were as quick as his fists. Then he might have a chance of—"

Boxing? She knew there had been a fight on the books, at one of Lucas' regular haunts in the East End, but what did that have to do with—?

A rueful sigh. "I must be going, old chap, Mother expects me—"

Lucas laughed. "Ah, yes, and one cannot disappoint Mother—"

Boots, echoing on the wooden floor, then muffled by the rug. Katherine moved before she was aware of it, darting away from the door and flinging herself across the nearest couch, landing with a muted *thud.* She assumed a posture of practiced lassitude just as the office door swung open and two gentlemen stepped into the parlor.

Lucas grinned when he saw her. "Fine day for it, Kitten."

"Lounging is a lost art, dear brother." She arched an eyebrow at his companion. "Percy."

"Kat." He smiled without warmth. His blond eyebrows were practically translucent in the late morning sun. "You've aged."

"And you've neglected to develop a set of manners."

"Now, children, play nice," said Lucas. "Percy, Graves will see you out."

Percy nodded. "Supper at the club?"

"Of course."

Once Percy was gone, closing the parlor door behind him,

Katherine looked at her brother. "Father would not be pleased to find you using his office without his permission."

Lucas gave a snort and sat down on top of her legs, ignoring her grunt of protest. Katherine wiggled and kicked, bracing one of her feet against his arm, but he did not react. "What Father does not know won't hurt him."

"Bold of you," said Katherine, still trying to free her other leg, which was beginning to go numb, "to take my complicity as a given."

"Bold or wise, Kitten?" Somehow, Lucas sank even more of his weight onto her foot.

"What are you doing," she said, "taking supper at the club? You heard what Father said last night, and racking up bills at the White Fox is hardly—"

Lucas rolled his eyes. "I cannot bankrupt us in a single evening."

Now it was Katherine's turn to snort. "If ever there was a champion—"

"Is this how you plan to spend the entire season?" Her brother cocked his head to one side. "Needling me?"

"There are far worse occupations." She flopped back into the cushions. "Lucas, I shall soon find myself without a foot."

"Your presentation at court cannot come quickly enough," he replied. "Distraction will suit you, I think. And it will spare the rest of us your meddling."

Katherine scowled at him. "Distraction? More like torture."

"Melodrama, however, does *not* suit you." Now, finally, he stood up, leaving her foot a tangle of pins and needles. "Mother is ecstatic."

Katherine did not dignify this with a response.

"And perhaps a few more dancing lessons would do you some good." Lucas flashed her a hint of his grin. "Your step is heavier than you think."

"I cannot understand your meaning."

"The floor in this room has sunken, Kat." Lucas gestured to the office. "There is a spare inch between the boards and the edge of the door. I saw your shadow."

Once again, Katherine chose silence, but she could not help the heat that rose in her face. Her throat burned with the truth of it all.

"You did not miss much." Lucas took an idle path across the room, his body a broad and noble line of swagger. "Scandal is thin on the ground, today."

"Two thousand," she said. "Two thousand what?"

"Pounds, dear sister." Again, that flash of a smile. "A loan. Or, rather, part of one. Toady hasn't paid his interest, and certain parties are looking to collect."

Katherine raised an eyebrow. "Sounds dangerous."

"Only if he turns out to be even more of a fool than he seems." Lucas paused by the door. "Where are Tom and Bran?"

"Garden." Katherine slouched back into the cushions. "They are fencing."

"Oh, how dreadful. I think I shall join them."

Once Lucas was gone, the air in the room seemed to thicken with an awareness of its own quiet. Since the family rarely used this parlor, the servants had not bothered to open any of the windows, let alone the curtains, and the room was bathed in a plush, lilac glow. Katherine looked around at the weathered furniture and the dust motes in the fleeting sunbeam, and could not remember the last time she'd taken tea here, or done anything here besides linger at the threshold of her father's office.

The light was dim, but would suffice. She reached into her bodice, plucked out a thin sheaf of paper, and unearthed a dull pencil from her slipper. It took her a moment to unfold and flip through her papers, until she found a blank space to suit her needs. Then she began to write, and the soft, scratching sound of her art filled the air.

3 May 1812

Nitwit & Lucas in F's office — disc. Toady (sp?) found in comprom. pos. (unclear), £2000 — loan?

Sal involved, intentions unclear

Mention "fists" — boxing? Boxing match?

A soft *snick* shot through the silence — the parlor door, opening. "There you are."

Katherine did not look up. "Is Mother looking for me?"

"Of course." Rita, Katherine's lady's maid, approached the couch, arms crossed against her chest. The muted light dulled her sharp features and the thin, feathery wrinkles in her face. "She seems to be under the impression that you are avoiding her."

Katherine slouched even lower into the cushions. "I cannot imagine why."

Rita sighed. "Who was it, then?"

"Percy," Katherine replied. "His social graces leave much to be desired."

"That is hardly surprising." Rita looked at Katherine's notes. "But did he bring news?"

"Nothing interesting." Katherine rested her pencil against her lip, frowning at her own scribbles. "Perhaps I am missing something."

"He has not been in town much longer than you, Kat. That is a short window for scandal indeed, and Percy has always been a dull gentleman."

Katherine met Rita's gaze. "No news out of his household, then?"

Rita shook her head. "His staff does not tend to gossip. Either he pays them a handsome wage, or he is as tiresome as he seems."

"How disappointing." Katherine folded up her pages and slid

them back into her bodice, then tucked her pencil into her slipper. "I suppose it is time I faced my fate."

Rita offered her a smile, radiating sympathy and amusement in equal measure. "Your mother is in her chambers."

"Of course she is. With a pile of dresses, no doubt."

"Come, now. There are worse things than a debut."

"I doubt that," Katherine replied, heading for the door. "I doubt that entirely."

THE KNIGHT FAMILY HOME SAT A GOOD DOZEN FEET TALLER than any other house in Mayfair, and gave its occupants the feeling of sitting in a crows' nest, or perhaps at the top of a teasing cliff. A cacophony of blues and grays dulled the obscene playfulness of the architecture, which was a study in tilting windows, hallways to nowhere, and a few misplaced staircases. From the servants' quarters on the top floor, one could see clear into Hyde Park; from Lucas' bedroom, a view of Buckingham Palace. When moving from one portion of the house to another, Katherine felt as though she were shifting between places, airs, and lives, caught between the framework of the city. Her own shadow would reach in one direction, even as she moved in another.

The house had belonged to the Knights for several generations, inherited from some faceless and quizzical great aunt or second cousin, someone with a penchant for the eccentric. For many years, Katherine had suspected that the house had never once been in 'new' condition — rather, that it had begun to crack and fall apart the moment the paint had dried. Each year, each visit, seemed to unearth new repairs, new oddities. Katherine's father often joked that the Mayfair house was his most costly investment, and far needier than any of his children.

It was a bit of a gamble, arriving at the house every season.

Sometimes Katherine wondered if there would be a house left at all, or if their carriage would come to a halt before a pile of bricks and crumbled plaster. Years before, the Knight children had made a game out of it — running through the dusty, muffled halls and cataloging what had fallen apart during the family's absence. Whoever had the good fortune to tally the highest number of repairs was entitled to first pick from the biscuit tray for a whole week, a prize as coveted as currency in the Knight household.

On more than one occasion, Katherine had wondered whether the Mayfair house kept its own crooked sentience. If it weathered and peeled out of sheer spite. The thought occurred again to her now, as she looked at a thin, spindling crack edging its way beneath the crown molding. Like ivy, or a spider's web.

"Kitten looked rather splendid in her gowns today." Mrs. Knight glowed in her seat at the end of the dining table. "A proper young lady."

Brandon snorted into his wine. "How disgusting."

"Yes, Mother," said Thomas, "you're putting us off our venison."

"Now, boys," said their father. His low, reedy voice slid along the dining table with its usual gentle irony. "As inconvenient as it may be, your sister is a young woman, which means that she is expected to fulfill certain obligations. Many of those occasions will be public, and require your attendance. I highly recommend you practice speaking of her in a respectful manner here at home, to best prepare yourselves for the inevitable shock of having to do so in front of others."

Katherine smiled. "I do hate to be such a burden, Father. Perhaps it would be better for us all if I did not debut."

He smiled at her in return. "A sporting effort, Kitten, but I'm afraid we have already paid for the gowns."

A chuckle went around the table. All of Katherine's gowns were second-hand, inherited from her vast array of female cousins.

"Think of your sons, Father," said Katherine. "Acting against their nature, for such a protracted period, is sure to affect their health—"

"We shall catch fever," said Thomas, with a grim nod. "And a persistent tremor—"

"Lumps," Brandon chimed in. "Lumps everywhere, even on our—"

"Boys!" Mrs. Knight was doing a poor job of concealing her smile. "Mind your manners."

Thomas gave a low groan, and affected a quaking tremor in his left arm. "You see, Mother, already it has started—" He slumped over his plate, knocking his knife and fork onto the table.

Both Katherine and Brandon leapt to attention, their napkins falling to the floor. "Quick," said Brandon, climbing up onto his chair, "check his pulse—"

Katherine grabbed her inert brother, shoving her fingers against his throat, ignoring the way he choked in protest. "His pulse is weak, Bran, very weak—"

"We must act quickly!" Brandon clambered across the table, narrowly avoiding the tureen of mashed potatoes. Two seats down, Mrs. Knight sighed. "Soon he will be paralyzed!"

"Tom? Tom?" Katherine tugged at him until she got him to slump backwards over his seat, his tongue lolling, his eyes rolling, his arm still shaking like a newborn fawn. She bit back a laugh and put her palm to his forehead. "He's burning up, Bran, hotter than the sun—"

"Heavens!" Bran put on a very serious face and knelt beside Thomas' plate, grabbing his brother's shoulder. "There is nothing for it, Kat, you know what we must do—"

"Of course, there is but one option." Katherine held up Thomas' knife, which was caked in gravy. "Amputation."

"Children," intoned Mr. Knight, reaching for his wine, "no surgery at the dinner table."

"Or without liquor to dull the pain," said Thomas, still staring into space with a slack jaw. "Father, please pass the whiskey."

"It is only an arm, Tommy." Bran took the knife from Katherine, the blade flashing in the candlelight, and held it above his brother's elbow. "You'll hardly feel a pinch."

"Yes, and the new one will grow back within a day," said Katherine. "A day, Tom!"

Thomas gave a great shudder. "Oh dear— I fear the condition is progressing—"

"You see, Mother?" Brandon rounded on Mrs. Knight, the tablecloth tangling under his knee. "You see what you have done?"

She shrugged. "Even if Thomas forfeits his arm, he must attend the Opening Ball. We are all expected — the young ladies cannot be expected to dance alone."

"Bran," said Mr. Knight. "Your venison is getting cold."

Brandon rolled his eyes and stood up, his free hand pushing a shock of dark hair out of his face. From Katherine's vantage point, he looked like a giant. "Kat is the one debuting, not us. I don't see why Tom and I have to be involved."

"Ah," said Mr. Knight. "But you would throw Lucas to the wolves?"

"Lucas is the eldest," said Brandon, as if it were the answer to every question in the history of the world.

"And the prettiest," said Thomas, coming out of his slump and wiping a smear of potato off his hand. "You should present *him* to court, instead of Kat."

"I can already imagine it." Katherine smiled. "I have the perfect dress to complement his figure. And the Queen would be terribly impressed by his high arches."

"You would not tease so freely if he were here," Mrs. Knight pointed out.

"Can you blame us for seizing upon the opportunity?" Katherine said, raising an eyebrow. She returned to her seat, tugging her skirts into place. "When it comes to his ego, Lucas is little more than a tyrant."

"As befits the son of a middling gentleman," said Mr. Knight.

"Richard!" Mrs. Knight's voice was full of reproach. Katherine hid her smile with a mouthful of spinach and potatoes.

"You indulge him and toy with us," Thomas said to Mr. Knight, reaching for his wine glass. "Is it any wonder we don't wish to participate in this charade?"

" 'Charade' is perhaps an exaggeration, Tom." Mr. Knight took a neat bite of venison. It was meaty, succulent, a fresh kill from their own estate. "Katherine is of age, which means that she must be presented."

Brandon snorted. "Sold at a meat market, you mean. Flashed about until she secures an appropriately wealthy husband."

"If she likes, yes." Mr. Knight cleared his throat, and Katherine watched the way he did not look at her.

Heat, unbidden and unruly, rose in her chest, turning her meal to lead. For all its jest, Brandon's comment was a little too honest. His words echoed around the cutlery and melted the present circumstances, replacing them with a tableau that was practically identical — the dinner table, Katherine and her siblings caged by their parents, the same venison roast steaming at the center of the table. Supper, the previous night, when Mr. Knight had looked up from his plate and spoken.

"Children." A simple call for attention, but full of such warmth and compassion. "I'll not mince words. The business is struggling, and we must tighten our belts considerably. I understand that London has always provided a wide array of diversions for this family, and I do want you to enjoy yourselves. Enjoy, but not indulge." He wiped his mouth and took his glass of wine in hand. "Restraint, perhaps, is to be the motto of the season."

Thomas had frowned. "Then why come to town at all? If we remained at Mosswood, perhaps we could be of some aid, Father."

"Your point, Tom, is a salient one. But matters are not so

simple." This was the moment that Mr. Knight had met his only daughter's gaze, and a silent, though ragged, understanding, had passed between them. "Kat is expected at court."

A simple sentence, yet full of such meaning. Katherine's father had been delaying her presentation for two years now; at eighteen, she was already ancient for a debutante. Any further stalling would only be seen as an insult to the Crown, an insult that the family could not afford, let alone entertain, even for the sake of fortifying their income.

And now, in this endless moment, as recollection and reality blurred in Katherine's eyes, she could hear everything that remained unsaid. That as a woman of reasonable intellect, some ability, and pretty, if plain, features, she embodied the Knight family's best hope of securing some sort of income. Income, and her family's salvation, in the form of a husband.

But no one would dare say it. To say it, to acknowledge the anxiety that hung over the family like a thundercloud, would undermine Richard Knight's determined and unshakeable nonchalance. Richard Knight had never been one to worry, and he would not begin to do so now.

"As far as meat markets go," said Thomas now, "it is a diverting one."

Brandon climbed down from the table and returned to his seat. "You are quite fanciful, brother. Blinded, perhaps, by the prospect of young ladies draped in feathers and finery."

"If that were true," said Mrs. Knight, gently tugging the tablecloth back into place, "Thomas might be the one to secure a match, not Kat."

Everyone laughed, even Katherine. And as the conversation shifted, turning on a steady and unfaltering axis, the moment of awkward and unacknowledged honesty faded, replaced by yet another warm evening full of laughter and wit.

THE CANDLES HAD BURNED LOW WHEN A SOFT KNOCK CAME AT Katherine's bedroom door. She looked up from her journal and watched as Rita slipped into the room.

"I heard about supper." Rita approached her slowly, and the gentle, orange candlelight shone against the sympathy in her gaze. "Seems that Bran was in a gaming mood."

"When is he not?" Katherine put down her pencil, slouching in her seat. "At least he did not put his shoe in the potatoes."

"Small blessings." Rita's hand went to Katherine's hair, which was falling out of its neat twist. "You look tired."

"Do I?" A soft noise of derision slid out of Katherine's nose, and she looked down at her own scribbles. "It was a long day, I suppose."

"You will need your rest, I think. To look your best for the Queen."

"Sleep can only aid so much, Rita."

A tug of the hairpin, and Katherine's hair fell in thin waves, spilling down her back. Longer than she'd worn it in years, grown out specifically for this season. It tickled the back of her neck and caught in the neckline of her gown, pooling at the small of her spine. She avoided her own reflection, cutting her gaze away from the mirror above her dressing table; she hated her long hair, and had to fight the urge to yank at it, to pull until she came undone.

For several ceaseless minutes, neither of them spoke. Katherine let herself be undressed and slipped into a night-gown. She let herself feel the cold bite of the water as it slid down her face, settling in the crease of her mouth, the hollow of her jaw. The pitcher, heavy and smooth in her hands, seemed to ache with the promise of the following day, and she wondered, for a fleeting moment, what it would be like to throw the pitcher across the room, to scream and to sob like a heroine who wasn't a heroine at all, but rather an object of torment and pity.

If Rita guessed at the nature of Katherine's whirling thoughts, she hid it well. Silence reigned as she stood behind Katherine, parted her hair, and began to brush.

A hundred strokes. The echo of Mrs. Knight, half a dozen years younger, stern and playful all at once, seemed to linger behind Katherine's shoulder. *A hundred strokes, every morning and every evening. A young lady's hair is her crowning glory.*

Pity, Katherine thought now, rolling her pencil between her fingers. *Pity it is not an actual crown. Perhaps, then, I would have some peace.*

"Seems you had a busy day."

A moment passed as Katherine worked to understand Rita's remark. Then her gaze snagged on her journal, on the rows of neat, regular writing. "Really?" She turned the page. "Middling, to tell the truth."

Rita gave a soft chuckle. "Sometimes, Kat, I wonder at the secrets you keep in those pages."

"It is hardly more than the stuff of gossip. A distraction, an occupation." Katherine had to work to keep disdain out of her voice. "It has only a fleeting value."

"Ah," said Rita, twisting Katherine's hair into a long, flat braid. "But a value nonetheless." She gave one of the strands a gentle tug. "You know, sometimes I think you are wealthier than half of London."

Katherine smiled then, and met Rita's gaze in the mirror. "You jest."

"I do not." Rita's own mouth twitched into a smirk. "Knowledge is power."

"For men, maybe." Katherine sighed. "For women, it is danger."

Rita tutted, and tied Katherine's braid with her favorite red ribbon. "Try to sleep, my dear." Her hand stroked a brief, feathery line across Katherine's head. "Try to calm that spinning mind."

"I will."

Later, when Katherine lay beneath her sheets, blanketed in

the false darkness of the London night, she listened to her own heartbeat. It was a steady, slow thump, soft in the back of her mind, and as she stared up at the canopy, her eyes tracing the embroidery she could not see, all she could hope for was a different bed, a different house, a different life. For a different night, a different day.

Any day would do.

 ❧　2　❧

Summer had begun, yes, but there was a chill underfoot. A cold seep from the mud, curling between the leaves and blades of grass, persistent as a cough. It snaked up from the ground, reaching for Katherine's toes, and she tucked her feet beneath her body, wrapping her blanket more tightly around her shoulders.

The air fizzed with the promise of dawn. It was near, but waiting, as if tensed for a signal. Katherine looked around, at the trees and the flowerbeds and the rosebush that had gone rather wild, noting what had changed over the winter. She could almost imagine this very scene, barren and lifeless, half-buried beneath the snow. She could see the holly, smell the mistletoe and mulled wine, taste the bitter promise of ice.

She never was one for summer.

"And what foul shade is this?"

Katherine looked up as Lucas approached. He moved through the garden with a stumbling fluidity, and his collar sat wrinkled and ajar. Still in his cups, then, and fresh from some party or other. "Good morrow, dear brother."

He hummed, pushing a hand through his disastrous hair. The

strands flopped against his forehead, coiled with sweat. "Couldn't sleep?"

Katherine sighed, and her stomach flipped. "No."

"I'm not surprised." He sat down beside her, and the bench swung lazily on its chains, the bough above them creaking with reproach. "But there are worse things, Kitten."

"Don't call me Kitten," she said, more out of habit than anything. Her eye caught the stubble on his jaw, the tired crease of his eyes. "Go on then, Lucas. Tell me what is worse than an audience with the Queen."

"Breaking in a new pair of boots, probably." Lucas leaned into her, jostling her with his shoulder. He smelled of wine and sweat and dirt. "Wet powder in a rifle."

She smiled. "Strawberries without cream."

"Mutton, with no gravy."

"Trousers, missing a button."

"How was supper?"

Katherine shook her head. "You were missed."

"Of course I was."

"Brandon..." The air seemed to tense. "He does not understand why I must debut. He knows it to be a farce, a masquerade. A means to an end."

"Brandon is soft." Wine had always heightened Lucas' lack of patience.

"He has a point, Lucas."

"There is never a point," he replied, dismissive. "Not in matters of the court. One does as one must do."

"But this isn't a simple matter of the court," Katherine said. "And I am sick of Father pretending it is so."

"We are all sick of things, Kat. Chief among them our own obligations."

She looked at him, looked at the line of her brother's nose. And she noted something she had not seen before. "Lucas," she said, "that savors most terribly of bitterness."

"Does it?" He huffed, a sardonic smirk sliding into place. "Temper your imagination, Kitten. It was just an observation."

Katherine watched him for another moment, trying, without success, to catch another glimpse of what she had seen in his face.

"Brandon is soft," Lucas said again, but with a duller edge. "He cares for you, and knows that you care little for matters of the heart, even less for marriage. He does not wish to see you suffer." He met her gaze, just for a moment, his eyes like pitch in the cloudy air. "And that is a sentiment I can understand, Kitten."

The corner of her mouth twitched. "Don't call me Kitten."

"You know," he said, in a lofty tone, "we seem to make a habit of this. Conferences in the garden, out of earshot from the house."

"Less a habit of conferring," Katherine replied, "and more a habit of my catching you in the act of indulgence."

"Not quite in the act," Lucas corrected her. "Dear God, never that."

"Don't be vile."

"There is no other way to be." He lurched forward, getting to his feet. The bench drifted in his absence, and Lucas reached for the chain, attempting to steady it. "Breakfast?"

And there it was — dawn, splitting through the leaves like a yawn. Katherine watched the yellow trickle through the gray, lightening the air and bringing the scent of dew. "Not for another hour, at least." She stood up, and the new light offered a fresh perspective of her brother's appearance. "Lucas, did you climb the back wall?"

"Yes," he said, glancing down at the streaks of filth across his trousers. "Graves neglected to leave the key in the gate. I must say, I have to have a word with Father about the state of that wall. The brick is nearly purple with moss."

"But it offers such a splendid accessory to your outfit." Katherine reached out and plucked a clump of said moss from his curls. "It suits you."

Lucas rolled his eyes and stepped towards the house, which sat quiet and blue behind the trees. "I'll change before breakfast."

"Not enough, I should think."

"Fiend." He almost smiled, then turned away, walking up the garden. His tread was steady, in spite of his indulgence, and his shoulders stooped with fatigue.

And Katherine realized then what she had seen flicker, like a bolt of lightning, across Lucas' face. It was fear.

⁂

"Two kings," said Katherine.

"No." Thomas held the cards aloft. "King and a jack."

Katherine frowned at her reflection. "Damn."

"Katherine!" Mrs. Knight shot her a warning glance. "Less of that language, if you please!" She swatted at Thomas' leg. "Boys, you should leave your sister alone."

Brandon yawned from behind his book. He lay like a spaniel on the chaise. "First, you demand that we participate in this nonsense. Now, you demand that we get out of sight. Which is it to be?"

"I meant," said Mrs. Knight, pained, "that you participate in the *social* events. And not in—"

"Primping and pampering?" said Thomas. Katherine watched in the mirror as he took a swig from his glass of Scotch and, with his free hand, reached for the deck of cards. "And honestly, Mother, we all know that tempering Katherine's language is a Herculean task."

"Sisyphean," said Katherine.

"I dislike you most immensely," he replied, then held up two cards, a silent question.

"Queen and a two."

Thomas checked, his eyebrows flickering. "Well done."

"Drink," said Brandon. Both he and Thomas took a swig from their glasses.

Katherine bit back a grin as Mrs. Knight flushed red. Rita stifled a chuckle while she pinned a section of Katherine's hair.

"Kat," said Brandon, looking at her over the edge of his book. "What have you done to your face?"

Katherine snorted, letting her smile surface. "You just noticed?"

"It is *rouge*," said Mrs. Knight. She bustled over to Katherine's dressing table, casting a critical eye, thumbing Katherine's cheek. Her touch was plush, chilly. "It suits her, does it not?"

Brandon was frowning. "She looks feverish."

"Yes, Mother." Thomas flicked the queen and the two onto Katherine's sofa. "Our sister appears to be in the throes of some mysterious illness. Perhaps my ailment is catching."

"*Honestly.*" Mrs. Knight ignored her sons' sniggering and turned another critical eye over her daughter. Katherine met her gaze in the mirror, and the moment held, tight as a piano string, before the corner of Mrs. Knight's mouth twitched and Katherine snorted.

"Oh, dear." Mrs. Knight leaned down, pushing the curve of her thumb across Katherine's cheek. "Perhaps it is a tad strong."

"A tad?" Katherine managed. "Mother, I look—"

"Stop!" Mrs. Knight trembled, her eyes glowing as she fought back a laugh. She rubbed at Katherine's cheek. "Never compare yourself in an unfavorable manner, my dear—"

"Oh, Lord." Katherine gave a sigh and sank back into her chair, giving up all pretenses of posture and comportment. "This will be a disaster."

"Nonsense." Mrs. Knight rubbed and nudged at Katherine's cheeks, doing all that she could to remove the rouge. A glance in the mirror revealed that she was unsuccessful. "You will be lovely, and the Queen will be..." A few moments passed before she settled on an apt descriptor. "Charmed."

Rita made an inelegant noise in the back of her throat. "Only if she's wearing a blindfold."

Katherine bit back a giggle as alarm, true alarm, flashed across her mother's face. "Oh," said Mrs. Knight, scrubbing more vigorously — Katherine winced — "surely we can make her—"

A knock sounded at the door, followed by Graves' low voice. "The carriage, ma'am."

Mrs. Knight straightened up, and Katherine watched her mother school her expression into something bright and determined. Nerves, unbidden and unwarranted, pooled in Katherine's stomach, and suddenly, she wished she'd managed to eat more than a bit of toast at breakfast.

And there. Hovering before her, trapped in the unbreakable silver of the mirror, was her reflection. Katherine stared at herself, at a creature familiar and unfamiliar, a creature suspended in a moment that, she feared, would never end.

Katherine hardly ever wore her hair like this, twisted and pulled into itself, curled atop the crown of her head into a bun so sensible it made her want to scream. Rita, with a touch both gentle and sweet, had woven a few thin white ribbons between the strands. They glowed against the dark chestnut of Katherine's hair, and she fought the urge to bring a hand to her head, just to confirm that what she saw was real.

Below her hairline, she met her own gaze. Her deep hazel irises gave little away, as did the thin, wide line of her mouth. *A beggar's mouth*, her grandmother had once said, on the tail end of a cruel cackle. There, her chin, with its half-buried cleft, and her cheeks, now stained a deep red. She could see Thomas' point — under ordinary circumstances, she would look deranged. But here, under the soft, clear sunshine streaming in through the window, she looked caught unawares, somehow, as if stuck with one foot out the door, on the threshold of something quizzical and new.

Katherine blinked — her eyelashes, which she had never considered or thought of once in her entire life, seemed darker, fluffier, striking against the line of her brows and russet of her face.

Oh Lord, she thought. *I look like—*

"Quickly, Katherine." Mrs. Knight ducked in front of the mirror, sparing a moment to tidy her own hair and straighten the sleeves of her gown. She was dressed in her finest, and that, suddenly, more than anything, showed Katherine the weight of the situation. Edwina Knight, wearing silk, looking like a lady, even if she wouldn't be seeing the Queen. "We mustn't be late."

"Oh, yes," simpered Thomas. His glass was empty, and he flung a few more cards into the air. "How dare we impose upon Her Majesty's time—"

"Hush, you!" Mrs. Knight fixed him with a fiery look, undermined by the curve of her mouth. "We'll have none of that mouth at the Opening Ball."

"Never." Thomas gave her a weary salute. "Wouldn't dream of it."

"I'll handle him," said Brandon, from behind his book. "He'll behave."

"And dance with the ladies?" pressed Mrs. Knight. Behind her, Rita grinned.

"God, yes," Thomas replied. "But only once I've had another drink."

"Steady on," said Mrs. Knight, a touch grim. "The night is long." She turned to Katherine. "Ready?"

Katherine took a breath, then got to her feet. The floor seemed to shift beneath her, a slight but unmistakable adjustment. It seemed to promise a change, a change beyond the twists in her hair and the crimson of her face — something tangible, something fundamental. She rocked back onto her heels, met her mother's gaze, and nodded.

"Yes," she said. "I am."

❧

NECESSITY, IT SEEMED, HAD CRAMMED ALL THE ELIGIBLE YOUNG ladies of London into a chamber the size of a butler's pantry.

"Ah." Mr. Knight turned his gaze about the room, scanning the sea of faces and tulle and feathers. His ruffled, unkempt hair stuck out like a boil against smooth skin — beside all the other fathers, he looked—

Katherine pinned down that thought and held firm as it struggled, then disintegrated. *No,* she told herself. *No, you shall not think of him in such a way. You shall not become someone so completely obsessed with their own appearance, with the appearance of their family, that you give in to cruelty.*

"Goodness." Mr. Knight, a touch helpless, bobbed to one side in an attempt to dodge an enormous feather. "It reminds one of a zoo."

"Courage, Father." But even to her own ears, Katherine sounded grim. "It is hardly a battlefield."

"On the contrary." He ducked down, his forehead level with her nose. "We appear to be on the defensive."

Katherine swallowed a giggle, and quite suddenly, the strange reality of the moment sank in. Here they all were, clustered like a bunch of chickens, trapped between the decadent walls of a gilded palace. The small room reeked of perspiration and perfume and anxiety, and a strange fog seemed to emanate from the crowd of people — a fog of heat, of scent, of dense moisture. Katherine felt as if she could smell what everyone had had for breakfast, the rouge that countless mothers and maids had patted onto waiting cheeks, the feet squeezed into ill-fitting shoes. She could smell skin and cloth and fear, and she fought off an abrupt shiver, her gaze fixed on what little she could see of the closed double doors. The doors that, if rumors were to be believed, were the gateway to her fate.

Mr. Knight straightened, tugging at his jacket — he must have been sweltering. Like her, he was watching the doors. "They are taking their time."

Katherine glanced behind them, at the enormous windows that made up the wall opposite, through which sunlight poured like a blade. Like everyone else in the room, she was beginning to perspire — her dress clung to the small of her back, and her hairline was growing damp. "A window," she said, gathering her skirts. "We need to open a window—"

She moved before her father could stop her, and pushed past the people clustered behind them. Ignoring muffled complaints and squeaks of surprise, Katherine burrowed across the room, using her elbows in the manner Brandon had always described as "dastardly." A few moments later, she stumbled to a halt before the windows, catching herself on the curtain rope and nearly running into—

"Ah." Katherine looked at the woman standing before her. "I see we had the same idea."

The corner of the woman's mouth twitched. She was a touch taller than Katherine, and about her age — Katherine's gaze lingered on her thin, bare hands, then on her dark eyes. She had never seen this woman before, but it seemed that this woman, too, was at her limit. Her arms were stretched overhead, grasping for something Katherine could not see. "There is a latch above," the woman said. "But it is far beyond my reach."

"How helpful." Katherine stepped closer to her and looked up, following her gaze along the muntins. This close, she could see the black hair curling at the nape of the woman's neck, wild and frizzy, and the sheen of her deep brown skin. The woman was dressed in lilac silk, and the color gave her complexion a wonderful, warm glow. She smelled oddly metallic, oaky — a scent so dazzling and puzzling, that for a moment, Katherine quite forgot where she was.

"It is no use," said the woman, shaking her head. "Without a ladder, we cannot open it."

"We could ask a footman," Katherine replied, glancing around for a helpful wig with shiny black shoes, but none appeared.

The woman gave a light snort. "They are all in the throne room, at least until the festivities begin."

"Well, then." Katherine met the woman's gaze. "Give me your hands."

Her eyebrow quirked, and something sparkled in her eyes. "I beg your pardon?"

"Like this." A horrid wave of heat rose to Katherine's face, but she ignored it, and held her own gloved hands out before her, palms up, fingers interwoven.

"Ah!" The woman glanced around them. "Quickly—"

It happened so fast that Katherine was hardly aware of her own body. Between one moment and the next, the woman knelt, her hands cupped before her in a silent offering. Before she could doubt herself, Katherine pushed her slippered foot into the woman's thin hands — thin, but surprisingly steady — braced herself on the woman's shoulder, and felt herself rise into the air.

Within seconds, Katherine was several feet taller than the rest of the guests. She wobbled a little, nearly banging her forehead on the glass, and steadied herself with a hand to the pane. Now, she could see the latch, and, more importantly, she could reach it. The metal was cool and obliging beneath the fabric of her gloves — she snapped the hook free, and grinned. "There!"

"Excellent!" Somehow, her companion was not even panting. She lowered Katherine in a fluid, steady movement, and Katherine jumped back to earth. The woman caught her, hands at her waist, and for some reason, Katherine went a bit breathless. Within seconds, the woman had the window open and swinging wide, inviting a sudden, perfect breeze.

They both sighed with relief, then flashed one another matching grins.

"Thank you," said Katherine. Around them, the crowd let out its own sigh as the fresh air wafted into the room. "For your assistance."

Again, that eyebrow went up, coy as anything. "My pleasure," the woman said, her voice low.

Katherine opened her mouth, but before she could speak again, a loud boom echoed through the chamber, and the double doors swung open.

And then, of course, absolute chaos erupted.

A great force — probably one of the debutantes — pushed Katherine deeper into the chamber, towards her father, and she barely managed to remain standing as the guests seethed towards the doors, rumbling and churning with their eagerness to be the first ones in the throne room. "One at a time!" barked a faceless voice — a footman, she guessed. "Form a queue!"

Somehow, in all of this, the woman in lilac had disappeared.

Katherine kept her feet and shoved her way through the crowd, retracing her steps. She dodged elbows and fans and feathers, and soon stumbled to a halt before her father.

"Kat!" Mr. Knight took hold of her. "Are you all right?"

"Yes, fine." She heaved a breath and put a hand to her pulsing cheek, then to her hair. "Oh— oh dear." Katherine met her father's gaze, bit her lip. "I seem to be dented."

They looked at one another, then snorted. As they began to laugh, the crowd shifted again, moving into something resembling a queue.

"Come, then." Mr. Knight took her hand and tucked it into his elbow. "It is time we walked into the lion's den."

3

Several hours later, Katherine reflected upon her presentation to the Queen, and thought that as far as things went, there had been worse disasters in the history of mankind. The Tower of Babel, for one, and perhaps the Flood, and Pompeii... the burning of the Library of Alexandria...

Katherine had managed to keep her feet, and to keep pace with her father, who, apparently, had the patience of a struck match. It had taken a remarkable effort not to lift her gaze, not to meet the dark, burning eyes sitting livid beneath a crown of gold and sapphires.

The Queen, everyone knew, never passed on an opportunity to make a statement.

And a statement she had made, scowling at Katherine like there were streaks of dung on her secondhand hem. But Katherine had curtsied — if her half-aborted movement could be called a curtsy — and waited, as she had been told to wait.

Silence had fallen, a pointed and bald silence. Katherine tried not to see the courtiers shifting and darting nervous looks at the throne.

Finally, the footman cleared his throat and repeated himself. "Mr. Richard Knight, presenting Miss Katherine Knight."

"Yes, I see." The Queen's voice rang with her lack of amusement. "Mr. Knight, how fare the herds?"

Mr. Knight blinked, as if surprised by the acknowledgment of his presence. "Well, Your Majesty, very well."

But the Queen did not appear to hear him. She was looking at Katherine, her eyes pinched. Another silence yawned, and then she spoke again. "Miss Knight. I suppose you will do."

Katherine had curtsied again, almost breathless with the urge to flee, to run, to sprint out of the room and rip the ribbons from her hair. That, and the manic urge to laugh.

Instead, she had tucked her hand into her father's elbow, and they departed at a steady, almost leisurely, pace. Katherine had forced herself to take a breath, to swallow her glee, and to pretend that her pride had not suffered a glancing blow.

Upon exiting, she had avoided the mirrors in the exterior hall of the throne room. No point in indulging herself, not now, when the illusion had been shattered like so much glass. Some part of her knew, had known for years, that she would never be the star of any room, the brilliant focal point of any season. She would be there, but not there, all within the same moment.

Now, her thoughts turned — or, rather, returned — to the question. The question of what the season would be like, if she were all but invisible to the other participants. Dull, yes, but it would have been dull regardless — the mere thought of dancing a jig, making small conversation, laughing at nothing, accepting a glass of watery punch — the mere thought was enough to make her skin crawl, to make her eyes roll and her body slump with derision.

But perhaps, Katherine thought now, as the carriage drew to a halt before an enormous manor house, the windows blazing with cheer and light. *Perhaps it will be easier this way.*

Across from her, her mother began to smile. "What a riot."

"Good God." Her father was peering out the window. Against the other carriages, theirs looked particularly northern and austere, built in a ruthless dark wood and lined with tartan upholstery. "Are the footmen wearing *golden* wigs?"

"Your gloves, Katherine," said Mrs. Knight, patting at her hair. Katherine could not remember the last time she'd seen her mother dressed like this — perhaps a Christmas many years before, the last Christmas with her grandmother. Mrs. Knight always dressed sensibly in the country — in thick, plain dresses with her hair in a braid. Worlds apart from the woman sitting here now.

Katherine obeyed, pulling on her detestable white stain gloves. These, too, she'd inherited from some cousin or other; she'd spent an afternoon sitting with Rita, repairing the tiny holes in the seams. A stray clump of thread dug into the nail bed of her pinky finger — Katherine had never been gifted at tying things off. "Where are the boys?"

"Not far behind, I'm certain," Mrs. Knight replied. "They took the pony and trap."

"I admire your faith," Katherine said. "In their sobriety and in their promise to attend."

"A mother knows," Mrs. Knight replied with a shrug. "Besides, Lucas is just as eligible as you, Kat."

Katherine snorted. "So are Tom and Bran, but if they so much as speak to a young lady, I shall eat my glove."

"It would be nice if Lucas settled down." Mrs. Knight clearly was not listening; like Mr. Knight, her gaze was fixed on the blazing edifice of the manor. "I would very much enjoy having a young lady about the house."

Katherine grinned, even as her stomach swooped in an ugly, fitful movement. "Goodness, Mother. If the insults are to be so thinly veiled, I shall require a glass of something alcoholic."

Their footman chose that precise moment to open the

carriage door, and a quick breath rattled through Katherine's lungs. *Come on,* she told herself. *Forward.*

The manor home was like a fairy castle out of a storybook — built of stone and dotted with ivy, sconces and lanterns creating eerie but warm pools of light. Music spilled out of the open windows, jaunty and welcoming, and the garden was dotted with moths and glow worms. Katherine watched as a handful of young men descended upon the front door, laughing and jeering, their white shirts a dull periwinkle in the late evening light. She felt a tingle of foreboding, then the growl of her stomach. She hadn't eaten since breakfast.

"Come, my dear." Mr. Knight took Mrs. Knight's arm, and for a moment, they made quite a picture — a handsome, happy, if somewhat homely, picture. "Let the season begin."

Katherine bit the inside of her cheek, straightened her shoulders, and followed her parents into the house.

Though even the word 'house' felt inadequate. As Katherine stepped over the threshold and into a vaulted foyer, she paused to wonder whether she was still in London, or if she had been transported to Paris without her knowledge. Her gaze raked over the lavish furnishings, the paintings, the footmen who were indeed wearing golden wigs.

"Oh, Kat!" Mrs. Knight was already preoccupied at a side table. "You must have one."

Katherine went to her side and fought a wince. "A dance card?"

"Yes!" Mrs. Knight took her hand and looped one of the infernal cards around her wrist. "Surely that will ease the path to conversation."

Sisyphean, Katherine thought. She managed a smile. "Lovely."

It seemed that the Knight family was fashionably late. Already, dozens of guests were milling around the rooms, glasses of wine and punch in hand, critical eyes falling on the young ladies and their delicate blushes. A few gazes followed Katherine's way, lingered, then moved along. She stood there for a moment, her ears ringing, then bit back a smile.

Perhaps invisibility was a blessing in disguise.

Katherine followed her parents into the next room, which seemed to be a parlor. Clusters of people and families were dotted around the space, ebbing between tables and armchairs and conversations and gossip. Within moments, it became obvious that Katherine's parents were somewhat out of their depth — they spent little time in London, and were not close to most of the titled families. Katherine glanced at faces familiar and foreign, and absolutely did not look for a tall, dark woman in a lilac dress.

Around her, the game of courtship was already beginning to play itself out. In the corner of her eye, she saw curtsies and smiles, blushes and bows. She wondered, in a faint, disinterested sort of way, if any of the young gentlemen would ask her to dance. The prospect was irritating, rather than exciting.

"Well, my dear." Mr. Knight turned to her. "Would you like me to make any introductions?"

"Father, I have little notion to whom you would introduce me."

"There is a list," said Mrs. Knight. "Did we not receive a list from my sister?"

Katherine glanced around; thankfully, it seemed that no one had overheard this remark. "I believe so, Mother, but I doubt that it is something we should advertise to London at large."

"A list?" Mr. Knight frowned. "A list of what?"

"God in Heaven," muttered Katherine, then, louder: "I am going to get a drink." With that, she turned and made her way to the table of refreshments.

No one paid her any heed as she took a glass of wine and swallowed half of it in a single gulp. It was hardly Scotch, but it would do. Another look around the room told her that her peers were not wasting a single moment — it seemed as if most of the dance cards were already half-full. Her stomach growled again, and she reached for one *vol-au-vent*, then another. The pastry was salty, thick with ham and some kind of cheese.

"Miss Knight?"

Katherine froze, then turned to face this newcomer.

It was a young man with a flop of brown hair, and his ready smile faltered at the sight of her bulging cheeks. "I— I wonder if we might be introduced."

Katherine swallowed thickly, her heart stuttering. "Yes, of course—" She turned, and saw that her father was already making his way towards them. "Father—"

"Kat." Mr. Knight drew even with them and shot the young man a flinty look. "Might I introduce...?"

"Mr. John Ransom," the man supplied.

"Mr. John Ransom, my daughter, Miss Knight."

"Excellent." Mr. Ransom seemed to rally, and he offered Katherine a smile. "I was wondering if we might dance together, Miss Knight."

"Certainly." She held out her dance card, and watched in a mute sort of horror as he wrote his name under the first slot. "But I think the orchestra—"

The orchestra chose that precise moment to blare a sudden wall of sound — a call, a signal, that the dancing was to begin.

"How timely!" Mr. Ransom offered her his hand. "Shall we?"

She was still holding the *vol-au-vent*. "I—" she began. "I—"

What followed, then, were some of the most excruciating minutes of Katherine's life.

Mr. Ransom seemed oddly keen to continue dancing with her, in spite of the way she flubbed a step, and, during a memorable moment, smacked him in the shoulder. They danced twice together, then again after the third song. When the music ended and Katherine gave what felt like her fiftieth curtsy of the evening, a sudden hush fell across the hall, followed by a low, steady murmur.

Everyone turned to look at the doorway, and Katherine did the same.

The crowd seethed, then parted. A young woman stepped into the room, a tiny circlet of silver glinting in her dark hair. She was beautiful, a classical line of chin and brow, her skin a rich, warm brown; she cast a sharp gaze over the crowd, and a demure little smile curled at the corner of her mouth.

The debutantes standing nearest to Katherine were scowling, mutinous. "It's her," one of them hissed. "The bloody Star."

Understanding, keen as a bee sting. Katherine looked at the woman, at the Star of the 1812 London Season, and couldn't help but feel that she seemed a bit familiar.

Mr. Ransom, along with every other young man in the hall, was fixated upon the Star. When the room shifted back to life, he didn't even spare Katherine a glance before he headed in the direction of the doorway, where the gentlemen were already swarming like flies. Katherine rolled her eyes and returned to where she'd left her parents, near one of the sideboards. And it seemed that their party had grown.

"Thank goodness," she said to Thomas, stealing his glass of wine. "You took your time."

"We got lost," he replied. His face carried a pleasant flush, the only sign of his inebriation. "No thanks to Bran."

"Excuse me." Brandon cut them a look. "I've never driven to this part of London before. I think I did very well, considering the circumstances."

Katherine frowned at him and Thomas took the opportunity to reclaim his glass. "You drove the trap? I thought Lucas—"

"Lucas has abstained," said Brandon. "You shall have to make do with the two of us."

"Abstained?" Katherine looked to Thomas, who met her gaze and shrugged. "Why?"

"Believe it or not, he did not make us privy to his decision," Thomas replied.

Katherine met her father's gaze, and did not miss the little frown of concern that flitted across his features, or her mother's. But they both recovered quickly.

"No matter," said Mrs. Knight. "We will have a wonderful time regardless of his absence, and he shall be green with envy come morning."

"Will he?" muttered Brandon. Quicker than a snake, Mrs. Knight darted out a hand and smacked the back of his head. "Ow! Mother!"

"Quiet," said Mr. Knight, in his customary low tone. "The night is young, and we must nurse our patience."

A crowd was still seething around the entrance to the chamber. The orchestra resumed playing, but only a half-dozen couples were on the floor.

"Who is she, then?" said Katherine. Her chest was warm, and her dress was sticking to her back. "This year's Star?"

"Lady Sophia Alwyn, better known as Sophia Johnson" said Thomas. He frowned when they all turned to stare at him, incredulous. "People were discussing it when I arrived, I hardly—"

"Johnson," said Katherine to her mother. "A common name."

"Quite," Mrs. Knight replied. "Her father, Lord Alwyn, is a merchant."

"A merchant?" Katherine fought the urge to glance across the room again. "I do not believe I've heard the name before."

It had nothing to do with believing — she *knew* she did not know the name, and that her brothers didn't, either. None of the gossip floating out through the backwaters of London's social clubs had told her anything about Lord Alwyn, a man who, apparently, had been granted his title, rather than inherit it.

"No," her father agreed. "From what I know, he is English by birth, but he made his fortune in Holland. The family returns now, with their three daughters, to formally enter English society. The eldest has just been married to an Englishman, so I suppose this is their second."

"I see." Katherine's fingers itched for a bit of paper. She could not ask, but she knew — by instinct, or by some learned skill, perhaps — that there was more to this situation than a simple change in scenery. A family without a title did not suddenly appear in English society, and at the Opening Ball, without due reason. And for their daughter to be named the Star, so soon after her own sister's wedding — surely, that too was no coincidence.

Katherine's gaze skirted around the room, and for a moment, she saw past the candles and the silk and the feathers. Instead, she saw the invisible strings tying family to family, man to man, debt to collectors. She saw the hidden tide of their world push and ebb and reorient itself around its newest guiding light — Sophia Alwyn, the Star of the season.

She would have to learn more.

❧ 4 ❧

"It is not like him." Mrs. Knight's voice was hushed, full of tension. "Not like him at all."

"You fret too much, my dear." But Mr. Knight's attempt at nonchalance was somewhat lacking. "Lucas is a young man, and he has an adventurous spirit. It is hardly surprising that he would prefer not to spend an evening with his family."

Katherine shivered, tugging her blanket more tightly about her frame. The light wool prickled against her skin, comforting and unnerving all at once. She was curled up on the steps outside the library, bathed in the ready darkness of the night. The time eluded her, but she knew it was almost three o'clock in the morning; it was unusual for her parents to stay up so late, even after a night of celebration.

They were worried, she knew. About Lucas.

For all his protesting and occasional behavior to the contrary, Lucas was, generally speaking, a reliable eldest son. For him to be absent two nights in a row, and to miss Katherine's Opening Ball, was out of character. He'd hardly even taken breakfast with them that morning; he'd only stayed long enough to swallow a few eggs and kippers, then had retired to his room with a massive pot of tea.

And he wasn't in the house. Not now, and he had not been for hours. No one had seen him since Thomas and Brandon's departure for the Opening Ball. Katherine could not remember the last time Lucas had vanished without so much as a word about his whereabouts — not even Graves knew where he'd gone.

Their mother worried. Had always worried. And Lucas knew that. For him to be so unthinking and cruel in his actions was—

"He has been different." Mrs. Knight's voice was muffled now, as if she'd spoken with her hand to her mouth. "Recently."

"Edwina." Gentle, pleading. "We knew this would be a difficult season, a difficult year. We cannot expect all of our children to take it in stride. Perhaps Lucas simply needs time—"

"But it cannot be a surprise to him," Mrs. Knight said. "Not when he's known for weeks, even months— He was in the meeting with you and Jeffords, for God's sake. And he knew how important it was for him to be there tonight, for the family to present a united front." A pause. "He knew what it would mean to Kat."

A prickle of emotion went up Katherine's spine, and she held her breath. Was she upset by Lucas' absence? She did not know.

"I doubt Kat even noticed." Her father's voice was warm, wry. "She had much to hold her attention."

"Yes," said her mother. "She did very well, and those young gentlemen—"

That was enough. Katherine stood without making a sound, and slipped down the stairs, gliding through the moonlit, empty house.

The passageways were even more infernal and maddening in the darkness — only a practiced tread knew which floorboards would squeak, which corners would cut, which doors would stub one's toe. Katherine kept glancing behind her, or to her right, or to her left. She could not shake the feeling that the house was moving when she did not watch it, shifting and turning and grinning behind her back. But it felt playful, not sinister. She knew these halls, these rooms, and could likely find her way even when blindfolded.

Perhaps she was blindfolded now, stumbling through the season with all the grace of a fawn. In spite of her family's early departure from the Opening Ball, and her own exhaustion, she had not been able to get to sleep. Energy and anxiety had pulsed through her body like blood, throbbing behind her eyes and in her tired feet. She'd climbed out of bed and made her way to the staircase with every intention of slipping out to the garden, not realizing that her parents were still awake. Now, their conversation only fueled the unease rippling in her stomach.

Lucas did not keep secrets, especially not from her. Even if he confided in Thomas or Brandon, secrets never lasted in the Knight household, not between the siblings. It could be frustrating, she knew, to have so little privacy, but she would not have traded it for anything. And she knew that Lucas felt the same way.

So — why? Why hadn't he confided in her? When they'd spoken in the garden that morning, she'd known that something was amiss, but hadn't thought to press the issue, not then. *Perhaps he wouldn't have told me, perhaps he would have lied,* she thought as she made her way through the darkened kitchen and out the back door.

Night, deep and succulent, draped over the garden like a blanket. Katherine bit back a shiver as she stepped into the cool grass, moisture beading at the hem of her nightgown, catching on the bare inch of her ankles. In moments like this, with a chill catching in her throat, it was almost impossible to remember that it was summer.

But the cold reminded her of home, of the country. She hugged her blanket to her chest and wandered through the trees and bushes, making her way towards the bench swing beneath the poplar tree.

The woolen blanket protected her from the moisture, and she sank into her seat with a sigh, her breath pooling gray in the air. Moonlight, silver and determined, cut through the branches and the leaves and the roses, throwing the space into stark relief and sudden shadow. The grass shone in a dim purple, and the distant line of the back wall was as black as eternity. Katherine took a breath, and wondered if this was the witching hour, an hour of fairy folk and secrets.

How fitting, she thought. *Hiding in plain sight.*

Without her permission, her mind began to turn, to sift through the events and the remarks of the Opening Ball. It seemed to be her instinct, now — to collect details and moments, to file them away for later inspection, even when she was preoccupied with the young gentlemen of London and Brandon's attempt to knock over the punch bowl. Katherine could look one way and hear what was happening in another, whether she wanted to or not. This skill, this preoccupation with the lives of others, seemed to be more than a passing fancy, and she did not quite know what to make of it.

Some time later — a couple of minutes, or perhaps an hour — there came a sound. A rustle, and a long, muted scrape.

Katherine froze, her heart giving a particularly painful throb. She stared into the darkness, at the fog curling around a thatch of evergreen shrubs. She knew that sound — it was the sound of the back gate opening.

The scrape became a sudden whine, cut off by a muttered curse. Katherine gulped, heard the gate latch, and wondered if she would ever find the courage to move, to run, to—

A figure appeared and began limping up the garden, towards her, towards the house. A hunched figure, silver moonlight splashing across its wide shoulders and unsteady feet. A figure with a mangled shirt, a torn jacket, and a splotch of blood across—

Katherine blinked, recognition overcoming her fear. "Lucas?"

Now he was the one who froze. He looked up the garden, his gaze resting on her, and he was close enough that she could see the way he kept his right arm tight to his body, the way he seemed to favor his left side. His face was swollen with cuts and bruises, and even in the darkness, she could see the guilty tilt of his mouth.

"Ah." His voice was dry, mangled. "Kitten."

She stared at him, uncomprehending. "Lucas, what on earth happened to you?"

"That—" He took another step forward and winced. "Is a very long story."

"I should fetch Brandon, you're bleeding—"

"No, don't—" Another wince, and he drew even with the bench. "Don't get up."

Katherine obeyed, bitter fear curling in the pit of her throat. He sat down beside her and bit back a pained moan, his breath coming in fits and pants.

Now that Katherine could look at him, it was obvious that he had been in a fight, and lost badly. Even the dulled moonlight could not hide what would soon be an enormous black eye. His knuckles were a disaster, and the cuts on his lower lip, cheekbone, and brow bone were obviously responsible for the blood on his shirt. He'd wiped away the worst of it, save for a sticky smear on his collarbone.

"Christ, Lucas." Katherine shook her head. "Were you robbed?"

"No." The ghost of a smile tilted his mouth. "But perhaps that would be the best story to tell Mother and Father."

"You would not tell them the truth?"

He did not reply, and under different circumstances, Katherine would have smacked his arm.

"I knew something was wrong." Katherine slid the blanket off her shoulders and draped half of it across his lap. "You were being exceptionally melodramatic earlier, even for you."

"Come along, Kitten, don't you know not to hit a man when he's already down?"

Katherine looked at him, at the line of his nose — their father's nose. At least it wasn't broken. "Lucas, you can tell me. Whatever the circumstances, I promise that you can rely on—"

"Your discretion, yes." He thumbed the cut on his lip. "I know, Kat."

"Then tell me." Her voice was low. "Tell me why you've come home in such a state of injury. If it is not the result of an accident or an attack, then I can only draw the worst conclusions."

"Perhaps your conclusions would be accurate."

"A gentlemanly disagreement?"

Silence.

"Lucas." She tried to sound soft, endearing, like their mother, and had no idea if it worked. "I will not think the worst of you."

Several moments passed before he spoke.

"I am in debt." Lucas looked away, into the trees. "Ferocious debt. This—" he gestured to his face— "was a warning. Or, rather, a promise. Of what is to happen if I fail to pay it back. And I cannot pay it back. I do not have the money."

"Debt," Katherine repeated. The word tingled on her lips, turning them numb. "As in— you mean what Father discussed with us at supper the other night?"

"No." He almost smiled, then winced. "Father does not know. This has nothing to do with the company, and everything to do with—"

"Gambling?"

Surprise flickered across Lucas' mottled features. "You know about it?"

"Yes." It was only a partial lie. She knew that he'd gambled before, more than once, with poor results. On fights, if she remembered correctly. Boxing matches. "But I did not realize..." The enormity of the situation sank in. Lucas had his own debts, and the family estate was under lock and key, under threat of running dry. His collateral had evaporated like dew in the sun, and he had nothing left to give. "Lucas, how much do you owe?"

"A lot." His voice was hollow. "More than a lot. I've been putting them off for a while; it was easier while we were in the country. But now..."

A shiver broke over her body, and it had nothing to do with the temperature. "You must tell Father."

"Kat, no—"

"Yes, it is the only option—"

"You know as well as I that it is anything but!"

"We have savings," Katherine said, with an unfounded certainty. "There must be enough put aside to—"

His laugh was sudden, harsh. "Oh, Kat. You are not so gullible, or so stupid. There is nothing left. Almost everything has been swallowed by the company, and what little is left over has to get us through the season."

She swallowed hard. "Not everything."

A pause as Lucas looked at her, uncomprehending. Then— "No, Kat."

"Yes," she said. "My dowry—"

"Don't even finish that sentence." His words were lethal, full of fire. "Your dowry is not to be touched. What is more, we both know most of it is in Mother's jewelry case."

"True." Katherine managed a shuddering breath. "She would notice, eventually, if some of the pieces went missing."

"And, more importantly, I want you to have that security, if you... if you make a match."

She almost smiled. "You flatter me."

"How was it? The *soirée?*"

"Middling. Though I did manage not to injure anybody on the dance floor."

"A feat in and of itself. I am sorry I missed it."

Her breath hitched. "What are you going to do?"

"I do not know." And now, she could hear his exhaustion. "But I doubt I shall reach an answer before I've had any sleep."

He had a point. Katherine nodded, forcing herself to focus on the issue at hand. "Mother and Father were still in the library when I came outside. I'll check if they've gone to bed." The last thing she wanted was for them to catch Lucas sneaking back in his present state.

"There's no need," he said. "I'll sleep in the drawing room."

"With bruised ribs? Absolutely not. You need a proper bed, and a wash." Katherine fought back a shiver. "Wait for me in the kitchen."

The house was silent as Katherine tiptoed up the stairs, craning her neck to sneak a peek over the landing of the second floor. Darkness seeped under the doorway of the library — it seemed that her parents had gone to bed. She took a quick, relieved breath, and continued up to the next floor, then slipped down the hall, past her own room, and through a pair of closed — but not locked — double doors.

Brandon slept like a dog, with his arms curled under his head. She had to shake him twice before he woke with a grunt. "G —'way."

"Bran. *Bran. Wake up.*"

"Kat?" Finally, he stirred, squinting at her through the murky shadows. She hadn't had time to light a candle, but she could tell that his hair was an absolute riot. "What is it?"

"It's Lucas," she hissed, flinging his dressing gown at him. "He's hurt."

That woke him up. Brandon frowned, then tugged on his gown. "Where is he?"

"Downstairs."

"Is he conscious?"

"Yes. But I'm not sure he can get up the stairs on his own, and I am not strong enough to catch his weight."

Brandon climbed out of bed and shoved a hand through his hair. "We'll have to be quick. Mr. Salk—" the cook— "wakes before dawn."

Lucas was waiting for them in the kitchen; he'd propped himself against the slumbering stove, his good hand hovering above the banked heat of the fire. When he saw that Katherine wasn't alone, he scowled. "I never agreed to visitors."

To his credit, Brandon didn't visibly react to the state of his elder brother, or ask a single question. "Don't make a fuss," he said. "I do this for all the damsels in distress."

Together, Katherine and Brandon helped Lucas climb the two flights of stairs to his bedchamber. Much to her relief, all was silent — their parents seemed to be sound asleep, and Thomas was snoring like a mule in his own chamber. By the time the three of them were safe behind a locked door, Lucas had gone pale from the effort, the dried blood a shocking brown against his skin. He sank down into his chair, hand clutching his side, and closed his eyes.

Katherine met Brandon's gaze, and saw all her own concern reflected back at her. She turned away and lit a few candles, then stoked the fire. Behind her, Brandon poured a fresh dish of water and unearthed a roll of bandages from the chest of drawers, along with a pair of sharp scissors.

"Go on, then." Lucas lolled in his chair, or, at least, attempted to. "Dissect me."

"Kat." Brandon met her gaze again. He looked quite serious like this, in spite of his creased dressing gown and floppy hair. Almost like an actual physician, which, Katherine supposed, was the best they could do, under the circumstances. At least Brandon had read some books on the topic, unlike her. "I can handle it from here."

"Oh, dear. I require handling?"

Katherine ignored Lucas and nodded. "If you need anything, knock."

"Polly want a cracker?" Their secret knock.

"Yes." She looked at her brothers, and even like this, piecemeal and sleepy before the fire, they seemed so solid and real. "We'll say his horse threw him."

Brandon nodded. "And he made his way home on foot. A touch inebriated."

"I'm sober as a skunk, you absolute arse."

Katherine continued: "You woke up when you heard Lucas come into his bedchamber, and you saw to his injuries."

"Of course," said Brandon. "Like the good brother I am."

"And I will learn about all of this at breakfast." Katherine glanced at the door. "Brandon, I will see you in the morning."

"Yes. I'll have Chauncey bring him something on a tray."

"*He* can hear you, and would like half a dozen kippers."

"Try to get some rest," Katherine said. And with that, she left the room.

Her bed had gone cold. She lay there shivering for several minutes, hunched beneath the sheets, staring up at the canopy. Now that she was alone, she had expected her mind to whirl and overflow, but instead, all was silent. A single thought occurred, then repeated like a prayer, as Katherine sank into an unwilling and sudden sleep.

What are we going to do?

❧

"AH, KATHERINE!" MR. KNIGHT OFFERED HER A SMILE AS SHE entered the dining room. "Brandon was just telling us all about his midnight escapades with dear Lucas."

"Oh?" Katherine glanced at Brandon, then at Thomas, who was sulking, and tried to keep her expression neutral. "What happened?"

"Lucas was thrown from a horse," Brandon said. "Not his own, thankfully."

"He overindulged," Mr. Knight went on. "And apparently forgot that he went to the club via coach, rather than mammal."

"Goodness me." Katherine sat down across from Brandon and began to fill her plate with eggs. "Is he quite hurt?"

"A little," said Brandon. "Mother is with him now."

A genuine smirk nearly broke through her careful facade — Lucas abhorred hovering and fussing, especially at his expense. She could imagine how foul his temper would be by midday.

"We're quite fortunate to have such a dab medical hand in the family," said Mr. Knight.

"You flatter me, Father." Brandon's modesty was genuine. "I still think he should see a proper physician, just to be safe."

The morning was watery but sunny, and enough light was coming through the windows for Katherine to see the tiny, careful look flit across her father's face. She doubted that they could afford to pay a physician, even for such a simple consultation.

"I am certain that Lucas will recover quickly," said Mr. Knight. "Let's save the physician the trouble of a house call." He wiped his mouth with his napkin and stood up from the table. "If you'll excuse me, my dears, the post is waiting for me in the library."

Once Mr. Knight was gone, and well out of earshot, Thomas turned his scowl on Katherine and said, "I can't believe you didn't wake me up."

She rolled her eyes. "Bran's the one who knows how to dress a wound."

"Yes, but I could have helped."

"No, you couldn't," said Brandon, reaching for the teapot. "You would have fooled around and knocked things over."

Thomas ignored him. "So what really happened? Lucas can handle a horse even when he's too drunk to walk. Hell, I've seen him ride blindfolded, and naked."

Ah — Lucas hadn't said a word to Brandon, then. Katherine

glanced at the open door, and Brandon caught her doing it. "Not now, Tom."

Thomas looked between them, and an understanding passed through the air. He went back to his breakfast and began talking of something ridiculous, like the races or the stock market.

Katherine sipped her tea and resolved to slip into Lucas' chamber before the close of the morning. She had no idea how truthful he wanted to be with Brandon and Thomas, and the last thing they needed were more ridiculous ideas.

Although, she thought, watching her brothers trade barbs, *perhaps a ridiculous idea is just what we need.*

INTERLUDE I — THE ISLAND, EAST LONDON

Rebecca squinted into the sun and wiped the sweat off her brow. It was one of those mornings, one of those delicious mornings, when she could taste the salt in the air, and just the salt, not the fug of coal, not the grime of the rotting wood, not the stale tang of spilt gin. Just salt, plain and bitter and so delightful, sharp in the summer breeze.

"A fine morning."

She waited a moment, then turned her head in the direction of the dock and offered a lazy salute. "Indeed, Father."

"You were up early." Lord Alwyn paused at the dock's edge, looking down into the ship. "I don't believe Harris—" their butler — "even heard the door."

"Early to bed, early to rise. Unlike some, I was not dancing until dawn." She flashed him a smirk. "How fares our dear Star?"

Her father smiled, and it carried an edge. In the sunlight, his dark skin had a coppery tint, and his teeth were a ruthless white. "I believe she is still sleeping, like your mother."

"Ah, of course." Rebecca picked up her rag and continued polishing the rail. "Even a Star needs her beauty rest. Have you taken the carriage in?"

"Yes, just now. The wheelwright told me that you did a remarkable job patching it up, given the circumstances."

She shrugged. "Mrs. Fawn—" the housekeeper— "wasn't too keen on the state of my dress. Mud and grease can stain, apparently."

"We are in your debt," Lord Alwyn replied, teasing. "Thanks to you, we were able to make it to the Opening Ball. And I am on my way to purchase another carriage. Why I thought just the one would suffice is beyond me."

"Live and learn, Father." Rebecca paused, the rag catching on one of her nails. "Did Sophia do well last night?"

"I believe so." His smile curled and warmed. "She made quite an entrance. And she danced with all of the most eligible gentlemen in London."

Just as she should. "Are we to have callers, then?"

"Most likely." Lord Alwyn looked at her, and he bent down, reached to nudge her sweaty cheek with his finger. "It will be your turn soon enough, Rebecca."

She snorted and pushed him away, an easy grin breaking over her face. "I can wait, believe me."

"Soon enough," he repeated. "Who knows? You might find you have an affinity for dresses and dancing."

"And perhaps a set of horns and a tail to match."

"Protest all you like." Lord Alwyn straightened up, brushing nonexistent dust off of his sleek, ribbon-trimmed jacket. "But I think you would enjoy these parties."

"Hardly," Rebecca replied, but her mind shifted, turning to the image of a flushed, energetic face, framed by glossy strands of dark, chestnut hair. And those hazel eyes, sparkling as if they carried a private joke. She curled her free hand into a fist, mimicking the weight of the woman's foot, and wondered, not for the first time, what her name was.

Perhaps it would be worth going to a party. If it meant seeing her again. Seeing her, and seeing how low that delightful blush would travel down her body.

Rebecca shook her head, banishing these thoughts to the sunshine. The ship swayed gently beneath her feet, grounding her in reality. "Will there be supper this evening?"

"A light one," he replied. "Before we depart."

"I shall be home by six, then. To spare Mrs. Fawn another nervous episode."

"So thoughtful of you." Her father made his way back up the dock. "Don't get into too much trouble!"

"Never!" Rebecca grinned again, and tipped her head back, letting the sun spill over her face.

❧　5　❧

Lucas appeared to be asleep, but his eyes flickered when he realized who was standing in his doorway. "Kat."

She paused, one foot in the hall. "I can return later."

"No." He cleared his throat, and shifted slightly on his pillows. "Come in."

It was late afternoon. The morning's sunlight had given way to a pressing and drizzly rain, but the air still carried a strange fug of warmth. Katherine closed and locked the door behind her, and made her way to his bedside.

"It is strange to see you like this." She offered him a thin smile. "An invalid."

Lucas slotted her a look that was misery and outrage rolled into one. "Don't."

"Sorry. How are you feeling?"

"If one more person asks me that—"

"Don't over-excite yourself, or I shall have to fetch Mother."

He muttered an oath not fit for indecent company.

"At any rate," said Katherine, "I am glad you're resting." She leaned back in her chair and propped her feet on his bed. "I gathered that you did not offer Brandon anything resembling an explanation."

"No," Lucas agreed. In the light of day, his face was mottled and ruinous. A puffy, purple-black bruise swelled his left eye shut, and the cuts on his brow bone and lip were an ugly, dull crimson. Brandon had closed the cut above Lucas' eyebrow with a few neat stitches, and Katherine had the fleeting thought that her brother would scar, and noticeably.

"Do you not wish to tell him the truth?"

Lucas paused, and the pause was almost enough to answer Katherine's question. "I do not... I do not know."

"We have to offer him an explanation of some kind. Both him and Tom. They already know that something is rotten in the state of Denmark."

Lucas dropped his gaze. She could see it — everything he was not saying. If he and Katherine lied, it would be the first time they concealed something from their siblings, and enclosed themselves in a solitary, shared secret. A sea change, a point of no return. A boulder on a hill. Sisyphean.

"They will not think ill of you," she said, her voice low. "I did not, when you told me."

A humorless smile flitted across his face. "You are not Bran. He..."

They both knew what he was going to say. Brandon idolized his eldest brother, and always had. Thus far, nothing had shattered that impermeable image, not even an ill-fated and semi-accidental visit to one of London's most notorious brothels, which had ended with a slap across the face and an Elizabethan ruff glued to Lucas' thigh.

"They will have ideas," Katherine said. "About how to help you."

"Yes. But whether those ideas will hold any merit—"

"We will think of something, Lucas. There is no other

option." She had to ask him, had to know. "What have your creditors threatened you with? If you cannot follow through?"

"Lots of things." He fiddled with the seam of his blanket. "I think they plan to extort Father, if all else fails. Pity they have no idea he is just as penniless as I."

Cold, seeping into her stomach. "They could do that?"

"Yes, Kitten. They can do anything they like. They know who I am, who my family is."

"No, I mean—" She licked her lips. "They are powerful, then, these people? Powerful enough to move in your social circles, and to guarantee your compliance?"

Lucas nodded, then winced — she guessed he had a massive headache. "They have connections, lots of connections. I believe they work for the Tyndale family."

"Tyndale." Katherine let herself taste the name. "Don't they own the racetrack up north?"

"Yes. And most of the gambling dens and half the pubs in London. And a brothel or two. And..." He was sheepish now. "The White Fox."

"*What?* When did they purchase—?"

"Last year. The previous owners were looking to retire, and had no family left to inherit. The Tyndales snapped it up."

God. This was getting worse than she'd imagined. "So you cannot hide."

"No," he confirmed. "They run half the city, and parley with the other half. They are watching my every move."

"Watching?" she repeated, that cold fear pooling in her stomach once again. "Now?"

"Probably." Lucas glanced at the window. "I know they have someone keeping an eye on the house. There might be a man in the garden as well."

The cold splintered and turned into panic. "You must go to the Continent."

"No, Kat—"

"Yes, the Continent. It is your only option. You can disappear, take a new name—"

"And leave Father without an heir?"

"No heir is better than—"

"Than what?" he snapped. "A dead heir?"

"You said it, Lucas. Not I." Katherine swallowed the wobble in her throat. "And I would prefer you in hiding to you..."

"Shuffled off this mortal coil, yes."

"And there's Tom. You are not the only heir to the Knight estate."

"No," he said. "But you and I both know Tom's in no fit condition for that level of responsibility. He would run the business into the ground."

"Then we seem to have gone in a circle," she bit out, "with no resolution in sight. If you will not leave, and you cannot pay — what else is left?"

Lucas put on a thoughtful, slap-worthy look. "Mustering an army?"

"We need money." Katherine felt the words, so full of simplicity and complication. "How can we get more money?"

"*I* need money," he corrected her. "This is not your problem to solve."

Katherine got to her feet and turned away from the bed, resisting the urge to throttle him. "Lucas, you made it my problem the moment you stepped into the garden. You made it *our* problem. The family's problem. I have as much right to solve it as you do. As does Tom, and Bran."

"I had no other choice — I could not have returned to the club after they set upon me. Quite apart from making a scene, the questions alone would have been enough to call our membership into question. We already tread a fine line as it is. No," he went on. "I had to come home."

"What about your friends? Percy, Ian, George?"

"They do not know anything," he said. "And I am going to maintain my silence."

"But they could give you a loan—"

"No!"

She turned in time to see Lucas flinch and slump back into his pillows — he'd spoken with too much force for his bruised ribs.

An uneasy silence fell. Katherine watched her brother take one slow breath, then another.

"No," Lucas said again, quietly. "I refuse to take on further debt. Quite apart from the personal stress, it would— tarnish our reputation. My peers would know, their fathers would know, and word would spread. The Knights are hard up for cash, and God only knows why."

"Then there is nothing for it," she said, frustration seething in her belly like a hurricane. "We need ideas, because this situation impacts all of us, especially me, Tom, and Bran. It is our future you gambled with, not just your own."

These words seemed to hit something, some hidden, sensitive tissue of his being. Lucas looked at her, and she almost missed it, the flicker of vulnerability, of shame, that passed over his features. But she knew he would not admit to it. Lucas Knight was too proud for that. He looked away, out the window, a muscle twitching in his jaw.

Katherine swallowed, forcing herself to move. She crossed the room, opened the door, and called out into the hall. "Tom, Bran? Can you come up here, please?"

"They won't hear you," Lucas said. "Not from the drawing room."

"They are not in the drawing room," she replied, going over to the sitting area in front of the dormant fireplace. Atop the table was a small tray of biscuits, all in Lucas' preferred flavors. She helped herself to one. "I asked them to wait on the landing."

Lucas cut her a glance, ice and flint in his eyes, then looked away again.

A rumble of feet, then Thomas and Brandon appeared in the doorway. They were confused, worried, and trying to hide it.

"Lucas," said Thomas. "Glad to see you mostly alive. Not many have survived the well-intended ministrations of Brandon Knight."

Brandon shot him a glare. "I shall let you bleed to death one day."

"Tom," said Katherine. "Could you lock the door?"

The request seemed to surprise him, but he complied. Once he had, and once a strained silence had fallen, absent of any sounds from the household around them, Katherine said, "As you may have guessed, Lucas did not fall from a horse."

"Of course," said Thomas, rolling his eyes. "In spite of my juvenile sense of humor, I was not born yesterday."

"I wasn't going to mention it," said Brandon, shooting Lucas a glance. "But I could tell that your injuries were not the result of a fall."

"No need to boast." Thomas gave Brandon a friendly shove and wandered over to the biscuits. "Go on, then, Lucas. Did you get into a scrap and come a cropper?"

Katherine met Lucas' gaze, and silently willed him to speak.

"It wasn't a fight," said Lucas. His words pulled like teeth. "Last night, I received a warning."

"A warning?" Thomas repeated, showering shortbread crumbs down his shirt. "What do you mean?"

Katherine took a breath, and reached for another biscuit. This afternoon was going to be a long and trying one. She should have rung for tea.

❦

THREE DAYS. THAT WAS ALL THE TIME THEY HAD.

Lucas had until Friday at midnight to cough up the money —

either in part or as a whole — and a failure to meet that requirement would end in dire, unspecified consequences.

Thomas and Brandon had handled the news well. After going a bit pale and quiet for several minutes, Brandon had sunk into one of the armchairs and told Lucas, under no uncertain terms, to hop the next boat to Calais. This had led to much disagreement and discussion — Thomas had begun pacing the length of the room — at the end of which, the four of them had come up with... nothing.

There were a few items they could sell, yes, but most of those items were heirlooms, little trinkets that would be almost impossible to fence (or so Lucas said), due to their obvious attachment to the Knight family. And, very little of what the Knight children had to hand was even worth selling — for the first time in her life, Katherine wished that she or her brothers were the indulgent sort, the type to spend dozens of pounds on silk clothing and jewelry. Disposing of such items was the simplest option, and least likely to garner attention.

We are too grim, Katherine thought as Rita pinned her hair. *Too grim, too Spartan. Too dedicated to a life of practicality and simple pleasures.*

"Are you well, my dear?" said Mrs. Knight from where she was perched at Katherine's desk. "You seem quiet."

Katherine offered a smile, and was pleased when the mirror told her it seemed genuine. "No, Mother. I was simply imagining what diversions this evening might hold."

"Plenty, I am sure." Mrs. Knight met her gaze in the mirror and offered a small smile of her own. "The Bainbridge family is well-known for their supper parties."

"Is it a supper party, then? And not a true ball?"

"Difficult to say." Mrs. Knight crossed out something on the list she was working on — matters to do with the household or the business, Katherine assumed. Mr. Knight would not know the first thing about what to pay the servants. "Supper is served at most balls, and most supper parties offer music and light dancing."

"Ah," said Katherine. "Then there is little, if any, difference between them."

"Only in what the hosts decide to list on the invitation." Mrs. Knight shook her head. "I am quite relieved that we are not hosting this year. It is such a bore."

Now, Katherine bit back a genuine smile. Her mother adored hosting, and refused to admit it. Katherine knew that the moment there was an engagement in the Knight family, the parties would be ridiculous.

"There has been quite a stir in the streets today, ma'am," said Rita. "It seems that Lady Hearsay is on the warpath again."

To Katherine's surprise, Mrs. Knight rolled her eyes. "That mongrel should have retired her quill years ago. She is nothing but a trouble-maker, and does more harm than good."

"Lady Hearsay?" Katherine repeated. "What on earth are you talking about?"

"Society papers," said Rita, raising an eyebrow. "Have you never heard of Lady Hearsay?"

"No, I—"

"Enough, Rita." But there was hardly any bite to Mrs. Knight's words. "No need to fill her head with such nonsense."

"Scandal sheets," said Rita, with a certain degree of relish. She reached into the pocket of her apron. "I confiscated it from Sally, ma'am, just this morning."

Mrs. Knight shot Rita a knowing look. "Confiscated for your own amusement, I think you mean."

"I resent that, ma'am," said Rita, all too cheerfully. She handed a thin, creased pamphlet to Katherine. "As long as there has been a social season, there have been gossip sheets. Written by anonymous hands and circulated among London's finest neighborhoods. They deliver all the news of the season and the debutantes, regardless of whether it is fit to print."

Unable to deny her own curiosity, Katherine cast her gaze over the pamphlet. It was only a few pages long, and printed on cheap, flimsy stock. The price in the upper right corner raised her eyebrow — definitely higher than she would have expected.

"Lady Hearsay has been writing for years," Rita went on, fiddling with the last bit of Katherine's hair. "She made the season of your mother's debut quite exciting, if I recall."

"Indeed, the cow," said Mrs. Knight.

Katherine stared at her mother. "No love lost between you, then."

"Not in the least," said Mrs. Knight, again performing surgery on the bit of paper before her. "Gossip-mongers have always done what they can to cast suspicion on the participants of the season, but few have gone as far as she. She seems to delight in tearing down the young women of London. A certain amount of intrigue and speculation is to be expected — after all, the drama is what sells the papers. But she goes too far, with little regard for the high cost of her claims. Of course, she has to bear none of the consequences."

"Your mother still nurses a grudge," said Rita to Katherine. "On behalf of a friend."

"Oh?" Katherine began to sift through her memories of her mother's friends. "Which one?"

"You do not know her." And now, a russet blush — one of anger, Katherine recognized — rose on her mother's cheeks. "She passed away several years ago."

Katherine nodded, feeling a twist of sympathy. "What was her name?"

"Joséphine." To Katherine's surprise, her mother's French accent was seamless. "She came from one of the highest-ranking families in the land. A French family. An unkind family, deeply unkind, to tell you the truth." Mrs. Knight cleared her throat. "But Josie was lovely. And she made a match, a love match, with a man of no title, no station. It was a scandal of the first order, only heightened by Lady Hearsay's delightful reporting on the matter."

"I see," said Katherine, glancing again at the paper in her hands. "Did Lady Hearsay ruin the match?"

"No," her mother replied. "I have no idea how they managed to secure it, to tell you the truth. Josie and I were the same age, but she debuted after I was married to your father, as she had three older sisters. I could only offer her my support from afar."

Nearly bristling with intrigue, Katherine bit back a tirade of questions. She had the feeling that her mother was hiding something, and resisting the urge to press her was like resisting the urge to pick at a scab. "Were they married, in the end?"

Mrs. Knight nodded. "I always liked him. He was a good man, and clever. He and Josie were quite a force to be reckoned with."

"But he was a commoner?"

"Yes, a physician, in fact. From the north." Now, a smile flickered over Mrs. Knight's face. "He had a wonderful brogue. It only slipped out when he had been at the wine, but my God..." She shook her head. "How we laughed."

It was strange for Katherine, to be sitting in front of her reflection when the air itself seemed to shift and blur, easing the lines between past and present. For a moment, Katherine felt as if she caught a glimpse of her mother, twenty-five years younger, waiting for the carriage to spirit her away to that evening's ball. Emotion, sudden and unbidden, pricked at her eyes, and she forced her attention back to the pamphlet. "This writing... it is clunky, to say the least."

"And inaccurate," said Rita. "Nine times out of ten. Most of it is mere invention, speculation. Sometimes it is quite obvious that Lady Hearsay works mainly out of second-hand whispers."

"You mean that she does not actually attend the events?"

"No," said Mrs. Knight. "But perhaps that is for the best. She is dangerous enough as it is, and hardly needs any more help."

"And people pay for this?" Katherine frowned down at a

sentence declaring that roasted swans had been served atop silver platters at the Opening Ball. "Even if they know it to be false?"

"Of course," Rita replied, now dabbing rouge on Katherine's cheek. "Boredom is the chief enemy of a successful season. But what else do the peers have to discuss, apart from each other?"

Katherine rolled her eyes. "Bonaparte, for one. The Americans, for another."

"Lady Hearsay must make money hand over fist," said Mrs. Knight. "Think of it — at least three copies a household, and dozens of households in the city. Not counting the servants and by-passers on the street." She let out a sigh. "Perhaps, then, I cannot begrudge her for not retiring. Not if there is good money to be made."

Rita smirked, then leaned down, under the pretense of straightening Katherine's silver necklace. " 'Tis a pity Lady Hearsay does not employ your services, Kat. You could offer her a most thrilling read."

Something like an idea began to churn in the back of Katherine's mind. She forced herself to nod, to smile like a lady. "Yes. Quite."

❧ 6 ❧

Once the idea came to her, it was impossible to shake, like a fly in her ear, or a shadow on a sunny day. It flew and tangled with other thoughts in the frosty current of Katherine's mind. She found it difficult to concentrate as she sat in the carriage, as she stepped into the Bainbridge manor, as she curtsied to her hosts and made her way to the ballroom. Tables were placed at even intervals, and she followed her parents towards an empty one, next to the wall. Away from the thrust of the evening's action, she noticed. An older couple she vaguely recognized approached the table — her parents' friends, she guessed — and Mr. and Mrs. Knight drifted towards them.

"Return to earth, Kat." Brandon, back from the refreshment table, offered her a smirk and a *canapé*. "Though I cannot blame you for searching for distraction."

" 'Distraction' is an understatement." Katherine took the *canapé* and stole Thomas' glass of wine, ignoring his indignant protest. "You must keep your heads," she muttered, emptying his wine into a nearby decorative plant. "Both of you."

"Why?" said Thomas with a scowl. "Dancing hardly requires concentration. Unless, of course, you're Brandon Knight."

"Does it require concentration to be simultaneously an arse and a bore?" Brandon said to his brother.

Thomas ignored him. "I agreed to attend the season," he said to Katherine. "No part of that agreement required me to be sober."

"Tom," she said, mustering a great effort to keep her voice low, "trust me on this. You can drink a little, but I need you to be functional when we get back to the house."

"Why?" said Thomas, but Brandon was already catching on. He nudged his brother and offered a mute shake of his head, his eyes wide.

"Oh." Thomas glanced between them. "I see."

Katherine, heedful of her nearby parents, leaned in and whispered, "I have an idea. It might only be an idea, nothing may come of it, but if it *is* worth something — we will need to act quickly, and decisively. Wine is the enemy of efficiency, not its ally."

"Says you," said Thomas, but he held up a hand in resignation. "Do not worry, Kat. I shall behave myself with unparalleled enthusiasm."

"If it distracts suitors from approaching our table," said Katherine, "by all means."

Thomas gave an artful pout. "Is our poor sister not enjoying her debut?"

"Bite your tongue," she hissed, darting a glance around the room. "If word spreads that I am of a disagreeable and unfriendly nature, then our chances of helping Lucas grow even slimmer."

"She says, while all but hiding behind her brothers."

Brandon was frowning. "What does your agreeability have to do with Lucas?"

Katherine said nothing, chewing the inside of her cheek. She forced her gaze to fixate on something across the room, something distant and unimportant. The blood thudded in her ears, just as the cogs and wheels turned in her brothers' minds.

"Good God, Kat." Brandon stared at her. "You cannot mean—"

"Bite your tongue," she whispered.

"No, sorry," said Thomas. "I am still quite lost."

"Be quiet," Brandon hissed, and he took Katherine's elbow. "Marriage is not the answer, Katherine. And if Lucas were here, he would explode at the idea of you—"

"It is our best option, Bran." She took a quick, flighty breath. "Our only option, if my idea does not hold water."

"Are you mad?" Brandon's ears were turning red while Thomas frowned, glancing between them. "You cannot be married in less than a week, Kat, it's—"

"Not less than a week," she agreed. "But quickly enough to liquidate my dowry and, if necessary, accept a small engagement gift from my new fiancé."

"None of that will matter," he replied, "if Lucas does not make a payment by Friday."

God, she wanted to scream, to throw something, to— "We need to prepare, Bran, for every eventuality. He may find a way to make this first payment, but what of the next? We need a long-term solution, and right now..." Katherine swallowed a gag of fear and steadied her voice. "Right now, I am our most lucrative commodity."

Something flashed in Brandon's eyes, something deep and indefinable, something that signaled — to her horror — of affection. "Kat." His spoke in a broken whisper. "How could you say such a thing?"

"I say it because it is true." A footman passed, and Katherine reached for a glass of wine. She downed half of it in a single gulp, relishing the warm burn in her throat. It surged through her belly, offering her courage. "Look around us. My worth, my price, is all that matters here. We aren't in the country anymore, Bran, where I can dress how I like and hunt and ride and carry on with you as if I am one of the men. If I did that here, they would take me to Bedlam."

Thomas stepped in, a genuine look of concern creasing his features. "Kat, if you are to marry, it should be for reasons that are personal, reasons of affection. Not this, not some attempt to rescue the family—"

A dry snort burst out of her before she could stop it, and Katherine swallowed the rest of her wine. "Clearly, brother, you are not well-educated on the purposes of marriage. Once upon a time, people wed for chickens and land. Our situation is the same, or close enough."

"I wish all we had to worry about was chickens," muttered Brandon, also reaching for a passing footman.

"This seems very unfair," said Thomas, giving Brandon and his wine a dirty look.

"Gentlemen," muttered Katherine, "I have not yet made up my mind, and I do not have any offers within sight. I am merely hedging my bets until we determine the feasibility of my idea."

"It is probably a terrible idea," said Thomas.

"Undoubtedly," said Brandon.

"Yes," Katherine agreed. "But it will be several hours before we can discuss the matter in full. Why not make the best of things, in the meantime?"

Thomas made a sound of derision. "You mean to dance?"

"Yes. I think so."

"How horrible."

"Come along." Katherine held out her hand. "You're the eldest brother, tonight. Mother and Father are occupied. Which means you should introduce me."

He winced. "Must I?"

She responded by taking his hand and all but shoving him towards the dance floor.

Brandon raised his glass at them. "An honorable sacrifice."

Thomas sighed but complied, and as they walked over the

polished floor, Katherine fought back a wave of revulsion, forcing herself to smile. All she could do was hope — hope that her idea might have some throttle, and save her from the prospect of marriage.

❦

THE CANDLE OFFERED LITTLE MORE THAN A WEAK, WARM circle of light as it hovered over the doors to Lucas' bedchamber. A floorboard creaked behind her, and Katherine shot Brandon a glare. "Sorry," he mouthed, his face ghoulish in the dim light, and beside him, Thomas rolled his eyes. The three of them continued to creep along the corridor, heedful of the room at the end of the hall, where their parents lay asleep. None of them said a word as Katherine gently turned the door handle, eased the door open, and slipped into Lucas' bedroom.

The space was dark, save for the light of a solitary candle beside his bed. Katherine guessed that he'd fallen asleep while reading — some sort of pamphlet was splayed across the covers, Lucas' eyes were closed, and his breathing came in a shallow, even tide. Her brothers followed her into the room, and Thomas locked the door with all the care of a father handling a newborn.

Katherine went to light the candles on the mantelpiece. "Wake him slowly," she whispered to Brandon, who nodded. "Tom, the corners."

The Mayfair house had a mischievous streak, and liked to carry whispers and secrets between rooms, spiriting them away on stray and unpredictable breezes. In an effort not to wake their parents, or expose their own craft, Katherine and her brothers had decided to implement a tactic they had not used since childhood — to stuff the crack beneath the door, and all the corners of the room, with blankets and pillows.

Thomas got to work, while Brandon gently prodded Lucas.

Katherine lit a few more candles and a soft, warm light began to pool through the room.

"Is this an ambush?" said Lucas, stirring. His voice was cracked and rough with sleep.

"Of sorts," Brandon replied. He helped Lucas to sit up, propping him against the headboard. "Kat's had an idea."

"Has she?" said Lucas. He squinted at where Thomas knelt in the corner, stuffing a pillow against the baseboard. "What the hell are you doing?"

"Covering our arses," Thomas replied. "We don't want to be overheard."

"Ah." Lucas looked at Katherine; his left eye was still swollen shut. "Is it treason, then?"

"Of the highest order," she replied, turning his chair towards the bed before sitting down heavily. "God in Heaven, my feet."

"A busy evening?"

"For another time." She propped her feet on his bed, and they throbbed in protest.

Brandon sat down beside Lucas and handed him a biscuit that seemed to materialize from thin air. "Kat did very well. Especially considering the depravity of our peers." He smirked at Thomas. "So did Tommy-boy."

Even in the dim light, Katherine could see Thomas' blush. "Shut up."

"Well, I'll be." Lucas grinned at Thomas as he sat down on the lounge at the foot of the bed. "Have you found a little lady to make an honest man out of you?"

"Gents," said Katherine, cutting off Thomas' reply. "Let's not waste time."

"The floor is yours," said Lucas, taking a bite of his biscuit.

Katherine paused to steady herself, a fresh wave of heat rushing to her face. Coming up with the idea was one thing — presenting it in full view of her brothers was quite another. "Are you... Are you familiar with society papers?"

"No," said Thomas and Brandon.

"Yes," said Lucas.

Katherine forced herself to breathe and pulled the rumpled copy of Lady Hearsay out of her pocket, tossing it onto the bed. "Gossip rags. All the society news that is fit to print for the season. Completely anonymous, and complete rubbish, from what I gather." She continued speaking as Thomas reached for the pamphlet, holding it up for the others to see. "But what matters is the circulation. The numbers are good, very good. You can make a tidy profit off even a small number of words, say less than three half-pages. And all of it is completely anonymous.

"This Lady Hearsay is the reigning champion of society papers. She has been around for years, long enough to have written about our mother's debut. The longevity of her career is especially remarkable, given that her reporting is often less than accurate."

"I can see that," said Thomas, pointing to the same sentence Katherine had caught, about swans being served at the Opening Ball.

"So what do you propose?" said Lucas. "Tracking down whoever Lady Hearsay might be and holding her at gunpoint until she coughs up her earnings?"

"No." Another wave of heat, building in Katherine's face. Her mouth went numb. "I propose that we enter the ring of society news ourselves. As her competitor."

A ringing silence fell after her pronouncement, and Katherine swallowed a spike of — of what, of trepidation? Of fear? Of panic? — as her brothers all turned to stare at her, incredulous.

"Gossip equals money," she went on. She had to keep speaking, before they remembered to put voice to their shock. "And when it comes to gossip, we are wealthier than half the families in London. I say we cash in, and quickly." Katherine reached into her pocket and unearthed a tightly-rolled furl of paper. "I have already written an edition that covers all of this evening's events, and more."

"More?" said Lucas, his voice low. "What do you mean?"

"She means Rita," said Brandon. "Don't you?"

Katherine nodded. "Rita brings me whispers from the servants across Mayfair and Kensington. It is a game of ours, a diversion — to gather information about our peers, to tuck away bread crumbs about their hidden lives. And that..." Now, horribly, her voice wavered. "That can be our insurance."

"What?" said Thomas, sharply. "What do you mean, insurance?"

"We never have to be obvious about it," said Katherine. "We do not have to show our hand. But if we indicate, through implication, that we have the ability to air the dirty laundry of the British aristocracy — it would keep us safe, and above inquiry, above suspicion. After all," she went on, "who would ever accuse the Knight family of knowing a single thing about the peerage?"

"No," said Thomas, tossing the pamphlet onto the bed. "No, Kat. It is far too dangerous, and far too great an undertaking."

"Wait," said Brandon. "Kat might be on to something. She's always scribbling in that journal of hers, and keeping notes about who says what and when."

Thomas looked at him, incredulous. "You cannot seriously consider this."

"Of course I will," Brandon replied. "Tom, do the arithmetic. Even if we charged less than this Hearsay person, we could turn a considerable profit, and quickly."

"It is not that simple," Thomas bit out. "None of it is."

"Lucas," said Katherine, breaking the tension. "What do you think?"

Lucas had been watching her, focused and unfocused all at once, while his brothers squabbled beside him. Now, something in his face shifted, and he said, "It does sound like a considerable risk, Kat, with very little promise of reward."

"How fitting," she said, before she could stop herself, "given that a similar action necessitated this conversation in the first place."

A silence fell, thick and awkward. Both Thomas and Brandon looked away, away from the silent argument playing out between their siblings. Katherine held her eldest brother's gaze, forcing herself to ignore the flash of hurt that had gone through his eyes.

"We have to decide," she went on. "And quickly. There is no point in discussing it any further if we are not in agreement."

"I'm for it," said Brandon. "It is the best idea we have had, and the only one that makes any worthwhile sense."

"As am I," said Katherine. "Obviously." She turned to Thomas.

He met her gaze and scowled. "Fine," he said. "But I give my approval under protest."

"Noted." She turned once again to Lucas, and waited.

When he spoke, his voice was bloodless. "We would have to tread carefully."

"Of course," Katherine said.

"And do whatever it takes to protect ourselves."

"Yes."

"Perhaps it's a bit mad," he said. "A mad venture."

"Of course it is," said Brandon. "But better to try something mad than to try nothing at all. I'd rather not put you on a boat to Calais."

"Nor I," said Katherine.

"Well," said Thomas, with a touch of his usual levity. "I wouldn't go that far—"

"We do not know anything about publishing a pamphlet," said Lucas.

"No," Katherine agreed. Her heart was racing, livid with the prospect of this endeavor. "We can make a few educated assumptions, but one of us will have to liaise with a printer as soon as possible. Incognito."

"Christ," said Thomas. "How do you propose we disguise ourselves?"

"A servant would attract the least attention," she said.

"A servant?" Brandon repeated, frowning.

"Ask Chauncey," said Lucas. "For a spare bit of livery. You could dress as an anonymous footman from the household of—" He looked at Katherine. "We never decided on a false name."

"The name comes later," she replied. "First, we need information."

"There is one assumption we can make," said Lucas. "Whatever agreement we reach with a printer, there will be an up-front cost for paper, ink, labor." He shook his head. "Which leaves us back where we started."

"No," said Katherine. Her mouth grew numb again. "Not quite." She cleared her throat. "The up-front cost will be minimal. We can pool our pocket money."

"That will not be enough, Kat—"

"Do not worry," she said quickly. "Do not worry about the cost of having it printed. I will handle it."

Another silence fell, and her brothers looked at her, then glanced at each other.

"I am not going to ask," Thomas muttered.

"Fine, then," said Brandon. "What is our first step?"

"The livery," she said. "And one of you visiting the printer. Before breakfast, if possible. In the meantime, we have to sort out the details." *I hardly know what I am doing*, she did not say, and she did not need to.

Brandon nodded. "I'll get to Chauncey in a few hours. In the meantime, I say we sleep?"

Katherine looked around at them, at her brothers, all of them tired and brilliant in the low light, and nodded. "We should begin meeting somewhere different. If we keep gathering in this room, Mother will grow suspicious."

"The parlor," said Lucas.

Thomas scoffed. "Right outside Father's office? You are mad."

"He's taken to working in the library. It has better light."

"The parlor will do for now." Katherine stood up, sliding the tightly rolled scroll of gossip back into her pocket. "Send for me when you return from the printers'."

The air seemed to tense as Brandon nodded, as they all went quiet and sat with the weight of their own plot. It was a mad idea, mad enough that it made her want to scream, madder still that her brothers had agreed to it, and so readily, taking her idea within a stride so sure that any other considerations now appeared ludicrous.

They have confidence in me, she realized, and that was the worst part of all.

Katherine left the room without looking at any of them again. Something had curdled in her stomach, something like nerves, and she could not bear it, she could not bear the possibility of naked hope showing on her face, and of her brothers seeing it, seeing everything in her heart. Because it was ridiculous to see anything in this, in a half-cooked plot and—

Her room was silent, her bed soft and cool. Katherine curled up against her pillow, and there, small and vulnerable beneath the night, she felt it, quickening beneath her skin. Something new, something tangled and thorny and impossible.

Something like ambition.

Katherine woke with a blurred mouth and a hand on her arm.

"Kat." Rita spoke in a low whisper. "Thomas is looking for you."

Katherine nodded and sat up, reaching for her dressing gown. "Follow me." The light was dim — she hadn't slept for more than a few hours. "This concerns you as well."

Mercifully, Rita did not say a word as they moved quietly along the corridor and down the stairs. The house was still cocooned in the hush of night, in the sleepy murmur between dawn and true light. There was no sign of her parents, and Katherine shivered at the magnitude of what was about to happen, but maybe— *Maybe*, she thought, reaching for the parlor door, *it was all a dream—*

She entered the parlor, and stopped short at the sight of Brandon in breeches, a trim shirt, a tricorn, and a pair of weathered boots.

"Morning." His smile jolted her, ruining the illusion. "Recognize me?"

"Barely."

"It suits you, Bran," said Thomas, from where he lounged by the lifeless fireplace. This room was even more dismal in the near-darkness. Thankfully, he struck a match and lit a few candles by his elbow. "Kat, you brought a guest."

"I did." Katherine shifted an inch closer to Rita. "It is easier than repeating myself."

"Bran," said Lucas. He was tucked into one of the sofas, stubbled and miserable. "Give us your news, quickly."

"I found a printer willing to take the work. A Mr. Beech." Brandon tugged a slip of paper out of his pocket and angled it toward the candles. "Or, rather, Mr. Beech's apprentice. It took some convincing, but he can guarantee our anonymity, as long as he is paid."

Shock had rendered Katherine nothing less than mute.

"How much?" said Lucas.

Brandon took a breath, and named a price. "For a hundred copies," he added. "I did not know how many we might want to—"

"A hundred," Lucas repeated, then nodded. "That seems reasonable. We cannot even guarantee that we would sell all of them—"

"I was wondering about that," said Thomas. "Surely we won't be the ones flogging them—?"

"No," said Brandon. "Mr. Beech has errand-boys. They will sell the pamphlets with the day's newspapers."

"What of the price?" Lucas glanced at his siblings. "Can we afford it?"

Here, finally, Katherine found her voice. "Yes."

His eyes were dark, steely, when they met hers. "You are certain?"

Katherine nodded. An odd kind of relief had flooded her veins — relief that this gamble was less of a gamble, and more a genuine plan — a plan to rescue her brother, if only— "We have to work quickly."

And they did.

Over the next half-hour, details and contingencies were plotted out to their infinite end. Brandon had the idea of under-cutting the market, and selling their pamphlets at a lower price per copy than Lady Hearsay, furthering their chances at turning a profit and increasing demand. After estimating their gross earnings, Brandon then accounted for the percentage that would be funneled back to Mr. Beech, his apprentice, and the errand-boys, and to Rita, for supplying information from the local servants. Rita, to her usual credit, did not react to any of the news beyond a simple nod. But she flashed Katherine a look that promised a later conversation behind a different set of closed doors.

In the end, even allowing for a low number of sales, they would be left with enough money for Lucas to make his first payment. Providing, of course, that the income found its way back to them in a timely fashion.

"Good grief." Thomas had been looking over Brandon's shoulder at the pages of sums. "I suppose we are lucky at least one of us paid attention in arithmetic lessons."

"How much notice does Mr. Beech need, Brandon?" Katherine unrolled her notes from the previous evening, feeling a sudden tremor at the sight of her own handwriting, handwriting that would soon be set in unyielding, black carbon. "How many hours?"

Brandon shrugged. "He needs it the night before publication, he said. To have it out with the morning edition. Latest would be ten o'clock, I think."

Katherine nodded. "We have time, then. More than I expected."

"Can we read what you've written?" Thomas fidgeted as everyone turned to look at him in surprise. "What? I think we should have some idea—"

"Yes." Katherine handed him her pages and turned to Lucas.

"I had another thought. The three of you can use the White Fox to your advantage."

"How do you mean?"

She smiled.

He groaned, tipping his head back into the cushions. "Katherine, if the Tyndales catch us eavesdropping on the cream of London's crop—"

"They won't catch you. And you need not behave any differently, or take any particular risks." She shrugged. "Don't men have a natural tendency to speak freely around other men?"

"She is right," said Thomas. "Gentlemen, especially."

"We will not report on anything too scandalous," Katherine went on. "But if I am keeping an eye on the ladies, it is only fair that you keep an eye on the men."

"A name," said Brandon, in the middle of checking his sums for the third time. "We still haven't got a name for this damned thing."

Katherine looked to Lucas, who looked to Thomas. And when nobody replied, Brandon glanced up, irritated. "It need not be ground-breaking. We just need a *nomme de plume*."

Thomas sniggered. "A *what?*"

"Any ideas?" said Lucas, to Katherine.

She shook her head.

"Well..." Lucas scuffed a hand through his hair. "We could keep in fashion, and call ourselves a 'Lady' as well."

"No," said Thomas. "We don't want it to seem like we are imitating this Hearsay person."

Katherine bit back a smile. "We don't?"

Thomas shook his head. "We want to distance ourselves, to stand out. Why not 'Madam?' "

"Madam what?" said Brandon, impatient.

"Kensington," said Rita. "It takes the scrutiny away from Mayfair, doesn't it?"

"Madam Kensington," Katherine repeated, feeling that same

feeling, something like nerves and hope tangled in her stomach. Spoken aloud, the name seemed to carry the same arcane tethering of a spell, an inertia, a promise. A new era, if she was given to indulging such fancies.

"Madam Kensington it is," said Brandon. "And are these her papers?"

"No," said Thomas. "These are her High Society Papers."

His siblings all laughed then, jeering and throwing pillows at him. Thomas grinned, his cheeks flushed, and perhaps it was all a bit fun, a bit meaningful, a bit meaningless—

"We can finalize the material later this afternoon." Katherine made for the door, Rita in tow. "In the meantime, I shall sort out our payment for Mr. Beech."

"And we must all put in an appearance at breakfast," said Brandon. "Earlier rather than later."

"Fine," said Lucas. "But one of you will have to carry me."

"You can walk perfectly well on your own, you sod—"

Katherine slipped out while her brothers were bickering, feeling Rita's gaze on the back of her neck. She led the way up the stairs to the second floor, down the corridor, and into the little cupboard just inside the entrance to the servants' staircase.

"This bodes well," Rita said, watching her root around in the sewing supplies.

Katherine said nothing as she unearthed a pair of scissors — large scissors, shiny and sharpened to a brutal edge, usually reserved for fabric. Ignoring Rita's raised eyebrow, she closed the passage to the servants' staircase, and made her way back to her bedroom.

Once the door was shut and locked behind them, Katherine turned to Rita and said, "I can explain everything."

"I sincerely hope so."

After breakfast, Rita met Katherine's gaze in the mirror with her jaw set and her eyes flashing. "Kat. I will say once more, and for the final time, that I do not approve."

"Noted." Katherine took a deep breath. "But if you refuse, I shall have to do it myself, and that could—"

"It *would* be a disaster." Rita shook her head and took the pair of sewing scissors in hand. "Are you— Are you completely certain—?"

"Yes. Even if our business venture falls through, we could use the money."

"Very well." Rita winced. "If you're certain—"

"I am." Katherine worked to keep her voice even. "Do it, please. Quickly."

Something horrible, something far too much like excitement and relief, churned in Katherine's stomach as she watched Rita lift the scissors in one hand and take one of her braids in the other. Katherine kept her gaze fixed on the mirror, hardly daring to breathe, as the shining metal closed around some of the twisted chestnut strands she had worked to grow for the better part of two years. *Snick* — a brutal, thin sound; a peculiar grinding sensation in her ears, in her scalp; and one of the braids fell away, drooping into Rita's waiting hand.

Rita sucked in a breath, then shook her head. She lay the cut braid on Katherine's bed, then returned.

Snick.

The other braid fell away, and with it went an unexpected weight. Katherine looked at the length of winding hair in Rita's hand, then back at her own reflection. Now, her hair hung halfway down her shoulder blades, shorter than she'd had it in years. Shorter, but not so short that she could not put it into a bun. The ends were sloppy, truncated, and yet she could not keep herself from smiling like a fool.

"I knew it." Rita lay the second braid beside the first and

wiped off the scissors with her apron. "You had an ulterior motive all along."

"I hardly know what you mean." Katherine *was* smiling now, properly, there was no point in denying it. Her fingers combed through her hair, her short hair, and it was delightful, wonderful—

Rita was smirking. "You were looking for any excuse to be rid of it." She went about wrapping the braids tightly in sheets of yesterday's newspaper. "Your mother would—"

"She will not know." They'd already discussed this. "She will never see me wearing it down."

"I shall tidy the ends when I return." Rita tucked the parcel into the pocket of her skirt. "Until then, keep out of sight, you minx."

"Of course, Rita, dear." And Katherine offered her her best grin.

Rita paused, then shook her head, a true smile softening her mouth. "I cannot decide whether you are mad or brilliant."

"Time will tell, Rita." Katherine reached for her journal. "Time will tell."

⁂

KATHERINE SLIPPED BACK INTO THE PARLOR HALF AN HOUR before she had to leave for the Donager supper party. She found her brothers in much the same positions they'd occupied that morning, but with rather wild hair — stress, it seemed, was in the air.

"Gents." She shut the door, locked it, and kicked the rug up against the threshold, blocking the gap between the edge and the floorboards. "How are we?"

"Not well," said Lucas. He had a glass of Scotch in hand. "Thomas has taken it upon himself to become something of a tart."

"I have not." Thomas looked up from his seat at the desk, his expression like a thundercloud. "And I do not appreciate the exaggeration, dear brother."

"Listen," Katherine said, holding up the envelope. "I have the money we need to place the order."

The effect was instantaneous — the three of them twitched to attention, staring at her in utter disbelief. But before any of them could voice a question—

"Brandon," she said. "If you can find a way to haggle with Mr. Beech in a manner— well, not untoward — it is best to be as polite as possible in such matters, and you must not be forceful, or rude, or— anyway, if you can haggle him down a bit, we might be able to put some of this towards Lucas' payment."

"Right," he replied. "I shall haggle in a manner becoming to a gentleman. Because that sounds reasonable and, well, *possible*."

"Yes, thank you." Katherine turned to Thomas. "Now, what was this about you being a tart? I see no rouge, no stockings—"

"Thomas has found a quill," said Lucas. "And — shock and horror — some ink."

Katherine raised an eyebrow at Thomas. His refined complexion took on the quality of a fresh tomato, and he rolled his eyes.

"I simply added a few things," he said, fiddling with the corner of a bit of paper. "To your writing, Katherine."

Katherine blinked at him, surprise overcoming her so completely that for a moment, her feet went numb. "I beg your pardon?"

"I am not changing it." Thomas pushed away from the desk and brought her a small stack of papers. "But I read Lady Hearsay after breakfast, and I realized that she— she implements such flowery language, and she takes on a very personal tone with her readers. She engages with them, and makes them feel as if she is letting them in on a secret."

"Mental." Brandon shook his head, not looking up from his sheets of sums. "He's gone completely mental."

Thomas flushed again, and Katherine saw the red creep up to his ears — something that had not happened since he was a boy. Thomas did not embarrass easily, not at all, and beneath the surprise, she felt a prickle of wonder — wonder that such a change, such a shift could occur.

"I see," she said, taking the papers from him. A quick glance told her that, true to his word, he had changed very little of the meat of her writing. He had added flourishes, and asides, that—

"Good grief, Tom, our mother has said no such thing—"

"What good is the truth, without a touch of intrigue?"

In spite of herself, Katherine snorted. "This is more than intrigue, this is—"

"What does it matter?" he said, with a bite of impatience. "It will sell. You know it will."

And he was right. If Katherine knew her peers at all, she knew that they would lap up the drama with a spoon. She nodded, handing the papers back to him. "What is the plan?"

"Given that you are occupied for the evening," said Brandon, "Thomas will draft a final, clean copy of the pamphlet. He and I will take it over to Mr. Beech once you and Mother have left, and Lucas will ensure that no one is any wiser to our absence. After we've returned, Tom and I will have supper in the dining room with Father and Lucas, to keep up appearances."

"And you have a disguise?" Katherine said to Thomas.

He nodded. "Chauncey found me something in the laundry."

"Well." Katherine glanced between the three of them and fought back a smile. She could hardly believe that here they were, working together, helping one another, with an endeavor so ridiculous it made her want to cackle like a monkey. "I suppose... this is it, gents."

"Yes," said Thomas. "Now leave us to our work."

She raised an eyebrow. "I shall see you when I return from the Donagers'."

"Bring us plenty of notes," said Brandon. "Oh—" He looked up. "And a slice of cake, if there's dessert."

"Cake?"

"Salk's gone off cake," said Lucas, by way of explanation. "God knows why. Brandon is taking it quite personally."

"I see." Katherine passed her envelope of money to Brandon and gathered her skirts. "I suppose I should join Mother."

"Please do." Lucas almost smiled. "Keep your ears open, Kitten."

❦   8   ❧

It would be poetic and somehow fitting to state that, paralyzed with anxiety and excitement and all the nervous moods in-between, Katherine did not sleep a wink that night, the night that Madam Kensington came into being. But instead, she slept like a troll — unmoving, hunched, snoring. Unaccustomed to the demands and late hours of the social season, she'd poured herself into bed with all the grace of a spilled drink, and pulled the covers over her head. Her aching mind, her aching feet, her aching stomach (which was not pleased by the rich food) were all hallmarks of her new station, and overwhelmed any concerns she might have had about Madam Kensington stepping into the world for the first time, shaky as a foal.

She woke later than usual when Rita pulled the covers off her head and exposed her to the dazzling, unexpected sunshine of the new day. Katherine squinted, rubbed a hand over her face, and grumbled, "What year is it?"

"1812, little madam, much to our disappointment." Rita was bustling around the bed, gathering various articles of clothing from where Katherine had left them strewn across the floor.

Behind her, Sally was shaking out the curtains, relieving them of dust and, no doubt, spiders.

"I suppose that is some comfort," said Katherine. She sat up, and was reminded of all the aches and pains bestowed upon her by the dance floor. A wince crawled up her spine as she rubbed her face again. "What time is it?"

"Just past eleven," said Rita. She handed Katherine's laundry to Sally and pulled a dusting cloth out of her apron pocket. "There is ever such a stir downstairs, Kat."

"Really?" Katherine met her gaze then quickly looked away again. "Whatever for?"

"It seems that there is a new publication in the city," said Rita. She began dusting the mantelpiece, not seeing the way Sally darted a glance at her. "Society papers."

"I see." Katherine fiddled with her braid, curling the end around her finger. She refused to admit to the excitement that was frothing in her stomach. "Are they quite full of scandal?"

"One supposes."

"Miss Katherine." Sally was looking at her with wide eyes. "Your hair."

Katherine met her gaze, then looked down at her very short braid. Damn. She'd forgotten—

"Terrible, isn't it?" said Rita, light as a feather. "That's what she gets for climbing in a tree."

"A tree?" said Sally, frowning.

"Yes," said Katherine quickly. "The— the sap. It became quite entangled in my hair, and would not shift for anything."

"There was nothing we could do," said Rita. "It had to be cut."

"Oh." Sally glanced between them, the corner of her mouth twitching. "How awful."

"Yes," said Rita. "And Mrs. Knight cannot find out, of course."

"Of course." Sally then seemed to steel herself. "Miss Katherine, it seems that these new society papers are daring, indeed."

"Are they?" Feigning ignorance was so enjoyable, Katherine

almost hated herself for it. "Has Lady Hearsay broken some great scandal?"

Sally shook her head. "It is not Lady Hearsay, Miss Katherine. It is a new writer, a complete unknown. No one has any idea who she is, but what is obvious..." A blush rose on her cheeks, along with a look of cheeky delight. "It is obvious that she knows what she is writing about."

"How exciting." When Sally turned away, Katherine shot a glance at Rita, and both of them shared a tiny, quick smile. "Time for breakfast, I think." She slid out of bed and sucked in a breath of fresh morning air. "And then, Rita, let's go for a walk."

⁂

NONE OF HER BROTHERS WERE AT BREAKFAST, AND KATHERINE was not surprised, given her lateness. As much as she would have liked to press them for all the details of their experience the night before, Katherine knew that they, like her, had to keep up appearances. Not that anyone would suspect the Knight children for behaving in a manner unseemly to their station — in fact, she was certain that if anyone thought a society family was directing the hand of Madam Kensington, the country-rough Knights would not even pass into consideration. But it was better, perhaps, to be safe, rather than sorry.

Besides, Katherine thought, as Graves and Sally cleared away the remains of breakfast, *if we are to continue this, we should get into the habit of covering our tracks.*

Speaking to the boys would have to wait until that evening, she guessed, when Brandon would return to the printer and collect their earnings. Then, she could hear everything. And, they would know if their endeavor, as silly as it might be, would turn a profit.

She could hardly keep a handle on her own impatience, which surprised and annoyed her. Katherine was not predisposed to bouts of emotion, or to heightened fits of fancy. To find herself so unmoored and so reckless — it was galling, frightening.

But it was difficult to feel frightened in the bright, rare sunshine of that delicious May morning. She smiled up into the sun, tilting her parasol back and away from her face, relishing the heat on her forehead and cheeks. Katherine had a habit of greeting the sun as she would an old friend, regardless of the season. Even in winter, she would pull her woolen muffler away from her face, feel the ice sting her cheeks, and grin up into the blinding gray sky.

"Come, dear." Rita's voice was thick with sarcasm. "You'll ruin your complexion."

Katherine never bothered with anything as silly as a parasol in the country. She only did so in London because it was expected of her, and because she tired of the scandalized, patronizing looks from the mothers. She opened her eyes and smirked at Rita, returning to the shade of her parasol. "If only the whole summer promised weather as jovial as this."

Rita shook her head as they both stepped onto the pavement, joining the flow of foot traffic through Mayfair. "It never does, Kat. Never."

This, too, was a common habit in the Knight family — taking a walk in the morning, passing through the market and along the houses that were more beautiful and stately than their own. Even now, Katherine could taste the warm, buttery flesh of roasted chestnuts from the market on Twelfth Night two years before, when she'd accompanied her father south for a sudden errand in the city.

But there was something different, today. Something in the air, in people's hands. The inaugural edition of Madam Kensington's High Society Papers, in printed flesh.

Katherine caught her first glimpse of Madam Kensington between the lace fingers of Lady Ednam. Lady Ednam was discussing something with a companion, her mouth curved with glee — gossip, primed and perfected. Katherine let her gaze slide along to the next young lady, and the next, then to a young gentleman and his wife, and even to a footman polishing the brass fixtures on a family's front fence. They all had Kensington in hand or in pocket. Katherine pressed her lips together, forcing back a smile, caught Rita's gaze, and continued down the road, past the homes and market stalls that she had known her entire life.

"—simply outrageous, can you believe—?"

"—had no idea that Val Bainbridge could—"

"—trod on her toes during the quadrille, to nobody's surprise—"

"Apparently, her father has promised a bushel of silver to anyone who—"

They were all discussing it. Everyone — peers, servants, merchants, and anyone in-between. Katherine's heart raced as she heard her own words swirl through the air, at once a parody and a reflection, an endorsement of her efforts. She took a quick breath, and tried not to stare, or to smirk, or to — God help her — let out a squeal of glee.

It was ridiculous, of course. To derive — satisfaction? pleasure? — out of such a fleeting, indulgent bit of nonsense. But perhaps Katherine could be ridiculous, just this once.

❧

BRANDON WAS GRINNING LIKE A DEVIL, HIS FACE SMUDGED with soot from the murky passageways of London. "We seem to be somewhat of a success."

"Really?" Katherine could have smacked herself for sounding so breathless. "Don't exaggerate, Bran—"

"I would never." He reached into his messenger pouch and withdrew a leather pouch swollen with coins. "If you do not believe me, then believe this."

Something within Katherine's body teetered and fell, plummeting to her feet. A strange beat kicked up in her ears as she stared at Brandon, at the undeniable evidence of their success.

"Holy Christ." Thomas' voice was hoarse, wobbly. "They bought it."

"It seems that all of London bought it," said Lucas, wry. He stood up from the couch and went over to Brandon, reaching for the pouch. It clinked as it settled in his hand, the coins within rattling like leaves in autumn. Katherine did not miss the look of wonder that crossed his face, before he schooled it into submission. "How much is there?"

Brandon named a figure that turned Katherine's knees to jelly. "And that's after Beech took his payment, and payment for the runners."

"But that—" Katherine gulped. Her face, her chest, her fingers — they had all gone numb, simply faded out of existence. "That cannot mean—"

Brandon nodded, unable to hide his glee. "We sold every copy. Every copy, plus another run of fifty."

"Another run?" Thomas sank into the couch, looking rather windswept.

"They sold out before noon," said Brandon. "Beech called for more copies. Then they sold out again."

"We are quite lucky, I think," said Lucas. "To live in a city full of such incurable gossips."

"It must be a fluke," said Katherine. She was hardly aware of her own voice. "This is the first time in years that they have heard from anyone other than Lady Hearsay. They were simply looking for something new."

"Perhaps." Brandon nodded. "But we would be fools to think that London will grow tired of Madam Kensington overnight."

"Meaning?" she said.

"He thinks our success will continue." But Lucas kept his expression impassive. "Now that Madam Kensington has arrived, it appears that she will stay."

"All the better for you, Lucas." Thomas glanced at his eldest brother. "There is hope in sight, is there not?"

Lucas looked at Katherine, then looked away, back at the money in his palm. His black eye had faded somewhat, and the bruising around his cuts had dulled to a faint, sickly yellow. In the twilight, he appeared to be growing out of the house itself, his shadow stretching towards the cracking plaster. "I suppose there is."

Something shifted in the air, some intangible and sticky. Katherine looked to Thomas, then to Brandon. A silent agreement passed between them, in a manner untested and yet seamless. The three of them looked at one another, and knew that Lucas could not be left alone with the money. Not even for a minute.

And perhaps there was something to it, this telling look. Something that trembled within their shared blood. Because Lucas, after taking a long, shaky breath, extended his hand, offering the pouch of money back to Brandon.

Brandon took it, slid it back into his bag. "This is all well and good. But how are we to deliver Lucas' payment? We are expected at supper."

Lucas scowled and looked every inch like some mythological beast. "There is no 'we,' Brandon. I will meet the Tyndales."

Thomas snorted. "You are not going alone—"

"Of course I am going alone!" Lucas rounded on his brother. "Don't be ridiculous—"

"If you think we are letting you set off all on your lonesome to face the wild animals who tried to eat you for supper, you're not nearly as clever as Mother says." Thomas grinned without mirth. "Give in, Lucas. You are fighting a war you cannot win."

"Let's go after supper," said Brandon. "I shall need to wipe down and change."

"And get upstairs without Mother or the servants seeing you," said Katherine.

"No matter," he replied. "They will assume I am in disguise. Sneaking off to woo a young lady."

Katherine could not help herself — she giggled.

"They might actually believe it," said Lucas, the corner of his mouth twitching. "In spite of twenty years' experience speaking to the contrary. We shall have to encourage their impressionable minds, Bran."

He blinked. "I beg your pardon?"

"He means theatrics, Bran." Thomas flicked a hand through the air. "A mussed collar, rouge on the shirt, a bit of perfume in the hair, yes? That sort of thing?"

Brandon's face curdled. "If I must."

"Rita will discourage any whispers that might threaten us," said Katherine. "We can rely upon her judgment in these matters."

"And what of her judgment in other matters?" Lucas looked at her. "You are certain you trust her involvement with this enterprise? A secret of such magnitude?"

She looked back at him, a bolt of nerves going through her stomach. Of all the unexpected— "Of course, Lucas."

The moment hung between them, tense as a new blade. Then Lucas gave a nod, stepping towards the windows. "After supper, then. When Father and Mother have retired to the library."

"And I am coming with you," said Katherine. A blush, horrible and untimely, rose in her forehead. "To the White Fox."

For the second time that evening, a silent conversation took place. Lucas looked to Brandon, who looked to Thomas, who looked back to Lucas. There was a bit of a sigh, and Katherine could see the moment of surrender, the moment when her brothers realized that they had to pick their battles, especially now.

"Fine," said Lucas. "But get out your trousers and cap. The moment these men see a lady in a skirt, they will pounce."

Katherine nodded, fighting back a shiver.

The clock on the mantel chimed the quarter hour, and they all glanced at the muted, dusty face. "Time to change," said Thomas. He swung himself to his feet. "See you all *sur la table*."

"You first," said Katherine. "Then Lucas, and I will come in from the garden. Brandon will join us last, and seemingly in a hurry."

Lucas gave a soft, genteel snort. "Father would not even notice if Bran came in with his trousers on his head."

"No," Katherine agreed. "But Mother would."

And they all knew that avoiding the keen and unremitting gaze of Mrs. Knight would be the key to Madam Kensington surviving the season.

⁂

KATHERINE WAS AWARE, MUCH AS SHE WAS AWARE OF HOW TO track a deer, that she had seen very little of London in her eighteen years of life. Her limited city experience had been shaped by the steady, unchanging scenery of their little road in Mayfair, by the repetitive and conniving halls of their family home. She knew Kensington, and the homes of her parents' scant number of friends. She knew the park, and the street, and the market.

She did not, however, know the White Fox.

The White Fox Club sat in the lower corner of Belgravia, austere and imposing in its solid white veneer. *Gentlemen Only* read the delicate gold sign beside the front door, and she guessed that the brass fixtures were polished by hand on a weekly, or even daily, basis. No part of this building had ever known the touch of something as foul as soot, as unseemly as smoke. She imagined that fingerprints left by its members upon tables or chess boards would vanish into thin air, buffeted away by nothing other than the building's own will. Within its walls, treaties were discussed, embargoes decided, trades offered. The White Fox contained some of Britain's greatest and most terrible secrets, and Katherine itched to climb a wall, open a window, and listen.

"Breathtaking, isn't it?" Thomas cut her a sly look. "I promise, it is unbelievably dull inside."

"You would say that." Katherine scuffed the heel of her boot against the cobblestones. "But I've heard the stories. Cigars with the Prime Minister and his Cabinet. Visitors from faraway countries. Evenings with the nicest ladies from Soho, procured most discreetly for your entertainment."

Something in Thomas' jaw tightened, and Katherine knew that her information was correct. He let out an unimpressed grunt. "Exaggeration and speculation."

She sucked her bottom lip between her teeth, forcing back a grin of victory. But in the late evening darkness, and away from the street lamps, Thomas would never have been able to see it. "If the Fox is so dull, why continue to go?"

"Do we have any other choice?" said Brandon. "It is expected of us, much as it is expected of you to attend tea parties and dance with eligible young gentlemen. And for all his complaining, Thomas does enjoy himself of an evening."

"Of course I do," Thomas replied. He leaned back against the brick building, slotting into shadow. "But I am one for the simple pleasures, brother. Cigar, Scotch, and conversation are all I need to enjoy myself. Unlike you, with your books—"

"At least a book does not make snide comments about my lineage—"

"Stop." Katherine went as still as a pointing hound. She stared into the darkness of the alley, into the space near the rear exit of the White Fox. There was a dart of movement, then a sudden, slippery beam of light as the door opened. Muted light — the light of lamps, not of a candle, she guessed —from a stairwell. As she watched, Lucas slipped out of the White Fox and into the alley, his white shirt a purple gleam in the darkness. The muted light of the stairwell pooled through the window beside the door and settled around him, a soft, orange glow.

Brandon checked his pocket watch, though Katherine knew that he would not be able to read it. "Right on time, I think."

They did not have to wait long. A mere minute passed before the rear exit opened again, and three figures joined Lucas in the alley. Two of them were... large. Large enough that, even in such low visibility, Katherine could see how they towered over her brother, who was not a small man to begin with. Lackeys, she guessed. Enforcers.

One of the men said something, and Lucas replied. The brick and the shadows and the hushed commotion of the street behind them swallowed the words. Katherine's ears strained to catch something, anything, but she forced herself not to move, not to shift as much as an inch. She was here as a courtesy, and she would not compromise Lucas.

Then, Lucas turned, glancing over his shoulder towards the spot where he knew his siblings lay in wait. Thomas hesitated, then stepped forward, taking the pouch of money from Brandon. He crossed the alley, his footsteps echoing along the cobblestones.

It happened in the space between breaths. The money passed from Thomas to Lucas to the men, and Katherine heard the faint rattle of the coins. It occurred to her that the men might want to count the money, but Lucas had assured her that this was unlikely — it was a gentlemen's debt, after all.

A long, tense moment. Katherine watched one of the men step towards the light of the rear entrance and fumble with the purse of coins. He stood there, doing something she could not see, though she guessed that he was checking whether the purse was actually full.

Whatever he saw seemed to be enough. The man stepped forward, said something else, and the he and his men retreated into the White Fox. Once the door swung shut, Lucas and Thomas hurried back across the alley.

"Is that it?" said Katherine as they approached, looking up into their shadowed faces. "Is it done?"

"Yes," said Lucas, as Thomas nodded. "We seem to be in the clear." He glanced over his shoulder again, back at the club. It seemed even more monolithic now, jagged and white as a tooth. Katherine looked at him, at the nerves he did such an excellent job of hiding, and looked away.

"Come along." Thomas took a step towards the road. "We should get home."

They all turned their backs on the White Fox. Lucas fell into step beside Brandon. Thomas kept pace with Katherine, glancing at her as the approaching street lamps offered greater visibility.

"It is almost strange to see you like this." The corner of his mouth quirked. "Perhaps I have become accustomed to seeing you in a dress."

"Perish the thought," she murmured.

They passed into the street; traffic was low, quiet for a Thursday evening. As Lucas and Brandon drew ahead, Thomas glanced at her and muttered, "I feared he was lying. About all of it. That it was all some ruse to obtain more cash..." He did not need to elaborate. The silence was enough explanation.

Katherine did not look at him; she could not bring herself to. Not when he had voiced the very fear that had been nagging at the back of her mind ever since Lucas had appeared in the garden. "So did I," she breathed.

Thomas looked at her. She could feel his gaze on her face. And together, they continued walking, slipping through the shadows of the street, leaving that inescapable but horrible thought scattered on the pavement, ready to be crushed by a passing wheel.

❧ *9* ☙

Madam Kensington's High Society Papers, No. 1

Well, well, well, my darlings... The London season is off to quite a remarkable start, is it not? Each year, I find myself expecting nothing less than the absolute highest standard of beauty, indulgence, and — of course — Rumor. And each year, I am never disappointed. This season promises to be quite thrilling indeed, a season of sly grins, lifted brows, *double entendres*. The Opening Ball brought us the Dawn of our annual Star, a bright and shimmering beacon amidst the lesser, duller planets of our delectable little orbit. We all watched with bated, hungry breath as she stepped into a room full of admirers, carrying with her a radiance so remarkable it threatened to blind us, stupefy us, bewitch us. There is no use denying the Queen's sharp, impenetrable eye in these matters — in moments such as this, where one is faced with proof beyond a doubt, it is all we can do to humble ourselves, to admit, in hushed tones, the power of her royal gaze...

"I THOUGHT YOU SHOULD HAVE A COPY." RITA SMILED AS Katherine ran her finger across the pamphlet. "For posterity, or whatever it is they call it."

Katherine smiled in return, unable to stop herself. Seeing her new name again, in the clear light of day, only solidified this strange and delightful path. The tip of her finger came to rest on the word 'Star,' and she felt it, the weight of the ink, of the paper. Of the future.

"Have you a plan, then?" Rita reached for a hairbrush. "For how Madam Kensington will sneak among the masses?"

"Of sorts," Katherine replied. "I shall keep my paper in my bodice, and my pencil in my shoe, as I have always done. The trouble is finding the right moment to sneak away, and to a space secluded enough that I might be alone for longer than a few minutes."

"It will become easier, I am sure," said Rita, "once you have a feel for the houses."

"I hope so. It is dreadful when I have to rely upon my memory, rather than my notes. I find that I forget certain details, and nuances."

"I would think that nuance matters little, in terms of gossip."

"On the contrary," said Katherine, wry, "it is all that matters." She slid the first edition of Madam Kensington into the top drawer of her vanity and locked it, then slipped the key beneath her unused jewelry box.

Rita hummed, twisting a lock of Katherine's hair around her finger. "I could ask some of the girls about the houses. Ahead of your attending the events, I mean. So you would know where to sneak away, where to hide."

Katherine met her gaze in the mirror. "Would that not raise suspicion?"

"No more than our usual conversation." Rita flashed her a

wink. "But I suppose I cannot fault your caution. I imagine the whole town is wondering who Madam Kensington might be."

A gentle snort broke free before Katherine could stop it. "Perhaps, Rita, but such imagining savors strongly of self-indulgence."

"Meaning?"

"Meaning..." Katherine swallowed, looking away from her reflection. "Pride can be a dangerous thing. It is best not to encourage it."

In her periphery, Katherine could see Rita flash her something like a frown. But then she looked away, back to Katherine's hair. "Have you heard about Lord Alwyn's new carriage? It is quite ornate, upholstered in a fine red brocade. Gold on the windows, that sort of thing."

"Really?" Katherine could not help herself — she glanced up, raising an eyebrow. "Why should they need a new one?"

The corner of Rita's mouth twitched. "I gather that the reason for our Star's tardiness at the Opening Ball was the result of an axle snapping *en route* from the palace."

"Goodness. It is a wonder they arrived at all."

"Ah," said Rita. "Only due to the efforts of Lord Alwyn's youngest daughter, if reports are to be believed. She worked with the footman and a passing stranger to repair the axle and get the carriage out of the mud." She shook her head. "One can only imagine the state of her dress."

A storm of questions threatened to roll through Katherine's mind. She blinked a few times, trying to match this new information to the events she had watched play out before her eyes. "But the youngest Lady Alwyn did not attend the Ball."

"No," Rita agreed. "She is not yet out."

"Then why was she in the carriage at all?"

"She attended her sister's presentation at court, I believe. Per her mother's request."

Katherine shot Rita a knowing look. "You have quite the songbird under your wing."

A wicked grin broke across Rita's face. "A young one. She has not yet learned when to hold her tongue."

"A lady's maid?"

Rita shrugged. "A kitchen maid. But it seems that the whole household knew of the incident. I am not surprised, given that it nearly ruined Lady Sophia's debut."

Katherine hummed, toying with her pencil. "I shall have to keep my wits about me, then. I would not have expected a ship as strong as the theirs to already have its leaks."

"There are worse ideas, you know," said Rita, "than forming an alliance with the Star of the season."

"Why, Rita." Katherine smirked. "You sound almost conniving."

"I should think you would share the sentiment." Rita pinned Katherine's bun into place. "Or have your priorities shifted?"

Ah. She spoke of Katherine's other plan — of matrimony. Something in the air had gone very dry indeed. Katherine's gaze lost its focus, hazed in the milky sea of the mirror. "No," she found herself saying. "They have not."

"There is no better place to find an eligible gentleman than at the skirts of the Star."

And Rita was correct, of course. Men clung onto Lady Sophia like limpets — if Katherine had a different temperament, she would have recognized the opportunity bestowed upon her by male fragility, and pounced. But something within her forced her away from such considerations, from an act of seeming cowardice.

"At any rate." Katherine slipped her pencil into her slipper. "This promises to be a most instructive afternoon."

"Worthy of Madam Kensington, do you think?"

Katherine met Rita's gaze and smirked. "Only time will tell."

THE ALWYN HOME, WHITEHILL MANOR, WAS ONE OF THE largest and newest houses in Kensington, and the sight of it — muted gray brick, sweeping windows, luscious gardens — was enough to leave Katherine breathless as she stepped out of her carriage. Behind her, she heard her mother give a low coo of approval. "Goodness, what lovely roses—"

Katherine plastered on a smile as they approached the front door, unable to shake the feeling that she was being watched. Paranoia could be instructive, on occasion, but now, she knew it to be the result of her newfound (if secret) fame.

Will it get easier? she wondered, stepping into the foyer. *Will I ever become accustomed to being seen, and not seen at all?*

Whitehill Manor was bright, airy, filled with tinkling chamber music and the melodious chatter of a dozen debutantes. Katherine and Mrs. Knight followed the stream of guests into the drawing room, a wide, elegant space furnished with tables and sets of tea.

"My." Mrs. Knight flashed Katherine a teasing look. "What a diverting afternoon we seem to have before us."

"Consisting of at least a dozen pounds of smoked salmon," Katherine replied, watching a tray of sandwiches go past.

Mrs. Knight nudged her elbow. "Come. Let us greet our hosts."

Katherine had attended tea parties before, affairs hosted by her family members or by an eager mother looking to form alliances. They all paled in comparison to this afternoon, this array — she caught sight of the delicate silver, the finest china, the sumptuous flowers, the decadent little tea cakes. Her mind whirred, filing away detail after detail, and her fingers itched for her pencil. But it would have to wait, of course, until she found a moment to slip out of sight.

It occurred to Katherine that perhaps she should go out of her way to familiarize herself with the Alwyn household. With Sophia being the Star, she imagined that the Alwyns would host a few more events, likely in concord with the eldest, newlywed daughter. Though perhaps the eldest had absconded to her country seat for the summer, as any newlywed with a grain of intelligence would.

Were the Alwyns an intelligent family? Katherine glanced around once again, taking note of faces and whispers, and resolved to find out quickly.

Lady Alwyn was standing with her daughter at the end of the room, before a wide bank of windows that looked out upon a well-kept garden. The sunlight spilled across their shoulders and highlighted the sienna undertone of their dark, gleaming hair. Katherine looked at Lady Alwyn and Lady Sophia, and noted that the resemblance was almost uncanny.

And... somehow familiar.

"Lady Alwyn." Mrs. Knight curtsied, an elegant little movement that surprised Katherine. "Thank you for inviting us to such a charming affair."

"Not at all, Mrs. Knight." Lady Alwyn smiled and inclined her head. "We are so thrilled to have you. Is this your daughter?"

"Yes." Mrs. Knight turned, and Katherine curtsied accordingly. "This is Katherine, my youngest."

"Ah." Something sparkled in Lady Alwyn's gaze, something like amusement. She spoke with an accent, soft and rolling — Dutch, Katherine guessed, though she was not certain. "I have heard quite a few stories about your other children."

Mrs. Knight offered a delicate laugh. "They certainly are an adventure, Lady Alwyn."

"I look forward to hearing about them this afternoon." Lady Alwyn turned to Sophia, and even more light spilled across her daughter's radiant expression. "This is Lady Sophia."

"Lovely to make your acquaintance," said Mrs. Knight, giving her a nod. Katherine copied her, keeping one eye on the hem of Sophia's gown. The fabric was nothing short of decadent.

Sophia smiled, her diamond necklace sparkling. "Likewise, Mrs. Knight. Thank you so much for joining our little tea party."

"It is our pleasure." Mrs. Knight seemed to hesitate, glancing around them. "Forgive me, but—" She turned to Lady Alwyn. "I was under the impression that you had another daughter."

If Katherine had not been watching, she would have missed it. The tiniest expression went flitting across Lady Alwyn's face, then Sophia's. It was a strange expression — a mixture of annoyance, embarrassment, and affection. Curiosity prickled down Katherine's spine.

"Yes, ah." Lady Alwyn gave an elegant sweep of her hand. "She will be joining us shortly, I am sure." Though she sounded nothing of the sort. "She is quite excited for the opportunity, of course, given that she is not yet out."

Sophia's smile widened into a grin, one of her teeth digging into her bottom lip. It was the smallest change, but it forced a laugh to burble within Katherine's chest — Sophia looked almost manic, as if she were stifling giggles. A silent, private joke was reverberating between Sophia and Lady Alwyn, and they both refused to acknowledge it. *How odd*, Katherine thought.

"The young ladies are seated at the far end of the room," Lady Alwyn went on, gesturing to the set of tables beside the dormant fireplace. "And the mothers are at this end. Take any seat you like, and do help yourselves to as much cake as you can stomach."

"Thank you, Lady Alwyn." Mrs. Knight smiled and curtsied. Once again, Katherine copied her, then fell into step behind her as they turned around and made their way into the thicket of young ladies and mothers.

Once she was certain they were out of hearing range, Katherine leaned towards her mother and muttered, "I think Lady Sophia's younger sister is in a spot of trouble."

"Rather more than a spot," Mrs. Knight murmured, then flashed a smile at the Countess of Morley. "I do not think her mother even knows where she is."

"How delicious," Katherine replied. "And how reminiscent of a life with Thomas."

Mrs. Knight sighed as they slipped between two tables. "Perhaps they would be well-suited to one another. We should introduce them."

Introductions seemed to be the item of the hour, as was proper, given the circumstances. Katherine took a seat between Lady Pembroke and Lady Cowdray, and, once they'd all exchanged a smile and a nod, found herself in the midst of a fierce debate about—

"He would never," hissed Lady Pembroke, stirring sugar into her tea. "He would not dare go to war. The embargo is already having a negative effect—"

"The embargo is nothing more than a short-term effort to stall the inevitable." Lady Cowdray took a very dainty bite of her biscuit. "A slap on the wrist, if you will. If President Madison is quite serious about stopping British involvement with the natives, he knows that trade restrictions will only go so far."

Lady Pembroke huffed, her curls fluttering around her face. "What do you think, Katherine?"

Katherine blinked a few times, still reeling from the shock of hearing such conversation at a *tea party*. "I— I—"

"Do not pay them any attention," said the young woman sitting across from them — Miss Spencer. Amusement curled around the bow of her mouth. "Treat them as you would a storm. Let them bluster and thunder, then blow themselves out."

Lady Cowdray snorted and, after checking that the mothers weren't looking, tossed a hunk of biscuit at Miss Spencer. "Don't be such a rat, you know you agree with me—"

They all stifled their giggles, and the conversation continued — a fierce debate, bristling with politics and candor and enough economic opinions to make Katherine's head spin. For a moment, she could only let herself feel surprised. Surprised, because she had never heard such conversation in a setting like this. The talk itself was familiar — topics and arguments that she explored with her own family over the evening's supper or a tray of tea in the library. But Katherine would never have dreamed, never have imagined—

"I have said it once," muttered Lady Cowdray, "and I shall say it again, someone needs to shoot him, or implement the guillotine, and have the whole mess over with—"

Perhaps Katherine's surprise was a touch shameful. Perhaps it was shameful not to expect her peers to have their own opinions, their own capacity to understand their circumstances and to reach nuanced conclusions. But none of Katherine's cousins had ever spoken like this, with such fearless conviction and candor, a candor informed by nothing less than a consistent dedication to information, to education— She had not expected it, to sit among these ladies and discuss war.

I cannot underestimate them, Katherine thought, popping a tiny cake into her mouth. *Not even a little. Not ever.*

But, as she began to consider how Madam Kensington might write about this afternoon at Whitehill Manor, a wave of foreboding took root in Katherine's stomach. She stared down at the fine china as that foreboding transformed into nothing less than realization.

She would have to lie.

If she were to continue masquerading as Madam Kensington, spinning the events of her life and the lives of these women into entertainment, Katherine would have to lie. If she were to be honest, candid about the thoughts and experiences of her peers, she would invite a widespread reaction of disgust, horror, perhaps even outrage. It could lead to the dissolution of engagements, or even worse consequences. And the last thing she wanted, regardless of her own personal attitude towards the season, was to invite discord among these people, among the young ladies and families she had known, even from a distance, for most of her life. She would not want to jeopardize their futures, their fates.

Lucas' folly and the birth of Madam Kensington had brought Katherine power. And now, she realized that she had to be extremely careful in how she used it.

Perhaps it was fitting, then, that at that precise moment, a low *thud* came from the nearest doorway. A young woman caught herself on the elegant door frame, then bent at the hip and pushed a shoe onto her foot. A woman dressed in lilac, her face flushed with exertion.

Something in Katherine went very cold, then very hot. All she could do was sit there and stare, because it was *her.* The woman from the palace.

The woman looked up, caught her gaze. A sharp grin broke over her elegant features. A brief, eternal moment as they looked at one another, immune from the tea party chatter. Then she winked, and heat flooded Katherine's face.

"Finally!" Lady Alwyn seemed to appear from thin air, sweeping between the tables and taking the young woman's elbow. "Come along, I must introduce you—"

"Must you?" the young woman replied, arching an eyebrow, but she allowed herself to be led into the room. She watched Katherine for another moment, as if indulging in a private victory, then looked away.

"Ladies!" Lady Alwyn put on a smile and raised her voice above the chatter. "Allow me to introduce my youngest daughter, Lady Rebecca. Do forgive her tardiness!"

The chatter rose to a chuckle and a hum of welcome. Katherine could only stare at the woman — at *Rebecca* — as her world shifted to accommodate this new information.

Lady Pembroke gave a delicate sigh, and when she spoke, it was wistful. "A beautiful family, are they not? Their bone structure alone makes me quite green with envy."

Katherine quietly agreed, staring at Rebecca while trying not to appear as if she were staring at Rebecca. Rebecca, meanwhile, seemed to harden beneath the gazes of London's ladies. She offered a little smile and a curtsy, but both were stilted, as if wrung from a starched cloth.

"I wonder if she shall be named the Star," said Lady Cowdray, watching as Lady Alwyn led Rebecca over to her table. "When she debuts."

"Some things do run in families," said Miss Spencer. "But it will all depend on Lady Sophia's match. A disadvantageous one could shift the family's entire trajectory."

Lady Cowdray tilted her head to one side, thoughtful. "Perhaps it would be quite terrible, then, to be named the Star. To live under such scrutiny, to determine the fate of your parents as well as your siblings."

"Speak for yourself." Lady Pembroke huffed into her cake. "I think it would be nice."

Katherine's ears throbbed as she forced herself to return her attention to the tea party at hand. She was here to collect gossip, not to turn herself in circles over a woman she'd barely met.

"Speaking of the Star's match," she said, reaching for her teacup, "are there any decent prospects on the horizon?"

❦

THE SOUND OF A DOOR CLOSING; A FAINT ECHO OF LAUGHTER. Katherine glanced over her shoulder, and after ensuring that she was quite alone in the outer hall, returned to her work.

She could barely read her own handwriting, but that did not matter. The details were all that mattered — they made the difference between Hearsay and Kensington, between belief and disbelief. Her mind churned with the afternoon's conversation, with all the crumbs she'd gathered from the ladies at her table, and from the ladies sitting around them. It seemed that Lady Sophia courted almost a dozen suitors already, and at least three had pulled to the head of the pack. Only time would tell which among them would be her selection, and Katherine wondered now, as she had earlier that afternoon, how much of the choice would be Sophia's, rather than her parents'.

Another burst of laughter echoed down the hall, and Katherine glanced out the window. The sun had shifted; she'd been absent from the tea party for a quarter of an hour, at least. With a sigh, she finished off her last scribble, then slipped the papers into her bodice, her pencil into her shoe.

A large, ridiculous landscape hung on the wall just outside the drawing room. She paused to look at the forest scene, fidgeting a little to get her pencil to sit correctly. Poised beside a tree, the doe was supple, its eyes glassy as it stared at something over Katherine's shoulder. A hunter, perhaps. Or a hound.

Then, quite suddenly, one of the doors to the drawing room opened, and Lady Rebecca stepped into the hall, letting out a huff of relief. She halted when she caught sight of Katherine, who now matched the doe in the painting — startled, wary.

"Hello." Rebecca eased into a smirk, stepping closer. "Are you lost?"

"No," said Katherine, her mouth dry. "I simply... needed some air."

"Ah." Rebecca nodded. "I understand." She walked over to Katherine, looking up at the landscape. "Dreadful, isn't it?"

"I—" Katherine bit back a grin. "I really could not say."

"My father has absolutely terrible taste in art," Rebecca went on. "One cannot fault the man, given all of his other strengths. But I wish he wouldn't splash it about in such a visible fashion."

"I suppose out of every fault a person could have," said Katherine, "poor taste in art is hardly the worst."

Rebecca's smirk stretched into a smile, and her eyes seemed to sparkle in the reflected light from the windows. "I never caught your name, at the palace."

"Katherine. Katherine Knight."

"Katherine Knight," Rebecca repeated. "A young lady with three older brothers. Their reputation precedes them," she added, at Katherine's raised eyebrow. "The ladies at my mother's table seemed quite preoccupied with throwing their daughters in the Knight direction."

Katherine could not hold back a snort. "A foolish endeavor, to be sure."

"Ah," said Rebecca. "Your brothers are not romantically inclined?"

Katherine shrugged. "Whether they are or are not is of little consequence. But any woman who would willingly entertain their company is, I think, somewhat..."

"Foolish?"

"Primed for disappointment," Katherine said. She was smiling as well. "When asked to describe my dear brothers, the word 'settled' does not come to mind."

"They are wild young things, then." Rebecca's voice took on a coy edge.

Katherine thought of Brandon climbing onto the dining table. "I suppose."

"And if they are wild, you are...?"

A bolt of *something* went through Katherine's stomach. "Here," she settled on. "I am here."

"A little more than that, I think." Rebecca stepped closer. "You are very talented at opening windows."

"You flatter me," Katherine said, trying and failing to calm her pounding heart. This close, she could see where the sun had left a haze of cheerful red across Rebecca's cheeks.

"I am not prone to flattery," Rebecca replied. "Merely honesty."

A sudden crash of laughter sounded from within the drawing room, echoing out from beneath the doors. Katherine winced before she could catch herself, and Rebecca noticed.

"Best in small doses," she said, nodding to the drawing room.

"I could not have put it better myself," Katherine muttered.

She shifted to one side, and, to her horror, her pencil went rolling out of her shoe.

She watched it trundle merrily across the floor and nudge against the baseboard. Panic, sheer panic, cut through her like a knife.

A pause. Then Rebecca bent down, picked the pencil up. "You dropped this?"

"Yes." Katherine took it from her, not meeting her gaze. She stared at the floor, her ears burning, wondering how she might escape—

Suddenly, the doors to the drawing room opened, and out came none other than Mrs. Knight. She halted, then brightened. "Kat! What splendid timing."

Yes, Katherine thought. *Splendid timing indeed.* She slipped the hand holding her pencil behind her back, out of her mother's sight.

"We have an invitation," Mrs. Knight went on, smiling. "From your mother, Lady Rebecca."

"Indeed?" came Rebecca's cheerful reply. "For what, pray tell?"

"Promenading," Mrs. Knight said. She turned to Katherine. "Tomorrow afternoon. Kensington Gardens. We shall bring the boys."

"How delightful!" Rebecca flashed them both a perfect smile. Only Katherine caught the cunning gleam in her eyes. "I quite look forward to meeting the famous Knights."

Mrs. Knight chuckled and gestured towards the drawing room; another gale of laughter burst through the doors. "Shall we return, ladies?"

"Yes," said Katherine, making her way past her mother. "I need a cup of tea."

She ignored the weight of Rebecca's gaze on the back of her neck. It prickled, keen as a bee sting, persistent as the sea.

INTERLUDE II — WHITEHILL MANOR

"That went very well." Lady Alwyn smiled at her own reflection as she reached for her hair. "Very well indeed."

"Yes, I think so." Sophia returned her smile from where she splayed across the chaise. "You seemed to have quite the conversation at your table."

Lady Alwyn edged a finger under her hairline, then pulled off her wig. She let out a sigh as she skated her hand over her short, thin natural hair, and said, "A dull one, but a necessary one."

"Dull?" Rebecca repeated with a grin. She lay on her mother's bed, a box of chocolates at her hip, her head tipped back over the edge of the mattress. "That savors of weariness, and so early in the season, too—"

"Hosting is never about entertainment," Lady Alwyn replied, sliding her wig onto its stand. "It is an investment."

Both Rebecca and Sophia gave a snort, rolling their eyes. They had heard their mother's lectures on this subject more than enough times.

"At any rate," Lady Alwyn continued, shooting them a pointed look, "we now have three invitations to supper, and guaranteed alliances with a handful of families."

"What good are alliances," said Rebecca, "when Sophia is competing with their daughters?"

"You might be surprised what can be achieved by a few clever mothers."

"Good God," said Rebecca. "I hope we shall never have cause to find out."

"Any word from Gertrude?" Lady Alwyn glanced at Sophia. "It has been nigh on a week since her last letter."

"*Nigh on a week,*" Rebecca parroted, and her mother's balled-up glove bounced off her nose in return.

"No," Sophia replied. "Perhaps today. I do wish she would come to stay with us in London."

Lady Alwyn hummed, nose-to-nose with her reflection. Her bare fingers skated the line of her brow, the line of her nose, checking for imperfections. "Not yet. It is too early in the season."

"Yes, Soph," said Rebecca, "haven't you heard Mother's secret rules regarding the proper timing of city visits?"

Another glove, hitting her chest.

"Gertrude's return to London will be a special occasion," said Lady Alwyn. "We may very well have to use it to our advantage."

Sophia frowned, and Rebecca spoke up, reaching for a chocolate. "She speaks of strategy, Saintie. A concept you and I know little about."

"You would know more," Lady Alwyn replied, dry as sherry, "if you spent more time at home and less time on that damned boat."

Rebecca feigned injury, clutching her heart. "*Mother, you wound me,*" she said in Dutch. "*You know I spend just as much time roaming around the city.*"

Lady Alwyn gave a heavy sigh, shaking her head. "Do not remind me. And you know the rules — English, please."

"What did you mean, before?" Sophia looked at Lady Alwyn. "About having cause?"

Rebecca watched as her mother slowed before the mirror, her

expression flat and pensive. Sophia's angelic face hung suspended behind her, a picture of innocence.

"I trust you girls," said Lady Alwyn. The early evening light caught her profile, made her dark eyes glitter. "And I am realistic. This social farce is ridiculous, but deliberate. And so, we must be deliberate as well. Every event, every invitation, is part of a larger picture."

Sophia was frowning. "But what does that have to do with—?"

"She wants to save Gertrude's visit," said Rebecca. "In case we are in need of a distraction."

"Why should we want to distract ourselves?" said Sophia. "Mother, you said we were to be diligent and attentive in our actions—"

"Not to distract *ourselves*, Saintie." Rebecca looked at her mother, at the square line of her chin. "To distract others. If it should be necessary."

"Oh." Sophia glanced from Rebecca to Lady Alwyn, something quickening in her expression. "I see."

"Good." Lady Alwyn turned away from the mirror and made her way to her changing screen. "I trust you both will be at supper?"

"Yes, Mother." Sophia stood up and stretched. "I think I shall take a turn around the garden."

Once she was gone, Rebecca looked at Lady Alwyn and said, "I apologize for my lateness, earlier today."

Lady Alwyn gave a soft scoff and stepped behind the screen. "Do you?"

"Well," said Rebecca, "I am hardly as punctual as Saint Sophia, but at least I made an appearance."

"A rough appearance." Then came the sound of Lady Alwyn shifting out of her dress. "You must put in more effort, Rebecca. There are a thousand eyes on our family. A thousand people waiting for us to trip, to fall."

Rebecca rolled her eyes, but she knew that her mother was right, in a way. "A promenade," she said. "With the Knight family."

"Yes. A gesture of friendship, and an excuse for Sophia to make their acquaintance."

"They are not titled." Rebecca picked up another chocolate and bit into the rich ganache. "Why should you want—?"

"No title," Lady Alwyn agreed. "But a powerful family, with old connections."

Rebecca hummed. "What do they do, anyway?"

"They are in business. Like us." Lady Alwyn stepped out from behind the screen, now wearing a more casual dress. "Chiefly in venison and pheasant, not to mention the pelts. And, if reports are to be believed, marmalade."

"Marmalade?" Rebecca repeated. Her mind's eye conjured the face, the careful hands, of Katherine Knight, and tried to match them to *marmalade*.

Lady Alwyn nodded, coming over to the bed. "They are worth knowing, and knowing well." She shot Rebecca a pointed look.

Rebecca sighed. "Understood."

"Now, leave me be for a while," said Lady Alwyn, skating her thumb over Rebecca's forehead. "I have some matters to attend to. I shall see you at supper."

This last remark was less a remark and more a directive. Rebecca got to her feet and said, "Yes, supper, of course." She slipped out of the room, smirked, and began to wander down the empty hallway towards her room.

And if her thoughts drifted back to the slight cleft in Katherine Knight's chin, she did not admit it.

🕱 10 🕱

"A productive afternoon," said Thomas, his gaze on Katherine's notes. "A productive afternoon, indeed."

"Hardly." She could not fight off a scowl. "It was all tea and nonsense."

"Are you still searching for a husband?" said Brandon. He lay sprawled on the couch, occupied with a small pile of cakes slightly squashed from their brief journey in Katherine's handkerchief. "I think we should inquire as to the marital status of the Johnsons' pastry chef."

"God save the London ladies from a man who thinks with his stomach." Lucas tossed a pillow at Brandon's face, getting a smear of *crème anglaise* across the ruff. "First Thomas, now you, sweet Bran—"

"There are worse sins, brother mine—"

"What was she like, then?" said Thomas to Katherine, not looking up. "The Star of the season?"

"Sweet enough to give one a toothache. As you will see for yourself, this afternoon."

"*Promenading*," said Brandon, turning the word into a slur. "I have never heard of anything so ridiculous—"

"Careful." Lucas gave a rather dramatic glance at the ceiling. "If Mother hears you, she'll make us do something even worse, like send flowers or write poetry."

"My condolences on your speedy recovery," Brandon replied. "But it is only fair that you suffer with us."

"Worry not, Kitten." Lucas smirked, highlighting the thin cut still healing above his brow. It made him look rather rakish, and Katherine guessed that the young ladies would be swooning over it soon enough. "We shall be on our best behavior."

"I doubt that entirely," she replied, though her cheeks burned with implied embarrassment. The thought of Rebecca meeting her brothers made her stomach curdle, though she did not know why.

"Listen," said Thomas. "We have yet to decide — how often is Madam Kensington to grace the streets of London?"

"More than once a week, surely," said Brandon. "If we are to turn a profit."

"Every other day?" Thomas suggested.

She sighed. "Invitations for the Knight family are somewhat thin on the ground."

"Meaning?"

"Meaning, I cannot be present at every event. I will have to rely upon reports from the servants, which take time to reach our household."

"And shouldn't we be wary of over-saturating the market?" said Lucas, teasing. "Giving the people too much Madam Kensington?"

"Success is a double-edged sword," said Brandon. "If our popularity increases, so will the cost of the materials."

"Twice a week?" Thomas wore a small, oddly mature frown. "Does that seem reasonable?"

Katherine let her mind turn for a moment, sifting through the invitations and letters she'd seen on her mother's desk. Today's promenade meant an excuse to watch all the other young entanglements in full view; she would have plenty to write about. "Yes," she said. "Twice a week. Mondays and Thursdays?"

Her brothers all agreed. None of them mentioned that her proposed schedule would give them ample time to ensure that they always had enough money set aside in time for Lucas to make his payments on Fridays. But they all shifted around it, this shared, silent acknowledgment of their circumstances, and took it in stride. *After all*, Katherine thought, smiling at Lucas as she sat down beside him, *who would protect him, if not his own family?*

❧

"GOOD GOD." THOMAS SQUINTED IN THE SUNLIGHT, HIS cheeks already ruddy. "It is even worse than I imagined."

"Pull yourself together." Mrs. Knight wore a smile both inviting and frightening. Katherine watched her mother's hand tighten on her little lace fan in an attitude that threatened a smack on the arm. "Imagine you are on a walk in Durham."

"A day's worth of sun here is a year's worth of sun in Durham," Thomas replied, sizing up Katherine's parasol. "I don't suppose you would be willing to share?"

Lucas grinned, and a few of the ladies within eyeshot blushed and giggled. "Hark at our tender little flower. Are you withering, dear Tom?"

"This weather is quite unseasonable," said Brandon, glancing around the park. "A spot of rain would be most welcome."

"God in Heaven." Mrs. Knight glanced around at the passing pairs and trios of London's finest. "You three complain more than a salon full of elderly women."

"An insult to elderly women everywhere," Katherine muttered. She copied her mother, surreptitiously glancing through the crowds of people, searching for a familiar face.

No sign of the Alwyn, and it was nearly a quarter past the hour. Perhaps—

"Mrs. Knight!"

As one, the Knight family turned. An unwelcome heat rose in Katherine's cheeks as she took in the sight of Rebecca dressed in pale cream and wearing a deadly smirk. Beside Rebecca stood her mother and her older sister, who was already causing a slight traffic jam. The two families halted before one another, taking each other in with careful, calculating looks.

Immediately, Katherine could not help but notice the differences between them. While she and her family were dressed in plain, sensible fabrics, the Johnsons wore the sleekest silks and the most delicate, playful jewelry. She counted eight diamonds alone on Lady Alwyn's neck, then another four on Sophia's. A gleaming, though not ornate, emerald glittered from Lady Alwyn's left hand, paired with a matching bracelet. Only Rebecca remained unadorned, and her dress, though still elegant and worth at least three of Katherine's, was modest in comparison to her sister's soft yellow satin. Unlike her mother and her sister, she wore her hair in a simple bun, without an ounce of ornamentation. And while Katherine had to admire the feathers and pearls threaded through Lady Sophia and Lady Alwyn's hair, she could not help but wonder how Rebecca had managed to avoid becoming the third piece in their matching set.

Rebecca met her gaze, and something about the curious tilt of her mouth made Katherine's tongue go dry.

"Lady Alwyn!" Mrs. Knight dropped into a curtsy. "So wonderful to see you again."

"Likewise, Mrs. Knight." Lady Alwyn inclined her head and smiled. "Forgive our tardiness. We are still learning the lay of the land."

"There is nothing to forgive." Mrs. Knight swept a hand towards her children, and in return, something like excitement swept through Katherine's stomach. "Please, allow me to introduce my other children. Lucas here is the eldest — do excuse his appearance, he is recovering from a fall off his horse."

"Goodness!" Lady Alwyn's eyebrow arched, and the corner of her mouth twitched. "I am most relieved to see you not permanently disfigured, Lucas."

"As am I, Lady Alwyn." He gave her a smile and a nod, his eyes twinkling in the sunlight.

"My next eldest is Thomas," Mrs. Knight continued, and Thomas gave an obligatory nod. "Then Brandon." Brandon did the same. "And, of course, Katherine."

"Of course," murmured Rebecca, and Katherine bit her tongue.

"A pleasure to make your acquaintance, gentlemen." Lady Alwyn turned towards Sophia. "My daughter, Lady Sophia. And her younger sister, Lady Rebecca."

Both the ladies curtsied, and Katherine did not miss the way her brothers all looked at Sophia as if they'd been hit over the head, simultaneously, by a small anvil. She bit her tongue again, but this time, it was to fend off a laugh.

"Come." Lady Alwyn stepped forward. "Let us take the air."

As one, the two families began to stroll through the park, following a pace that Katherine would hardly classify as a 'walk' and would instead refer to as a 'slug on an energetic day.' Somewhat to her surprise, Thomas fell in step beside Sophia, flanked by Lucas, and struck up a conversation about water lilies, of all things.

Rebecca, meanwhile, smiled at Brandon and said, "I am thrilled to make your acquaintance, Mr. Knight. Miss Knight has told me so much about you and your brothers."

Astonishment welled in Katherine's stomach, but before she could do little more than blink owlishly at Rebecca, Brandon offered a self-deprecating smile and said, "You flatter me, Lady Rebecca, in part because you lie so beautifully. Kat never mentions us if she can avoid it, especially in mixed company."

Rebecca let out a laugh, her eyes sparkling with delight. "Tell me of the your family, then. Where do you hail from? And why should your sister refrain from conversing about her brothers? Is it perhaps a reflection of your stolid, genteel natures?"

"Ah," he said. "I see our reputation precedes us."

"To a certain extent, yes."

"We are the bane of Durham, Lady Rebecca," Brandon replied. "A little town in the north that has long wished it could evict the Knight family."

"You do us a disservice, brother." Katherine gave her parasol a lazy twirl, the shadow flashing over Rebecca's shoulders. "Without us, the natives would have dozens of deer tormenting their pretty village square."

"You are a hunting family, then?" said Rebecca.

"All British families are hunting families, Lady Rebecca. Though I must admit that our enthusiasm for the sport is rather unmatched."

"Blood thirst," Rebecca said with a nod, a grin playing about her mouth. "A rare quality among the aristocracy."

Katherine snorted, and Brandon gave a chuckle. "Just you wait," said Katherine, "until the engagements begin. Then you'll see a bloodsport."

"What about your family?" Brandon said to Rebecca. "It is no secret that the Johnson family is rather new to London."

"No," Rebecca agreed. "We are quite a group of mutts. We traveled frequently," she added, at Brandon's questioning look.

"Ah," said Brandon, and Katherine made a mental note to skim the trade papers in her father's library. "Outrunning our dear friend Bonaparte?"

"You could say that," Rebecca replied, with another hint of that grin. "These wars have made it difficult for families in the world of trade."

Have they? Katherine thought, looking once again at Lady Alwyn's jewelry, at Sophia's fine satin. If their family had struggled, it did not show.

"You say your family traveled," said Brandon. "But your father is English, is he not?"

"He is. And my mother is Dutch, as you could probably tell from her accent."

"Oh!" Brandon could not hide his keen interest. "Can you speak it? Dutch?"

Rebecca chuckled and said, "*Dat hangt af. Wat wil je dat ik zeg?*"

Brandon practically vibrated with delight. "You must teach me."

"Oh, must I?" Rebecca teased.

As they continued to poke at one another and, in Rebecca's case, fire off bits of Dutch, Katherine slowed her pace. She fell a few steps behind, casting a furtive glance around the park. Beside the pond, she could see Lord Suffolk and Lady Elizabeth trading sweet nothings and blushes; near the willows, Lady Stewart and Lady Ednam stood together and smiled prettily up at Lord Warwick and Sir Addison. Her fingers itched for a pencil, but she spun her parasol instead. Then her gaze wandered from the debutantes to their families, to their escorts and mothers. Like Katherine, everyone was watching, and pretending that they weren't.

This is ridiculous, she thought, with the casual indifference of a seasoned hunter. *This is utterly ridiculous. A farce that would turn the Bard in his grave.*

But now, this farce was her family's bread and butter. It was a peculiar and oddly humbling thought. Katherine shook her head, and felt a tendril of emotion snake up her throat. How strange, to remember the night before her debut, when she had insisted that such folly, such gossip, was worthless, nothing more than a passing fancy. A distraction, serving only to root herself in the present, and to turn her gaze away from her fate.

Perhaps I am destined, she thought, *to eat my words.*

And yet, Madam Kensington did not offer a guarantee of stability. Katherine had heard many tales of how fickle London society could be — any day, the tide could turn, and the peers could find some new amusement, perhaps a new source of gossip. It would be reckless and arrogant to believe that Madam Kensington's nascent success would continue. And that meant... she and her brothers needed—

Katherine glanced to her right, and saw Mr. John Ransom smiling at her from beside the pond. Her breath caught, and her ears began to ring.

Yes. A contingency plan.

"Is it very exciting, then?" Brandon was saying to Rebecca. "To be back in England?"

Rebecca smiled, but it seemed to be a shield, hiding or protecting some other emotion. "That depends upon one's definition of 'exciting.' "

"Fair enough," he replied, with a dip of his head. "Were you born here?"

"No, in Amsterdam — my family has traveled my entire life. We have lived in more cities than I can remember."

"But you do not have a Dutch accent," Katherine blurted, before she could stop herself.

Both Brandon and Rebecca turned to look at her — they had not realized she was listening. Rebecca's smile gained a teasing edge as she said, "No, Miss Knight. I am a shape-shifter. I never carry one accent or one language for very long — I step into port, and into my new voice."

"You can speak many languages, then?" said Brandon.

Rebecca gave a shrug. "Some better than others. I lose a language quickly, if I do not hear it every day. But I can pick it up again just as quickly."

Shape-shifter indeed, thought Katherine. With effort, her memory dredged up some French and Italian conjugations — echoes of her time under the tutelage of Mistress Hedge, a horrible governess who had tried and failed to educate Katherine on matters of modern language. The word 'subjunctive' floated through Katherine's mind and she winced, returning her attention to the games of attraction and flattery. She noted a handkerchief passing from the hand of Lord Warwick to Lady Stewart, and the way Sir Addison looked on with sparks of jealousy in his eyes.

Katherine's game was a repetitive one, and soon, she found her attention pulled instead to the weather, to the breeze slithering between the trees, carrying a northern bite. She smelled the roses and the lilies, broken only by a cool edge of ivy, and heard the nearby pond lolling merrily against the shore. Birdsong, brilliant and unbroken, poured through the trees, accompanied by the hum of insects. The grass sprang and cushioned underfoot, reaching towards the sunbeams.

Tracking would be playfully simple. No real challenge. Katherine smirked to herself, imagining the look on her peers' faces if they saw her stalking a six-point stag through their lovely little park. Not that she would be seen — she was always well hidden, even while in plain sight.

The thought of being on a hunt made her breath catch. She could almost smell it — boot polish, fresh mud, damp wool, cold steel, musky tallow.

But it would be months before she returned to the country. Months before she could varnish her rifles, scrub her boots, run with the hounds. Months before the rain would swallow her, before the fog would cling to her skin. Months before she would be alone, perfectly alone, in the great wilderness beneath the sky.

Katherine swallowed, and once again shifted her gaze across the park. With a roar, her surroundings returned to her, along with the nearby conversation.

"I miss it greatly," Rebecca was saying. "I have not been able to practice since we left Amsterdam, and I fear I have grown very rusty."

"How fortunate," said Brandon. "Thomas and I are quite weary of one another's competition. We need fresh blood."

"Oh?" Genuine excitement seemed to rise in Rebecca's voice. "Are you certain?"

"Absolutely." Brandon was smiling. "I can guarantee you would offer a better challenge than most of the young gentlemen in London."

Rebecca made a wonderful noise — something between a snort and a laugh. "I can guarantee that as well, Mr. Knight. And I've not even met most of them."

Katherine frowned and met her brother's gaze. "What on earth are you plotting now?"

"Fencing," he said, grinning. "Lady Rebecca fears that she has grown rusty."

"Fencing?" Katherine repeated, a fresh heat rising in her face. She glanced at Rebecca. "You can fence, Lady Rebecca?"

"Aye," Rebecca replied, with a dollop of smugness. "I certainly can."

Something — a protest, an exclamation, a clever remark — withered and died in Katherine's throat. She could only watch as Brandon turned to Rebecca and said, "Tomorrow, after church?"

"Indeed," said Rebecca, then glanced ahead of them. "But do not tell my mother."

11

Katherine watched Rebecca dodge Brandon's jab and perform a neat somersault, her boots catching the edge of the flowerbed. Brandon's grin flashed in the sunlight as he lunged, only to find his strike blocked by Rebecca's foil. A brief struggle, then Rebecca punched Brandon in the knee, rolled to her feet, and continued the attack.

"Lady Rebecca fights like a wolverine," said Lucas. He was sitting beside Katherine on the hanging bench, enjoying the cool shade and wearing a thoughtful look.

"Yes." Katherine's mouth was dry, and she forced her gaze elsewhere, to the cluster of lilies growing wild beneath the oak. "I suppose she does."

"Is it normal, I wonder." Lucas watched Rebecca's foil jab Brandon in the arm. "For Dutch women. Women from the Continent."

"To fight like wolverines?"

"To fence," he replied. "To wear trousers and boots instead of skirts and slippers."

Another flash of heat, seething through Katherine's stomach. She found her gaze pulled back to the slim curve of Rebecca's legs, clad in those patchy, stained trousers. One or two curves in particular were quite diverting, and Katherine forced herself to look away again.

"I wear trousers," she said, though it hardly seemed to matter now that she knew no one could wear trousers as well as Rebecca. "And boots."

"Yes, but in the country. Not in town. Well, not where anyone of consequence might see you." Lucas tilted his head to one side, a portrait of consideration. "Do you think she would ever wear them to a ball?"

"If you named the right price." Katherine sighed. "But I am certain Lady Alwyn would never allow it."

"Something tells me that Lady Rebecca might be quite adept at subterfuge." Lucas met her gaze. "She came on foot, you know."

"Yes," said Katherine, "I know."

For she had. Rebecca had arrived at the Knight house between one moment and the next, sauntering up to the front door in her trousers and shirtsleeves, grinning like she had a secret. She carried a small leather brace of foils, and wore a faded, disreputable tricorn. Katherine knew for a fact that Graves had mistaken Rebecca for one of Brandon's young gentleman friends, and that Rebecca had not done a thing to correct the assumption. Though how anyone could get a glimpse of her mouth or her cheekbones and think she was a man—

"I must admit," said Lucas. "I did not..."

"Recognize her?" Katherine shook her head. "Nor did I."

And a part of her knew what it meant. Knew that by allowing them to see her like this, Rebecca was extending a branch of trust. And that trust had come quickly, in spite of the Johnson family's secretive and protective nature. Perhaps Rebecca had seen something among the Knights, something to inspire confidence in their silence, or their complete lack of concern over such matters. Though what that might have been... Katherine had no idea.

"They are very different," Lucas went on, returning his attention to the bout. Rebecca was now chasing Brandon around the roses. "She and her sister."

Katherine nodded. "Our Star."

A smirk played across Lucas' mouth. "They are alike in beauty," he said, somewhat to her surprise. "Though clearly not in temperament."

"Perhaps that is a good thing." Katherine glanced at the windows, checking to see if Mrs. Knight was watching, then slouched in her seat, leaning her head against the back of the bench. "Sophia seems far too docile for her own good."

"Do you speak as Katherine Knight?" said Lucas, his voice low. "Or as Madam Kensington?"

"Both," said Katherine, before she could stop herself. "I am still learning the rules of this world, but I do know that *naïveté* does not mix well with the machinations of courtship. Everyone is watching Lady Sophia, and waiting for an excuse to tear her down."

Lucas shook his head. "A bloodsport indeed. And what, dear Kitten, would you say if the Star was a dear friend of yours? Would you be so forthcoming in your judgment, your advice?"

"Yes," she said, though without conviction. "I like to think that I would. Being the Star is rather more of a curse than anything else."

Lucas shot her a look — a look of indignation. "A harsh censure, indeed."

"Love matches are rare to begin with, Lucas," said Katherine. "Sophia lost any hope of securing one the moment she was named the Star. The season is a political machine," she added, "and the engagements are its oil. As the Star, she is expected to make the most advantageous match, regardless of her own feelings."

"An odd metaphor indeed." Lucas brushed a flurry of spent blooms off his trousers. "Kitten, your speech savors of cynicism."

"Give it time." Katherine smirked as Rebecca knocked the foil out of Brandon's hand. "Soon, my cynicism will scream, rather than savor."

"Yield!" cried Brandon, flinging his arms into the air. His shout echoed around the garden, rattling the branches and the blooms. "Good God, I yield!"

Rebecca began to laugh, the tip of her foil hovering a bare inch from Brandon's chest. Her smile caught in the sunlight, and for a moment, in spite of her odd, drab clothing, she looked every inch an Athena, braced in the attitude of victory.

Katherine's mouth went quite dry again, and she forced herself to smile, offering a bit of applause. Rebecca's gaze flashed to hers, and then she offered Katherine and Lucas a small, obsequious bow.

"My turn, I think," said Lucas, getting to his feet. His grin was easy and wide, self-assured. "It will be an honor to be defeated by the noble Lady Rebecca."

"By all means," said Brandon. He hauled himself to his feet. Rebecca took his hand and they shook like good sportsmen, then Brandon reached for his discarded foil. "Spare the rest of us the trauma."

Rebecca laughed again, a delightful, pealing sound, and swished her foil through the air. Whether in encouragement or warning was difficult to discern. "You speak in such dramatic terms, Mr. Knight. Is that a familial proclivity?"

"Probably." Lucas shrugged off his jacket and reached for his favorite foil. "Let's see if you give me reason to indulge."

Rebecca eased into her fighting stance, her foil flashing in the sunlight. "*En garde.*"

The bout began, and Katherine forced her attention to return to the novel lying open in her lap. She could hardly pass the whole afternoon watching Rebecca demolish her brothers, as enticing as the prospect might be.

A distraction, she corrected herself, glancing up as Rebecca leapt over a cluster of lilies. She landed neatly, and grinned like a tiger. *She is a distraction, not a prospect.*

And a threat, perhaps, to Madam Kensington. Katherine had originally intended to spend the afternoon finalizing her draft for the following day's edition, but now it would have to wait.

A distraction, she told herself again, her gaze finding but not reading the neat, printed lines within her novel. The words sat before her, dull and without meaning, as she pondered the weight of the moment, of Rebecca's insistence at spending time with her brothers. *Why is she here?* Katherine could not help wondering. *She hardly knows us, and she could call on any family in London. And she could probably find another fencing partner, or even an instructor to match her abilities.*

Unbidden, her mind returned to that image of Rebecca, sauntering up to the house in those damn trousers and that damn hat. The tricorn alone had carried the unmistakable air of adventure, of a life apart from the London season. Rebecca had traveled through the city by herself — and, assumedly, with the knowledge, even the permission, of her family. Did they really allow her to swagger about London without an escort, without so much as a sniff of protection? It was unthinkable, and certainly beyond anything Katherine had ever experienced.

Something curled and burned in her stomach. She refused to admit that it was envy.

A light tea was served a short while later, in the drawing room. Katherine stood beside the long windows, gazing out at the garden, her fingers itching for her pencil. Their visitor was diverting, yes, but Katherine's patience was wearing thin.

Thomas let out a loud, guttural moan and splayed face-first into the sofa cushions. "I am quite dead," he said, his words muffled by the down.

"Such theatrics, brother," said Lucas, though he had a cold compress draped across his forehead.

"I am going to have a word with Father," said Brandon. He took a gulp of tea and stuffed half a scone into his mouth, looking like a wretched little rag doll. "Our tutors are full of—"

"I appreciate the compliment." Rebecca smirked from where she sat at the card table, slicing apart an apple with her pocket knife. She looked every inch a rake, slouched with her leg hitched over the arm of her chair. The top two buttons of her shirt had come loose, either by accident or by design — it was quite warm in the drawing room. The collar of her shirt pulled low, exposing a flash of her clavicle. "And here I thought the Knight boys might present a challenge."

Thomas gave another grunt. Lucas tossed him a biscuit.

"Where did you learn?" said Brandon, pouring her a cup of tea. "Who taught you?"

Rebecca shrugged. "I've had several masters over the years. Once I learned all I could from one, I moved on to the next, leaving their egos much the worse for wear."

A soft snort fell from Katherine's nose before she could stop herself. She bit back a smirk, then glanced up to find Rebecca looking at her, amusement flashing in her eyes.

Katherine looked away.

"And your father..." Brandon squinted at Rebecca. "Allowed...?"

Rebecca nodded, now buttering a scone. "Encouraged it, as a matter of fact. He is not particularly... traditional."

Thomas surfaced from the cushions, his face creased and ruddy. "Your sisters. Can they—?"

Rebecca shook her head. "No, Sophia was always more... domestically inclined. Gertrude, however, is one for archery. She can hit a bullseye thrice in a row from a hundred paces, and she can run faster than anyone I know." She sighed a little, lifting one shoulder. "I think a life in high society is a touch wasted on her."

Thomas looked at her for a moment, then shook his head and returned to his cushions. "Amazons," he muttered.

Katherine bit back a smile and reached for a scone.

The conversation continued, but Katherine turned away, leaning against the window as she looked out into the garden. From here, she could see the bench hanging beneath the tree, swaying in a slight breeze. Her imagination conjured an image of herself and Lucas, wrapped up in the pre-dawn. Trading barbs and worries.

A week ago.

A lifetime ago.

"Penny for them?"

Katherine jumped, nearly dropping the remains of her scone. She met Rebecca's gaze, and refused to look at the space where her collar had ridden low. "Beg pardon?"

The corner of Rebecca's mouth twitched. "Your thoughts."

Katherine managed a bland smile. "They are hardly worth an entire penny, Lady Rebecca." She looked over Rebecca's shoulder. "You appear to have killed my brothers."

"Ah." Rebecca eased back onto her heel, cutting a smirk at the boys, who were wallowing in their own misery. "They'll live, I think."

That scent again — metallic, oaky, warm. A reminder of close, warm rooms, of mulled wine, of the cupboard under the stairs at Mosswood Heath. Familiar and yet alien. It seemed to cling to Rebecca like a second skin. Katherine fought the urge to lean in.

"Fencing does not interest you, Miss Knight?"

It took a moment for Katherine to catch up. "I suppose not."

"What is it, then?" Rebecca took a bite of her apple slice, the sweet scent bursting in the air between them. "That holds your interest?"

Katherine almost smiled. "A rather personal question, before drinks have been served."

"Oblige me." Rebecca nudged her arm. "You are a country

woman, are you not? I hear there are many diversions to be had in our more rural environs."

"Perhaps," Katherine allowed. Then, something tweaked her memory, and she cast Rebecca a sidelong look. If she could not write, perhaps she could do a bit of research. "Apart from being a skilled fencer, I hear that you are gifted in the area of mechanics."

"Mechanics?"

"Carriage repair."

"Ah." Rebecca took another bite of apple. "News carries in this city."

"Such a heroic gesture," said Katherine. "I'm certain it made several gentlemen quite green with envy."

"That is hardly an achievement," said Rebecca. "These Englishmen are quick to temper. It shows their insecurity, I think." She met Katherine's gaze and shrugged. "There was nothing to it, really. I'm quite good with my hands, and I can rig together a snapped axle."

A tendril of heat snaked up Katherine's neck, which had nothing to do with— *good with my hands.* "Have you much experience mending carriages?"

Rebecca offered her a sudden, cheeky grin. "No."

Then, the sound of a door on the floor above— "Kat! Boys! Where are you?"

Katherine sucked in a breath, Thomas bolted up from the cushions, and even Lucas showed signs of life. Katherine met Brandon's gaze and together they said: "Mother."

"Quickly—" Katherine put a hand to Rebecca's arm. "If she sees you—"

Rebecca had the good sense to look alarmed. "Yes, we can't let that happen. My foils—"

A flurry of movement. Then—

Rebecca, one foot out of the drawing room window, brace of foils lying in the flower bed below her, tricorn perched on her head. "Thank you for the tea." She offered Lucas a lazy salute. "Another time?"

"Most certainly," he said, reaching for the window's latch.

Katherine was standing behind him, and she almost missed it.

Rebecca flashed her a wink. Then she jumped, and was gone.

"Quickly, Kat—"

"I am," she bit out, her quill flying over the page.

Thomas was hunched over her, reading as swiftly as she wrote. "Add something there," he said, pointing to the end of a sentence. "A flourish, some flowery word—"

Katherine forced herself to breathe as ink splashed across her fingers. Sweat pooled in the small of her back, along her hairline. She had never been this anxious before in her life. A cramp was twisting along her arm, around her wrist, and she let out a grunt of frustration—

"There!" Thomas all but shoved her away the moment she finished the final sentence, and hurled himself at the paper. He threw in a few wild scribbles, muttering to himself, then grabbed the sheet of paper and held it aloft. "Bran!"

Brandon swooped in like an eagle, his expression thunderous. "Not again," he spat, cutting them a ruthless look. "Never this late—"

"We know!" Katherine cried, but he was already gone, sprinting into the hall. She slumped in her chair, panting, as Thomas shoved a hand through his hair, getting ink on his forehead.

Lucas looked at them both and raised an eyebrow. "Seems that we should be wary of distractions." He walked over, two fresh glasses of Scotch in hand.

Katherine took hers and swallowed the measure in a single

gulp. She handed the glass back to him, breathing in the burn of the liquor, and ignored his gaze.

After Rebecca's departure, Katherine and her brothers had been unable to escape their mother's attention until after supper. The final drafting of Monday's pamphlet had been little more than a mad dash, a race to beat the clock. Katherine's heart still thundered in her ears, unable to believe that the mayhem was over.

"It sounded dull." Lucas passed her a fresh pour and clapped Thomas on the back. "The Johnson tea party."

Katherine glanced at him, then away. She shrugged. "It was... as expected."

Lucas nodded. "Though it seems that Lady Rebecca is not what we expected, not at all."

"No," said Thomas. "Quite the opposite of Sophia."

"Indeed." Lucas swirled the contents of his glass, his expression pensive. "And it seems that she wants to be our friend."

"God only knows why," said Thomas.

Doubt even He does, Katherine thought, leaning into her Scotch.

12

The rouge was still drying on Katherine's cheeks when a booming knock sounded at the front door of the house. Katherine jumped, her gaze flashing to her mother's — normally, she could not hear anything from the ground floor, let alone a knock. Her mother frowned, a crease appearing between her brows, and said, "It is probably a delivery boy. Carrying a message, perhaps."

Katherine nodded, and took an unsteady breath. It did not help to ease her nerves, foolish though they might have been. "An invitation?"

"Possibly." Her mother reached forward, brushing a stray hair away from Katherine's forehead, then rested her hands on Katherine's shoulders. "We shall have to visit my sister soon."

Katherine flinched, as if warding off a fly. "Which one?"

"Linda," said her mother, the name tight in her mouth. She cleared her throat. "In fact, we should call on all of them."

A groan leaked out of Katherine's mouth, and she slumped back into her mother's touch. "Why can't they come to us? At least here we can sneak away, or feign some disturbance—"

Mrs. Knight offered her a humorless smile, and gave her a

playful poke in the back of her neck. "Oh, but you see, that would never do! Our house is not nearly grand enough to receive such guests of note."

Katherine groaned again, playing it up until her mother gave a genuine grin.

"Edwina!" Mr. Knight, from below. His voice hit Katherine with a jolt — strange, to hear it at such a volume, and heavy with such fear. "Boys! Come here at once!"

Both Katherine and Mrs. Knight froze, their good mood vanishing. They looked at one another in the mirror, then leapt to their feet. Katherine ran out into the hall and saw Brandon and Thomas surface from their rooms, their faces riddled with confusion. Mrs Knight dashed to Lucas' room and the door opened just as she reached it — Lucas appeared, his dress shirt half-buttoned, a disgruntled Chauncey behind him. "What is it?" said Lucas, frowning at all of them. "What happened?"

Katherine hurtled down the stairs, her brothers on her heels. As she ran, her brain pounded, trying to make sense of the situation— Her father would not call to them like this, not in such a manner, not on the verge of departure, unless something terrible—

The last time he had, it had been her grandmother.

Katherine all but leapt down the last few stairs, landing with a gasp just a foot away from her father. He stood like a crane in the foyer, Graves at his side, and they both wore grim expressions.

"Children." Mr. Knight looked at Katherine, then at the boys, and finally, at his wife, who lingered a few steps above them. He cleared his throat. "I will not mince words. Mr. Perceval has been killed."

"Assassinated," added Graves, his voice low.

Katherine blinked at them, her brain struggling to catch up. Mr. Perceval — she only knew of *one* Mr. Perceval — no, surely not—

"The Prime Minister?" managed Thomas.

"Where?" said Lucas. "When?"

"The House of Commons," said Mr. Knight, and nodded again when his wife stifled a gasp. "In broad daylight. Just a few hours ago."

"But—" Brandon gaped at him. "Who would—?"

"A discontented man." Mr. Knight's tone was dismissive, sharp. "A madman, for all we know."

"They sent word," said Lucas, with the air of one catching up. "His Cabinet. They are afraid." He stepped forward, and even in his state of rumpled half-dress, he cut an imposing figure. "They are worried the assassin did not act alone."

"Yes." Mr. Knight nodded. "For one, the Luddites are cause for serious concern. They could see it as an opportunity, an excuse."

"Perceval's Cabinet thinks it might happen again," said Brandon. "The riots."

"The burning," said Mrs. Knight, so quietly Katherine almost missed it.

"This evening is canceled," said Mr. Knight. His expression had tightened into familiar, militaristic lines. "No one is to leave the house."

"Father." Thomas stared at him. "You cannot be serious—"

"I am perfectly serious," Mr. Knight replied, cool as steel. "If our peers have any sense, they will postpone tonight's events and, with any luck, the rest of the week's."

"What do you propose we do?" said Katherine, finding her voice at last. She could not restrain a wave of absurd indignation. "Hide under our beds?"

Her father did not rise to the bait. "We lock the doors, reinforce the windows, and do what is necessary to protect ourselves, if it comes to that."

"And will it?" said Brandon. "Come to that?"

"I doubt it," said Mr. Knight. "But I said the same thing thirty years ago."

Katherine met her father's gaze, just for a moment, and saw everything he did not say.

As one, she and her brothers followed their father towards the rear of the house, to a small cupboard hidden by a long, unremarkable curtain. Mr. Knight produced a small key from his waistcoat pocket — his children, his wife, and even Graves had copies of the same key, and now Katherine had the thought that she should keep hers closer to hand. He unlocked the cupboard, revealing a wide, shallow cavity mounted with hooks and narrow shelves. Rows of gleaming metal and wood twinkled out at them.

"We will keep to our chambers," said Mr. Knight, handing a rifle first to Graves, then to Lucas. "And take up a watch. We have to keep an eye on the garden as well as the front drive."

"Easy enough," said Thomas. He stepped away from the group and aimed his rifle at the far wall, checking the sights. "Between the seven of us."

"Six," said Mr. Knight, passing Katherine her rifle. "I want Graves in the basement with the other servants."

Katherine looked at him, about to protest that he should at least let the servants sleep, then remembered that their chambers were on the topmost floor. In the event of a fire—

"Shouldn't we stay together?" she found herself saying, even as her fingers performed their well-learned movements, touching and checking the rifle. It was hers, in fact, properly hers — a gift, on her sixteenth birthday. But she wasn't allowed to keep it with her in the city. Lock and key was always the rule. "I seem to recall some sort of idiom about there being strength in numbers."

"I agree," said Mrs. Knight, taking a rifle in hand. A restrained wince crossed her features; this was one aspect of country life that she did not particularly enjoy. "We shouldn't be separated."

Mr. Knight nodded, now handing out pistols to the boys. "Very well. Shall we keep to the ground floor?"

Lucas shook his head. "Keep Katherine upstairs. She is the best shot."

For a moment, the absurdity of it all hit Katherine like a wave. Or, rather, what she imagined a wave would feel like — she had never been to the sea. Half an hour ago, she had worried about how she would sneak around the evening's festivities, and find the odd corner to let Madam Kensington come to life. Now, her family was talking of defending their home against riotous and violent intruders. She shook her head, and pressed her thumb against the soft, smooth wood of the rifle's stock. A life in London was an odd one indeed.

The rest of it was decided very quickly. Mrs. Knight would stay on the ground floor with Thomas, and Brandon with Katherine on the floor above. Lucas and Mr. Knight would likewise keep their watch from the ground floor, patrolling the perimeter and staying within earshot of everyone else.

A life in London, Katherine thought again, once she was perched in the window seat behind the staircase, near the entrance to the disused parlor. *What a life, indeed.*

From here, she had an excellent view of the front drive and the street. She could also see the edge of the garden. Above all of it sat the familiar skyline of Mayfair, and beyond it, the rest of London, the brick and stone seeping into a dull lavender in the sunset.

It was a warm night, as if Nature herself had felt the folly of human treachery, and indulged them. Teased them, even. Heat, Katherine knew, could be the worst kind of encouragement.

"I cannot believe he's dead," said Brandon. He lay on the floor beside her, rifle easy by his leg. They both knew he could mount and fire it in a second, if necessary. "Killed."

Katherine hummed her agreement. "Unprecedented." Which she knew to be correct. She may not have paid attention in matters of language, but Katherine Knight knew her history.

"He must be mad. The fellow who shot him."

"Perhaps."

"I wonder if he shall take a plea," Brandon went on. "An insanity plea."

Katherine did not reply. She wondered what the papers would say, in the morning.

As if he'd heard her thoughts, Brandon smiled. "What will Madam Kensington have to say about it?"

She glanced at him, her touch skirting the familiar carvings of her rifle. "Do not jest, Brandon."

"I do not jest at all, I simply—"

"Madam Kensington shall make due mention of the tragedy, as any other publication would." Katherine sighed. Near the end of the gravel drive, a squirrel hesitated, washing its face. "But it is possible, Bran, that London will be far too preoccupied with their own political theater to take any notice of Madam Kensington."

"Oh." His voice dropped as he realized what she implied. "Oh, *damn*—"

"It is a selfish consideration, I know." Katherine leaned her head back against the wall, her gaze not straying an inch from the front walk. "But it is one we have to make."

Because of the money, she did not say. *Because we might not be able to afford a day of losses.*

Brandon sighed. "I suppose we can count on the support of those who did not care for Mr. Perceval. They, at least, will tire quickly of the obituaries and the articles."

Katherine hummed again. "But if all the events are postponed, Bran, Madam Kensington will not have anything to write about."

A silence fell, and Katherine became aware of the cricket song. It seemed to grow, slowly but steadily, to replace the sound of the birds, of the breeze. She breathed in, and tasted sun, soot, the roses from the garden. Lilies and grass. "Has Father ever spoken to you about it?"

"About what?"

"The Riots."

Brandon shook his head. "If he has, it's been... in passing."

Of course. How does one begin to discuss a night like that? For that was what it was — a weeklong night, seven endless days that had melted together into a grim, seething mass. "Mother will not discuss it, either."

"But she was not in London," Bran pointed out. "Not properly. Not like Father was."

Katherine sighed. "No. She was not."

Another silence fell. Crickets, a breeze. Stirring leaves and fading sunlight.

"I wonder what Rebecca is doing." Brandon's smirk was audible. "I wonder if she is standing behind her front door, rapier in hand."

"I would not be surprised. I doubt we are the only family waiting for something to happen."

"As *assassination*." Brandon pulled out the word, as if he were testing it. As if he could not believe it to be true. "We are living in history, Kat."

"I suppose we are, dearest Bran."

And the thought was oddly comforting.

⊗

KATHERINE WOKE BETWEEN ONE BREATH AND THE NEXT, THE chilly glass pressed against her face. She blinked once, twice, the early morning a sea of colors behind the window.

"You fell asleep." Rita's voice was low, and she put a hand to Katherine's shoulder. "The night passed quietly."

"Indeed it did." The words were slurry in Katherine's mouth. She eased her face away from the window, and winced at the sharp ache in her neck, her shoulder. Even her lower back had seized in disapproval.

Rita watched her grumble and roll out her shoulders. Her lined face was even paler than usual, a stark contrast above the neat gray of her uniform.

Katherine glanced up at her. "Did you get any sleep?"

"A bit." A thin smile ghosted over Rita's mouth. "As much as one can in one of those kitchen chairs."

"I should have told Graves to let you stay in the drawing room."

"He wanted us where he could see us," Rita pointed out. "Not that I blame him. One cannot be too careful, in this day and age."

Katherine rolled her tender neck, and found her gaze drawn to the floor, which was mysteriously devoid of her brother. "Where's Bran?"

"In the parlor," said Rita, nodding to the doorway opposite. "Making a mess of one of the nicer couches."

"The rat. He was supposed to keep me awake."

"Worry not. I heard some snoring on my way up here — I don't think anyone was able to resist the temptation."

"A quiet night." Katherine glanced over her shoulder, out the window. "Surprising, I think. Certainly not what we expected."

Rita clucked her tongue. "No part of the past twelve hours has been what we expected."

Katherine met her gaze again, ignoring the protest from her neck. "How are you, Rita?"

That thin smile reappeared, twitching the corner of Rita's mouth. "Muddling through."

"Brandon is worried. About Madam Kensington."

"At a time like this?"

"If there aren't any *soirées*," Katherine said, "then Madam Kensington has nothing to write about. Which means that we won't have any pamphlets to sell."

A crease appeared between Rita's brows. "I see."

"And if the servants are kept inside," Katherine went on. "There won't be any whispers."

Rita looked past her, out the window. "Give it two days, and the peers will forget that anything ever happened to shatter their little world, or that poor man's heart."

RITA, AS USUAL, WAS NEARLY CORRECT.

Two and a half days later, just as the evening was sinking into the night, Katherine heard a rustle from the garden wall. From her seat on the swinging bench, her view was somewhat obstructed by the oak, and by the fact that sunset had come and gone. A bolt of nerves went through her stomach, and her hand shifted along the bench, her fingertips resting on the butt of her rifle. It could just be a squirrel, and she did not want to—

A thin figure, flitting beneath the oak. It paused when it caught sight of her, and she realized what she was looking at — stained breeches, and a weathered tricorn.

Katherine let out her breath as another bolt went through her — nerves again, though tinged with something else.

"Ah." Rebecca smiled at her, sauntering out of the shadows. "I thought it was you."

"Good evening, Lady Rebecca."

"Hush, now." Rebecca feigned a crouch, as if dodging her own name. "I am undercover."

Katherine bit back a smile. "To what do I owe the honor of this visit?"

Rebecca came up the garden, closing the distance between them. Her gaze snagged on the rifle resting beside Katherine. "It has been a distressing week. I wanted to see how your family was faring, given the state of things."

"Kind of you," Katherine replied. "I assume your household, like ours, has been in a state of—"

"Isolation? Panic?" Rebecca nodded. "Quite so."

"Then I can understand your desire for fresh air." Katherine watched her. "It must be difficult to be housebound when one is accustomed to wandering where one pleases."

Tell me, she wanted to say. *Tell me why you wanted to call upon a family you hardly know. Tell me why it is worth the risk.*

Rebecca's expression did not falter, though her gaze once again flitted to the rifle.

How did you know? Katherine wanted to say. *How did you know about the garden wall? How did you find it in the darkness?*

"There will be a ball," said Rebecca, her voice low.

"Will there?"

Rebecca nodded, her face dipping in and out of shadow. "The peers are... weary of hiding. And the Queen is eager for the season to continue."

Curiosity pricked Katherine's ears — it seemed that Rebecca's family was well-connected, indeed. Impressive, given their short tenure in Britain.

"Keep an eye on the post," Rebecca went on. Then, it seemed, she could stand it no longer, and gestured to the rifle. "Is that your brother's?"

For the second time that evening, Katherine let her fingers graze her rifle, and she watched a shiver work its way over Rebecca's shoulders. "No," she said. "It is not."

A silent understanding passed through the air between them. Rebecca took a breath, met Katherine's gaze. Her eyes were inscrutable in the near-darkness.

And the darkness was only deepening. Rebecca seemed to sense this, and took a step back towards the oak. "I should be on my way."

A tug, deep in Katherine's belly. "Are we to expect fencing lessons?"

Rebecca gave a sudden grin as she backed away. "Of course. Saturday."

"Saturday," Katherine echoed.

Rebecca tipped her tricorn, hand to brim, then ducked behind the oak and was gone.

❧ 13 ❧

First thing the following morning, the Knight family received an invitation to a party that evening. Katherine met Lucas' gaze over breakfast — Madam Kensington had gone to print the day before, as planned, and had sold an encouraging number of copies. Nothing close to their profits from the week before, or even from Monday, but it would be enough for Lucas to scrape by and make his payment that evening.

Mrs. Knight tutted at the invitation, then stuffed it under her plate. "I cannot help feeling that this is in poor taste."

"Poor taste or not," said Thomas, "it would be worse to not attend."

He had a point. The Knight family could not afford to ignore an invitation, even in an unprecedented political climate. Doing so would jeopardize their precipitous social status, and, Katherine recognized, be a bit of a death-knell for Madam Kensington.

"Well," Katherine muttered, so that only Brandon could hear her. "We would not want to be rude."

Mr. Perceval's assassination seemed to be a taboo topic amidst some circles and a source of morbid fascination amongst others. Katherine overheard no fewer than a dozen theories about the motivations of his assassin, and decided to sprinkle a few into her next edition. Then, she watched with keen eyes as Lord Francis Dashwood presented Lady Sophia with a pink camellia. Around her, the ballroom rustled and swelled as a tide of whispers rose through the air, paired with wide eyes and tilted smiles. For the moment, it seemed, nobody was discussing Mr. Perceval.

Sophia blushed, just as she was meant to, and offered Lord Dashwood a neat little curtsy. Behind her, Lady Alwyn watched the scene unfold with an impassive expression — Katherine could not tell if she was pleased, or displeased.

Because it was no secret — Lord Dashwood was a perfectly respectable gentleman, but his title was far from the highest on offer. Katherine was certain, beyond any reasonable doubt, that he would not be Lady Alwyn's top pick. Sophia did have plenty of other options. Every day, it seemed, another set of gentlemen callers would make the rounds at Whitehill Manor. Rebecca had told the Knights as much between their fencing bouts, rolling her eyes at the "dozens upon dozens" of bouquets currently occupying her sunroom.

"It is all very well for them to simper and recite poetry and preen like a bunch of peacocks," Rebecca had said, oblivious when Brandon spluttered through a mouthful of water. "But I do wish they'd get a move on. Cowards, the lot of them."

Cowards, Katherine thought again now, watching as the crowd shifted and the orchestra readied its instruments. And then, to her surprise, a gentleman walked up to her with a ready smile and a nod.

"Miss Knight."

Beside her, Katherine felt Lucas bristle, then school himself. "Buckmaster."

"Knight." The gentleman — Buckmaster — nodded again. "Be so kind as to introduce me to your sister?"

"Certainly," said Lucas. "Katherine, may I present the Viscount Buckmaster?"

Katherine curtsied, dropping her gaze, ignoring the thud of surprise that ricocheted through her body. "How do you do?"

"Very well, thank you." Lord Buckmaster nodded to the dance floor. "Would you oblige me, Miss Knight?"

"Of course," she managed, offering her hand.

The dance itself was adequate, and Lord Buckmaster entertained himself by discussing his stamp collection and asking her about the weather in the north. But just when she thought she'd escaped, another gentleman approached Lucas, flashing a grin and a ready hand.

Then, it happened again. Three dances, three gentlemen. And when Katherine managed to catch Lucas' eye, he looked just as confused as she felt.

She had never received so much attention, never. Not even at the Opening Ball.

Finally, between a waltz and a reel, she managed to escape. Katherine hastened to the refreshment table, where she saw a friendly face.

"I know," said Miss Spencer, the moment Katherine was within earshot. She passed Katherine a glass of wine and some sort of *vol-au-vent*. "It is happening to all of us."

"Us?" echoed Katherine, before taking a gulp of wine.

"Us," said Miss Spencer, nodding at the crowd. "Everyone who attended the Alwyns' tea party. Christ," she muttered. "It's as if a damn guest list was printed in the paper."

An ugly swoop in Katherine's stomach, but she had no reason to worry. She had not mentioned any of the guests by name in either edition of Madam Kensington. Wherever the leak had sprung, it had not come from her.

She took a bite of her *vol-au-vent*, chased it with wine. "You do not think—? They are trying to woo us to—?"

"To get within spitting distance of Lady Sophia? Yes," said Miss Spencer, her voice low and grim. "Yes, I rather think they are. Now that they believe us to be part of her inner circle."

"Oh!" Lady Pembroke came stumbling out of the crowd, her face flushed, her eyes sparkling. "What a wonderful evening it has been!"

"Has it?" Miss Spencer handed over the obligatory glass of wine, then nodded at the dance floor. "You're in high demand, I gather."

Lady Pembroke nodded and giggled into her wine. "Yes. I can hardly feel my feet."

Katherine and Miss Spencer exchanged a look, and the *vol-au-vent* seemed very dry in Katherine's mouth.

Buck up, she told herself, forcing herself to swallow. *This might end well.* And there were worse ways to secure a husband.

Though it was hardly a compliment if the match came as a result of someone settling for her instead of Sophia Johnson. Katherine frowned at the thought of watching a look of resignation, of disappointment, crossing the features of a man like Viscount Buckmaster. Of having to see that look, or some echo, some version of it, across the table from her every morning, every evening. Of having to share a life with that look, to share a bed—

A shudder rolled through her, settling low in her back. Katherine pushed the rest of the *vol-au-vent* into her mouth, her eyes watering from the stale pastry and the idea of sharing a marital bed with a man. She'd known for a while now, for better or worse, what that would entail, what it would ask of her. The obligation, the sacrifice. The endurance.

And she knew, just as she knew to breathe, that she did not want it.

But want was a very small thing in the face of tradition, of formality, of saving her family's estate. A small thing, indeed.

"Well?" Miss Spencer was saying to Lady Pembroke. "Your mother must be happy."

"Sparkling," Lady Pembroke confirmed. "Though it hardly matters, if none of the gentlemen come to call."

And there — the secret, understated rule of the season. Flirtations on the dance floor were not a promise or a guarantee. A man had to appear at one's front door with flowers in hand and a head full of compliments in order to merit any due consideration.

How would they feel, Katherine wondered, watching two couples smile and spin each other around, *if we were the ones picking them?*

Lucas appeared, skirting the edge of the dance floor. She noticed the tilt of his mouth, the loose lock of hair drifting over his forehead — he was discomposed, and she knew not why.

"Sister." He drew even with her, nodding at Miss Spencer and Lady Pembroke. "Ridley would like to dance with you."

She blinked at him, still unable to understand her newfound popularity. "Very well."

"Enjoy it, Miss Knight," said Miss Spencer, smirking in farewell. "While it lasts."

Katherine and Lucas made their way back across the ballroom, slipping between parents and families and conversations laced with wine. "What did she mean?" muttered Lucas.

"It is happening to all of us," Katherine replied, side-stepping a tray of *hors-d'oeuvres.* "All the young ladies who attended the Alwyns' tea party. We are in sudden and inexplicably high demand."

A few moments passed before Lucas spoke. "You know why, as do I."

Katherine bit back a sigh. "Do not let it affect your mood."

"No," Lucas returned. "Why shouldn't I be thrilled about every young rake in London using my sister to get to the Star?"

"At the very least, it keeps me occupied. And do not be so

quick to condemn your peers, Lucas. After all, we cannot know their true motivations."

Lucas clenched his jaw but did not reply. They reached the midpoint of the ballroom, where yet another gentleman was standing near the sideboard. He had quite a chin, and Katherine had to remind herself that it was impolite to stare.

"Lord Ridley." Lucas gave him a nod. "My sister, Miss Katherine Knight."

"Charmed," said Katherine, dropping into a curtsy.

"Likewise, Miss Knight." Lord Ridley offered her his hand. "Might we dance?"

"Of course, Lord Ridley." Though could she really say anything else? At the last moment, Katherine leaned in towards Lucas and whispered, "Don't you have somewhere to be?" Then she turned and allowed herself to be led onto the dance floor.

Very well, she thought, as the music began. *To war.*

❧

THE GARDEN WAS A RIOT, A CACOPHONY OF CLASHING METAL and shouts of delight, groans of dismay. A flash of silver as foil met foil, a scuffle of grass and mud as feet made a hasty retreat.

Watching from her table and chairs beneath the willow tree, Katherine could not deny that she was smiling, and had been for quite some time. A dozen paces away, Rebecca feinted left, then smacked Thomas across the leg with her foil, ending the bout.

"You cannot trust your opponent!" Rebecca reached for Thomas' arm, adjusting his stature. "Always assume that I am the opposite of what I seem."

He huffed, and gave her calf a playful jab with his foil. The hazy rain swarmed around his hair, crusting the strands in droplets. "Simple enough, when you're in those trousers."

Rebecca chuckled. "A break, then?" She looked at Lucas and

Brandon, who were slumped on the hanging bench, then let her gaze wander over to Katherine.

Katherine looked down at her needlepoint, which she'd hardly touched over the past hour. The cool, damp air had a sharp edge to it, and it seemed to catch in her throat as Rebecca ambled over, the picture of ease.

"Well?" Rebecca was grinning, her shirt once again slouching low over her collarbone. "Are we entertaining?"

"I doubt I need answer that question," Katherine replied. "Perhaps a day will come when one of my brothers bests you. That would be entertainment indeed."

"Such a day is far off, Miss Knight." Rebecca stepped closer, her gaze skirting over the table and its scattered contents. "Are you an artist?"

Katherine could not keep herself from snorting, could not keep a genuine grin from breaking free. "Good God, no. But pretending to be has its benefits."

Rebecca shot her a questioning look, and Katherine glanced over her shoulder at the windows of the house before leaning closer.

"My mother," she said in an undertone. "She worries that if I spend too much time with the boys, I shall abandon what little femininity I still retain." Katherine flicked a hand toward her needlepoint, her scattered sketches. "This is to appease her."

Something like mirth sparkled in Rebecca's eyes. "An admirable ruse. And an admirable effort." She stepped closer, her head tilted to one side as she considered one of the drawings, a relief of the side of the house. "You nearly have it."

"Oh, you—" But then Rebecca reached for a charcoal pencil, and Katherine's voice died in her throat.

With a few firm, confident strokes, Rebecca rendered a splendid recreation of Knight house. A second later, she had the windows, and the odd turret on one side. Then she licked her thumb, and smeared the curtains into place. "There," she said, a smudge of charcoal on her chin.

Katherine blinked a few times, her face oddly hot and her mind stuck on the pink flash of Rebecca's tongue. "Good God," she managed. "Is there anything you cannot do?"

Rebecca looked up, and a genuine smile crossed her face. "Waltz."

Katherine laughed. "It is easier than it seems."

"That is what Sophia tells me, but I never know if she is trying to soften the blow. To tempt me into joining the season."

"I suppose it is only natural. I imagine debuting alone, in a foreign country, with only a few acquaintances, is no easy feat."

Rebecca gave a light scoff. "Our circle of acquaintances grows each day. Sophia has no cause to feel lonely."

"I see. Has Lord Dashwood made a convincing argument thus far?"

"He certainly thinks so." Rebecca leaned against the table, scratching a few absent-minded shrubs in front of her little Knight house. "He's brought her flowers and her favorite chocolates. And he makes her laugh, of all things."

"Is that not ideal?" said Katherine. "To share a sense of humor with one's beloved?"

"I suppose," Rebecca conceded. "But I cannot shake the impression that he is a great, prancing fool."

Katherine could hardly control her grin. "Harsh censure, indeed."

"I will admit, my standards are somewhat ridiculous." Rebecca sighed; beneath her hand, the willow tree had erupted into life. "I cannot think any man my sister's equal."

Surprise overtook Katherine, and for a moment, she could only stare at Rebecca. "I see."

"Sophia certainly likes him best," Rebecca went on. "Out of all of them."

Katherine nodded. "And... your mother?"

"Has yet to make up her mind." The corner of Rebecca's mouth twitched, and her hand stilled. Her gaze lifted to the scene before her. "Is this the extent of your family's diversions? Fencing and would-be sketches in the garden?"

"No," Katherine said, before she could stop herself. "We are much more lively in the country, but we have our ways here in London."

"Ways," Rebecca repeated, shooting her a sly look. "Such as?"

A tremor like champagne went through Katherine's stomach. "You shall have to visit us after supper," she blurted. "Nothing proper happens after supper."

"Very well." Rebecca said it like she was taking on a challenge. "After supper, then. Sometime next week." Suddenly, she leaned down, close enough for Katherine to see the impish tilt of her eyes, to smell that intoxicating blend of metal and warm wood. "I'll be sure to make use of a window."

14

**Madam Kensington's High Society Papers,
No. 4**

oodness me, my dears — we had ourselves quite a diverting evening, did we not? It seems that London is all too eager to forget the grim fate of its Prime Minister, and to instead entertain itself with games of flattery and courtship. One would have to be quite blind to have missed the way a certain dark-haired Beauty gleamed and shone in the direction of her Raven, a handsome specimen most adept at making her blush. A handsome Raven, yes, but perhaps not the best that England has to offer — our corvid ruffled many a feather in the ballroom, spiking tempers and jealousy as he strolled past. We can only wonder if his courtship is genuine, and if our Beauty is as taken with him as she seems — she is an enigmatic little thing, and particularly adept at hiding her hand... Dear readers, we can but speculate, though soon enough, the tides of the season will shift, and reveal the treasures lurking in their ever-reaching depths...

KATHERINE FLIPPED THROUGH A STACK OF PAPERS AND WINCED when one of them sliced through the pad of her thumb, drawing a thin line of blood. She sucked at the cut, grabbing the papers with her other hand and shifting them down the table, away from her. She then reached for the nearest ledger — a copy of business tax records, dated some thirty years previous — and hefted it open, its dusty spine cracking with a wheeze.

On days like today, Katherine was quite thankful for her father's troubling habit of collecting any and every book that might cross his path. His usual maxim, *You never know when they might come in handy*, was proving quite true today.

The Knight family library — at least, the one in London — reminded Katherine somewhat of an attic. Books were packed into the dark, ancient shelves, stuffed into every available space and crevice. Where the shelves surrendered, the books overflowed onto the floor, stacked and piled wherever they could fit. The library offered little in the way of furniture; Katherine sat in an old, squashy armchair at an old, dull desk that rivaled their dining table in size. Comfort and modesty ruled the space, and the high ceilings offered a cocoon of shadows, buffeting the shelves and lending the room a cozy air. A dented, enormous globe dominated the far corner, bleached by the sun from the nearby window and stained from careless cups of tea. From the mantelpiece, a bust of Cicero frowned upon his little kingdom; from the wall, a pair of antlers burst forth.

Mrs. Knight had made her attempt to tame the space. Before the fireplace sat a long, comfortable couch, fencing in a low table and a pair of matching armchairs. Katherine could hardly count how many evenings she and her family had passed before the fire, playing cards and games and trading stories of imaginary places.

Now, she sat in the library alone, surrounded by stacks of books and papers that had remained untouched for years. Her eyes itched from the dust, and her fingers twitched with the urge to take notes. But she couldn't, not for fear of being caught.

Her fear was silly, perhaps, but she could not deny it. She could not deny it, because she had spent the better part of a day working through as many records as she could find, and had unearthed only a handful of whispers about Lord Alwyn.

Or, as he'd been up until the year before, Mr. Maximus Johnson, a merchant who specialized in sea-based shipping and textiles. A London native with a background not worth mentioning, he'd found himself entwined with Hobbes & Co., an import-export company, and worked his way up through the ranks — first a runner, then an apprentice, then an assistant. When the owner passed away, the company had fallen into Maximus' ready hands. He'd made some changes, as far as Katherine could tell, and within a handful of years, had tripled their profits.

Then, he'd sold Hobbes & Co. Relocated to the Continent, opened a new import-export business, partnering with a handful of wealthy financiers. A year later, he married Anneke van der Meer, daughter of a prominent solicitor. And somehow, in the twenty-odd years since, Maximus Johnson had made money hand over fist, as evidenced by his London residence, his household, and the appearance of his family.

It could be false money, Katherine thought now, flipping through the tax records. *He could be building a mountain of debt.*

But such a revelation would surprise her. Her hands stilled as she found the correct page, as she saw the registered earnings of Hobbes & Co. during Lord Alwyn's final year at the helm. The figures only confirmed what all the other scraps of information had told her — he seemed, by all accounts, to be a diligent businessman, one with a clever nose for profit. Selling the company at such a successful stage was an odd choice, perhaps, but doing so had given him the funds he'd needed to invest in his second venture in Amsterdam and requisition a new fleet of ships.

Katherine's gaze wandered to the globe, where it traced the

fading coastline of the Netherlands. *Amsterdam*, she thought. *Why Amsterdam?*

Then, the sound of footsteps in the hall. The door to the library opened, and Lucas poked his head in.

"Ah, Kitten. There you are. It's time for supper."

She must have missed the gong. "Am I very late?"

"Not at all. Father is still wandering in from the garden." Lucas pushed open the door, leaning against the frame. "Seems you've been busy."

Before she could respond, he crossed the room, reaching for a pile of papers. "Good grief," said Lucas, raising an eyebrow. "What do you want with all this nonsense? Profit and loss margins from 1785, market trading indexes—"

"It is nothing, Lucas." Katherine stood up, snatching the papers out of his hands. She gathered them into a pile and pushed them beneath a book, avoiding his gaze. "I was simply checking a fact from today's paper."

"Lying is an art, Kitten," he said, moving to look at the open ledger, "and one you have yet to master. Hobbes & Co.," he read aloud, while Katherine scrambled to shove the ledger away from him. "I do not believe I'm familiar with that particular enterprise."

Katherine did not reply, gathering several volumes in her arms and taking them back to their shelf. Her silence, it seemed, only encouraged matters.

"We both know I am a gambling man," Lucas said. "And I'm willing to bet you're looking into someone. Have I caught Madam Kensington in the act of sniffing about for her newest prey?"

Katherine shot him a scowl. "Must you characterize me in such a beastly manner?"

"Of course." Lucas gave her a look that she did not like at all — a keen look, a knowing look. "Does this inquiry have anything to do with our new acquaintance?"

A blush flooded Katherine's face, and she hated herself for it.

She crossed to the door, knowing that Lucas would follow. "What would give you that impression?"

Lucas snorted. "Only that you have been on tenterhooks these past couple of days, waiting for her to appear at our drawing room window."

"If I were... on tenterhooks," Katherine said, now heading down the stairs to the ground floor. "Can you blame me for it? When the most exciting event this season has been the sudden demise of our beloved Prime Minister?"

"I suppose there is some truth in that. But only some."

When they reached the bottom of the stairs, Katherine turned to face her brother. "If you have something to say to me, Lucas, say it and be done with it."

"I have nothing to say," he replied, arching his scarred eyebrow. "But to warn you that some friendships are best left... where they lie."

Katherine frowned. "Meaning?"

"Lord Alwyn is a powerful man, Kitten. Certainly more powerful than any Knight in England." He hesitated, then took a step towards the dining room. "Tread carefully."

After a moment, Katherine followed him, unable to shake the feeling that somewhere, between those dusty pages and cracking spines, she'd missed something.

◈

KATHERINE LOOKED HER BROTHER IN THE EYE AND TOOK A long, burning swallow of Scotch. Thomas matched her, his gaze unwavering as the liquor passed down his throat. Before her, his hand twitched in the air; even his fingers seemed to have a snide, teasing air.

Katherine inhaled, then exhaled slowly, lifting her own hand to meet his. "Prepare to die a quick and painful death."

"Not today, I think," Thomas replied. He blinked a few times, and she could see the sweat beading at his temple — they had been here a while, and the room was stuffy.

"Lucas," said Katherine. "Open a window, before Princess Tom comes over faint."

"Bold words. You're the one who collapsed at the sight of—"

"Everyone faints on their first hunt, Tom," said Lucas, opening one of the drawing room windows. "And Kitten felled a six-point buck to your four-point."

"Well?" Katherine said to Thomas, wiggling her fingers.

Their hands met, and the war began.

Katherine clenched her teeth, her elbow digging into the pliant wood of the card table. But she held Thomas' gaze, refusing to drop it for even an instant, even as her arm burned with tension. She kept him there, at a stalemate, for a few moments, then a few moments more. Longer than she'd anticipated. Then—

"My word," came a wry, familiar voice. "What a scene this is."

"Give them a minute," said Lucas. "It never lasts long."

"How dare you, brother," Katherine forced out, sweat pooling at the small of her neck. She tried not to look at Rebecca, who was climbing in through the window. "We both know I have bested all of you."

"Surrender," said Thomas, pushing her hand half an inch past the midline, back towards her own arm. "Wave the white flag."

"Never." Katherine clenched her jaw, the liquor buzzing under her skin, and mustered the fading strength in her arm — this was her third match of the evening. She gave a mighty push, and managed to force him back a spare inch towards his own side. Thomas gave a muffled grunt, then flexed, and it was over. He slammed her hand down onto the table, and Katherine's arm went limp, yielding to his triumph.

"Damn you," Katherine hissed as Thomas stood up from the table and let out a shout of triumph.

"Katherine beat him last week," Lucas said to Rebecca. Rebecca, dressed in her usual motley trousers and shirt, was standing beside him, wearing a thoughtful expression. She caught Katherine's eye and smiled, then gave her the slightest wink.

A fresh heat crawled over Katherine's chest and neck. She turned away, taking her glass and making her way to the sideboard, where the Scotch was waiting.

"Hah! Yes!" Thomas pumped his fists in the air, his face flushed and his smile wide. "Victory, sweet victory!"

"Not for long." Brandon took Katherine's seat and flexed his hand.

The Scotch sloshed into Katherine's glass, dripping over her fingers. Katherine rolled her eyes and considered her right hand. It was bright red and still throbbing from the effort of arm wrestling. She sucked the Scotch off her thumb and wandered over to the nearest sofa, slumping into the cushions with none of the grace she'd inherited from her mother.

"Buck up, Kitten," said Lucas from across the room. "It was a sporting effort."

Katherine ignored him and stared up at the ceiling, refusing to look at her brothers or at Rebecca. A slick, hot thud ricocheted through Katherine's body, vibrating along her arms, and she reflected that, perhaps, she'd had quite a bit to drink.

I am entitled to wallow, she told herself. Her feet were heavy, and her eyes throbbed in the dull candlelight. *Wallow, wallow, wallow.*

Madam Kensington No. 4 had sold well the day before, which was a consolation, she supposed. With Perceval's assassin returning into the hands of his Maker, London seemed to forget that such an act of catastrophic violence had even occurred. All of the peers were once again most concerned with the tidal shifts of the season, with engagements and promises and sly, flirtatious looks. Katherine had seethed over her own handiwork, her own flippancy in the face of a lynchpin in British history, but had seen it through regardless. *What does this make me*, she had wondered the previous night, lying in the darkness of her bedroom. *What have I become?*

Monday's earnings were tucked into a hidden compartment of Brandon's dresser, as was now their standard procedure. In her second full week of life, Madam Kensington was just beginning to break even. Katherine hoped that if the coming Thursday edition sold as well as Monday's, she might be able to finally pay Rita for her services. She was certain that Rita's whispers from the Bainbridge household had been the key to No. 4's success.

"Good Heavens. You scowl most beautifully."

Katherine glanced over the rim of the sofa. Rebecca stood by the armrest, a coy smile playing about her mouth. Behind her, Thomas and Brandon were mid-match, glaring at one another from bright red, sweaty faces.

"I have every right to scowl," Katherine replied, tapping her finger against the rim of her glass. "You, however, have no right to tease me for it."

Rebecca chuckled under her breath. "It was a compliment, Miss Knight. I would never dream of teasing you."

"Good grief." Katherine pressed her free hand to her forehead. "I can never parse sarcasm when I am in my cups. Go pester Lucas."

"Pester?" Rebecca leaned against the armrest. "You do me a disservice, Miss Knight."

"*Miss Knight*," Katherine mimicked her, before she could stop herself. "Call me Katherine, for the love of God. It is hardly worth pretending anything about this is proper, especially not when you are wearing those damn trousers."

A pause, long enough that Katherine almost forgot that Rebecca was there. When Rebecca spoke again, her voice had dropped, and it carried a soft edge. "Very well," she said. "Katherine."

A shiver snaked along Katherine's spine, but she did not let it show. She stared up at the ceiling and swallowed hard, her heart giving a sickening throb.

"Rebecca!" Lucas, from the card table. "Come along, it's your turn—"

"Coming," said Rebecca, and a moment later, she shifted away from the sofa.

Once she was gone, Katherine tapped her finger against her glass again, wondering if perhaps the best way to avoid a farewell was to simply fall asleep.

And a quarter of an hour later, she did.

❧

KATHERINE WOKE TO THE SOUND OF SOMEONE SITTING DOWN across from her, the rattle of a teacup in its saucer. She opened one eye, winced, then opened the other.

"Morning, Kitten." Thomas looked far too cheerful. He cracked open the newspaper and raised an eyebrow. "Did we have an enjoyable evening?'

"Get away from me."

"You've had a bit of mail." Thomas pointed with his foot to the low table between the sofas, where lay a letter with her name on it. "Cannot imagine why."

Katherine frowned at the letter, trying to ignore the invisible splinters attempting to pierce her skull. She steeled herself, picked up the letter, and broke the seal.

A minute later, Thomas said, "Anything noteworthy?"

Katherine lowered the letter, her heart pounding in her throat. "Mr. Ransom has invited me," she said, through a very dry mouth, "for a walk in Kensington Gardens."

Thomas looked at her for a moment, his expression unchanged. "Ah," he finally managed. "Generous of him."

A very odd ringing had begun in Katherine's ears. She blinked a few times, wondering if she was still asleep, still dreaming. It was then that she noticed a blanket pooled in her lap, over her legs.

Thomas watched her tug the blanket away and said, "That was Rebecca's handiwork."

Katherine's stomach gave an unhelpful swoop that had nothing to do with her indulgence the previous evening. "What?"

"She was worried about you catching cold, if I remember correctly." Thomas smirked and returned to his paper. "Cushioning your wounded ego, I think."

"I see."

"You should get a move on," Thomas said. "I doubt Mr. Ransom finds tardiness very attractive in a potential wife."

For once, Katherine's wit failed her. She forced herself to her feet and left the drawing room, unable to shake the image of Rebecca standing above her, looking down.

INTERLUDE III — WHITEHILL MANOR

Rebecca winced, swore under her breath, and sucked on her finger. She tasted copper, rolled her eyes at her own clumsiness. Outside her open window, the birds sang.

"There you are!" Sophia waltzed into the room, a vision even in her plain muslin gown. She flopped onto Rebecca's chaise and let out a most artful sigh. "Have the days always been so long?"

Rebecca glanced at her sister, coy. "I think the days are unchanged. Your patience, however, is shorter than ever."

"You wound me," Sophia deadpanned. "What are you doing? Are you *sewing?*"

Rebecca muttered another curse and picked up her needle. "Hardly a novel occurrence, sister. I darned your stockings, did I not?"

"You have never darned a thing in your life."

"No?" Frowning, Rebecca prodded at a clump of thread she could not remember creating. "I've repaired many a canvas. And how different could it be, really?"

"Those are *sails*." Sophia came over to her, gently lifting the needle and the trousers out of her hands. "Let me. At this rate, it will be full of holes."

Rebecca sighed and surrendered, slouching back in her armchair. "Never thought I would need to be rescued by Sophia the Saint."

"Worry not, I won't tell any of the other sailors your shame." Sophia unpicked a few of Rebecca's clumsy stitches. "Are you certain it is worth the trouble of repair? These trousers are—"

"Yes." Rebecca tilted her head back and looked up at the ceiling. "I like those trousers."

"*Really?*"

"Soph."

Sophia tutted like a hen and began her work. Her needle flew through the fabric, faultless and precise. "You've been keeping late hours."

"Have I?"

"At least promise me you aren't getting into any trouble." Sophia held up the torn trousers as evidence.

Rebecca waved her hand in dismissal. "No trouble, I promise. Just a bit of a diversion with the Knight boys."

"Oh?" The eagerness in Sophia's voice pooled like honey. "What sort of diversion?"

"Fencing."

Sophia scoffed. "Rebecca—"

"What? I'm following Mother's orders, aren't I?" Rebecca shifted in her seat, ignoring the unsteady prickle in the back of her neck. " 'They are worth knowing, and worth knowing well.' "

"Not well enough to fence with, surely." But Sophia continued her work. "Do you... enjoy their company?"

Unbidden, the image of Katherine, slack with slumber, her nimble features tucked into a cushion, rose in Rebecca's mind. She blinked several times, but was unable to shake it. "Yes," she said, then cleared her throat. "Yes, I suppose I do."

Sophia hummed. "Well, at least it keeps you off the streets. I cannot bear the idea of you wandering into the wrong sort of area."

Now, Rebecca flashed her a grin. "This, from the young lady who knew the roads of Amsterdam better than I did."

"Do not be ridiculous, Rebecca."

"My habits are of little concern, Saintie." Outside, a robin chirped. "I am not out. The people of London do not care how I spend my time, so long as I do not embarrass the family."

"You are quite wrong about that." Sophia looked up, her gaze inscrutable. "If you were seen, Rebecca—"

"I am never seen," Rebecca said. "And if I am, I am not recognized."

"For now," Sophia replied. "But the more time you spend in public, at court, the more memorable you will become." She leaned forward, her needle stilling. "You must promise me. To be careful."

"Of course, Soph—"

"I mean it." Sophia looked at her for another moment, then dropped her gaze back to her mending. "It may not concern you, but it concerns me."

Rebecca looked at her older sister. Looked at her, then slowly sat up. "He is going to propose, isn't he? Your handsome little Raven?"

Sophia blushed, suddenly and deeply enough that Rebecca could see it in her neck, her cheeks. "That is not for me to speculate, Rebecca, I merely want to be—"

"Careful," Rebecca said, then gave a nod, smirking. "I see."

A beat passed, then two. The birdsong continued, and Sophia's blush did not fade.

"You are head over heels, Saintie. Absolutely gone on him, aren't you?"

Sophia shot her a mutinous look, then cast an anxious glance at the door, which was not closed. "For God's sake, Rebecca—"

Rebecca's eyebrows scaled her forehead and she gaped at her sister. "You mean she does not know? You haven't told her?"

"What am I supposed to say?" Sophia hissed, stabbing quite

savagely at Rebecca's trousers. "You know she does not favor him, would rather see me matched with any number of other gentlemen—"

"But if you are in love, Soph—!"

"It does not make a difference!" Sophia looked up, her eyes shining. "And you cannot tell her, Rebecca!"

"Of course not," Rebecca said, dropping her voice. "Of course not, Soph, I would never—"

"We have a chance," Sophia went on, then took a shaky breath. "We have a better chance if she does not think that our... regard for one another... has anything to do with it. Mother likes numbers. And if Francis can convince her—"

"Francis?" Rebecca repeated, smirking again. "Using Christian names, are we?"

Sophia's blush deepened, and her needle flashed in and out of the fabric.

"Do not worry," Rebecca went on. "I shall not breathe a word, Saintie. Of any of it."

A few moments passed, then Sophia closed her eyes and nodded. "Thank you."

"I am happy for you." Rebecca smiled. "I never thought you would find a love match in this God-forsaken country."

"Nor did I," said Sophia, grimly enough that Rebecca had to stifle a laugh. "It is a dull sort of place, is it not?"

Rebecca did laugh then, snorting like a pig. "And you wonder why I seek out the challenge of the Knight boys."

"Are they friendly, at the very least?" Sophia glanced up, her blush fading. "Are they kind?"

"Yes," Rebecca said. "Very kind." *Distracting*, she almost said, thinking of Katherine's tongue, and the way it had flicked along the curve of her thumb, chasing a droplet of Scotch.

"They seem an insular sort of family," Sophia continued. "Not many of my acquaintances know them very well."

Rebecca nodded. "They prefer the country."

"I see." Sophia tied her thread and bit it off in a clean, pragmatic movement. "And which of the brothers do you prefer?"

A roaring heat overtook Rebecca's ears. "What?"

"There is no use denying it." Sophia shot her a wink and shook out the trousers. "Why else would you be so determined to spend time with them?"

Rebecca's mind stuttered, unable to catch up with this shift in the conversation. "Sophia — that — that is hardly—"

Sophia smiled and stood up, handing her her trousers. "Now you know how it feels when you ask me about Francis." She turned away. "I will be in the sunroom, if you would like to join me for tea."

Rebecca watched her sister leave. Outside, the birds continued to sing.

⁂ 15 ⁂

Madam Kensington's High Society Papers,
No. 5

Shine your shoes, fillies and colts, and prepare yourselves for a most diverting afternoon! The going promises to be good indeed — neither wet nor heavy underfoot — and filled with opportunities to take the lay of the land. The season is still young, but rapidly threatening towards spinsterhood — when will an engagement finally shatter our calm waters, bringing tidal waves of delight to our most dull and distempered lives? Perhaps I exaggerate, my darlings, but do we not ache for something new, something stupendous, to break the torpor of what has become a most dreary season?

Undoubtedly, my dears, we cannot deny that some of our fillies are off the pace — but, the same must also be said of our colts. Where is their courage, their bravery in the face of true love? I do wonder, on occasion, whether they have any interest in the season at all — any interest in romance, in the art of wooing, or in making one's beloved sigh and coo. As we gather in our crowds to watch the finest beasts race to their content, we must consider the most pressing questions of the season. Who among us is already washed out, and ready to make their retreat? Who will be scratched from the season altogether, and returned to obscurity? Who has been rated, only to surge to a late-season prominence? And finally, who will be kept under wraps, and come out ahead when we least expect it?

৩৩৫৩

KATHERINE STEPPED OUT OF THE KNIGHT CARRIAGE AND FELT A fresh wave of butterflies roll through her stomach. She squinted against the sunshine — a surprise, given that the previous night had offered nothing but rain — and inhaled the fresh scents of mud, grass, sugar... and horse dung.

Unlike her brothers, Katherine had never been to Ascot. She glanced around, taking in the crowds of her peers, the wooden stands, the stalls of vendors flogging pamphlets and iced buns and lemonade. From this distance, she could just see the edge of the track, and the stands rapidly filling with attendees. Another wave of butterflies, the thrill of the unknown; she imagined the thunder of galloping hooves, the heave and rattle of the horses gulping for air—

"Katherine," her mother hissed as she stepped down onto the gravel drive. "Parasol!"

Katherine bit back a curse and opened her damned parasol, lifting it above her head. A quick look told her that none of the other mothers had noticed her flub — she squeezed the handle, her webbed lace gloves digging into her palm.

"Good going," Thomas said, stamping the ground. "Not too muddy."

Katherine scoffed as Brandon and Lucas descended from the carriage. "As if you know a damn thing about horse racing."

"Katherine!" Mrs. Knight did not bother to drop her voice

this time. "What would Mr. Ransom think if he heard that sort of language?"

Katherine rolled her eyes and turned away, unable to deny the spike of *something* that jolted through her belly at the thought of seeing Mr. Ransom again. True enough, they had passed a pleasant enough time in Kensington Gardens, but she dreaded the thought of seeing him again, of having to make conversation, to smile and laugh in the pretty way that all proper young ladies did.

Worse, she dreaded encouraging him. Encouraging him, when she had little to offer, to promise. Even less than what she could offer herself, as consolation for betraying her own heart.

"Rotten weather," Brandon grumbled, while Lucas grinned and took in their surroundings. "Mother, if you continue to insist upon taking me out into the sunlight, I shall bury myself hip-deep in the mud at Mosswood and never ride south again."

"Is that a promise?" Mrs. Knight replied, as Mr. Knight joined them.

As one, the Knight family ventured into the crowds, trading smiles and nods with the families they knew. Katherine caught more than one glare from young ladies who, she presumed, were a bit stuck on Mr. Ransom. He was handsome, and a rather good prospect, in spite of his lack of a title. He had a larger income than some of the peerage, she knew, thanks to her own research and her brothers' diligent snooping at the White Fox. And Mr. Ransom had taken an interest in *her*, of all people. An attraction she could deny no more than she could deny her own repulsion.

As if he could hear her thoughts, Brandon piped up: "Where are we meeting the man of the hour, then?"

"At our seats," Katherine replied, refusing to blush. She clenched the handle of her parasol again, grateful for the burn in her palm.

"Best behavior, boys," said Mrs. Knight, through a gleaming smile. "I must admit, I am a touch surprised. No sign of our Star."

Another swoop in Katherine's stomach, as Thomas said, "The Alwyns are always fashionably late. What better way to make an entrance?"

Their seats were in the middle of the stands, partly shaded by a fabric canopy. The air swam hot and murky, thick with the tang of the dirt and the rough, warm scent of horses. Katherine found herself thinking of the stables at Mosswood, of Beatrice. She swallowed hard, and looked out at the track, at the faultless expanse of green. She should have been paying attention, she knew, to her peers, to the compliments and smiles flitting around her. But she could not bring herself to do it.

"Good afternoon, Knight family."

And there he was, as tall and charming as ever. Mr. Ransom, giving her father a nod. Katherine noted three young ladies nearby shooting him not-terribly-sneaky glances. She bit back a smile and looked up at him. "Hello, Mr. Ransom."

"Miss Knight. You look splendid, as always."

He was sweet as well as charming, because Katherine was wearing one of her plain muslin dresses, in a light blue pattern several years out of date. "You are too kind, Mr. Ransom."

"A splendid day for it," Mr. Knight said. "Won't you join us, Mr. Ransom?"

"Certainly." Mr. Ransom took the empty seat beside Katherine, and if she were a different person, perhaps she would have felt something other than a tickle of dread. "Are you a fan of the ponies, Mr. Knight?"

As their conversation continued, Katherine returned her gaze to the track. A faint ringing filled her ears, and it was several long moments before she realized that Thomas, who sat to her right, was muttering something.

"This is dull already." He leaned back in his seat, glancing around the tent. "We need a bit of proper entertainment."

"Do we?" Katherine replied in a murmur. "Has horse-racing become a leisurely sport since last I checked?"

He shot her a look that said, *You know what I mean.* "Perhaps Lady Edith will throw an insult at her sister, or better yet, her cousin." His glance flickered over those seated nearest to them. "Or perhaps Lady Cowdray will catch her skirts on the railing and find herself in a compromising position."

We need something, was the unspoken message. *Some bit of drama, of persecution. Something that will sell better than an average day at the races.* Katherine had already been forced to pad the day's edition with frivolous language; she feared what might happen to their sales if she did so again.

"Fear not," Katherine muttered, only half-listening to the conversation between Mr. Ransom and her parents. "Our Star will appear soon enough, and give us something to talk about."

Thomas hummed. "Better yet — perhaps Rebecca will bring her rapier."

The image alone was enough to make Katherine snort like a pig. She could just see it — Rebecca leaping atop a bench, or better yet, a horse, swinging said rapier and demanding that the jockeys race each other on foot. A pirate of the season, a foil to her older sister.

"Ah," Thomas said then. "Speak of the Devil."

A slight hush fell as a warm, beaming light appeared below them. Katherine had to squint as Sophia, dressed in a radiant, tooth-aching white, seemed to hover up the steps to the stands. Behind her were her parents, and—

Katherine swallowed, her mouth going dry. She looked at Rebecca, who was dressed in a yellow so pale it was reminiscent of fresh cream, and could hardly bring herself to look away. Rebecca was so different like this, with her hair in that neat little bun, a pair of the finest satin gloves on her hands. To see her was to see a strange, warped echo of the woman who tipped her tricorn and grinned like a thief. To see her was to not see her, and again, that odd feeling swept through Katherine's stomach.

Exhilaration, she thought, and wished she'd brought a fan.

She and Thomas watched as the Alwyns made their way through the stands, pausing and speaking to lords and ladies as they went. Mr. Ransom had the good grace not to stare as Sophia smiled and stepped into the row of seats below the Knights.

"Miss Knight!" Sophia dipped a tiny curtsy. "How lovely to see you!"

"Lovely indeed," Rebecca said from behind her. Only Katherine caught the smirk lingering in the corner of her mouth, coiled with all the self-assurance of a cat.

"Are you a fan of the races, Miss Knight?" Sophia went on. Katherine tried not to stare — this close, it really was like looking into the sun. "Or did these devils drag you along?"

Lucas feigned a blow, putting a hand to his heart. "Lady Sophia, you wound me dearly."

"Such harsh censure, brother," said Thomas, giving Sophia a doleful look. "And from so tender a lady."

Rebecca hid a snort, while Sophia gave a good-natured sniff and said, "What sweet brothers, to speak over their sister with such ease."

"I do enjoy the races, Lady Sophia," said Katherine. The words caught like dry crumbs in her mouth, and she tried not to meet Rebecca's gaze. "My brothers, of course, could not say the same."

"Very sporting of them to attend," said Rebecca, arching an eyebrow. "Generous, even."

Then, a blast of sound — the warning horn, from the track. The crowd stilled, then an excited murmur ripped through the stands.

"Quickly, dear." Lady Alwyn appeared beside Sophia, Lord Alwyn just behind her. She nodded at the Knights, then turned to her daughters. "Let us take our seats."

Somewhat to Katherine's horror, the Alwyns sat down in the row below the Knights. Rebecca took the seat directly in front of

Katherine; she could see Rebecca's back, where her thin, tiny curls hovered above the skin of her neck.

Katherine forced herself to take a long, deep breath. It did not help.

"Fascinating history, you know," said Mr. Ransom, apropos of nothing. He smiled at Katherine. "Horse racing."

"Oh?" she managed, then squeezed the handle of her parasol yet again.

"It was King James II who famously transformed it from a pastime to an organized sport. He established Newmarket as the headquarters of racing in Britain."

"Oh?" said Katherine again. "How interesting—"

Rebecca glanced over her shoulder at Mr. Ransom and said, "Right town, wrong king."

He looked at her askance. "I beg your pardon?"

"Newmarket was established as the seat of British racing," Rebecca said, "with the first cup race in 1634." She glanced at Katherine. "Under the reign of King Charles I."

The silence that fell could have been cut with a pin. Beside Katherine, Thomas stifled a snort, and Brandon cleared his throat.

Katherine stared at Rebecca, unable to parse the emotions rolling through her stomach. *What are you doing?* she wanted to scream.

"Ah," said Mr. Ransom. "My mistake."

"An easy one to make," Rebecca replied.

"I do not believe," said Mr. Ransom, his voice mild, "that we've been introduced."

"No," Rebecca agreed, looking back down at the track. When she spoke, she tossed the words over her shoulder. "But you are Mr. John Ransom, are you not?"

"Yes—"

"Lady Rebecca," she went on, with all the interest of a passing fly. "My father is Lord Alwyn. My sister, I believe you have already met."

And then, thank God, the race began.

Katherine barely registered it as the horses streaked past the stands, as the crowd roared in her ears. All she could do was stare at that stripe of Rebecca's neck, at the curls floating along her hairline, and feel an anger so astute it was almost blinding.

Anger... and perhaps gratitude.

The horses thundered, the crowd roared, and Katherine watched the sly game of looks between Lady Sophia and Lord Dashwood. Then, it seemed, someone won — the course erupted with cheers and applause, and even Katherine's brothers leapt to their feet.

Katherine hastened to stand up, clapping.

"Remarkable, wasn't it?" Mr. Ransom was saying, smiling his good-natured smile. "And to think, these horses are descended from the same five stallions. They are all related, distant cousins, if you would believe it."

"Three stallions," said Rebecca, and when she glanced over her shoulder, there was something like fire in her eyes, even though her expression remained placid. "Not five."

Thomas snorted again, but did a poor job of stifling it. A horrible heat rose in Katherine's face; she looked at Rebecca, and when Rebecca finally met her gaze, it was like looking at the point of a knife.

"I see," said Mr. Ransom. His expression had shuttered, and a few moments later, he bid the Knight family a hasty farewell, barely even glancing at Katherine. She opened her mouth to say goodbye, but he turned and left, cutting through the crowd. Katherine shut her mouth and dropped her gaze, staring down at her own feet. A door had just closed, she knew, and likely would never open again.

She said nothing as her family exchanged pleasantries with the Alwyns, as her mother laughed and her father shook hands with

Lord Alwyn. She did not meet Rebecca's gaze, nor Sophia's, but instead fixed her eyes upon the crowds, scanning for the usual whispers and movements of intrigue. Thomas was watching her, she knew, searching for something in her face.

When the Knight family departed the stands, Katherine felt as though a hot edge was burning between her shoulders. She tried to ignore it, listening to her brothers' chatter as they approached the line of market stalls.

"How charming!" Mrs. Knight turned to smile at her children. "Shall we take a look around, before heading home?"

Lucas and Thomas immediately walked towards the beer tent, and Brandon wandered over to a book vendor. Mrs. Knight cooed over a luscious set of silks they could not afford, and Mr. Knight followed her, smiling in an indulgent sort of way.

Katherine took a breath and stepped out of the foot traffic, then tilted her parasol back and lifted her face to the sun. She closed her eyes, taking another breath, and tried to calm her thundering heart.

Then, a presence behind her. Quiet on the plush grass. "Katherine?"

Katherine opened her eyes and turned to face Rebecca, her earlier anger returning with a vengeance. "I hope you're pleased with yourself. Mr. Ransom is likely to never speak to me again, after your little performance."

Again, that edge in Rebecca's eyes, and she took a step back, surprise flickering over her face. "Katherine, John Ransom is a fool, and a pompous fool at that. Forgive me for thinking that you would not want to waste your time upon such a person—"

"That," Katherine bit out, emotion welling like cotton in her throat, "was not your decision to make, Rebecca."

Rebecca looked at her, and Katherine hated how much she could see. "You do not like him, Katherine. You never have."

Words failed Katherine. She could only stand there, gripping her parasol as if it were a lifeline. Around them, the crowds of peers took no notice.

"Katherine," Rebecca said again, her voice gentle. She stepped closer, her hand twitching as if she wanted to reach out, take Katherine's arm. "I did not mean to upset you—"

"Good day." The words fell like stones from Katherine's mouth. "Good day, Lady Rebecca." With that she turned and walked away, melting into the crowd. She tried not to think about what she was leaving behind, or the look on Rebecca's face when she'd spoken to Mr. Ransom.

Because Katherine and Madam Kensington knew all too well what that look had meant.

Jealousy.

"Rise and shine, sleeping beauty!"

Katherine could only glare as Rita tore open the curtains and exposed the day in all its foul, gray glory. A ceaseless and cowardly rain pattered at the windows, banishing the prospects of an afternoon spent in the garden. She chose not to mention the fact that she'd been awake for several hours already, her mind churning with those last few words she'd exchanged with Rebecca.

I did not mean to upset you.

Rita offered a smirk, lighting the candles on the mantelpiece. Without sunlight, the halls and rooms of the Knight house became quite impenetrable. "Has the season already exhausted its delights for you, my poppet?"

Katherine replied by rolling onto her stomach and tugging her blankets over her head.

"Madam Kensington seems cheerful enough," Rita continued. "I suppose we should be grateful that she shares none of your unfaltering gloom."

A noncommittal grunt unearthed itself from Katherine's throat.

"It would be best to cheer up by breakfast," Rita said. She tugged the blankets off and swept her finger across Katherine's forehead, as if to smooth away her scowl. Her touch was feathery, plush. "Your mother will say something."

"My mother always says something."

" 'pon my word — she speaks." Wry, Rita leaned against Katherine's headboard and gave her a knowing look. "Something happened at the races."

Katherine rolled her eyes and turned away from Rita, forcing herself out of bed. A yawn cracked her jaw, and she stretched, reaching for the flimsy plaster in her ceiling.

"I must admit," Rita went on, "I did not think that Ascot, of all places, could be the scene of such annoyance. Unless, of course, your brother found his way to the odds."

Katherine shook her head and yawned again, eyes watering. Thomas had been glued to Lucas' side the entire time for that precise reason.

"Well," said Rita, with the air of one giving up. "I suppose I shall look forward to reading about it in Madam Kensington's next edition."

A sudden, ugly swoop in Katherine's chest as the realization took hold. She would, of course, have to write about her own embarrassment, especially given how public it was. Her peers had seen, had taken note of the shifting tides. If it were anyone else, any other debutante, Katherine would not hesitate. She could not make an exception for herself.

"Yes," Katherine managed, turning towards her pitcher. "I suppose you will."

❧

Breakfast was its usual cheerful affair, thick with conversation about the races and politics. Katherine listened here and there, catching only the occasional snippet. She focused instead upon the rich yolks of her eggs, the salty bite of her bacon. She watched Lucas demolish two of his kippers and winced, wondering what on earth the women of London saw in him.

And, of course, she felt her mother's gaze, incessant on the side of her face. But she ignored it. With Thomas between them, Mrs. Knight could not interrogate Katherine without drawing the attention of the entire table.

Mr. Knight met Katherine's gaze over his teacup. "A dreadful day, isn't it?"

She smiled. *The weather. Of course, the weather.* "Yes, Father, especially after such a resplendent afternoon yesterday. But I suppose we are lucky for any sun at all."

He nodded at his newspaper. "Apparently, we shall see some sun again tomorrow, even the day after. Optimism, I think."

"And do you dare be optimistic?" she said, reaching for her tea.

"I dare indeed," Mr. Knight replied. "I was thinking we might take the horses."

The breath caught in Katherine's chest as she looked at her father. "Really?" They never brought the family horses to London — the expense of stabling them was too high — and instead used the horses kept by their neighbors.

He nodded, offering her a sly smile. "There is a most temperamental mare who's aching for a good walk."

Katherine glanced at the windows, at the pitiful rain, then turned back to her father. "I will bundle up quite warmly, and wear my best boots."

Mr. Knight chuckled. "It is too wet, Kitten. Tomorrow, perhaps."

"Father! You tease me so cruelly."

"But spare you, I think," he said, with a knowing glance at the opposite end of the table. "From a certain degree of scrutiny."

Katherine fell silent at that, her fingers tightening around her teacup. She was all too aware of her mother's gaze, tangible even from this distance.

"Worry not," Mr. Knight went on, dropping his voice a little. "I shall not ask you about it. Though I will say... I was not impressed by Mr. Ransom's conduct."

Somehow, Katherine found the air to say, "No?"

Mr. Knight shook his head. "It is a feeble man indeed, who finds such ruin in a simple error of his own design. He is arrogant," he settled on. "And weak-willed. Not an ideal match for my Katherine, I dare say."

To Katherine's surprise, genuine emotion welled in her throat. She blinked a few times, and nudged her father's hand with her knuckle. He nudged her back, flashing her the hint of a smile, and returned to his newspaper.

☙❧

THE NIGHT AIR WAS DAMP, CHILLY, AND CARRIED THE MUSKY tang of coal. Katherine breathed deeply, smelling river muck and gin and all the other things that the nicer parts of London tried to hide behind white brick and brass finishings. She smiled, almost gleeful with the taste of it, and nudged her shoulder against Thomas' arm.

He smirked at her, no more than a twitch of movement under the flare of the nearest street lamp. "You're cheerful."

"Can you blame me?" Katherine replied, tipping her face up to the sky. "It stopped raining."

They were within spitting distance of the White Fox — she could see the towering, glossy monolith, and the spare few carriages loitering in the road before it. Katherine looked at the burning amber windows and ached, once again, to put her ear to the door.

"Perhaps I have grown bored, brother," she went on. "Of petticoats and dancing."

"Of men like John Ransom?" Thomas shook his head and glanced behind them. "I think, Kitten, Rebecca did you a favor."

"Regardless," Katherine replied, ice dripping into her tone, "it was not one I asked for. Or one that we could afford."

Thomas, wisely, said nothing after that.

It was pure luck, Katherine supposed, that they had not been invited to any events that evening. Luck, or perhaps misfortune — Madam Kensington needed fresh material, of course, just as a crocodile needed fresh meat.

"Have you heard anything about him at the Fox?" said Katherine. "Lord Alwyn?"

Thomas frowned, then shook his head. "Nothing. I'm not even certain that he is a member."

Odd indeed. The White Fox had become the haunt of every high-ranking man in British society; membership opened nearly any door in London. Anyone who overlooked it would be a fool.

Katherine thought, then, of the scant bits of information she'd managed to collect about Lord Alwyn. His life, his business, his marriage. All of it calculated, all of it precise. She thought of Lucas' warning, of the enigma of the Johnson family, and their ascendance to the Alwyn title.

More, Katherine thought, as she and Thomas slipped into the shadows behind the White Fox. *I shall have to learn more.*

⁂

THE DRY WEATHER HELD THROUGH THE FOLLOWING MORNING. A rough dew broke against the mare's legs as she charged through the ferns and bracken, startling a family of blue jays. Katherine grinned, the air roaring in her ears, cutting across her face. It felt like autumn, in a way — the chill, the brutal edge, the merciless sting across her skin — and she savored it as Brandon would savor a last bite of pastry. Her breaths came in shallow, determined pants as she pushed the mare further, faster. The mare was thrilled to obey, charging through the undergrowth with the tenacity of an arrow, her body steaming against Katherine's legs.

Some minutes later, they reached a break in the trees — the boundary of the park. Katherine slowed the mare, clucking to her and stroking her mane. The mare snorted as she drew up short, nosing at a nearby patch of crispy, dew-soaked grass.

Mr. Knight appeared a few moments later, panting from atop his borrowed horse. His cheeks had flooded cherry-red in the early morning chill, and his eyes were bright with exertion. He grinned at her as he drew even with her. "How does she handle?"

"Like a dream," Katherine replied, giving the mare another pat on the neck. "She wants a tough hand, though. I can see why she gets restless."

Mr. Knight hummed in agreement. "The city is no place for horses." He turned his horse towards the park, going at a gentle walk, and after a moment, Katherine followed him.

They traced the line of the grass, passing behind trees and benches. The park itself was empty; a fog still lingered above the ground, whispy and curling in the lavender light. Katherine looked across the grounds, and her imagination supplied the crowds of debutantes, the clusters of suitors. Her mind's eye played out a dozen variations on the same theme, and she watched them all.

"I gather you were in the library the other day," her father said, drawing to a halt. "Looking at the stock market indexes, of all things."

A jitter of nerves went through Katherine's stomach, and she ignored it. "I stumbled across something in the paper, and in the process of trying to answer my question, I found myself falling down quite the rabbit hole."

"I see," he replied. "And was this rabbit hole illuminating?"

For a moment, Katherine weighed her options, then decided to take a risk. "Not very. This seems to be one area where our personal collection is somewhat lacking."

Mr. Knight smiled a little. "Fair enough."

"Where might one go?" Katherine went on, ignoring the heat that flooded her chest, threatening to curl up her neck. "For more information on such a topic?"

"About the market?"

"Business," she settled on. "Trades and acquisitions of the past thirty years. Including overseas commerce."

Mr. Knight flashed her an eyebrow.

"Hypothetically," Katherine added, the heat reaching her face now. "Hypothetically, where would I find more information?"

Mr. Knight let out a sigh and tilted his head to one side — he was thinking. "Well," he said, nudging his horse away from a patch of thistles, "the offices of the Exchequer would be the first place to look."

Katherine nodded. "Of course."

"Or, I suppose, His Majesty's Treasury."

Something within her began to deflate, going slack with defeat.

"Or... have you heard of Lord Hartford?"

"No."

"Old family," Mr. Knight said with a nod. "Older than the Tudors, with the family tree to prove it. Lord Hartford is... well. He is a bit eccentric."

Now it was Katherine's turn to raise her eyebrow. "Eccentric?"

"The Hartfords have always had their hands in the money, one way or another. Nobody knows how much they're really worth. The markets, to him, are like horse races to other men. He follows them with a manic fervor. And Lord Hartford has always been very cozy with our dear Exchequer. I would not be surprised if he knew more than the Prime Minister, or the King."

"Does he," Katherine said, her mind churning.

"I have heard rumors about his library." Mr. Knight nudged his horse into a walk, and Katherine followed, her mare snorting in reply. "He guards it closely. But they say he has the whole history of our money hidden in his shelves."

Katherine smiled then. "Father, this is sounding more and more mythical by the moment."

"I suppose it does. But I imagine it to be true. A family like his does not survive very long without learning a few tricks."

"It sounds as if Lord Hartford is a man of singular interest," Katherine said. "Has he any diversions, apart from counting pennies? Or is he a recluse, buried in his piles of dust and money?"

"He is a reclusive sort," Mr. Knight admitted. "Though he golfs."

"Golf," Katherine repeated. How unhelpful.

"His wife," Mr. Knight went on, "is his precise opposite."

"Really?"

He nodded. "Lady Hartford is one of the most determined busy-bodies I have ever had the misfortune to meet. Hosting is her favorite pastime, and she never turns down an opportunity to parade about her gilded furnishings. They host a ball every season," he threw over his shoulder, putting his horse into a canter.

Katherine stared at him, her heart leaping with undue hope. She put into a canter as well, the undergrowth breaking against her mare's hooves. "Really?"

"We've already received the invitation!" Mr. Knight called to her, now a dozen feet away. "A fortnight from now, at their London home."

"A fortnight," Katherine repeated, pushing her mare to go faster, further. "A fortnight."

THEY RETURNED TO THE KNIGHT HOUSE, MUD-SPATTERED AND rosy-cheeked, just as clouds descended from the sky and buried the city in a buzzy, intermittent rain. Mr. Knight made a joke as they crossed the threshold, and Katherine was still laughing when they drew even with the dining room, from which came the chatter of some very familiar voices.

Ice, piercing bitter and sudden through her stomach, down to her hips.

Rebecca was here.

Katherine halted mid-step, her laughter faltering, but her father did not seem to notice. He shucked his coat, shaking off the fresh droplets of rain, and handed it to Graves.

"A hot bath, I think," said Mr. Knight. "For us both."

"Very good, sir. I'll inform Rita."

"And I will take breakfast in the library," said Mr. Knight. "Kat?"

She glanced at him, her mind churning with recognition, with shock, with outrage. "I shall join you, Father."

He frowned, taken aback. "Are you certain? Your brothers—"

"Are occupied," Katherine replied. "They have a guest."

Mr. Knight glanced at the open door to the dining room, then nodded. "See you in the library, then." He went upstairs, and Graves disappeared.

Katherine turned back to the dining room, steeled herself, and walked in.

The table was a riot, a mess of laughter and grins and cups of tea. Katherine's brothers slouched over their half-eaten break-fasts, the picture of lions at leisure. She steeled herself as she approached the table, focusing on the picked-over platter of bacon.

"Ah, Kitten!" Thomas flashed her a grin. "Fresh from the hills of London."

"Yes," she replied, reaching for the tongs. She ignored the gaze burning into her from the other end of the table.

A brief, awkward silence fell. Katherine picked up a piece of bacon and bit off the end, stepping away from the table. "Where's Mother?"

"The market," said Thomas. "She'll return before the rain sets in."

"Join us?" said Brandon, his tone light but wary. From beside him, Lucas watched her, silent and maddeningly keen.

Katherine offered Brandon a tight smile. "No, thank you." Here, finally, she looked at the end of the table, and met Rebecca's gaze. "It seems the table is already full."

Rebecca's eyes were clear, dark pools in the dim light from the windows. She was dressed like a lady, wearing a simple gown and not a stitch of jewelry, not even her gloves. A stark opposite to Katherine, who wore her riding breeches, boots, and an old sweater. Even from this distance, Katherine could see something hidden in Rebecca's face, something impossible to parse. Something a little too much like hurt.

Katherine took another bite of bacon and felt a tendril of satisfaction rake through her body. "Good day, Lady Rebecca. I do hope you enjoyed your visit." With that, she left the room, the back of her neck burning.

❦   17   ❦

"I wish you would tell me," Mrs. Knight hissed behind her cup of tea, "what on earth happened between the two of you—"

"Nothing!" Katherine hissed in return, for the third time in as many minutes. "Nothing happened, Mother—"

"I simply do not believe you." Mrs. Knight put on a wide, if manic, smile, and reached for a biscuit. "A gentleman like Mr. Ransom must have a reason for making such an impolite and hasty exit."

Katherine returned the false smile, glancing at where her Aunt Linda was still busy at the table, doing Heaven knows what. "And what reason could he possibly have, Mother? Was I not a model young lady? Did I not simper and smile and bat my eyelashes, just as he should like?"

Mrs. Knight also glanced at her sister, then shifted her skirts and kicked Katherine, hard, in the ankle.

Katherine jumped like a startled mare, nearly dropping her teacup. "What," she managed, "what the *hell*—"

"Language." Mrs. Knight sipped her tea, unfazed. "Sister," she said, raising her voice. "Have you found it?"

Aunt Linda straightened up, her expression fixed in a state of gentle surprise. "Pardon?"

Mrs. Knight took a deep breath, then said, louder: "Have you found it?"

"Ah! Yes! It was in my sewing basket, of all places." Aunt Linda smiled, swanning across the room, her ancient silks and feathers carrying the strong scents of cosmetic powder and sherry. She was only a few years older than Mrs. Knight, but the difference might as well have been a decade or more. Where Mrs. Knight was sturdy, vivacious, and grounded, Aunt Linda was fragile, fanciful, and indulgent. And as prone to birthing daughters as Mrs. Knight was prone to sons.

Mrs. Knight reached for the scrap of fabric in her sister's hands. "Oh, Linda. You know you ought to keep it somewhere safe."

"My sewing basket is very secure," Aunt Linda replied, her voice mild. She sat down opposite her sister and reached for her cup of tea, which she drank from a saucer. Having watched her dose it with no less than four sugars, Katherine could not hold back a wince.

Mrs. Knight sighed and gently unfolded the length of lace. Even to Katherine's eye, the fabric was old and delicate, yellowing and so frail it seemed almost translucent in the weak sunshine filtering through the window.

"Beautiful, is it not?" Aunt Linda smiled at Katherine, mistaking her expression for awe. "For all her faults, our mother was most skilled with a pair of needles."

Katherine stared at her aunt. "Grandmama made this?"

"Yes," said Mrs. Knight, casting an appraising eye across the lace. "I believe she referred to it as her greatest accomplishment."

Aunt Linda hummed, still smiling. "Certainly a greater accomplishment than any of her children."

Mrs. Knight gave a snort. "Indeed." She held the lace up to

the light and frowned. "This might be an exercise in futility, Linda."

Aunt Linda's smile flickered. "That would be a shame."

"Where did you hear of this trick?" Katherine said, her gaze tracing the delicate stitching.

"Rita," Mrs. Knight replied, somewhat to her surprise. "It is an old wives' secret, apparently."

The parlor door opened, and one of the maids appeared, carrying a thick white jug.

"Ah!" Aunt Linda stood up and clapped like a little girl. "What perfect timing!"

The three of them bent over the dining table. Mrs. Knight lay the piece of lace in an oblong china dish, then reached for the jug. Aunt Linda took a quivering breath as Mrs. Knight poured a stream of thick, creamy buttermilk into the dish, covering the lace entirely.

Katherine raised an eyebrow as her grandmother's best stitching disappeared. "This feels a bit... scandalous."

"Nigh on illegal," Aunt Linda chimed in.

"It works," Mrs. Knight said. "Supposedly." She set the pitcher down and looked into the dish of cream.

"We shall be haunted," Katherine said. "By our most beloved Grandmama."

Aunt Linda giggled and Mrs. Knight smiled. "Can you imagine it?" said Mrs. Knight. "She would be in chains, of course, as all spirits are."

"Chains and her bathrobe," said Aunt Linda. "Even though we buried her in her best silk."

"How long do we wait?" said Katherine, glancing at the clock on the mantelpiece behind them. She and her mother had been there for more than an hour already, and the day was fading.

"A quarter of an hour, I think," said Mrs. Knight. "Even longer, if we want the buttermilk to work to its fullest extent."

"Very well." Katherine made for the door. "I believe it is time I visited my cousins."

"Oh, what a lovely idea!" Aunt Linda beamed at her. "They will be so delighted to see you!"

Katherine rolled her eyes as she stepped into the hall, leaving the parlor door open behind her. The pale blue walls and gilded trim seemed to mock her, as if they were aware of her own family's austerity and found it amusing. Aunt Linda's house — Mockingbird Hall — was a handsome, if over-furnished, beast. Katherine eyed one of the gilded hall tables and the endless rows of shining portraits, quietly pricing everything in her head. It was an old habit, one she'd developed as a means of surviving endless hours in overwrought houses.

Her cousins spent most of their time upstairs, in a little wing designed for their personal use. Katherine heard them before she saw them. She rolled her eyes again, then reached for the door to their parlor.

"—give it back! Give it back, you wretch, or I'll smash your favorite mirror—"

"Seven years bad luck, idiot — seven years bad luck!"

"Maggie!" Prudence's face was quite red, and her hair had risen in a cloud of sulphuric anger. "Give — it — back!"

"No," Maggie replied, dangling a thin, leather-bound volume in the air. "No, I don't think I will."

Prudence let out a shriek and leapt over the sofa. Maggie, giggling like a devil, paused only to give Katherine a kiss on the cheek before running away, darting into the hall and thundering up the stairs. Prudence followed, bellowing, and Katherine sighed, wandering over to the nearest armchair.

Amanda glanced up from her book as Katherine sat down. "You look tired."

Katherine smiled. "Lovely to see you as well, dear cousin."

"You bring us news, then? Of the tantalizing season?"

Amanda, two years younger than Katherine, had yet to debut.

And — as Katherine knew — she had little desire to do so. "Only if it is welcome."

"Oh, it is welcome!" Maggie came running back into the room, then flopped across the sofa. The little leather book was nowhere in sight. "Most certainly welcome, dear Katherine."

"Pay the thief no heed, Katherine," said Amanda, marking her place in her book with her ribbon. "She has airs above her station."

"Tell us everything," said Maggie, her eyes wide and fiendish. "Every single detail."

"Don't," said Amanda. "I am quite excited for my impending spinsterhood, and refuse to be convinced otherwise."

"Well, after these past few weeks," said Katherine, "spinster-hood sounds quite enticing."

"Maggie," said Amanda. "Where's Prudence?"

"I locked her in the airing cupboard." Maggie grinned at Katherine. "Now, tell us everything. Has Lucas fallen in love?"

Katherine snorted and shook her head. "It would take a miracle for him to love anyone other than himself. He is a peacock by nature, and fans his feathers only at his own reflection."

Amanda smiled. "What of Tom and Bran?"

Katherine put on an expression of mock thoughtfulness. "Bran cares only for the pastries, and Tom only for the wine."

"I suppose I should not be surprised. But what about you, dear Kat? Any prospects on the horizon, waving a white flag?"

"No." And there came the feeling again, the feeling of failure and relief, mingled into one. "But that is hardly surprising, given the fact of Lady Sophia, a Star among mere rocks."

"Really?" Amanda's tone grew coy. "That is not what I hear from a friend of mine."

A throb, deep in Katherine's throat. "A friend?"

Amanda slid a very familiar pamphlet from beneath her skirts. "A certain Madam Kensington."

Katherine attempted to smile as Amanda held up issue No. 6, creased and wrinkled from being hidden, she was certain, in at least three different pockets. "What nonsense."

"Hardly!" Amanda flipped to the second page and cleared her throat. " 'It seems that our little Sparrow, having recently found favor with a handsome Eagle, has been cast aside again in favor of songbirds sporting a more brilliant plumage. One can only wonder at the reason behind such a change in heart — perhaps the Sparrow's siblings flashed their feathers in warning, sending a clear, if veiled, message. Whispers abound where the Eagle might next take roost. We can only assume that he might find a more suitable — and welcoming — perch.' "

Hearing her own words thrown back at her made Katherine want to wince. "Oh, am I this mythical Sparrow?"

"Of *course!*"

"And the Eagle is Mr. Ransom," Maggie chimed in. "Everybody knows, Kat."

"Everybody," Amanda confirmed.

"I thought you cared little for the diversions of the season, dear cousin."

"Yes," said Amanda, rolling her eyes. "Except when it comes to *you*, Kat."

"We never expected you to find a match," Maggie said, so earnest it was almost painful. "Let alone with someone like Mr. Ransom."

"You flatter me, Margaret," said Katherine, feeling as if she were playing tennis. "And here I thought Mr. Ransom was quite lucky to find favor with *me*."

"But he turned you aside!" Maggie replied. From the hall, there came the sound of distant, muffled shouting and thumping. Prudence's patience had evidently waned. "He must have found you lacking in some way, or you insulted him most dearly."

"Maggie!" Amanda's eyes flashed, and she stifled a surprised laugh. "Don't say such horrible things to your cousin!"

"I do not mind," said Katherine, slouching back into the cushions. "It is quite entertaining."

Maggie rolled her eyes. "Are you really not going to tell us what happened?"

"Nothing happened." Katherine kept her tone even and calm. "There was no great falling out. We simply... did not get along."

"Liar," said Maggie.

"*Maggie!*" Amanda laughed. "Oh, Kat, I do apologize for my sister's willful and spiteful nature—" She flung a cushion at Maggie.

Katherine grinned. "It will be a blessing to her, in this world."

"Don't you wish to be married?" said Maggie, ignoring her older sister. In the hall, Prudence continued to thump and bellow.

"Do you?" Katherine countered. "Don't we all? Is it not the natural state of every woman who is born on this earth?"

Maggie snorted. "I think marriage sounds quite boring."

Katherine did laugh then, while Amanda shook her head. "Goodness, Mags, you are quite a bundle of contradiction."

"Did he propose?" Maggie pressed. "Did you refuse him?"

A tightness crawled into Katherine's throat, and her laughter faded. "No, he did not."

"Worry not, dear Kat." Amanda's voice was filled with kindness, and she put a hand to Katherine's arm. "I am sure another option will present itself."

"Yes," said Katherine. "Indeed."

On rare and wonderful occasions, Mrs. Knight could have remarkably good timing. One of those occasions presented itself a few moments later — she came into the parlor, her arm around the shoulders of a very red-faced Prudence. "I found this little troll locked in the airing cupboard. Can anyone explain how that might have happened?"

"No, Aunt Edwina," said Maggie, wide-eyed and innocent. "How horrid."

"Mmm." Mrs. Knight gave Prudence a reassuring pat on the

back, evidently not believing a word out of Maggie's mouth. Prudence, meanwhile, gave Maggie a glare that could kill. "Amanda, glad to see you looking so well."

"And you, Aunt Edwina." Amanda shot Katherine a glance. "We were just hearing all of Katherine's news about the season."

Mrs. Knight arched an eyebrow but her impassive smile did not flicker. "I am certain she has many a story to tell. But I am afraid I must steal my daughter, ladies."

"Has the buttermilk worked its magic?" said Katherine.

"No," Mrs. Knight replied, "but Chrysanthemum—" Aunt Linda's favorite cat— "has licked up all the buttermilk and, in the process, swallowed the lace."

Katherine gaped as her cousins gasped. "God in Heaven. What is to be done?"

"Something quite distasteful," Mrs. Knight said. "That involves calomel." She gestured to the hall, a movement so simple and yet full of such long-winded suffering that Katherine almost smiled. "Come along. All hands on deck."

Katherine shook her head in resignation and stood up. "Pray for me, Amanda."

"As always, darling." Amanda raised her hand in farewell. "And don't let that dreadful Eagle get you down."

"Eagle?" Mrs. Knight said to Katherine, once they were in the hall. "What on earth does she mean?"

"Nothing," Katherine said quickly, keeping her gaze on her feet. "Nothing at all."

The Knight house, that evening, was silent and warm.

Spare few thoughts crossed Katherine's mind as she wandered from room to room. Her parents had retired early — the Chrysanthemum incident, it seemed, had sealed her mother's fate for the night. Mrs. Knight had taken three glasses of gin with supper, and hardly touched her food. She'd spent most of the meal staring into the grain of the dining table with the expression of a woman haunted.

The boys had found the story uproarious, of course, and had spoken of little else as they ate, ignoring their father's protests. Katherine had no doubt that Chrysanthemum and his digestive history would live in infamy under the Knight roof.

Then, after dinner, when their parents had gone upstairs—

"We're off." And something in Brandon's face had been kind. "Lucas and Tom want to go to the Fox, after we drop off the pages."

Katherine had nodded, even as a frown pulled at her mouth. She knew that her brothers had to show face at the White Fox every so often, for the sake of appearances (and Madam Kensington's accurate ear), but she could not ignore a prickle of foreboding whenever they did.

"We will be careful," Brandon had assured her. "No more than two glasses of brandy."

She'd smiled, then. "Very well."

He'd stepped back, with something else in his face. "Are you certain you're all right?"

"Yes, Bran," she'd said, nudging him towards the door. "Yes, go—"

But now that Katherine was, for all intents and purposes, alone under this mischievous roof, she could not help feeling a bit desolate. Melancholy. Lonely.

It is the night, she thought, as she wandered into the empty and silent drawing room. *The night and the conversation.* Maggie's words, as guileless as they had been, were still rattling around in her head, sealing her fate.

She could not shake the feeling that Mr. Ransom had been her only chance. A fleeting glimmer of hope, swept out from beneath her feet. Replaced by a sense of loss, of inadequacy, of relief. Of anger.

Anger, because Rebecca had been right. And Rebecca had saved her, in her strange and utterly singular way.

The drawing room glowed a dim orange, bathed in the light of the two candelabras Graves had left burning. Almost as if he'd known that Katherine would find herself in here, alone and in need of company.

Katherine retrieved a glass and the decanter of Scotch, then sat at the card table and pulled out her favorite deck of cards. She took a sip, shuffled, and dealt herself solitaire.

This routine was familiar, if stale — normally, this was an activity reserved for winter evenings, when she could not sleep and all her brothers were already in bed. Katherine ached for a bit of snow now, as the warm air drifted across her face. Snow, a blanket at her feet, a crackling fire. But she settled for the stifling breeze, the haze of sweat on her brow. Even in her nightgown and thin robe, with her hair drifting across her shoulders, she felt sticky, overcooked.

Katherine won once and lost twice. She refreshed her glass, and noted that the candles had burned halfway. Around her, the shadows lengthened, tickling at her ankles.

And there it came. A flicker, a dancing shift in her peripheral vision.

Katherine looked up, and met Rebecca's gaze.

Rebecca was standing outside the open drawing room window, evidently caught between one moment and the next. One of her hands was raised, as if considering a knock on the glass, but her expression was hesitant, wary. Watchful.

She had not been standing there long, Katherine knew. The thin, gauzy curtains rippled around the sill, trailing out into the open night, catching the edge of Rebecca's arm. Katherine cleared her throat and looked back down at her cards. "Well. Are you coming in?"

Rebecca seemed to hesitate, then she climbed in through the window, nimble as a cat. "I was not certain I was welcome," she said, her voice low.

Katherine said nothing, overturning a queen.

Rebecca glanced around. Tonight, she wore her usual trousers and shirt, and she took off her tricorn. "Forgive me. I had expected—"

"My brothers are at their club." Katherine looked up, and Rebecca stilled. "I am afraid you are stuck with me, this evening."

The corner of Rebecca's mouth twitched, and some of her bravado returned. "Lucky me."

A tremor ricocheted through Katherine's stomach and she looked down again. The action was somehow physical, as if thumbing an invisible wire that ran through the air between them. "Would you like a drink?"

"Of course." Rebecca wandered over to the sideboard; she

turned away, and Katherine noticed, with a shock, that her hair was short. Extremely short. It barely grazed the edge of her neck. But how—?

Katherine blinked a few times. No — a wig?

Impossible. It was Rebecca's real hair, undoubtedly — the same color and texture, those tight, maddening curls thinner and finer than Katherine's pinky nail. There was simply less of it.

Rebecca came over to the card table, glass in hand. A smile played about her mouth. "Your hair. It is shorter than I expected."

Katherine huffed, looking through her cards and not seeing any of them. "I could say the same to you."

"Ah." Rebecca gave a rueful sigh and ran her hand across the back of her head. "You have uncovered my secret."

"You cut it?"

Rebecca shook her head. "It is but another accessory. Like jewelry. And I did not bother to wear it this evening."

Ah. She wore a piece, then, something she could clip in and take out.

"Katherine." Rebecca's voice softened. "I cannot pretend to enjoy speaking with you like this. As if we are strangers."

"What are we then?" Katherine replied, flipping over her next card.

"Friends." But even that sounded tentative. "At least, I hope we are."

"I thought you wanted a drink."

A sigh eased through Rebecca's shoulders, and she reached for the decanter. She poured herself half an inch of Scotch, then looked at Katherine as if to say, *Well?*

"A friend," said Katherine, testing the word, "would not have interfered as you did. Would not have jeopardized a chance at a great happiness."

"Happiness?" Rebecca repeated. "Katherine, let us not entertain this farce. Doing so would insult our intelligence."

A thrum of anger went up Katherine's arms, settling in her

throat. "Do not pretend to know my wishes, my desires. My circumstances."

"I pretend nothing." Rebecca looked into her eyes, so calm and assured that it made Katherine tremble. "I saw it for myself. In your face."

Katherine swallowed, words caught in her throat.

"You did not like John Ransom, Katherine. Not enough to marry."

"What I feel," Katherine managed, "is none of your business."

"Is it?" said Rebecca lightly.

A strangled laugh broke out. "Your arrogance knows no bounds."

"Perhaps. But it is the arrogance of a friend." Rebecca sat forward, sipped her Scotch. Katherine refused to watch the pull of her throat. "If I acted in error, Katherine, then I apologize. With an exception."

"An exception?"

"Yes." Rebecca put her glass aside and propped her arm in the middle of the table, elbow resting on the surface and hand held aloft. "If what you are telling me is a true measure of your feelings, your conviction in John Ransom and his lackluster heart, then prove it."

A moment passed as her challenge hit home. "You must be joking."

"I am perfectly serious."

"You want me to prove my own conviction," said Katherine, "with arm wrestling?"

"One match is all I ask." Rebecca was smug and inscrutable. "After all, I missed my chance at beating you last week."

Outrage joined the anger billowing in Katherine's veins. Outrage, and — intrigue. "Fine." She squared up to Rebecca and lifted her hand, propping her elbow on the table. She looked at Rebecca's palm — thin, pale, corded with callouses and a scar near her wrist — then met her gaze. "One match?"

Rebecca nodded. "And then I shall leave you quite alone."

With the feeling that she was jumping off a cliff, Katherine took Rebecca's hand. Her skin was warm, dry, and her smirk broadened as Katherine's frown deepened. She gripped Rebecca's hand, and Rebecca answered in kind — she was strong. Stronger than Bran.

But Katherine refused to panic. She had to win, even if she no longer remembered what it was she was fighting for. Everything had become small and meaningless in the feeling and the scent of Rebecca's skin.

Any other fight, she thought. *This is like any other fight.*

Katherine clenched, and Rebecca did the same. Katherine pushed, and Rebecca did the same.

Katherine glared at her. Rebecca did not return the favor. Instead, her face was open, guileless. Showing an emotion so deep, so sincere, that it was as if she were naked, laid bare and without a shred of pretense.

Katherine sucked in an unsteady breath, a sudden heat pooling in her stomach. A heat that had nothing and everything to do with the vise-like grasp of Rebecca's hand, the glimmer of possibility in Rebecca's gaze.

"This means nothing," Katherine said, her words brittle as she struggled against the brutal force of Rebecca's arm.

"Of course," Rebecca replied. She hunched forward over the table. Her face was close enough that Katherine could see the tiny little mole beneath her left eye. When she met Rebecca's gaze, a bolt of something — something like panic and fear and delight, all mixed together — hit the base of Katherine's spine. "Nothing."

Katherine broke, and Rebecca slammed her hand down into the table. But gently. If such a thing were even possible.

Rebecca pulled away, though she lingered, her fingers a scant few inches from Katherine's arm. She did not speak, but her smug triumph was tangible.

For a long moment, Katherine sat there, looking at her opponent, her body a roiling mess of feverish emotion, her arm tingling and aching from the battle. "Damn you," she finally said.

"Yes," said Rebecca, smiling now in her crooked way. "I promise I—"

But the world would never hear Rebecca's promise. Because Katherine all but lunged across the table, seized Rebecca by the collar, and kissed her.

For a split second, Rebecca froze, going stiff with shock, but then a most delightful sound came breaking out of her throat, a sound of exhilaration and relief— Katherine swallowed it, pushing her hand into Rebecca's curls, sucking on her lower lip, and Rebecca grabbed her, her hands tangling in Katherine's gown—

The kiss was artless, sloppy, a testament to Katherine's inexperience. A roaring heat had overtaken Katherine's face, and her mouth fumbled at the corner of Rebecca's lips. Then Rebecca broke away and pulled Katherine around the table, pressing her up against the edge. Katherine gasped — all she could feel, all she knew, was the searing brand of Rebecca's arm around her waist, the possessive weight of Rebecca's hand in her hair. Rebecca's nails raked across Katherine's scalp, her eyes flashing like a predator's before she licked into Katherine's mouth.

It was all Katherine could do to keep standing. She quivered as Rebecca's tongue swept over her teeth, along the roof of her mouth — her hands fumbled at Rebecca's waist, at the small of her back, desperate to cling to this moment for as long as she could—

Rebecca pulled back, kissing her cheek, then her hand tightened in Katherine's hair— a gentle tug, sending a fissure of delight down Katherine's neck.

"God." Rebecca's voice was rough, muffled as she nuzzled at Katherine's jaw. "Katherine—" She licked her way down Katherine's neck, her teeth grazing the skin.

Shuddering, Katherine tangled her hands in Rebecca's hair,

pulling her closer. Rebecca's hips pressed into hers, a solid and redeeming weight, searing hot even through the layers of clothing. An embarrassing mewl crawled out of Katherine's mouth as Rebecca kissed the base of her neck, and she could feel Rebecca's smile—

Rebecca lingered, ghosting her mouth over Katherine's bare clavicle. Another shudder overtook Katherine's body, and she arched her spine, breathless and shameless, letting her head fall back and her eyes slip shut. Her breasts pressed into Rebecca's chest; the pull and friction of the fabric against her sweaty skin was almost too much to bear.

Katherine could only imagine what she looked like in Rebecca's eyes. Needy. Supplicant. Her pale skin flooding pink, following the line traced by Rebecca's mouth. But she did not care. She clung to Rebecca, desperate and—

"God," Rebecca said again, low and like a curse. "Look at you—"

Something between them seemed to break. Rebecca pounced on her, licking up Katherine's neck with a ferocity that left her reeling, gasping into the thick, stifling air. Teeth and tongue worked over Katherine's skin, leaving a wet path that caught cold and brought goosebumps. And when Rebecca reached Katherine's face, her devilish mouth paused, hovering just a breath away from Katherine's lips.

A moment passed, then two, and an ache so keen it felt like death pulled through Katherine's body. She tilted forward, another embarrassing sound breaking out of her throat, something like— "Please—"

Rebecca buried her in a kiss, her mouth swollen and fierce against Katherine's. She sucked on Katherine's tongue, and stars burst beneath Katherine's eyelids— she would die like this— she would die, or—

A thud, followed by voices. Voices from the hall.

Rebecca pulled away, looking over Katherine's shoulder at the drawing room door. Her hair was a mess, her mouth plush, her eyes shining. "Shit—"

Katherine blinked a few times and tried to breathe. "My brothers—"

"I should go." Rebecca looked at her, and her expression made Katherine squirm.

Katherine forced herself to nod. "Yes, quickly—"

Rebecca took her hand. "I shall see you—"

"Tomorrow." Katherine squeezed her fingers. "At the garden party."

"Yes." Rebecca's chest heaved, and she nodded. "Yes, of course —" She stepped away, out of Katherine's reach, and it was like the sun going behind a cloud. "Tomorrow."

Katherine could only nod, her heart thumping in her ears.

Then Rebecca jumped out of the window, and was gone.

Katherine took a long, shuddering breath and stepped away from the table, her hands numb and her face tingling. She looked down at her own chest, at the ruddy cast of her skin, and pressed her hand to it, as if she could mimic the weight of Rebecca's mouth. Her body, it seemed, was still within Rebecca's spell — the space between her thighs was damp and swollen, and she could see her nipples through the fabric of her nightgown. Meanwhile, the voices in the hall grew louder.

Katherine gave herself a shake and tugged her robe closed, crossing her arms against her chest. She turned just as the drawing room door opened and Thomas came in.

"Kitten!" His surprise was evident, his body loose with liquor. "You're still up."

She tried to smile. "I was playing solitaire."

"Yes, I can see." Thomas came over to the table, where the remains of her last game lay bare and somehow telling, she thought, in the low light. "You were thirsty."

He tapped Rebecca's glass, and Katherine's stomach jolted.

Thomas glanced at her, teasing. "Two glasses?"

Her smile did not falter. "I poured one for the devil."

Lucas and Brandon came into the room, swaying and chuckling. They both stopped short when they saw her, then their smiles widened. "Kitten!" said Lucas. "What a lovely surprise! Care to join us for a game of whist?"

"You'll have to play without me," she replied, drifting closer to the door. "I am quite exhausted."

"Spoilsport," said Brandon, getting a fresh glass from the sideboard.

Lucas lingered by the door, and he took Katherine's hand as she left. He looked into her face, concern evident in his gaze. "Are you all right?"

Katherine refreshed her smile and nodded. "Yes. Just tired."

Lucas looked at her for another moment, and she knew she had not convinced him. But he nodded. "Sleep well."

"And you, brother." Katherine let go of his hand and slipped into the hall, then fled upstairs, her heart in her throat.

Finally, behind the safety of her locked door, she flung herself across her bed and stared up at the ceiling, unable to think of anything save for Rebecca's mouth.

❧ 19 ❧

Morning arrived softly, with a gentle patter of rain. Katherine listened with a distracted ear, her body a churning mess of heat and nerves. She'd tossed and turned for much of the night, sleeping in fitful, messy snatches, her mind awash with memories. Memories and sensations, touches and kisses. She replayed the events in the drawing room over and over again, unable to breathe without thinking of the way Rebecca had tasted. Katherine's fingers drifted across her own mouth, down her neck, over her chest, tracing the spots that Rebecca had kissed. Her body buzzed with the knowledge, the terrible and wonderful knowledge, that she had tasted something new, and would never recover.

But exhaustion did not touch her. She lay in bed as the rain grew, then faded, as a weak sunlight began to streak across the garden, and energy crackled through her. A sleepless night, it seemed, was the price of having kissed Rebecca.

Katherine let out a long, lingering sigh, and once again put her hand to her lips. She worried, perhaps needlessly, about forgetting the feeling of Rebecca's mouth on hers. And she wondered, perhaps necessarily, about what would happen next.

Foolishness did not run in the Knight family, for all that her brothers' behavior might suggest otherwise. The Knights were shrewder than they looked, with a hard, knowing edge disguised by affability. Katherine knew well enough that kissing another woman, as she had kissed Rebecca, was quite illegal.

Illegal, yes, but full of a feeling and promise that Katherine had never felt before. Full of a simmering want that could not even compare to the tepid feeling she'd had towards men such as John Ransom. A want that burned as keenly as a wound, that pulled and reared and left her aching, shivering, reaching.

And what was this want? Was it fleeting, misguided perhaps? Was it borne of proximity, of frustration, of a determination to prove something, to win something? Did Rebecca care for her at all, or had Rebecca's passion been borne of competition, of a moment so charged, so fraught, that it undermined all propriety?

Katherine trembled and rolled over to look at the ceiling. A spider's web clung to the cracking plaster, shining silver in the dim sunlight. She had to ask herself the same questions. Katherine, who had never been touched, never been kissed — did she see Rebecca as little more than a pair of hands, a lingering and enticing flash of decadence, of indulgence?

Had she more experience in the realms of attraction and adoration, she might have been able to probe her own motivations with greater acuity, greater precision. *Madam Kensington would know*, Katherine thought, giving a sardonic chuckle. Madam Kensington would pick apart this mess like a surgeon, laying Katherine and Rebecca bare with only a few slashes of her brutal quill. Meanwhile, Katherine could only lie in her bed, fawning and muddled and as useless as old ink.

She waited until she heard her brothers make their way downstairs before joining them for breakfast. And when she sat down at the table, Lucas shot her a sharp glance, his gaze far too keen.

Katherine ignored him, buttering her toast. She could feel her mother's gaze on her face as well, and hoped that her blush had faded somewhat.

The conversation that morning had much to do with Napoleon. Katherine listened and ate, contributing little. It was strange to sit in her usual chair, at her usual spot, in the same house, after such a colossal shift in her world. Nothing was the same, and yet nothing had changed.

She wondered if Rebecca was sitting down to breakfast as well. She wondered if Rebecca had slept, if she, too had tossed and turned, bewitched by the few moments they'd stolen together. Bewitched and beset by the never-ending tide of questions, of doubts.

But perhaps I am not the first woman she has kissed, Katherine thought, stuffing a piece of bacon in her mouth. Rebecca had hardly been a blushing, fumbling idiot the night before. The way she'd moved, the way she'd kissed, the way she'd picked apart Katherine's seams — all of it spoke to some experience, though where and how she'd gotten it — and with whom — was a mystery.

"Katherine," said Mrs. Knight. "Are you planning to join us this afternoon?"

Katherine blinked a few times, her mind whirring back through the conversation. "For the garden party? Of course."

Mrs. Knight offered her an appraising look. "I did not want to assume. You seem a bit... out of sorts."

"Do I?" Katherine refreshed her tea. "Apologies, Mother. I had trouble sleeping."

Now Mr. Knight frowned, surfacing from behind his paper. "Are you quite well, Kitten?"

"That is all this family needs," said Brandon. "A summer 'flu."

"I feel perfectly well." Katherine's cheeks were flaming now, contradicting her assertion. "I am simply a bit tired."

"Very well." But Mrs. Knight did not seem convinced. "Perhaps a bath would help."

"Sounds lovely. I'll have a word with Rita." Katherine stood up from the table, feeling as if everything, the full truth of what had happened last night, was written across her face. And without waiting for her mother's response, she picked up her teacup and quickly left the dining room.

⁂

RITA CAST HER A SHREWD LOOK. "ARE YOU CERTAIN YOU FEEL well, Kat?"

Katherine rolled her eyes and snatched a towel off the rack, rubbing herself dry with a militaristic determination. "For the love of God, if one more person asks me that question, I cannot be held responsible for my actions."

"No need to get snippy, Miss Madam." Rita leaned against the dresser. "It is strange to see you so out of sorts."

"Bound to happen eventually," said Katherine, disappearing behind the changing screen. "This damn season tests dignity and reason alike." She reached for her chemise and her stockings. "At least I no longer have to suffer the attentions of John Ransom. That, more than anything, might have cost me my sanity."

That made Rita raise an eyebrow, just as Katherine knew it would. With any luck, whispers of her disappointment and discontent would be flitting around the city by dusk. Perhaps it was a touch petty, a touch toothless, but Katherine found that she cared little. If John Ransom could be impolite enough to dismiss her without so much as a goodbye, she could return the favor.

Rita deftly wove a handful of daisies into Katherine's hair. Then came the rouge, and when Katherine looked at herself in the mirror, she felt a spike of nerves, of hope.

Would she catch Rebecca's attention like this? Or better yet, would she catch it and keep it?

Katherine made her way downstairs and was surprised to see

Thomas waiting for her in the foyer, wearing a fresh shirt and a trim jacket. He'd even combed his hair.

Katherine went down the last few steps, her gloves in one hand. "Are you accompanying me this afternoon?"

"Yes." His jaw clenched. "I drew the short straw."

Katherine grinned. "Oh, you poor sweet thing."

"Shut it." Thomas glanced at her, then lowered his voice. "Do you have your pencil?"

She nodded, scuffing her heel on the floor. "Secured. And my papers are in my bodice."

Thomas made a face, but nodded. "It is a pity the rain stopped. It might have spared us this suffering."

"Now, Tom," said Mrs. Knight, appearing at the top of the stairs. "You promised you would behave."

"I never." Thomas smirked and leaned against the banister. "But perhaps my good behavior can be negotiated."

Mrs. Knight chuckled. "Oh, I know better than to attempt to negotiate with you." She reached the bottom of the stairs and smiled at Katherine, showing none of her earlier concern. "You both look lovely. Shall we?"

The garden party was hosted by the Hedgeworth family, a family apparently named after the most obvious feature of their garden. Katherine raised an eyebrow at the boxwood maze visible from the front drive — it was the largest she'd ever seen, certainly in London. The hedges were tall, taller than Lucas, and dense as a shadow. From behind the maze came the sounds of a party, and the light, trilling music of a string quartet.

"Good Heavens." Thomas scowled. "This appears to be a most overdone affair."

"Yes, it does, doesn't it?" Mrs. Knight sighed, unfurling her fan. They had paused at the edge of the garden, just before an open gate that bore a sign reading, *Join us!*

Thomas produced a small flask and took a quick swig. Then, somewhat to Katherine's surprise, he passed the flask to their mother. Mrs. Knight took it, swallowed a gulp of what Katherine guessed was Scotch, and passed it back to Thomas.

"God in Heaven." Katherine looked from her mother to her brother and back again as the flask disappeared inside Thomas' pocket. "I am surrounded by heathens."

"Sometimes one needs to fortify oneself, Kat," said Mrs. Knight, clearing her throat and stepping into the garden. "Come. Let us face the lions."

The crowd was much the same as any other gathering for the season. Katherine cataloged the familiar faces, taking quick note of tensions, smiles, flirtatious looks. Ladies and gentlemen drifted between tables and platters of light *hors d'oeuvres* and pots of tea. The light, playful music seemed to tease and ebb the guests, encouraging conversation and turns about the garden. Katherine hid a smile and tilted her parasol forward, bringing the shade over her face and chest. Some instinct told her this would be a most entertaining afternoon.

Their hosts were cheerful and quite smug with their apparent success. Katherine listened to her mother make the usual niceties and curtsied when she was supposed to. But she glanced across the garden whenever she could, searching for a familiar face, listening for a familiar laugh.

Nerves, fresh and brittle, ricocheted through her stomach. She tried to swallow them, with little success. *Tomorrow,* they'd agreed. But where was she? Where was Rebecca?

Katherine followed her mother around the lawn, trading greetings and small talk with various families. Thomas spoke with a few of the gentlemen, but he kept close to Katherine's side, telegraphing a message of protection that Katherine supposed was quite fitting.

Finally, she caught sight of Lady Alwyn, who stood at the other end of the garden, flocked by her usual crowd of admirers. Beside her stood Lady Sophia, radiant as ever in the shifting sunlight. But there was no sign of Rebecca — Katherine's stomach flipped, then curled in upon itself. She looked away, and followed her mother to the edge of the maze.

Thomas sighed as they sipped at glasses of punch. "How much longer?"

"At least an hour," said Mrs. Knight.

As their conversation continued, Katherine leaned back against the hedge and tried to take a deep breath. She could not assume, could not read anything into Rebecca's absence — but how could she not, when they'd agreed, when Rebecca had looked at her like—?

"*Pssst. Katherine.*"

Katherine blinked a few times, then dropped her chin. No. Impossible.

"Don't turn around," Rebecca whispered from behind her, seemingly from within the monolithic hedge. "I need your help."

A fire erupted in Katherine's face. She blinked a few times, wondering if she'd lost her mind. "What on earth with? And why are you hiding?"

A soft sound of frustration. "I shall explain later. Can you ask your brother to take Sophia on a turn about the garden?"

"*What?*"

"Later," Rebecca whispered again, the urgency evident in her voice. "Please, Katherine. Sophia will say yes, I promise."

"Very well." Katherine shook her head and approached Thomas, taking his elbow. "Tom, why don't you ask Sophia to take a turn about the garden?"

He looked at her as if she'd grown a second head. "What?"

"She seems quite bored. I am sure she'll be grateful for the distraction."

Mrs. Knight stepped forward. "I shall join you, and keep Lady Alwyn company."

Thomas frowned, but nodded. "Very well."

"Go, now." Katherine gave him a gentle push towards Sophia. "Don't keep her waiting."

Thomas glared at her but obeyed, and set off across the lawn, Mrs. Knight tailing him. As Katherine watched, he approached Sophia, who flashed him a glittering smile. They conversed for a moment, then Thomas offered his arm. Moments later, he and Sophia set off in the opposite direction, tailed by their mothers. Everyone else stared after them, then began to whisper.

Satisfied that her work was complete, Katherine took a gulp of air and turned on her heel, marching into the hedge maze. Time to face her fate.

And her fate, it seemed, was waiting for her.

Rebecca stood a few yards away, half-buried in the hedges, wearing her lilac dress and a pair of intricate lace gloves. A precise and delightful opposite of the Rebecca who had crawled through the window the night before. The moment she saw Katherine, something like heat and need went across her face, and she smiled, as if relieved. "Hello."

"Hello," said Katherine, a tingling numbness scaling up her neck. Here, out of sight and far from the other guests, she drew closer to Rebecca, protected by the shade and the density of the leaves. She caught that same, heady scent — metal and oak — and fought the urge to press her mouth to Rebecca's cheek, to drink her in.

"Thank you," said Rebecca, a touch breathless. "For your help. It is a long story, but Sophia needs someone to distract our mother from Lord Dashwood."

Katherine nodded, though she did not understand. She stepped closer, close enough that she could feel the warmth of Rebecca's body, see the heave of her chest. "You look well."

The corner of Rebecca's mouth twitched. "As do you."

A silence fell, broken only by the steady sounds of the birds, of the breeze, of a thousand things that Katherine did not hear. All she could feel, all she could know, was the sight of Rebecca among the leaves, and the naked yearning in her face.

They stood there for a short eternity, hardly daring to breathe.

But a fire ebbed in Katherine's chest, pooling in her belly, then in her hips. Her hands throbbed with the urge to reach, to grab, to—

"Rebecca," she began, but she did not finish.

Rebecca surged towards her, capturing her in a sudden, delicious kiss. A moan caught in Katherine's mouth as the heat built and broke, shattering across her body. She wrapped her arms around Rebecca, pulling her closer, sucking on her bottom lip. Rebecca's hand cupped her jaw, her neck, and when Rebecca pulled away to kiss her ear lobe, Katherine shook.

"Quickly," said Rebecca, her voice raw. "Not here—"

She took Katherine's hand and pulled her deeper into the maze, further away from the party and into the shadows. They turned one corner, then another, until they found themselves in a dead end. Around them swam the now-distant sounds of the party, of dignity and charm, a reminder of the risk they took in doing this, even out of sight—

I do not care— Katherine managed to think as Rebecca pulled her close, pushed her back against the hedge, *I do not care in the least*—

"Katherine," Rebecca murmured, one hand finding Katherine's hip, the other cupping the back of her head. "Katherine—"

Katherine tangled her fingers in Rebecca's skirts and pulled, moaning when they crashed together, hip-to-hip. And they kissed, slippery and needy. Katherine shook as Rebecca's tongue slid along hers, teasing and sinful, pressing but not urgent.

Rebecca pulled away to kiss Katherine's cheek, her neck. "I thought I would go mad," she managed, nipping at Katherine's earlobe, "waiting for you."

Katherine almost giggled, squeezing Rebecca's hips. "Really?"

"Yes," Rebecca murmured. "I could not sleep at all. It was infuriating, to lie there and think of you, of your mouth, and not be able to kiss you."

Katherine swallowed hard, trying to summon a coherent thought. "I— I felt the same—"

Rebecca let out a sigh full of all the yearning Katherine felt, her breath ghosting across Katherine's neck. "We do not have much time."

Summoning her courage, Katherine slid her hands up Rebecca's back, tracing the light, firm muscles of her shoulders. "Then make the most of it."

A fearsome, half-feral noise came out of Rebecca's throat and she pounced, rabid as a hornet, kissing Katherine until she could hardly breathe. The world tilted and spun, reverting its axis to the fierce heat of Rebecca's mouth — all Katherine could do was cling to her and hope that she would not float away, unmoored by this new reality.

And then, Rebecca tugged at her, tilting her hips forward, grabbing Katherine's bum. A fresh heat rose in Katherine's face, but she swallowed her surprise — Rebecca's mouth dropped to her neck, then to her chest, where she traced the same line she'd found the night before, pulling a fresh shiver out of Katherine's body. In an instant, understanding went through Katherine like a thunderclap — Rebecca was recreating the moment.

Putting Katherine where she wanted her.

Katherine's mouth fell open on a silent moan as Rebecca's tongue slid dangerously and deliciously low over the exposed swell of her breasts. She could only watch and pant like a fiend as Rebecca licked over one of her many moles, one sitting just above the edge of her *décolletage*. Then, Rebecca bent lower, and nosed the fabric directly above Katherine's nipple.

Katherine twitched, her hips hitching against Rebecca's, and the sound of their skirts catching in the hedge felt somehow scandalous. Rebecca tilted her head back to look up at Katherine, a fiendish grin sliding over her features.

"What I would do," Rebecca murmured, licking again at the delicate rise of Katherine's breast, "if I had you, a bed, and a locked door, for but an hour."

With the feeling that she was bargaining with a devil, Katherine said, "Yes."

Rebecca's grin flickered into a frown of confusion. "Yes?"

Katherine reached, fumbled with Rebecca's hand. She brought those deft, calloused fingers to her mouth, grazed them over her lips. "What if I said yes? To... that?"

"I—" Rebecca swallowed, her expression flickering from confusion into naked wonder. "Dear God, it is as if you were made to tempt me."

Something rather like courage overtook Katherine, and she smiled. "Perhaps I was."

A low hiss spilled from Rebecca's mouth, and she ducked her head to Katherine's chest, as if to muffle it.

"Tonight?" said Katherine, still ruled by that bolt of courage and more than a little want. She pressed her fingers into Rebecca's shoulder blades, and her mouth to Rebecca's knuckles.

A brittle laugh. "I cannot." Rebecca straightened up, shifted away. "We are hosting a supper party. I am expected to attend, and play nicely."

"Oh." Disappointment, keener than anything, twisted Katherine's stomach.

Rebecca's hand shifted, the plush of her thumb pressing Katherine's cheek. "Tomorrow?"

Katherine looked at her, and felt every single place they were touching. "Yes."

Rebecca took a slow, unsteady breath, and backed away, slipping out of Katherine's grasp. "We should part ways, Katherine, until then. For both our sakes."

"I will write to you." Katherine licked her lips, felt how swollen they were. "With instructions."

"Dear God," Rebecca breathed again, then turned away, her shoulders a brittle line. "Wait ten minutes before you follow me."

"Yes." Katherine took a great gulp of air as Rebecca disappeared from sight, and attempted to gather herself. But some things were easier said than done.

A quarter of an hour later, she rejoined her mother under the shade of a pear tree. Thomas was still mingling with Lady Sophia, and they'd drawn a flock of admirers. An audience for their timely charade.

"Good grief." Mrs. Knight took Katherine in with a single look and raised her eyebrow. "Are you quite certain you're well?"

"Oh, yes, Mother." Katherine glanced across the garden, where Rebecca stood beside Lady Alwyn. Even from this distance, Katherine could see the blush on her neck, the few loose hairs drifting along her temple, and felt a small curl of satisfaction. "I am very well indeed."

INTERLUDE IV — AMSTERDAM, APRIL 1812

Rebecca looked down into the city below, her gaze lingering on the half-lit storefronts, the twinkling street lamps, the nearby ebb of the canal. Salt lingered in the air, salt and fish and metal, and she could hear the rattle and thud of the warehouse down the road. The street teemed with life, with men and women and mugs of good ale. Laughter, shouting, singing. She breathed in, then out, and felt the air of the night on her bare skin.

"You are quiet." A mouth on her shoulder, a hand on her neck.

"Thinking."

Lotte hummed. "What about?"

"About this place. About Amsterdam." She glanced over her shoulder, meeting Lotte's gaze. "I do not want to leave."

Lotte smiled, sympathetic. "I know." She kissed Rebecca's hair. "You could run away."

Rebecca snorted, then rolled away from the open window, pulling Lotte close. Beneath them, the old bed groaned. "I could. But I would never see my sisters again."

"When is Gertrude's wedding?"

"The day we arrive."

Lotte cursed quietly, under her breath. "And what about you?"

"Me?"

"Do you have a nice English gentleman waiting for you?" Lotte's hand slid along Rebecca's stomach, slipping between her legs. "An old man ready to pump you full of babies?"

Rebecca smiled, rolling her hips, pushing Lotte's hand where she wanted it most. "No."

"Good." Lotte bent down, kissed her. "I will miss you, you know."

"I bet you say that to all your clients."

Lotte grinned, her teeth against Rebecca's neck. "Never."

Later, Rebecca dressed slowly, pulling on her trousers and her shirt with reluctance. From the bed, Lotte watched her like a sleepy cat, her eyes half-lidded but sharp, her legs splayed and her belly, her breasts, barely hidden by the sheet. Any other night, Rebecca would have climbed on top of her, unable to resist. But not tonight. Tonight, she had to return home. She had to pack.

"I feel..." Rebecca looked around the room, at the second-hand furniture and the low-burning candles and the velvet curtains. She knew it so well. "I feel like something is waiting for me. Across the sea."

"Maybe something *is* waiting," murmured Lotte. "Maybe it is your fate."

Rebecca tried to smile, buttoning her shirt. "I fear I will be very lonely in England."

"I do not think so. You will find someone, Rebecca."

"Really?"

Lotte nodded. "Perhaps that is what is waiting for you. A person who will be everything you want and need." She smiled, a little sad. "Not someone like me. Someone permanent."

Rebecca swallowed and was glad that she did not love Lotte. She reached into her pocket, withdrew a few coins.

"No." Lotte put up her hand. "Your money is no good here. Not tonight."

"Are you certain?"

"Yes."

Rebecca lingered, reaching for the door. "I hate goodbyes."

"I know." Lotte's throat bobbed and her eyes glittered. "*Wees voorzichtig*, Rebecca."

With that, Rebecca left, and did not look back once.

$$ \text{❧} \quad 20 \quad \text{❧} $$

Katherine paced in front of the windows, hardly daring to breathe. A steady, merciless blush had risen to her face an hour before and showed no signs of fading. Her stomach twisted in and out of endless knots, and her heart gave the occasional flutter, as if to ask what, precisely, she was doing.

Katherine was unable to come up with an answer.

The previous night, she'd sent a letter to Whitehill Manor, unsigned. *Third from the left*, it had read. *Half-past midnight*. If anyone other than Rebecca had intercepted it, it would not have made a lick of sense. But Rebecca would know. Rebecca *had* to know.

I am possessed, Katherine thought, not for the first time. *Enchanted. Bewitched and bewildered.* It was the only explanation for her behavior, her preoccupation. It was as if she were in thrall, beholden to a power that was not her own.

Down the hall, the crooked grandfather clock chimed the half-hour, and a fresh wave of butterflies swept through Katherine's stomach. She halted mid-step, and nudged open the curtains.

Outside, the night was black and riddled with stars. A faint breeze stirred the garden, and a little moonlight splashed across the grass, the patio. There was not a soul in sight.

Katherine took a long, trembling breath and turned away from the window, trying not to panic. What if Rebecca hadn't received her letter? Or, worse, what if she had received it and not understood—?

Tap tap.

Katherine turned, and saw a familiar figure standing just outside the window. She swallowed, gathered what remained of her wits, and undid the latch.

Night air poured in, bringing the sound of crickets and the smell of the river. Rebecca was but a smile in the shadows, dressed in a dark pair of trousers and a gray shirt. Her scent pooled in Katherine's face, stronger than before — metal and oak, sun and salt. "Evening."

"He—hello." Katherine stepped away, giving Rebecca room to climb into the house.

"Third from the left," whispered Rebecca, glancing back at the window. "I can see why you chose this one."

"It is the easiest to sneak through." Katherine closed the latch, tugged the curtains back into place. "One of Lucas' preferred methods of entry, if he is in his cups."

"Why does that not surprise me?"

"Follow me." Katherine glanced around, wary of the servants. "Be careful of that floorboard. And that one. And the one by the drawing room."

Rebecca gave a low chuckle that twisted Katherine's stomach. Her fingers found Katherine's and squeezed. "Does the house not like intruders?"

"You are hardly an intruder. The house has a mind of its own."

Katherine led them down the hall, around the corner, up the stairs. "Be very quiet," she breathed as she and Rebecca tiptoed up the carpet-covered steps.

"Your brothers are home?"

"Bran is." Katherine paused at the top of the stairs, glancing at the crack beneath the library doors. All was dark. "He stays up late reading."

"Worry not." Rebecca squeezed her hand again. "I have a light tread."

Together, they went up the next flight, then across the landing. Katherine nudged open her bedroom door — she'd left it unlatched — then darted in after Rebecca. Only once her door was closed and locked did she breathe again.

She stood there for a moment, hands pressed to the wood. Then she turned to face Rebecca, her heart throbbing in her ears.

A coy, teasing smile was playing about Rebecca's mouth. Katherine had left a few candles burning, and now, the warm, lush light spilled across Rebecca's features, highlighting her cheekbones, her chin, the slope of her elegant neck. A quiver wormed its way through Katherine's chest, down to her stomach.

"Katherine." Rebecca glanced around. "Why are there pillows and rugs piled around your bedroom?"

"Sound travels in this house." Katherine cleared her throat. "Through the baseboards and the walls." Here, finally, she forced herself to take a step closer. "I did not want us to be overheard."

"No?" Rebecca quirked an eyebrow. "Will we be very loud?"

"I—" Katherine's breath hitched. "I do not know."

"Well." Rebecca came towards her, pausing only a few inches away. Shadow overcame half of her features, leaving her inscrutable. "You've given me what I asked for. A bed." Rebecca shot said bed a pointed look. "A locked door." She leaned in closer. "And you. Wearing the most delicious nightgown I have ever seen."

Katherine could only look at her and try to breathe, butterflies and something heavy, something like lead, pooling in her stomach.

Rebecca pressed her forehead against Katherine's, put her

hands to Katherine's hips. Her touch was warm, weighty. "And now, Katherine. It is your turn to ask me for something."

"Oh?"

"Yes." She squeezed Katherine's hips. "You have not done this before, have you?"

"No."

Rebecca nodded, then slowly exhaled. Katherine could see the tension in her frame, almost as if she were holding herself back. "You must tell me what you want. And if you do not have the words... Then you must show me." She brushed her mouth against Katherine's, little more than a promise of a kiss.

Another tremble worked through Katherine's body, and she tried to grasp the situation. "I want..." Her voice was ragged, her throat raw with feeling. "I want you to kiss me."

Rebecca might have smiled. She brushed her mouth against Katherine's, another tease. "And?"

Katherine let her eyes slide shut. "I want you to touch me."

"Where?"

"Everywhere."

Rebecca took a soft, shaky breath, her hands pressing into Katherine's hips. "Katherine— if I— if I touch you somewhere you would not like me to touch, or— if I do anything you would not like me to do, then—"

"I will tell you." Katherine opened her eyes and wrapped her arm around Rebecca's shoulders, skating her nails across Rebecca's back. "I swear."

"Good."

Katherine stepped away, slipping out of Rebecca's grasp. As Rebecca watched, she climbed into her bed, and the familiar scent of her bedding grounded her. She lay back against her pillows, and felt the strap of her nightgown slide down her shoulder. "I want..." She tried again, her voice a little more steady. "I want you here."

Rebecca took a shuddering breath and nodded, reaching for

her boots. Once she'd wrestled them off, she climbed into the bed, watching Katherine with something like reverence. She moved slowly, carefully, as if waiting for Katherine's protest. When none came, she settled over Katherine's body, one leg between Katherine's and her face mere inches away. Her eyes glittered in the candlelight, and Katherine's stomach did a somersault, butterflies spilling down her legs.

"Now..." Katherine whispered. "Kiss me?"

Rebecca let out a sound of relief, a sound of wanting, and closed the distance between them, fastening her mouth to Katherine's.

The kiss was blistering, aching, full of so many things that Katherine could not name. She shook as Rebecca's tongue parted her lips and swept across her teeth, her hands reaching to skate up Rebecca's back. She could hardly believe that Rebecca was still fully clothed — she herself felt more naked now than she'd ever been in her entire life, bathed in the soft candlelight and Rebecca's shadow. Katherine skated her tongue across Rebecca's lower lip, then Rebecca's hand tangled in her hair and tilted her head to the side, deepening the kiss, and a moan caught in Katherine's throat.

Rebecca pulled away, pressed her mouth to Katherine's temple. "Steady," she whispered. "This house has ears."

"And we have pillows." Katherine pulled her back down, kissed that delicious bottom lip, her nails digging into Rebecca's shoulders.

A quiet laugh rumbled in Rebecca's chest, her breath huffing against Katherine's cheek. "I could have you like this for a week and still not be done with you."

A riotous heat overtook Katherine's face, and her brain stumbled around a response. Rebecca only chuckled at her expression, her mouth kissing a trail around Katherine's eyes, nose, cheeks, jaw. And finally, her neck.

Katherine arched into the touch, tugging at Rebecca's shirt. It was yet another echo from the other night — she all but shoved her body into the air, telegraphing a silent message.

Rebecca's teasing, warm mouth slid along the bare slope of Katherine's chest, kissing and sucking, dragging her teeth over the same mole she'd found the previous day. She nuzzled at the neckline of Katherine's nightgown, pushing it even lower, and Katherine squirmed, cupping Rebecca's head. Her loose strap slid further down her arm, finally exposing her breast.

Rebecca watched. And then — *sweet Lord* — she licked her lips.

When her mouth met Katherine's skin, it was gentle, teasing. She grazed her lips over Katherine's breast, drawing closer to but not touching her nipple. She let out a sigh as Katherine tangled her hands in her hair, all but pulling her down, and the gust of air against Katherine's skin made her tremble. Rebecca noticed, glancing up at her with eyes full of heat, then bent her head and licked.

Katherine's spine bowed and her mouth fell open on a silent moan, pleasure jolting through her belly to settle, low and pleased, at the crux of her thighs. She was not ready for it when Rebecca did it again, licking her over, teasing and sucking her nipple until it swelled and peaked. She just buried her hands in Rebecca's hair and tried to hold on, her body pulsing in time to the slick rhythm of Rebecca's tongue.

Rebecca pulled away, humming low in her throat. She thumbed at Katherine's other strap, then pulled it down, leaving her bare-chested and gleaming. Then she smiled, and sucked Katherine's breast into her mouth.

A wild, garbled sound tore out of Katherine's throat, and she curled upwards, pushing her body even closer to Rebecca's. Rebecca sucked and sucked, and Katherine's heartbeat roared in her ears. She could hear her own breathing, the slight shifts of their bodies against the bedding, and it all built into a heady, swirling mixture of indecency and want.

Then Rebecca's mouth, leaving a teeth-laden mark on the underside of her breast. The tiny jolt of pain was clarifying, intoxicating. "Shall I touch you anywhere else?"

"Yes," Katherine gasped, her hips twitching.

"Where?"

"Anywhere—"

Rebecca leaned back, settling on her knees, her hands resting on the edges of Katherine's torso. Her eyes still blazed in the low light, so intent that Katherine almost squirmed. Then she reached down, her hand finding Katherine's bare calf.

It was the smallest, gentlest movement. But that single touch went through Katherine like a shockwave — she felt it in her scalp. She felt it because she knew what it meant. A point of no return.

Rebecca watched her, impenetrable, as she slowly slid her hand up Katherine's leg, beneath the skirt of her nightgown. Panting like a fiend, Katherine watched her in return, and twitched when Rebecca's hand passed over her knee, reaching her thigh.

"Have you ever done this?" Rebecca murmured. "To yourself?"

Katherine tried to swallow. "Not— not really. I've tried, without much... success."

Rebecca arched an eyebrow, her other hand coming to rest on Katherine's breast, callouses grazing Katherine's swollen nipple. "Success?"

"I never... seemed to get anywhere."

"I see." Rebecca thumbed her nipple, smiled when she twitched. Then she bent down and kissed Katherine as her lower hand slid the rest of the way up.

Her touch was gentle, tentative. Rebecca hummed into the kiss — it vibrated down Katherine's throat, loosening the tendrils of tension in her hips. She let herself melt into the feeling as Rebecca's thumb slid along her sex, teasing her apart.

Warmth and weight. Soft, but tangible. And when Rebecca's fingers dipped, Katherine gasped.

Rebecca hummed again, mouthed at her jaw. "So eager for me, Katherine." Her fingers stroked, then twisted, and Katherine gasped again, jolts of pleasure ricocheting down her legs as her eyes slipped shut. Rebecca's head dipped, teeth raking across Katherine's breast, and another delicious bolt, cascading down to sit low in Katherine's belly.

Katherine curled into her, hips twitching. Stars exploded behind her eyelids as Rebecca's fingers slid up to the top of her sex, then came to rest on her swollen clit. Rebecca tapped, and Katherine's belly trembled. Then she circled, and a moan tore out of Katherine.

She could feel Rebecca's smile against her throat, Rebecca's callouses against her breast. "It seems you are getting somewhere already."

"Be quiet," Katherine bit out, then moaned again when Rebecca crooked her thumb and pressed.

Her thumb, steady, while her fingers curled, almost tentative, at Katherine's entrance. A finger circled, then slipped inside.

Katherine trembled. Her body seemed to swallow Rebecca's touch. An ache stretched within her, an ache for more, and from the way Rebecca hummed, pleased, Katherine knew it was obvious.

"So eager," Rebecca murmured again. "Have you been thinking of this, Katherine?" A nipple, eased between two fingers, then squeezed.

Katherine could only moan in response, her heart beating in her face. Another finger, slipping inside to join the first. Katherine could hardly believe how wet she was, how ready to surrender to least of Rebecca's attention. Her hips stuttered, then pushed down into the touch, encouraging and loose and so wanton she could scream.

Fine, then, her scrambled mind managed to think. *Let me be wanton.*

She raked a hand into Rebecca's curls, pulled her close, pushed her tongue into Rebecca's mouth. It was artless, but Rebecca made a wonderful, broken sort of noise, and her touch quickened, sending fresh sparks into Katherine's belly. Her other hand squeezed again, and Katherine gasped into her mouth, her tongue catching on Rebecca's teeth.

Together, they lurched. Together, they burned.

Pleasure built like a furnace in the small of Katherine's back. Her heart beat in tandem with the vicious circle of Rebecca's thumb, and a fresh sweat broke on her brow, in the slope of her spine. She could feel every inch of her body and every bit of Rebecca's touch. Rebecca's fingers dipped in and out, building a slick precipice that pulled Katherine to a rocky, high summit. Under the ceaseless swirl of Rebecca's thumb, Katherine twitched, pleasure coiling over her, around her, squeezing her like a ruthless snake. Her body tensed, clenching around Rebecca's fingers, and Katherine felt Rebecca's answering moan deep in her chest, in her mouth.

"Rebecca—" Katherine's voice was hoarse, wrecked. She shuddered, her hips rolling, grinding up into Rebecca's hand.

"That's it," Rebecca whispered, her breath hot on Katherine's ear. She sucked at Katherine's neck, tongued her collarbone, grazed Katherine's nipple with her teeth. That mouth— all trouble and reward, rolled together into a tantalizing, ruinous—

"Oh—" Something in Katherine's stomach crested, something bright and full of heat— She chased it, her body grinding into Rebecca's touch, fluid and real and so overwhelmed— "Oh—"

Rebecca kissed her as she came apart, swallowing all of Katherine's breathless, decadent sounds, her tongue skating the edge of Katherine's lip. Her hand stilled, as if to savor it, while Katherine rolled, bucked, shook, and fell still, the heat finally pouring out of her.

The world tilted, and Katherine opened her eyes. She looked up into Rebecca's glossy gaze, into a face riddled with as much want as she felt. Sparks fizzed in her hips, her teeth, and she brushed her mouth against Rebecca's chin.

Rebecca's breath caught, and her fingers slid out with a soft sound that seemed ridiculously loud. A wave of emptiness overcame Katherine, stronger than she would have expected, and she wrapped her arms around Rebecca's waist.

And then, she watched as Rebecca brought her hand to her mouth and licked. Then she moaned, her eyes sliding shut in apparent pleasure.

Katherine's face throbbed, and she slid a hand over Rebecca's stomach, up to the low collar of her shirt. "I want to see you."

Rebecca tugged her hem out of her trousers and pulled her shirt over her head, tossing it onto the bed. She straddled Katherine, half-naked save for a set of boneless stays, the light of the candles spilling across her skin. Her gaze was like pitch, like a challenge and a caress, and threatened to swallow Katherine whole.

The air hitched in Katherine's lungs. Her hand rested on Rebecca's belly, skated over the edge of her waist. Rebecca was as thin and agile as a bow, muscular and angular, with none of Katherine's gentle curves. And yet, something twinged deep between Katherine's legs, and she fought the urge to squirm.

Rebecca's stays were fastened with a neat little knot. Katherine nudged it with her finger. "May I?"

Rebecca's chest heaved, and she nodded.

A tug, and the stays loosened, bowing away from Rebecca's body. Katherine could only watch, stupefied, but then her hand moved, pulling the length of fabric down Rebecca's arms. Her hand stilled, then moved again, tentative.

Rebecca's chest heaved afresh, and her eyelids fluttered.

Her breasts were dainty, slight. Smaller than Katherine's. Her skin, warm and smooth, a touch sweaty. Katherine ached to taste her, but for now, she settled with thumbing over Rebecca's nipple, teasing it until it peaked.

"What about you?" Katherine whispered. "Can I—?"

Rebecca shook her head, nudging Katherine's other hand away from her trousers. "Not tonight." She smiled, indulgent. "But soon." A gust of air left her, and she rolled her narrow hips. "Not tonight," she said again. "Tonight, I want you to watch me." Her gaze raked over Katherine's body. "I want you to see what you do to me."

Katherine tried to remember how to breathe. But she settled for watching as Rebecca tugged open her trousers and slid her hand between her legs.

And when Rebecca moaned, the whole house shook.

"Touch me." A gasp. "As I touched you."

Katherine obeyed, a strange tingling sweeping over her face. She could hardly believe this was real, Rebecca writhing over her like a siren, like a woman possessed.

"Perfect." Rebecca gasped again, hips twitching. Beneath Katherine's touch, her body seemed to come alive, to sing with promise and reckless abandon. Her hand worked, steady and ruthless, over what Katherine could not see. And Katherine burned with it, the need to feel, to touch, to drink Rebecca in until they both overflowed.

"You enjoyed it," Katherine whispered, squeezing until Rebecca shook. "Watching me."

Rebecca nodded, unsteady. Her eyes glittered in the candlelight, as if to issue a challenge. *And?* she seemed to say. *And what if I did?*

Katherine licked her lips. Rebecca's weight against her body was steady and sure, a reminder that this was real. She must have looked a picture — bare-chested, sated, flush with the first true pleasure of her life, trapped between the legs of another woman. And Rebecca seemed to enjoy it. Her gaze tracked over Katherine's body, over her breasts, her neck, the slope of her brow.

What would happen, Katherine wondered, *if I followed her?*

Her own touch was softer than Rebecca's, lighter. She traced the tip of a single finger over the curve of her own breasts, down the line of her sternum. She saw, felt, and heard Rebecca's breath hitch, as if torn by the sight before her. Katherine smiled, and goosebumps erupted as she remembered the feeling of Rebecca's mouth.

"I enjoy watching you," Katherine whispered, and Rebecca shivered. Her touch slid further up her own breast, and pinched.

"God." Rebecca moaned again, her hand working furiously. Katherine imagined that she could hear Rebecca's body, wet and sliding open, a slick press in the evening air. She imagined replacing Rebecca's hand with her own. Or with her mouth.

With one thumb, she circled her own nipple. With the other, she did the same to Rebecca.

"Oh." Rebecca's chest hitched, and something like lightning seemed to crackle in the air between them. "Oh, Katherine—"

Her whole body seized, then seemed to rattle, shuddering apart at the seams. She gasped, lurching against Katherine, then slumped onto the bed, catching her weight on her elbow. And when she looked at Katherine, it was with eyes like midnight.

Katherine smiled again, reaching to cup her cheek. "There you are."

For a long time, Rebecca only blinked at her. Then: "You are a quick learner."

"I do as I please."

"Yes." Rebecca swallowed. "Yes, I noticed that."

Then, horribly — a sound from the hall. The sound of a door.

Katherine's stomach dropped. "That's Bran."

Rebecca offered her a smile. "Worry not. I have a light tread." She leaned in, gave Katherine a kiss so simple it was almost chaste. Then she rolled away, reaching for her shirt.

Katherine tried to feel anything other than dismay. "You are leaving?"

"If I do not leave now, I will stay until midday, Katherine." Rebecca got to her feet, putting on her stays. She tied them shut with a single hand. Katherine did not blush at the sight of those nimble fingers, knowing where they had just been— "Next time, I shall be a much more self-indulgent guest."

"Next time?" echoed Katherine, her stomach jumping with something like hope.

"Yes." Rebecca met her gaze. "If you would have me."

"Of course."

When Rebecca smiled, it was like a sunrise. She pulled on her shirt, buttoned her trousers. It was almost as if nothing had happened.

"Be careful," Katherine said. "He is probably in the kitchen."

Rebecca nodded, picking up her boots. She looked at Katherine for a moment, then ducked in and kissed her, urgent and needy. When she pulled away, Katherine could see the flush in her cheeks, the spark in her eye. And something within her body buckled, heavy with sudden emotion.

"Soon," Rebecca whispered. "Katherine."

And with that, she vanished, the door shutting quietly behind her.

21

Madam Kensington, it seemed, had become a woman of business, of repute. A figure known and unknown, tantalizing even to the most priggish of London's gentlemen.

"Not a single word of politics or money was spoken for half an hour, Kitten." Lucas smirked and poured himself a Scotch. "These gentlemen are quite enraptured."

Katherine shook her head. "I cannot believe it. I would never have assumed that they even read the pamphlets."

"They certainly do," said Thomas. "But they have the servants purchase it for them. Can you imagine if they were spotted engaging in such matters of gossip?"

"Beech wants us to increase the circulation," said Brandon. "To five hundred."

A ringing silence filled Katherine's ears. She could only blink at her brother. "What?"

"Five hundred copies," said Lucas, nodding. "Twice a week."

"He cannot keep up with demand, Katherine." Thomas smiled, and it had a self-satisfied edge. "The households of

London's finest want more of Madam Kensington, and who are we to deny them?"

"If we do this," said Katherine. "If we increase circulation, I want to give Rita a greater share of the profits."

Lucas frowned. "Why?"

"The risk," said Brandon. "She jeopardizes her position, and our identity, by making the inquiries that she does."

Thomas seemed to think for a moment. "Rita might be the most dangerous person we know."

Brandon snorted. "She could give Madison a run for his money."

Katherine winced. "Circumstances are dire, then?"

"Quite," said Lucas. "There have been rumblings of... well."

"People have been moving their money around," said Brandon. "Hedging their bets."

"You cannot mean," said Katherine. "War?"

Lucas nodded. In the dull light filtering in through the rain hitting the windows, he seemed very sober and grim. "Indeed."

Katherine looked at him for a moment. This was a welcome distraction from the fact that a thousand Madam Kensingtons would be flitting around the streets of London each week. "England can do quite a few things," she said. "But simultaneously fighting two wars on two separate fronts—"

"It is madness," said Thomas, in a tone of deep boredom. "As if dear old Bonaparte weren't thrilling enough—"

A laugh burbled out of Katherine's throat. Her face had gone numb. "That means more soldiers."

"Yes." Lucas sat down on the couch with a sigh. "More soldiers."

"Emmett. Gordon."

"Yes." Brandon slouched into the cushions. "It is only a matter of time."

The thought of her cousins going to war was sobering enough that, for the first time in the past day, Katherine was not thinking of Rebecca. And then, she felt absurdly grateful that her brothers had never needed to consider the opportunities afforded by enlisting in the military.

"Will it happen soon?" she said.

"I will be surprised if we do not receive a declaration of war within a fortnight," said Lucas.

"Madison," said Thomas, "is not a man who waits."

"And we are a country without a Prime Minister." Katherine shook her head. "What a time for him to strike."

"Boys!" Mrs. Knight came into the parlor, and stopped short at the sight of Katherine. "And Kat. We have been invited, rather at the last minute, to supper."

A pause as Katherine allowed the implications to sink in. "Aunt Linda?"

"Yes," said Mrs. Knight. Her children groaned in unison, and she gave them all a very pointed look. "And I expect you all to be on your best behavior."

"I would attend, Mother," said Lucas, glass of Scotch pressed to his forehead, "were I not deathly ill."

"And I," said Thomas. "Positively ghastly, Mother."

Mrs. Knight's nostrils flared. "You will attend even if I have to hammer you to a wooden frame and shove you through the front door."

"Good Heavens." Lucas tilted his head to one side. "Am I the Son of God, in this scenario of yours? That feels rather profane."

"You can repent your sins tomorrow, before the pulpit. In the meantime, you will make nice with your cousins, even Prudence, and not a word will be mentioned of Chrysanthemum and his remarkable digestion. Not a *word*," she repeated, when Brandon opened his mouth to protest, "on pain of my telling Mr. Salk to refrain from making his Victoria Sponge." Mrs. Knight clapped her hands together, the sharp sound ringing through the parlor. "Now, get dressed, and be ready to leave in fifteen minutes." With that, she swept out of the room.

"Fair warning," said Katherine, standing up with a sigh, "Prudence and Maggie will ask you ten thousand questions about the season."

"A last minute invitation," said Thomas. "That seems ominous."

"Does it?" said Brandon.

"It is out of pity," Katherine told him. "Since the Knights were not invited to this evening's supper party at Uphill Manor. Our dear Aunt Linda has seen fit to make us seem rather in higher demand than we are, at least according to her skewed logic."

Lucas took a sip of his Scotch and shook his head. "She needs Amanda to be married, and quickly. Anything to distract her from our existence."

Katherine followed her brothers out of the parlor, and in the corner of her eye, caught an echo of Rebecca, slipping through the hall in the shade of the night, her collar askew and her face flushed with pleasure. Katherine looked away, burying a smile, and tucked the memory away for later that night, when she would be alone.

❧

IT WOULD BE ACCURATE, PERHAPS, TO CLAIM THAT KATHERINE had thought of little else besides Rebecca in the past thirty-six hours. But it would be even more accurate to claim that she had thought most of Rebecca's hands, Rebecca's mouth, Rebecca's eyes. Pieces of the person, rather than the whole, because considering the whole would be far too overwhelming a reminder of what had passed between them on Friday night.

If Katherine thought of Rebecca in her entirety, she would, in short, simply faint.

So, when Katherine entered her family's usual church on that fateful Sunday, less than two days after her evening with Rebecca, she almost collapsed on the spot when she saw the entire Alwyn family sitting in the third pew.

"Good Heavens, Kitten." Thomas caught her elbow with a scowl. "Mind where you step."

"Sorry," she muttered, managing to right herself. A horrid blush swept up her neck and settled in her cheeks, and Katherine ducked her head, hoping that her bonnet would hide the worst of it. Thomas pushed her along the aisle, forcing her into the church.

The Alwyns, thankfully, were too far away to have noticed the Knights. The Knights were just another handful in a large crowd of parishioners, buried by other families. But everyone was watching the Alwyns, and trying to hide that they were watching the Alwyns.

"Goodness me," said Mrs. Knight. "It's Lord and Lady Alwyn. I wonder why they are here."

"Going to church, my love," said Mr. Knight, earning a snort from Brandon and an eye-roll from Thomas. "What else?"

Even now, amidst the crowds of Sunday families and pious widows, the world seemed to orient itself around its Star. A beam of sunlight appeared and trickled through the stained glass, anointing Sophia Johnson in a radiant halo, highlighting her elegant profile and the delicate swoop of her smile.

But as the Knights settled into their usual pew, halfway down the aisle, Katherine only had eyes for Rebecca, or, more accurately, for the back of Rebecca's head. Rebecca was wearing her lilac dress, and it conjured unhelpful memories in Katherine's mind. She and her brothers took their seats, and Katherine felt a stab of longing so acute that it nearly made her gasp.

And then, Rebecca turned, glancing behind her. Within seconds, she spotted Katherine. Katherine watched, her stomach leaping into her throat, as the corner of Rebeca's mouth twitched into a smile. Then, Rebecca winked, and turned back to face the pulpit.

KATHERINE WAS NOT A PIOUS PERSON BY NATURE, AND AS A habit, paid little attention to sermons. But today, she heard not a word of what the vicar said, and barely knew where she was. Once it was over, she followed her family out of the church, and stopped short when Lady Kemp waved them over.

"Mr. and Mrs. Knight! What a wonderful coincidence." Beaming, Lady Kemp stepped aside, revealing that she was standing with the entire Alwyn family. Katherine stared, mute with shock, at Rebecca, who smiled like a cat. Beside her, Sophia glittered; behind her, Lord and Lady Alwyn stood poised like they had walked right out of a painting. "I was just inviting Lord and Lady Alwyn to a little last-minute garden party this afternoon," Lady Kemp went on. "Won't you join us?"

"Certainly," said Mrs. Knight, hiding her surprise well. She smiled at Lady Kemp. "How kind of you."

"No matter, Mrs. Knight, the whole congregation is invited!" Lady Kemp turned her slightly manic grin back towards the Alwyns. "We must make our new members feel welcome!"

"Splendid," said Mrs. Knight, but Katherine did not hear her. A strange roaring had filled her ears, and she could not seem to look away from Rebecca. Rebecca, who looked at her as if she were something to be eaten slowly, decadently, with a dollop of whipped cream.

LADY KEMP'S GARDEN PARTY WAS MUCH THE SAME AS ANY other. Katherine slipped from group to group, flower bed to flower bed, avoiding the gentlemen and hiding behind the debutantes. It was not an ideal crowd for romance — there were far too many elderly parishioners, and the vicar had commandeered an entire corner of the garden for a long-winded lecture about some obscure bit of Biblical verse. Madam Kensington had little to observe, beyond a couple or two sneaking off into the garden.

Katherine did catch occasional glimpses of the Alwyns, who were the shiny new toy passed from guest to guest. She assumed they were fielding question after question about their family, their trade, their estate, and had to admire Lord Alwyn's tenacious, good-humored attitude towards such bold interrogation. Beside him, Lady Alwyn wore a thin smile tinged with warning, and Lady Sophia fluttered her fan, drawing the gazes of half the party. And Rebecca...

Katherine quickly turned away before she could be caught staring. Seeing Rebecca dressed like this was unnerving and yet fitting; the lilac silk made her skin sing in the sunlight, made Katherine want to pull that sleeve down and press her mouth to Rebecca's artful shoulder. But that would be impossible, of course. Her mind whirling, she quickly passed through the garden and into the house, hopeful for a bit of respite.

The empty hall echoed her steps, reminding her of her precarious position. If anyone were to suspect— if anyone were to learn — it would be catastrophic. A death sentence for her family's tenuous foothold in society. Katherine bit her lip, checked to see that the long hallway behind her was still empty, and slumped against the wall, fighting to catch her breath.

Pull yourself together, she thought. Now was not the time to wonder when she might have Rebecca to herself again, to wonder what new edge Rebecca might find for them both. Nor was it the time to consider, yet again, what this new and frightening attachment might mean.

Now was not the time to remember what Rebecca had looked like, half-naked and bathed in the light of the candles. Shining and writhing like Katherine would be the end of her.

Katherine did not hear the footsteps, nor did she realize she was not alone until it was too late, until the newcomer was but a few paces away from her. Only then did she gasp and straighten up, a thousand excuses dying in her throat as she met Rebecca's gaze.

The air swelled between them, tenuous enough to snap with a pinprick. Rebecca's gaze raked over Katherine with all the tenacity of a blade. When she finally met Katherine's eyes, her mouth curled again, an echo of that devious smile.

Katherine looked at her, her chest heaving as she fought for air, for sanity. Want, pure and cold, swept through her to settle low and ready in her belly.

"I—" she began, with no idea of what to say. "I—"

But Rebecca finished for her. She closed the distance between them, pushed Katherine up against the wall, and kissed her.

A strangled noise burst out of Katherine's throat. She grabbed at Rebecca, pulling her closer until they were pressed together. Rebecca gripped the back of her head, licked past her lips, swirled her tongue until Katherine shuddered. The kiss was wet, sloppy, and full of such yearning that Katherine thought she might very well die.

The air filled with their snatched breaths as their kiss deepened, grew filthier. The heated press of Rebecca's body was yet another reminder of the other night, and Katherine groaned anew at the memory of Rebecca's touch, clinging to Rebecca's shoulders.

Rebecca pulled away, gasping, "God, how I have missed you."

"And I you." Katherine bent her head, kissed Rebecca's cheek, jaw, ear, catching a glimmer of that scent — metal and wood. "Has it only been two days?"

"The longest days I have ever known." Rebecca squeezed her hips, rocking them together. The pressure was tantalizing, skating the edge of just enough, and Katherine throbbed. Rebecca looked at her with blown, half-lidded eyes and murmured, "Should I stop?"

And Katherine, caring not that they were in full view of

anyone who happened to wander down the empty hall, shook her head. "No," she whined, "please. I cannot wait any longer—"

Rebecca leaned in, bit Katherine's lip, then soothed it with a sweep of her tongue. "Hitch your leg," she murmured, "around my hips."

Katherine obeyed, trembling, and bucked when she felt Rebecca's hand slip beneath her skirts. Even though stockings and pantalettes, Rebecca's touch was full of heat and reassurance. But they did not have the luxury of time — Rebecca closed the rest of the distance between them, and put her hand to the bare crux of Katherine's legs.

A moan, buried in the dip of Katherine's neck. Rebecca dragged her teeth along the skin, her fingers sliding through the slick warmth of Katherine's sex. She did not have to state the obvious — Katherine was far gone, long past rescuing.

A shudder rolled through Katherine. Her hips lurched into Rebecca's touch, demanding more, and Rebecca's fingers slid into her body, her thumb coming to rest on Katherine's clit. She sucked Katherine's tongue into her mouth, and set a steady, merciless rhythm.

Katherine heaved, her head spinning. Pleasure whipped through her with a ferocity that was almost painful — her head snapped back, banging into the wall, but she did not feel it. All she could feel was the tight circle of Rebecca's thumb, the thick pressure of her fingers. Rebecca fell upon her with a growl, licking her way up Katherine's neck, biting her breast through the fabric of her dress.

And Katherine could imagine it. Could imagine what it would be like if they were both naked, without a stitch of excuse between them. The idea alone made her shake anew, made her want to rip Rebecca's lovely dress to pieces.

Pleasure surged like fire on fresh, dry wood, setting Katherine ablaze from top to toe. The feeling was nothing and everything like the other night — now, she'd begun to learn the signals of her own body. She could retrace the paths of desire and see where they began, where they led. And as she looked into Rebecca's eyes, seeing nothing but that ruthless, blazing want, she knew that her destination was closer, much closer, than she might have thought.

"Oh—" Katherine gulped, cool air hitting her forehead, her sweaty neck. Sparks burst in her back, her feet. "Oh, Rebecca—"

"There now." Rebecca's thumb worked in a vicious, slow circle; her mouth came to Katherine's. "Quietly, love, quietly—"

Katherine's startled moan was swallowed by an indulgent, lingering kiss. Rebecca hummed, and kissed her again, twice, three times, before pulling away. Her face was flushed, her eyes livid with chambered pleasure. Beneath Katherine's skirts, she shifted her hand, kissing Katherine's cheek when she winced at the feeling of loss. Rebecca eased Katherine's leg down from her hip, tugging her skirts back into place.

Katherine could only watch her, spent and fizzing. She could hardly believe she was awake, that they had—

"Well." Rebecca crooked a grin. "If that is how we will always greet each other, I think we are very well-suited indeed."

22

Katherine's mind spun, first from 'well-suited' to 'always' to 'greet,' then returned to 'well-suited.' Without saying a word, she grabbed Rebecca's hand, pulled her down the hall, and opened the first door she saw.

The door opened on a parlor, if her cursory glance told her anything of use. The curtains had been drawn, leaving the space bathed in a dim, purplish light. As soon as the door closed, she pushed Rebecca up against it and kissed her, doing her best to mimic what Rebecca had done earlier, swirling her tongue in that obscene manner. Rebecca let out a soft huff of surprise, her hands coming to squeeze Katherine's hips, at once an encouragement and a question.

"I want to," Katherine tried to say, a fresh heat rising to her face. It had nothing to do with her own pleasure and everything to do with Rebecca's. "Tell me, please. What to do."

Rebecca took a long, shuddering breath. "You need not," she whispered, "if it is too soon—"

"Rebecca, if I do not get a hand on you in the next thirty seconds, I shall become quite difficult."

A chuckle, then Rebecca tugged at her own skirts, her hem

fluttering over Katherine's hand. "Do as I did." She kissed Katherine's nose, cheek, chin. "If you insist—"

"I insist—" Katherine bit out, fumbling with Rebecca's skirts, kissing her again and again— "God in Heaven, do I insist—"

The space between Rebecca's legs was warm and damp, much like Katherine's. A searing heat met her finger as she stroked the space between the seams of Rebecca's pantalettes. Rebecca hummed, her head tipping back to rest on the door, and Katherine took that to be encouragement. Hesitant, she slid a finger upwards, parting Rebecca's short, tense curls, and paused when she felt—

Rebecca inhaled sharply. "There."

A small, hardened nub. Katherine was struck by how similar Rebecca's body felt to her own; similar, but different all the same. She fumbled a little, repositioning her hand, and pressed her thumb to Rebecca's clit, tracing a slow, soft circle.

Rebecca inhaled again, a smile ghosting across her mouth. Katherine kissed it, then pulled away in time to hear her say, "Faster, if you don't mind."

"Demanding," Katherine chided her, but obeyed. She slid her index finger lower, teasing apart Rebecca's sex. The searing heat grew and grew, as did the slick, intense moisture. She reached the place where Rebecca's body gave way, and gently pushed her finger inside.

A half-broken moan fell out of Rebecca's mouth. Katherine kissed her, all teeth and a little tongue, then slid her finger out, and in again.

Rebecca's body opened before her in a pressured, ceaseless slide. Her hips twitched in tandem with the movement of Katherine's thumb, and a fresh trickle of wetness pooled around Katherine's finger. Katherine watched Rebecca, overwhelmed by the ease of her pleasure and the hooded look Rebecca gave her, a look that spoke to nothing short of bone-deep desire.

Is this what they all chase? she thought, dipping her head to mouth at Rebecca's chest. *When they sneak off into bushes, into empty rooms, behind doors?*

For the first time in her life, Katherine understood it.

She felt as if she could see the pleasure building in Rebecca's body. Rebecca rolled against her hand, murmuring an occasional instruction, an occasional word of praise. And when her breath caught, when her hips stuttered, Katherine knew that she was close.

And then, suddenly, she shuddered and gasped, "Kiss me, Katherine— kiss me—"

Katherine did. Because she would give Rebecca anything she asked for.

Silence overcame Rebecca as her pleasure crested and crashed — her chest lurched, and a broken gasp worked its way into Katherine's mouth. She sucked gently on Rebecca's lower lip, holding her through it, loving the weight and the twitch of her sex. Like Rebecca had, she kept her hand still as the pleasure faded, and only when Rebecca quieted, sighing against her cheek, did she withdraw it.

Rebecca watched as she brought her fingers to her mouth and licked, tentative. "God in Heaven," Rebecca murmured. "You were made to unmake me."

Katherine licked again, then sucked. The taste was clean, bitter. A bit salty. And she enjoyed the way Rebecca was looking at her, at once astonished and riled.

There, in that moment, as they stood in the empty, shadowed parlor, hidden from the world around them, Katherine knew that they were standing on opposite ends of a precipice. Poised across from one another, daring each other to take that final, reckless leap into the unknown.

What am I? she wanted to say. *What am I, to you?*

"We should return... to the party." The reluctance in Rebecca's voice was palpable.

Katherine smiled, then leaned in to nudge Rebecca's cheek with her nose. "Should we?"

"I cannot believe I am saying this, but yes."

Katherine pulled away, took her hand. "Do you not trust me behind a closed door?"

"Not in the least, dear Katherine."

Katherine sighed dramatically, batting her lashes. "I suppose I can be convinced. If..." She took a quick breath, mustered her courage. "If you can promise me something in return."

Rebecca's eyes were like ebony. "Anything."

"Promise me that you will continue visiting me. At night," said Katherine, "as well as during the day."

Indulgence, in the form of a smile. "Of course."

"And..."

"And?" Rebecca teased her, squeezing her hand. "Two promises, then."

Fresh butterflies, coursing through Katherine's belly. "Promise me that if you must break my heart, you will do it quickly, and cleanly. And..." She took another breath, and tried not to feel anything very much at all. "Sooner. Rather than later."

The way Rebecca was looking at her defied words. It certainly went beyond any flourish of Madam Kensington's. One gut-wrenching moment passed, then another, before Rebecca spoke in a low voice. "I promise, Katherine."

Katherine smiled at her, and did not feel sad. With her free hand, she reached for the door. "Shall we?"

Together, they walked out of the parlor, and into the summer evening.

❧

Mrs. Knight, unfortunately, never missed a thing. Over supper that evening, she turned to Katherine and said, "You seem very friendly with Lady Rebecca, dear."

A horrible heat rose to Katherine's face. Her brain whirled like an overcome racehorse, and she almost blurted a protest, but then — *The truth*, she thought. *Lies are always best when they are couched in the truth.*

"Yes," she said, then cleared her throat. "We are friends, Mother."

"Lovely," said Mrs. Knight. "Though I must admit, I am somewhat surprised—"

"Don't be," said Lucas, and he shot Katherine a smile. "Lady Rebecca is a little more eccentric than she lets on. We all enjoy her company."

"And she is lonely," blurted Katherine. "Given that she is not yet out."

"Of course." Mrs. Knight, with her tribe of sisters, could understand all too well the struggle of sitting at home when the season was in full swing. "We should invite her to supper."

Katherine wondered if she had simply died at the table. Died, and gone to hell.

Mrs. Knight smiled. "Really, we should invite her entire family, but I know how busy they are. Lady Rebecca will make a good starting point."

Lucas gave a funny little cough. Beside him, Brandon fidgeted, then reached for his wine to cover it. "I am certain Lady Rebecca would love to receive an invitation," said Lucas. "If you think that we are—"

"Suitable," said Katherine.

"Yes," said Lucas. "Suitable for company."

"It will be excellent practice, at any rate," said Mrs. Knight. "With a lady from such a refined family. You will learn much from her, I think."

"Yes," said Brandon, his voice a little high. "Yes, certainly." He turned towards the other end of the table. "Now, Father. Have you heard anything more from the Battens?"

Katherine did not hear her father's reply, or the ensuing

conversation about the most recent litter of beagle pups. She poked at her peas and tried to imagine Rebecca here, at this table, wearing a dress and conversing with Mr. and Mrs. Knight.

A shudder raked over her, and she barely suppressed it. Taking supper with Katherine's family would be a strange experience for them both, but perhaps Rebecca would enjoy herself. She seemed to delight in taking risks, and in playing a part.

Katherine's hand tightened of its own accord, almost curling into the memory of Rebecca's body. But she forced her mind away from thoughts of that afternoon, thoughts of those stolen moments in Lady Kemp's disused parlor. She could not think of it, for the sake of her own sanity.

After supper, in the safety of their own disused parlor, Lucas stood behind her and said, "Have you heard anything about Lady Sophia?"

Katherine paused mid-sentence, ink splattering across her knuckle. "No. Why? Have you?"

He sighed a little, as if rueful. "Not as such. It is more... whispers. From the White Fox."

"Whispers?" Katherine turned to look at him properly, her heart giving a funny tremor. "Such as?"

"They are... unkind."

"We have long since established my tolerance for matters that are less than savory," said Katherine. She glanced at Brandon, then Thomas. "Have either of you heard anything about this?"

"No," said Brandon, and Thomas was frowning. "I do not know what he's referring to."

"A few of the gentlemen..." Lucas winced, as if his words had hooks. "A few of the gentlemen have implied that her virtue..."

Thomas looked mutinous. "You dare to question Lady Sophia's honor?" he bit out.

"I would not," said Lucas. "But some are. There is doubt. Amongst certain circles."

A horror, a seeping dread, wormed into Katherine's stomach. "And is there reason for it?"

"Malicious gossip," spat Thomas, lurching to his feet. "The product of jealousy and spite."

"No," said Lucas to Katherine, giving Thomas a pointed look. "Not as far as I know. It is but a rumor, though it seems to be... growing."

"Tell me," she said. "Tell me all of it, Lucas."

He sighed, and for a moment, he seemed every inch the eldest son. The light of the candles threw the lines of his face into sharp relief, aging him beyond his years. "There is debate about the timing of her family's arrival in Britain. If her parents staged it, and secured her position as the Star, so as to increase her chances of a match that met their standards."

"But any family with half a brain would do that," said Katherine.

"Some people think it was rather rushed." Lucas glanced at her. "As if her parents were trying to... cover up some more indelicate matters."

"To outrun a rumor," snapped Thomas. "A story. Following her from Amsterdam."

Lucas nodded. "Or a lover. One, perhaps, they did not approve of."

Katherine's mind whirled. She could, unfortunately, understand this perspective. Given the circumstances of the Alwyns' arrival and their sudden ascendancy, it was only natural for the peerage to speculate. Thomas was right, in some ways — jealousy would keep the wheel of gossip turning for eternity. But to imagine that there was some truth in it, that Lady Sophia — Saint Sophia, as Rebecca called her — would jeopardize her future and the status of her family... No. Impossible.

"If this were true," said Katherine, "then why is she not yet married?"

"Yes," said Brandon. "Wouldn't they want to wed her off as quickly as possible?"

Lucas shrugged. "Who's to say they have not tried? Would any of you believe that Lady Sophia would agree to a match she did not want, without at least putting up a fight?"

Brandon snorted. "If she is anything like her younger sister, absolutely not."

"Lord Dashwood," murmured Katherine, before she was even aware of thinking it. All her brothers turned to look at her. "Perhaps he is the reason for the delay. It is no secret that Lady Alwyn does not approve of him."

"True," said Lucas. "Have they announced anything?"

"No," said Katherine. "No, not yet." She tried to think of a moment, any moment, from that afternoon, when she might have overheard some remark from Lady Alwyn or seen a look of disapproval. But no — all she could remember was Rebecca. The sight of her. The taste of her. Katherine shook her head, dislodging the memory. *Distraction.* "At any rate," she went on. "I think we can all agree that Madam Kensington would never stoop to print such unfounded slander."

"Yes," said Thomas at once, and was quickly echoed by his brothers. "Leave such drivel for the mongrels at the White Fox."

Brandon smirked at him. "You mean us?"

"Yes." Thomas reached for the decanter of Scotch. "Us."

The following night brought an eerie but undeniable sense of calm. Katherine sat before the windows of her room, looking out into the garden, and breathed. Honeysuckle, rosemary, jasmine. Wet grass — for it had rained all day — fresh mud, and even the scent of rotting wood. It was still high summer, but already the trees had begun to decay, discarding the remnants of their cyclical lives to the uncaring ground. Katherine wondered how it would feel to shed oneself, to die, for a season, then to grow back anew, buds and leaves splitting the skin. She wondered if the trees could taste the earth they grew in. She wondered if they could feel each others' roots, stretching.

A hand on her shoulder. "Are you ready for bed, Kat?"

She shivered. "Yes, I think so."

"My goodness." Rita offered her a little smile. "I interrupted quite a deep thought."

"I suppose." Katherine stood up from her armchair, the floorboards creaking under her feet. "I think I have a difficult time understanding it." She glanced at Rita. "Love."

"Oh." Rita's smile took on a teasing, knowing edge, and she reached for the corner of Katherine's bedding. "Has someone been bitten by Cupid's arrow?"

"A countless number of my peers," said Katherine. "But not me."

Rita tugged the bedding open, gave her a look that was a little too shrewd for Katherine's liking. "What is it you do not understand?"

"The risk." Katherine got into bed, hugging her knees to her chest. "Are they not afraid of the hurt? The pain?"

"Heartbreak, you mean?" At Katherine's nod, Rita pursed her lips. "Well. I am hardly an authority in these matters, but I have heard that it is just another part of love. You cannot have one without the other."

"Then why fall in love at all?"

Rita offered her a sympathetic smile. "And that, I believe, is the question that we've been trying to answer for as long as... well. For as long as we've known there was a question."

And when Katherine was alone, sitting beneath the night, she began to wonder if she herself was gambling, and with something far more precious than money.

❦ 23 ❦

"**A**msterdam must have been quite a thrilling place to grow up," Mrs. Knight was saying, smiling over her wine glass. "I hear it is a very diverting city."

Rebecca returned her smile, radiant in the light from the candelabras. She'd worn her rich cream dress, and it made her skin sing. "I suppose it was," she said. "I enjoyed it immensely."

"Do you miss it?" said Mrs. Knight.

"Every day," said Rebecca, then glanced at Katherine. Something nameless sparkled in her eyes. "But England has been very welcoming. And the weather is quite familiar."

Mr. Knight chuckled. "It is so temperate here in the south. You should come north, and experience a true winter."

Brandon sighed. "I so long for a good blizzard."

Laughter echoed around the room. Katherine tried not to watch Rebecca, and concentrated on cutting her mutton properly. It would be just the thing to slice her own hand open.

"I have heard many tales of the north," said Rebecca. "Do you prefer it to London?"

"Yes," said Thomas and Brandon, in tandem with Lucas' "No." That set everyone off again, and Katherine hid a smile, unable to deny the tendril of delight snaking through her. She had not expected supper to go so smoothly.

And a part of her could not help but love seeing Rebecca like this. At ease and enjoying herself with Katherine's family. It made Katherine feel— made her hope—

"London has its perks," said Thomas. "I will grant that much. But there is nothing like walking into a good country pub at the end of a long day in the hills. A pint of bitter, a hot steak and kidney, right out of the oven. What more does a person need?"

"And the air." Brandon shook his head. "Fresh enough to wake a hibernating bear."

"If you keep on in the style of Wordsworth," Lucas said to him, "I shall become quite violent."

"You enjoy London, then?" said Rebecca to Lucas.

"Immensely," he said, stretching the word with relish.

"Ignore him," said Brandon in a stage whisper. "He only cares for the more savage city delights."

"Boys," chided Mrs. Knight. "Don't frighten our guest."

"Worry not, Mrs. Knight," said Rebecca. "I am not easily spooked."

Katherine watched Thomas stifle a snort, and Lucas grinned, cheeky as anything. She, meanwhile, bit the inside of her cheek, unable to shake the memory of Rebecca in her fencing gear, threatening to slice off Brandon's ear.

"I suppose that offers some peace of mind." Mrs. Knight gave Rebecca another smile. "How did you spend your time in Amsterdam?"

"My parents kept me and my sisters quite busy," Rebecca replied. "We had tutors in six subjects, as well as dancing, drawing, and needlepoint."

A stunned silence followed this remark. Katherine could not help but look at her mother. *Six subjects*, she thought, and it seemed that Mrs. Knight was thinking the same. *Six subjects, while I barely learned three.*

"Six." Mrs. Knight recovered a little. "My goodness."

"Literature, mathematics, music, history, foreign languages, and…" Something seemed to catch in Rebecca's throat, as if she'd swallowed a bit of vinegar. "Etiquette, of course."

"Of course," Mrs. Knight echoed. She looked down the table at Mr. Knight, who was just as stunned. "How wonderful, for your parents to be able to give you such a rich education."

"Foreign languages?" said Mr. Knight. "As in, multiple?"

"Yes." Rebecca nodded. "French, Italian, Prussian, Spanish… We traveled quite a bit, as a family, and my father was always entertaining guests from all over the Continent. My sisters and I learned out of necessity as much as anything."

"Good Heavens." A smile twitched over Mr. Knight's mouth. "You are quite gifted."

Rebecca gave a self-deprecating smile. "Oh, you are kind. No, my sisters are much more impressive, I assure you. I may have learned how to play the piano and stitch a rose, but I would hardly say that I excelled."

"What do you enjoy, then?" said Mrs. Knight, in a bid to return to less intimidating topics. "If such domestic activities are not of particular interest?"

Again, Rebecca glanced at Katherine, but so quickly that she almost missed it. "Walking, I suppose." A chuckle, now, and she reached for her glass of wine. "I very much enjoy exploring cities. I could spend my whole day walking and never grow tired of it."

Mrs. Knight gave a light laugh, some color returning to her face. "Just like our Katherine. Though she is a country girl through and through — you should see her in her tartan."

Heat, exploding in Katherine's face. She dropped her gaze to her food and prayed for a change of subject, any change of subject—

"Tartan?" Smug, teasing, edged with a fondness that Katherine could not have imagined. When she looked up, Rebecca was grinning at her. "I thought only the Scots wore tartan."

"Well, we Knights do have some Scottish blood," said Mr. Knight. "But keep that a bit hush-hush, Lady Rebecca."

"Of course," said Rebecca, her voice dropping to an exaggerated whisper. "I would never dream of exposing you."

Mr. Knight smiled at her, genuinely charmed. The conversation continued, then turned, as Katherine knew it would, to the unavoidable.

"Ridiculous in the extreme," Lucas was saying. "The idea that going to war will solve any of the territory disputes is short-sighted at best. Madison cannot accept that he is governing a country too large for his pitiful government, and that any hope of keeping it all to himself is sheer lunacy."

"He knows we are weak," Thomas replied, settling into his usual track. "He knows that Napoleon is testing Britain as it has not been tested before, and he sees this as an opportunity to strike. What he hopes to achieve is rather beyond my understanding, but that's America for you."

"Personally," said Rebecca. "I cannot fathom why our government is so invested in a wild land across an entire ocean when there are families and children starving in British cities."

One could have heard a pin drop. Katherine stared at her, trying to understand what had just happened. But Rebecca simply smiled, reminiscent of her sister.

"Well." Lucas seemed to flounder. "There are untold resources in America. Untold opportunities. It is an option we must explore, before the damn Yanks take control of everything."

"Must we?" Rebecca lifted one shoulder in an elegant shrug and took a sip of wine. Katherine did not watch the long line of her throat. "I think we are committed enough to handling the situation on the Continent without embroiling ourselves in a land that does not belong to us."

Something like glee was brewing in Katherine's stomach. She could hardly contain herself — forcing away her smile was like having a toothache.

"But does it matter?" said Thomas, frowning. "When they have declared war?"

"The Yanks, as you call them, have not declared anything," Rebecca replied. "President Madison has called on his Congress to declare war. If it wishes, Congress can ignore his request."

"Ridiculous," muttered Lucas. "Absolutely bizarre."

"Do you think it will happen?" Katherine found herself saying. She drew Rebecca's gaze, and held it. "Do you think the Americans will declare war?"

"I think," said Rebecca, "that the Americans are keen to prove themselves. They have been watching our dance with Napoleon, and are looking for a fight."

And for a moment, it was just the two of them. Seated across from one another at a table, talking, a shared meal between them. In a space so intimate it went beyond the call of any sensual desire Katherine had yet known.

But then the moment faded, and the conversation turned away from the question of war, terrible war. Katherine looked down at her plate, then glanced at her mother. Mrs. Knight was watching Rebecca, and the look beneath her placid smile was one of calculation, of surprise. Of admiration.

SEVERAL HOURS LATER, BRANDON LINGERED IN THE DRAWING room window, the evening breeze ruffling his shirt collar. He'd undone the two topmost buttons, and a blush had risen in his neck, a sign of that evening's particular indulgence — port wine. "I think she made a few excellent points," he was saying. "And I must admit, I agree with her."

"I agree that war is not the answer," said Lucas. He was splayed on the couch, his hair tousled, wearing a spectacular scowl. "The last thing I want is for Emmett and Gordon to see combat. But to discount the opportunities afforded by an entire continent—"

"Not again, please, for the love of God." Thomas threw a pillow at him. "We have heard this enough times."

"Oh." Brandon straightened up, put a hand to the open window. "Steady on—"

A hand appeared, then an arm. Brandon gripped Rebecca's elbow and helped her climb in through the window. "Thank you," said Rebecca, brushing a bit of dirt off her trousers. "Sounds like I ruffled a few feathers at supper."

Katherine's gaze raked over her, drinking her in. Rebecca had changed in the garden, out of her gown and into her usual dark trousers and shirt, and she'd taken out her hair. Her short curls hazed at her temples, her neck, and Katherine ached to nuzzle them, to press her nose to Rebecca's collarbone and breathe in the scent of the night on her skin. Rebecca caught her looking, and flashed her a tiny, private smile.

Something within Katherine quivered, and she swallowed hard. "Pay them no attention. You did wonderfully at supper. They are just upset that you bested them."

"I would not say 'bested,' " grumbled Thomas. He went to pour Rebecca a drink.

"I had wondered about your family's preference for Scotch," Rebecca said, watching him. "Though I suppose it does make sense, now."

"Wine will do in a pinch," said Thomas. "And we have a friend at the distillery near Mosswood."

"So it is an economic decision as well." Rebecca grinned. "I suppose I can admire that."

"Admire away." Thomas handed her her glass and returned to where Katherine was sitting at the card table. "Now—" He picked up two cards and held them aloft, their painted backs facing Katherine.

She looked at them for a moment. "A six and a Jack. A Jack of clubs."

"Damn! Lucas, that's your turn."

Rebecca looked from Thomas to Lucas, then back again. "What is this?"

"Two-Card Charlie," said Brandon, then he hiccuped. "A Knight original. We hold up two cards, and Katherine has to guess what they are. If she guesses wrong, she has to drink. If she gets them right, we have to drink."

"And Kitten is uncommonly gifted at guessing correctly," said Thomas. "Her talent is nigh on supernatural."

Rebecca shot Katherine a look of surprise, and Katherine shrugged.

In response, Rebecca raised her glass, and an eyebrow. "Well, then. Off to the races."

❧

Katherine gasped as her back hit the trunk of the tree, the bark digging into her exposed skin. Her hands fumbled for purchase on Rebecca's hips, and when their mouths met, their teeth bumped together.

"Rebecca—" Katherine pulled away to glance over her shoulder. "Rebecca, someone will see—"

Rebecca buried a laugh in her collarbone, tugging at her skirts with a ferocity that made Katherine shudder. "Who, the fairies at the bottom of the garden?"

"Well—" Katherine blinked a few times as Rebecca's tongue did several wonderful things to her neck, then to her breasts. "Our gardener—"

"Is in the kitchen, as well you know." Rebecca leveled her with a look, impetuous in the cool light of the morning. "If you truly want me to stop—"

Katherine replied by grabbing her lapels and yanking her in

for a deep, succulent kiss. Rebecca hummed into her mouth, her fingers digging into Katherine's hips, pulling their bodies flush. This was hardly their first time together — and the past week had been illuminating indeed — but each time, Katherine could not seem to fathom that this was really happening, that she could have Rebecca like this, all to herself—

"You just had me a few hours ago." Katherine panted into the dip of Rebecca's neck, felt Rebecca's hand begin to gather up her skirt. "You cannot want me again already—"

"Can't I?" Rebecca's eyes were like pitch, even in the daylight; her hand like a brand through the fabric of Katherine's pantalettes. "Do you recall what I said to you?" She sucked on Katherine's bottom lip, let it go with a *pop*. "Last night?"

Of course Katherine did. She could all too *clearly* recall shuddering her release under Rebecca's hand, only to open her eyes and see Rebecca watching her, then murmuring: "Next time, you will be doing that on my mouth."

She trembled again now as Rebecca said, in her matter-of-fact way, "I could not wait, Katherine. I could not wait—"

"Here?" Katherine hissed, even as she rolled her hips and scraped her shoulder blade over the bark. "Now?"

Rebecca responded by dropping to her knees, lifting Katherine's skirt, and disappearing beneath it.

Breathe, Katherine told herself, as she felt Rebecca's breath on her leg. *Breathe.*

The past week had been a blur of evenings spent with and without Rebecca. Even the night of Rebecca's supper with the Knights, she'd pretended to leave after playing Two-Card Charlie and snuck up to Katherine's room instead, all hands and fingers and that merciless, Scotch-laden mouth. They'd begun to learn one another between the walls of the Knight house, and Katherine was quite addicted to the sight of Rebecca in her bed.

This, however, was new.

"Rebecca—" Katherine darted a panicked look around, even

as Rebecca gently tugged the seam of her pantalettes apart. The garden was deserted, yes, and it was still quite early, but—

"Worry not," Rebecca murmured, her breath hot on Katherine's inner thigh. "I shall be very thorough." With that, she licked along the seam of Katherine's sex, and Katherine whined.

It felt familiar, yet like nothing she'd ever felt before. Rebecca licked her slowly, carefully, teasing apart her folds to worry at her clit. With every roll of her tongue, a little shock traveled up into Katherine's stomach, fizzing along her spine, up over her scalp.

Slick, sensuous. Unimaginable heat and the wet warmth of Rebecca's mouth. The steady, thick pressure of her tongue, pushing and rolling in that slow, unfaltering way. Rebecca's hands came to Katherine's thighs, gripping them and gently nudging them apart.

A moan caught in Katherine's throat as her head fell back against the tree trunk, her feet sliding a little in the damp grass. Rebecca hummed, and Katherine felt it in her body, felt it vibrate through her hips. A fresh heat overtook her face as Rebecca hummed again, then shifted, her mouth trailing lower.

When her tongue slid inside Katherine's body, it took all of Katherine's effort not to jump like lightning. Her hands skated across her skirts, trying and failing to find purchase on Rebecca's shoulders. She settled for gripping the tree trunk behind her as Rebecca's tongue slid in and out.

Rebecca pulled away, kissed her inner thigh. Her mouth was wet and swollen against Katherine's skin. Then she found her way back to Katherine's clit, and sucked. All Katherine could do was cling to the tree and pray that when she fell apart, she would do it quietly.

And Rebecca teased her. Waited until her hips lurched with want. Moved away from her clit to suck on her labia, soft and gentle, then hard enough that she saw stars, before finally returning to where Katherine wanted her most. Her tongue rolled in small, unforgiving circles, in a careful, delicate rhythm.

When her pleasure finally arched and burst, it felt like cold rain on Katherine's hot skin. Shattering over her in a way that was sudden and yet familiar. Her breath stuttered, and she let out a trapped, singular moan, her legs squeezing Rebecca's face.

Katherine stilled, and from beneath her skirts came a dark chuckle. Rebecca kissed her inner thigh again, then pulled away and resurfaced, Katherine's skirts fluttering down around her smug expression. Something slick glistened on her chin, and she looked—

Katherine gulped. *Lord, she shall be the end of me.*

She could only watch as Rebecca wiped her mouth and said, "I have been thinking about something you said the other night." Rebecca looked up. "Have you truly never been to the ocean?"

Katherine shook her head.

"But you can swim?"

"Mostly. There is a pond up at Mosswood."

Rebecca winced, but was still smirking. She rose to her feet. "I suppose we shall have to work on that. But until then... Have you ever been on a boat?"

"No."

"You should come with me," said Rebecca. "On a clear day."

Katherine stared at her. "You have a boat?"

"I keep a boat at the Island." Rebecca's smirk took on an edge of pride. "She's all mine. A gift from my father."

Her mind spinning, Katherine managed to say, "All right. After the Hartford Ball."

"Ah." Rebecca sneered. "A night to end all nights."

"Is your sister excited? It is less than a day away."

"Call me insane, Katherine." Rebecca leaned in, trapping her against the tree. "But I do not wish to discuss my sister at present."

Some of the feeling was returning to her face. Katherine cupped Rebecca's cheek, stroked the delicate line of her cheekbone. "What can I..." She licked her dry lips. "Can I touch you?"

"If you so desire." A kiss on her nose, then her chin. Then Rebecca's fingers tangled in her hair, curling around the strands, and *pulled*. "Your chin—" Rebecca spoke in a broken whisper, rekindling the flame between them. "Makes me feral—"

And very little was said after that.

❧ 24 ❧

Hartford Hall was a lavish, rolling estate. Its facade spoke to generations of wealth — layers upon layers of history and influence coalesced into a broad and intimidating symbol of the British aristocracy. As Katherine looked up at the towering edifice, with its blazing windows and seething cheer, a sour taste pooled in the back of her throat.

Thomas stood beside her on the front drive, straightening his cuffs. Behind them, Mr. and Mrs. Knight were disembarking from the carriage, aided by Brandon and Lucas. "Well," Thomas muttered, "is Madam Kensington ready for the night to end all nights?"

"Yes." Katherine declined to mention her other motivations for the evening — namely, sneaking into Lord Hartford's library. "Though I doubt much of note will occur."

"You never know, Kitten." Thomas was smirking. "Our peers might surprise you." He glanced around, ensuring that they would not be overheard, then muttered, "I have it on good authority that Lady Hartford has stocked the garden with flamingos, and they have run quite rabid. And apparently, the smell is atrocious."

"Rabid flamingos?" Katherine watched as Miss Spencer and

her parents walked up the massive front steps. "Perhaps one of us shall be attacked."

"Either way, I doubt we have to worry about this edition selling well." Thomas dropped his voice to a whisper. "Everyone in London wants to hear what happens at the Hartford Ball."

That was an understatement. Perhaps the understatement of the century. Though whispers were abound that Lady Plumhurst's Masked Ball, or the Eventide Ball, would be the most remarkable nights of the season. Katherine would have to keep her wits about her this evening, and take diligent note of even the most mundane details.

Strange, to think that this was her power, now. To condemn or to elevate the lives of those around her. Strange, when in her life as Katherine Knight, she could do nothing much of note.

Katherine was shaken from her thoughts when Lucas offered her his elbow. She attempted to smile and allowed herself to be led into the house, her heart skipping a beat as they passed through a foyer with cathedral ceilings.

Heavens, she thought, taking in the finery and the decadence and a thousand other things. *What a night we have ahead of us.*

In many ways, it was like any other ball. She was introduced to their hosts — Lord Hartford barely even glanced at their family, and Lady Hartford's cheeks were so rosy Katherine rather suspected she would have been thrilled regardless of who had darkened her doorstep. The crowd was already thick with guests, and Katherine noted several new faces. Or, at least, new to her.

"That," Lucas murmured in her ear, nodding towards a cluster of older gentlemen, "is a collection of trustees from two of London's largest banks."

Katherine tried not to show her reaction. Money, it seemed, was an intrinsic part of this household. "What on earth could they want with an evening like this?"

Lucas shrugged. "I imagine that if Lord Hartford says jump, they ask how high."

And that was just the beginning of it. Over the course of the next hour, Katherine's brothers pointed out enough members of London's financial industry that it was a wonder the stock market was still standing. It was all Katherine could do to hide her excitement, her hope that the answers about Lord Alwyn were hidden somewhere within these walls.

As she passed from room to room, invisible amidst the crowd of dancers, a thought pressed at the back of her mind, much as it had for the past few days. Katherine's curiosity about Lord Alwyn and his family could not, it seemed, be sated, even in the face of her newfound entanglement with his youngest daughter. All too easily, she buried herself in endless and circular refrains of worry, of morbid interest. Should she feel guilty for wanting to unearth the past of Rebecca's father? Worse, should she feel guilty for not feeling guilty at all?

For Katherine, loyalty was not a foreign concept. It was bred into her bones, and ran in her blood. It was proven on a weekly basis when she helped her brother earn the income he needed to avoid a grisly fate. These were all indisputable facts — facts of life, facts of Katherine's own self. And this, perhaps, was what compelled her to pursue her line of inquiry, in spite of any misgivings she should have felt about it.

Katherine had discovered a new kind of loyalty. A loyalty to the truth. And, by extension, a loyalty to her own determination, her own conviction. She knew that there was more to Lord Alwyn than met even the most careful eye, and that she owed it to herself — possibly even to her family — to do a little digging. Knowledge like this could protect the Knights, should Lord Alwyn decide to take advantage of their friendship.

This conviction, in the end, was what propelled her away from the party, towards the shadowy, dark halls in the rear of the house.

Katherine had not been idle the past few days, in spite of her inebriation when it came to all matters involving Rebecca. She'd put a word in Rita's ear, and had received a half-dozen in return.

Snippets and whispers that sketched a fragmented but discernible picture of Hartford Hall, and where one could find the ground-floor entrance to the main servants' staircase.

A startled breath slipped from Katherine's mouth as the hidden door swung open beneath her palm. She looked into the opening, which was dimly illuminated by a light many floors above, then glanced behind her at the empty hall. From a great distance, it seemed, came the sounds of the party; laughter, conversation, music. Before her, a narrow wooden staircase ascended to the heavens, disappearing into a plush semi-darkness.

Something like excitement trembled in Katherine's gut. She gathered her skirts, rubbed her heel against the pencil stowed in her shoe, and slipped into the hidden passageway.

At once, the shadows swallowed her. If it weren't for the light from far above, she would not have been able to see her hand in front of her face. The servants, of course, would be able to flit up and down these stairs in the pitch darkness. Katherine clung to the pocked bannister and put her other hand to the smooth wall, guiding herself up to the next floor.

The door was tiny, buried in the wall, signaled only by a thin handle with smooth edges. Katherine fumbled with it for a moment or two, her heart beating a tattoo in her ears, before finally finding purchase and pulling it open.

She stepped into a hall that was a mirror reflection of the one she'd left on the ground floor. Katherine glanced around, caught her bearings, and turned right towards a massive pair of wooden doors that gleamed even in the relative darkness. Her footsteps were muffled by a thick rug underfoot, and the door's brass handle was cold to the touch. She pushed down, then forward, and the door silently swung open.

Before her bloomed the largest library she had ever seen. Built in a rich, dark wood, shelves lined the walls from the floor to a ceiling so high she had to crane her head back to see it, broken only by a balcony that wrapped around the room, creating a second floor. The room itself stretched the entire width of the house; the curtains were drawn, omitting any moonlight that might have eased her path. Through the darkness, Katherine could make out occasional formless lumps or shapes — furniture. Heavy and, she guessed, utilitarian.

Katherine took a quick breath to steady herself, smelling tobacco and paper and wood ash, then walked a few paces to the left, bumping into the sideboard. She reached into the top drawer, just as she'd been instructed, and felt the glossy surfaces of a dozen new candles. A moment later she had one in a candlestick and a match struck. As the wick flared to life, the spines of a hundred books bloomed like leaves, and the furniture gleamed.

Now, Katherine thought, eying the shelves nearest to a fearsome-looking desk. *To work.*

Lord Hartford was meticulously organized; he kept his catalog of source material in a banking ledger, each entry numbered and sorted like a proper library. But, the entries were all in a strange half-cipher. It took Katherine the better part of half an hour to crack his code, then another half-hour to track down the different materials. When she finally sat down at Lord Hartford's enormous desk, surrounded by ledgers, newspapers, business reports, and a half-dozen lit candles, sweat clung to her brow. All the while, the party continued downstairs, getting louder by the minute.

And then, Katherine sat down and began the monumental task of sifting through business and trade reports from Lord Alwyn's final year in England.

At first, Lord Hartford's records had little more to offer than what she had found in her family library. She tracked the same trend of growth, of undeniable enterprise and profit, ending in the healthy, if sudden, sale of Lord Alwyn's first business, Hobbes & Co. Undeterred, Katherine flipped to the stacks of pages enumerating imports to the London docks five years after Lord Alwyn's departure, and began scanning for ships incoming from

Amsterdam, looking for the name of Lord Alwyn's Dutch company.

There. A few ships full of textiles, salt, and a few crates of wine. Very little of value.

She flipped to the following month. Precisely thirty days later, another import of textiles, salt, wine. And then an export, from London to Amsterdam, via the same ships — wool.

Katherine frowned, then skipped ahead a month, then another month. Every thirty days, the same transaction littered the ledgers from the London harbors. The same valuation declared, over and over. But not, she noticed, in an amount that could explain Lord Alwyn's obvious wealth, even accounting for growth over a period of nearly two decades. If Katherine's arithmetic was correct, his ships seemed to make enough to break even, with a tidy, but minimal, profit. Not enough to buy his wife and daughters a collection of silk dresses and diamonds. Certainly not enough to purchase a country estate.

True, there were not many records detailing day-to-day trade in Amsterdam. But a quick search of Lord Hartford's collection of foreign newspapers showed the steady rise of the Johnson family. It was not obvious, of course, but she only had to look for mentions of 'M. Johnson' in the society and business articles. The name, English among Dutch or French, stuck out like a sore thumb. And she watched as M. Johnson climbed ladders and made business deals, sliding ever-closer to the ruling social class of Amsterdam. She watched as he married — a tasteful, short announcement — and welcomed children. And she watched when the wars with Napoleon began, and M. Johnson only seemed to profit. To profit, when countless businessmen began to fall.

Katherine paused at the end of the newspaper article, the Dutch words swimming before her eyes. The air suddenly felt very thin, and a bit chilly. The sounds of the ball did not reach her.

Is it possible? she thought, the air catching in her throat. *Is it possible that Lord Alwyn is a smuggler?*

The pieces fit together, well enough that Katherine could not refute them. How else could she explain Lord Alwyn's countless years of growth, in a time of economic woe? It was common knowledge that smugglers had seized upon the Continental System with relish, taking the sanctions as a ripe opportunity to make a quick fortune. Lord Alwyn was well-suited to it — he had a fleet of ships, countless business contacts, familiarity with British ports and officials. He was charismatic, ruthless. And he had an excellent mind for numbers.

She guessed that the ships traveling to and from London were carrying far more than what was stated on the customs ledgers. And she could only imagine what Lord Alwyn might be shipping around the Continent — he owned enough boats to reach a half-dozen ports each day, if he so wished. Perhaps he was even smuggling weapons, artillery. Opium, liquor. Anything and everything that the tariff-strangled Continent might desire.

An untold amount of time passed as Katherine sat at Lord Hartford's ridiculous desk, trying to talk herself out of such a ridiculous conclusion. There had to be another explanation for his wealth. Perhaps an inheritance from a kindly, elder member of Dutch society, an inheritance never disclosed in the papers, or announced in a turn of language beyond her comprehension.

But Rebecca had never mentioned such a thing. In fact, she had never mentioned much of anything to do with her family's wealth, or their meteoric rise. She seemed to care little for money at all, a preference demonstrated by the clothing she chose for herself and her blatant disregard for finery. If she was aware of her father's business — licit or illicit — it did not seem to trouble her. But, Katherine had to remind herself: perhaps Rebecca knew nothing of these matters. Perhaps Lord Alwyn kept his business apart from his wife and children. Perhaps he did so for the sake of their safety.

Katherine had to imagine that smuggling came with its own set of risks, of dangers. *I wonder*, she thought, slumping back into her chair, *if that is why they left Amsterdam, and married Gertrude off so quickly. If they were determined to see their daughters safely ensconced in British households before some untold consequences reared their heads.*

But a sound interrupted her thoughts. Giggling, and footsteps echoing down the hall.

Panic tore through Katherine — two people were coming towards the library, and quickly. She had seconds; there was no hope of hiding her research — she blew out the candles and dropped beneath the desk, hunching in the footwell. And then, to her mounting alarm, the library door opened, and her visitors stepped inside.

"Well, look at this." Coy, playful. "A large, empty room, far away from the party."

A chuckle, the sound of hands on fabric. "You tease me so deliciously."

The footwell was cramped and warm. Katherine's hip dug painfully into the corner of the desk, and she had to bend her neck at an awkward angle. But none of that mattered, because she recognized those voices.

Lady Sophia. And Lord Dashwood.

Her panic fizzed, and was soon replaced by a mounting horror. Katherine put her hand to her mouth, muffling her breathing and burying a squeak of surprise. For the two of them to sneak away like this, on one of the most important nights of the season—

"You tease me just as well," said Sophia. "Need I remind you of the other night?"

"No, darling." The sound of a kiss. "I believe my memory is as strong as ever."

They both went silent, their words replaced by the unmistakable sounds of kissing, of hands catching in clothing. Katherine squeezed her eyes shut, her stomach rolling. This was the last thing she wanted to hear, the last thing she wanted to know—

Sophia let out a sigh, edged with a moan. "I wish we could be alone, properly alone." A gentle thud — she sat down on a couch, and was joined by Lord Dashwood.

"Soon, darling." More kissing. "Sooner than you think."

"Not soon enough," Sophia bit out, her voice tinged with anger. "I wish we could elope."

A soft hum. "You would not do that to your family, Sophia."

"No. I would not." But she did not sound convinced.

They again ceased speaking, and Katherine tried her best to cover her ears. But the footwell only seemed to amplify the horrifying sounds coming from the other side of the desk. The wet smack of their mouths, their heavy, decadent breathing. Soft, occasional moans, and the telltale rustle of skirts. But then, to Katherine's surprise—

"Stop." Sophia's voice was low, feathery. "Francis—"

"My love?" He kissed some part of her, and Katherine tried not to think what.

"I—" Sophia's breath hitched. "I have something to tell you."

Another rustle. Katherine imagined him sitting up, then cursed herself for imagining anything at all. "Sophia." There was a serious note in Lord Dashwood's voice. "You are trembling."

"Am I?" A shaky laugh. "I cannot feel it."

A silence fell, save for Sophia's uneven breathing. A short eternity seemed to pass, and then she spoke. "I am... late."

Katherine's stomach fell to her feet, and she barely stifled a gasp. A thick roaring filled her ears, and she almost missed—

"Late?" Lord Dashwood's concern was as palpable as his confusion. "What do you mean?"

"I mean... that my... my monthly courses..." Sophia's words were like broken glass. "Are a week late."

Horror, fresh and bitter, reared in Katherine's stomach. But her limbs were frozen. All she could do was crouch beneath the desk and listen to the end of Lady Sophia's entire world.

"I..." Lord Dashwood's voice was hoarse. "I see."

"Yes." And Katherine had to commend Sophia — her voice did not tremble, and as she spoke, a newfound strength seemed to rise through her. "The sooner our engagement is announced, the better."

"Are you certain?" He spoke with a hushed reverence. "You are with child?"

A humorless chuckle. "I am not certain of anything, Francis. Except, I suppose, of my feelings for you." She sighed. "We were foolish. To think ourselves above the consequences of our desire."

Lord Dashwood did not reply. Then a strange, muffled squeak — Sophia's.

"Francis — what are you—?"

But Lord Dashwood seemed to be beyond words. There came the sounds of kissing, then more kissing, and an embrace.

"Francis—"

"If only we were on a ship." His voice was wrecked with emotion. "I would wake the captain myself, in spite of the hour."

Sophia made a sound of breathless surprise. But whatever she said next, Katherine did not hear it. Did not hear another thing that passed between the couple in the spare few minutes they remained in the library, until they departed, whispering to one another. She heard nothing because she chose to hear nothing, could not bear to hear another moment.

She waited a minute or two after their departure, to ensure that they were truly gone. Then, in the silence, Katherine crawled out from beneath the desk, her knees and her neck screaming their protest. She slumped against the side of the chair, taking a long, deep breath. The air still smelled of the smoke from her candles.

The Star of the season was pregnant. And Madam Kensington had gotten the exclusive.

❧ 25 ❧

"Chop-chop, Kat." Thomas passed by her, Scotch in hand. "Now is not the time for writers' block."

Katherine took an unsteady breath, her quill jittering in her fingers. She watched the ink catch along her cuticle, pooling in the dip of her nail bed. It would stain. Her mother would notice. Rita would know how to get rid of it in time for breakfast.

She looked up and into the flame of the candle on the desk. The flame quivered, and it seemed to taunt her.

What a terrible thing it was, to have a secret. Worse still, to find yourself the guardian of someone else's. To have another person's life at your mercy.

Perhaps she should have expected it. Perhaps she should have known that this summer, more than any other, would be a summer of deception. Of mistakes made and counted. All too frequently, Katherine found her mind returning to that fateful morning in the garden, when Lucas had confided his greatest shame. She would never forget the look in his eyes, the fear and the relief. She could just imagine seeing that same look in Sophia's gaze. Worse, she could imagine deepening it, with the worst kind of betrayal.

Katherine could not deny the facts. If Madam Kensington were to announce, or even hint at, Lady Sophia's newfound circumstances, the edition would sell like no publication in London had ever sold before. Enough to build a small fortune. Perhaps enough to pay the rest of Lucas' debt, or to put a dent in the Knights' limping finances. Any businessman — any Lord Alwyn — would make the decision in a heartbeat.

But Katherine could not. Even just the thought of betraying Lady Sophia was enough to make her stomach turn. She could not bear the idea, let alone imagine the consequences. If Lord and Lady Alwyn found out the truth about their Star—

No. She would not follow this path again. These thoughts had tormented her, ceaselessly and ruthlessly, for the past night and day, robbing her of sleep and appetite. For hours after the Hartford Ball, Katherine had remained awake and wretched, tossing and turning until midday. She felt feverish, ill, strung like a cheap violin. Tense and ready to snap.

How could she even question it? How could she even entertain the notion of betraying Rebecca's sister? The fact that she could was perhaps the most troubling matter of all.

"Kat." This from Lucas, who was watching her from the nearest couch. His shrewd gaze was unfaltering. "You seem discomposed."

Katherine took an uneasy breath and freshened her quill. "The Hartford ball left much to be desired."

"Did it? I seem to recall adequate music, decent food, and an ungodly amount of wine." His words were dry, pointed. "I also seem to recall my sister disappearing for half the night."

"Thank goodness Mother and Father had a bit too much wine," said Brandon to Katherine. "Otherwise, they would have had your head on a pike."

"You must have overheard something worthwhile," said

Thomas, leaning against the desk. "In all your time away."

Katherine's stomach twisted, and she did not look up from her work. Her brothers had no knowledge of her pursuits in Lord Hartford's library, and she had no intention of telling them. Lucas' disapproval alone would be fuel for a lifetime of grief. And she could understand why — prodding at the matters of a suspected smuggler was dangerous enough. When taken with the fact of her family's attachment to the Alwyns, the risk was undeniable. The idea that she would even *entertain* such a risk spoke to her own selfish curiosity. A fresh wave of disgust welled in Katherine's throat, and she swallowed hard, unable to dislodge it.

How was she any better than Lucas at the gambling tables? Perhaps she was not, in the end.

"I gathered little of consequence," she said. "It was a very mundane evening. I snuck away in an effort to try and bolster my minimal findings, without luck."

"I saw Lady Pembroke make a bit of a fool of herself," said Thomas. "She seems keen to be wed, with little concern for who it is she meets at the altar."

Lucas snorted. "Cavendish is just as terrible. I believe he has no less than three young ladies at his beck and call, with no intention of making up his mind."

"Write whatever you can," Thomas said to Katherine, nudging her with his elbow. "Not every edition will be our best."

"What about our Star?" said Brandon. "Any whispers on a match?"

"They will have to announce any day now." Lucas stood up, wandering over to the window. "She and that idiot Dashwood could hardly be any more obvious."

Thomas scoffed. "Lord and Lady Alwyn would never agree to that match. Sophia could have anyone she pleased, without settling for Dashwood."

"Why, Thomas," said Brandon, coy. "Do I detect a hint of jealousy?"

Color flared in Thomas' cheeks, and Katherine could not help staring at him. "What you detect is outrage," Thomas replied. "Justifiable outrage, might I add. If the Star of the season settles for a man at the bottom of the barrel, what hope do the rest of the young ladies have?"

Lucas snorted. "You are so delightfully full of shit, Thomas. It is a wonder you do not burst at the seams."

"Forgive me for thinking of our own sister," Thomas fired back. "The Star sets the example, and Katherine deserves her best chance at a worthwhile match."

A nonexistent match, Katherine could not help but think. The gentlemen seemed to avoid her like the plague. Not that she particularly minded. Not when she had Rebecca in her bed, in her shadow, in her mouth. She did not mind at all.

"Write about Lady Pembroke," said Lucas, returning to the couch. "She will love it, and we should endear ourselves to our peers."

"What is this 'we' nonsense?" said Thomas. "You have never so much as lifted a quill—"

On and on they went, bickering like crows. But Katherine paid them little heed. She put her quill to the paper, and began to write.

And between one moment and the next, Lady Sophia's secret was condemned to dust.

❧

London, it seemed, could occasionally remember that it was, in fact, summer.

A brilliant, dazzling sun beat down upon Katherine's shoulders as she wound her way along the docks, following a hand-drawn map no bigger than her palm. She was surrounded by groaning, bobbing wooden ships, some of them larger than buildings, and the air reeked of salt, fish, and something bitter. Katherine squinted against the light, her skin hazed with sweat, and checked the map once more. At the end of the dock, she turned left, then—

"Ahoy!"

Katherine halted near a set of steps, looking down. Seeing nothing apart from the dock, the water, and the deck of a ship, she looked up instead. And nearly fainted.

"Rebecca!" The word came in a very unbecoming shriek. "What are you doing up there?!"

Rebecca laughed, jolly and uncaring that she was a good twenty feet off the ground. She swung around a rope and began to climb down the enormous mast.

Katherine could only watch, horror-struck, as Rebecca returned to the deck of her ship. "Come aboard!" Rebecca called, waving at her.

Katherine gulped and went down the steps. The dock seemed to sway beneath her feet, and she tried not to think about it. She was already a little nauseated at the prospect of seeing Rebecca for the first time since she'd overheard Sophia's news.

This close, the river seemed quite green and clear — odd, when she was accustomed to thinking of it as gray and foul. She could see barnacles and lichen clinging to the hull of Rebecca's boat, which was less of a boat and more of a—

"Ship." Katherine rounded on Rebecca, who was leaning against the railing of the ship's deck, grinning. "Rebecca, this is a *ship*."

"Aye, sailor."

"When you said you had a *boat*..." Katherine hovered on the dock, a good foot away from the gangplank. "I imagined a sort of... dinghy."

Rebecca gave an exaggerated gasp. "She did not mean it, dearest." She seemed to be speaking to — and stroking — the ship. "My lady is but an ignorant landlubber."

"Shall I leave you two alone, then?"

Rebecca's grin resurfaced. "Come aboard, I've got everything ship-shape."

"Are you going to speak in nautical puns the entire time?"

"Not in the least." Rebecca extended her hand over the gangplank, and what a narrow gangplank it was. It appeared to bob in the air, in tandem with the gentle current, and Rebecca seemed to notice Katherine's hesitation: "It is as easy as anything, Katherine, I swear."

"All right," Katherine replied, unconvinced. But then an enormous thatch of fur hopped up onto the ship's railing and gave a yowl like a breaking tree branch.

Katherine stumbled backwards, out of Rebecca's reach. She gaped at the creature, speechless.

Rebecca, meanwhile, only chuckled. "Oh, come along, that's just Meddie!"

"Meddie?!"

"Medusa. Ship's cat. A bit long in the tooth, but still the best mouser I've ever had." And then Rebecca began *scratching the creature's head.* An odd noise came out of Medusa's chest, a noise reminiscent of a rock fall. "She is harmless, Katherine."

Katherine gave a high, tremulous laugh. "Not if you are a mouse, apparently."

Rebecca was delighted. "Are you frightened of cats?"

"No," said Katherine, a little too quickly. "No. Cats and I just... get along best... from a distance. A long distance," she added, as Medusa walked along the railing, getting closer to her.

Rebecca gave a hearty laugh and scooped up Medusa, who looked rather like a mop head. She put the cat down at the other end of the ship, then returned to the gangplank with her hand outstretched, a familiar gleam in her eye.

Katherine took a deep breath, then Rebecca's hand. And slowly walked on board.

Right away a familiar scent overcame her, pouring from every inch of the deck. Metal and oak — *wood polish*, she realized now, seeing the rich, gleaming planks. She looked at Rebecca, and could envision her polishing every piece of the ship by hand. Rebecca looked back at her, and Katherine realized that Rebecca was completely at ease.

"Welcome aboard." Rebecca squeezed her hand, leaning closer. They were still within view of everyone from the dock, but it was not a busy day, and in her trousers and shirt, Rebecca looked like a man. Katherine met that dazzling gaze, and felt a tremor from her hips all the way to her toes.

"Does she have a name? This ship?"

"Anna Maria. After the first woman to attend university in Amsterdam."

Katherine let her surprise show. "Is that an aspiration of yours?"

Rebecca snorted, her grin edged with humor. "Hardly. But I rather like the idea of being the first woman to do something."

Of course. Katherine took a few steps, and was surprised by how steady the deck was beneath her feet. "Tell me about the Anna Maria. Is she a recent gift?"

"Yes, for my eighteenth birthday. I only had her for six months before we left Amsterdam."

"And what do you do with her?" Katherine ran her hand along the nearest banister, admiring its smooth, glassy surface. "Sail the Thames?"

"On a fine day, certainly. But most of the time, I run errands for my father, just as I did in Amsterdam."

Errands. The word caught in Katherine's mind like a bee sting, and she had to wonder if Rebecca was hinting at something more... salacious. Would Lord Alwyn really involve his own daughter in his black market trade? "You can sail this ship yourself?"

"I keep a small crew, though I had little need of them today." Rebecca's hand, sliding around Katherine's waist.

Katherine trembled but smiled, trying to hide her unease.

"You are not frightened, then? Of being out on the water?"

Rebecca looked at her, something flashing in her eyes. Something observant, but not yet wary. "You ask many questions, Katherine."

Katherine gulped, and prayed that her anxiety did not show in her face.

Rebecca squeezed her hips, and her voice softened. "Are you nervous?"

"Me? Never." But Katherine could not help glancing up at the mast, where Rebecca had been suspended with such gaiety. It was a welcome distraction from the horrible truth of what she knew, and what she could never say. Then, a hand on her chin, tilting her head back down to earth.

The warm heat of Rebecca's touch was matched only by the spark in her gaze. She leaned closer, her lips parted, as if to drink Katherine in.

"I would take you anywhere in the world, Katherine." She spoke in a low, reverent tone that made Katherine's toes curl with delight. "Anywhere you wished."

A smile broke free before Katherine could harness it. "You say the most ridiculous things."

"And I mean them." Rebecca was looking at her in a way that defied words. "Katherine."

Something like wonder caught in Katherine's chest, and it took all of her restraint not to close the distance between them and kiss Rebecca, there in the sparkling light of the Thames.

Rebecca squeezed her hand again. "Would you like to go below-deck?"

In spite of everything, Katherine rolled her eyes. "Rebecca—"

"I know, I know, I could not resist—"

Rebecca led her across the deck, towards a darkened doorway. Katherine had to duck as they went down a short flight of stairs, Rebecca's hand her only guide through the shadows. A few lamps burned at intervals, illuminating a series of passages, and a snug space that had to be living quarters for the crew. But Rebecca continued on, leading her around a corner, and there came another door. Behind it lay a cozy cabin built for one, including a bed. With tangled sheets and blankets.

Katherine's mouth went dry at the sight of it. Even now, after all the time they'd spent together, each new meeting brought its own tangle of anxiety and delight, as if it were their first encounter all over again. She looked up as Rebecca closed the door and tugged aside a shade, revealing one blazing porthole, then another. The white sunlight cut through the room like a blade, illuminating the sparse furnishings. Katherine saw a miniature ink pressing of a city — she guessed Amsterdam — on a shelf by the bed, along with a chipped enamel mug, a chess rook, and a small threadbare teddy. On the tiny desk in the corner lay a few books, a scattered pile of papers, a forgotten quill, a half-empty bottle of rum.

This, it seemed, was Rebecca's home.

And when Rebecca looked at her, it was with an expression of acute want, of a passion so deep that it rattled Katherine to her core. Rebecca paused for a moment, as if to savor it, then closed the distance between them and kissed Katherine, pushing her up against the wall.

And Katherine let her. *This,* she thought, as Rebecca sucked on her tongue, *this is what I know.*

It was different from all the other times. Slower, yet faster. For all their shared escapades, Katherine and Rebecca had never been fully nude in front of each other. But there, in the depths of the ship, that changed.

When Rebecca's hands went to Katherine's stays, Katherine shook. Then she shook again when Rebecca touched her like she was gold, like she would melt if handled too roughly.

They said little, if anything. Instead they spoke by kissing, gasping, pushing and pulling. Closer and closer, until all Katherine knew was the taste of Rebecca's skin, and the incessant, plush heat of her mouth. She closed her eyes and longed to bury herself in this, in the ecstasy of Rebecca's body. To escape, to hide, perhaps forever.

When the time came, it was Katherine who pressed Rebecca into the sheets, straddling her as she ground their bodies together. Nerves flew through her — she hardly knew what she was doing, but Rebecca was watching her in this way that made her feel—

Rebecca gasped as Katherine lurched, clinging to her hips. Katherine could smell her, brilliant and metallic, now mixed with something sharp and salty, and she bent down, kissing Rebecca until neither of them could breathe.

Rebecca had her hands in Katherine's hair, her face against Katherine's cheek. And Katherine felt her surprise as she slowly slid down Rebecca's body.

"Katherine." Rebecca's voice was heavy with pleasure. "You do not need—"

"I know." Katherine pressed a kiss to her inner thigh, nosed the curls at the apex of her legs. "But I very much want."

And she let that want guide her, pulling her into Rebecca's body like a siren's song. For the first time in her life, Katherine decided not to think at all, but rather to feel, and to trust that, in spite of her inexperience, she would find a way to make Rebecca feel as she did. Not just pleasured, but seen.

To her surprise, when she first put her mouth to Rebecca's sex, Rebecca shivered, her belly quaking beneath Katherine's hand. Katherine looked up at her, and Rebecca met her gaze with a half-lidded look of pure heat. But there was something more. Something tender. Something vulnerable.

Everything shrank within the scope of that look. Everything became small and unimportant. Even Katherine's guilt.

The moment held between them, silent and full, then Katherine rolled her tongue, Rebecca moaned, and it broke.

❦

"Ah, Kitten." Lucas looked up when she came into the dining room. "You are just in time."

"Oh?" Katherine took her seat and reached for the toast and bacon. "For what?"

"The morning news." Lucas flapped his newspaper most dramatically, earning an eye-roll from Mr. Knight. "There has been an announcement."

"And are you going to share it, or force me to duel you for the paper?"

"It is wonderful news," said Mrs. Knight, beaming. "The best."

"Lady Sophia is engaged." Lucas was smirking, and only his siblings knew why. "To Lord Dashwood from Kent."

For a moment, Katherine could not muster a single sound, let alone a word. A thousand thoughts tumbled through her head, and all she could hope was that they did not show on her face. But she recovered, smiled, and said, "The first of the season, and what a match!"

"They are a lovely couple," agreed Mrs. Knight. "Their children will be beautiful."

Katherine managed a chuckle, a wave of nausea going through her stomach. "Indeed, Mother. Beautiful."

"Their wedding is set for Saturday next," said Lucas, handing the paper back to Mr. Knight. "A special license, apparently. One does wonder why."

"Because they are in love, Lucas!" Mrs. Knight tutted. "Honestly. Your cynicism will come back to bite you one day."

Thomas stood up from the table, nearly knocking over his tea. "Excuse me." His voice was brittle. "I have an appointment." And with that he swept out of the room, leaving his breakfast untouched.

Katherine watched him leave, then glanced at the newspaper in her father's hands, making special note of the date.

This was it. The day that she became a liar.

INTERLUDE V — WHITEHILL MANOR

Rebecca glanced down the hall, relieved to find it empty. She crept along, balancing a plate in her hand, until she reached her sister's door. One final glance, just to ensure that she had not been followed, then she put the key to the lock and slipped inside.

Sophia gasped at her from her seat by the window. "Rebecca! How—?!"

"I lifted the key off Mrs. Fawn." Rebecca closed and locked the door then, with a flash of inspiration from Katherine, tossed a blanket from the bed onto the floor, blocking the gap between the door and the threshold. "Have you eaten?"

Sophia gave her a look that was part fondness, part irritation. "A few hours ago, yes."

"Good. Then you should eat again." Rebecca pushed the plate of food into her sister's lap and sat down across from her, taking in her appearance. Sophia was dressed, her hair swept into a tidy bun, her hands steady. She sat in the clear, gray light from the window, leaving nothing to the imagination. "You look tired."

"Believe it or not, being confined to one's room hardly bolsters the spirits."

Rebecca winced. "She will come around, Saintie. Sooner rather than later."

Sophia gave a hollow laugh and picked up a slice of plum. When she spoke again, it was in Dutch. *"You say that either out of kindness or pity, but not honesty. You know our mother as well as I do, Rebecca. She will never forgive me."*

"Do you need it? Her forgiveness?"

"I suppose not. I never meant to hurt her, Rebecca." Sophia ate the piece of plum, the juice catching at the corner of her mouth. *"What I did was foolish, I know. But in the moment—"*

"Oh, good God, please spare me the details—"

"In the moment," Sophia went on, flashing her a pointed look, *"it felt like the best... the most natural thing in the world."* She sighed. *"Of course, I was not thinking of the potential consequences."*

Rebecca watched her sister. *"You truly love him?"*

"From the moment I met him." Sophia caught Rebecca's look and smirked. *"I know you will say it is ridiculous, absurd. But I cannot explain it, Rebecca. I can simply tell you how it felt."*

"And how did it feel?"

Sophia paused, looking out the window at the rain. It was a cold, unseasonable day — the precise opposite of the day before. Sophia's hand drifted to rest low on her belly as she spoke, and Rebecca wondered if she was aware of it. *"It was not like... a lightning bolt, or the earth moving, or any of those silly things you read about in love stories."* She met Rebecca's gaze. *"It was like a rock dropping into a pool of water. A solitary moment, rippling out to touch everything else. I met him, and knew that I would never be the same. It was almost as if we had known each other before, in a forgotten life, and were meeting again."* She shook her head. *"I felt as if I recognized him, Rebecca."*

An unexpected wave of emotion throbbed in Rebecca's throat. "That sounds nice," she managed to say.

Sophia shot her a playful, teasing look. "Oh? I was expecting you to call me a fool, or a half-wit." She took up another piece of plum, bit into it with relish. "You never were one for romance."

Rebecca scoffed, grinning as the well of emotion faded, along with the hazy memory of Katherine laughing on the deck of the Anna Maria, her face gleaming in the sunlight. "You do me a disservice, Saintie." A pause, then: "Can I name the baby?"

"No," said Sophia, without missing a beat. In Dutch: "*There may not even be a baby. It is too early to know for certain — all this fuss might be for nothing.*"

"*What is certain is that I will be the best aunt in the entire world,*" said Rebecca. "*Leagues ahead of Gertie. Can I take the baby on the boat?*"

"*Not if you want to keep your hair, no.*"

"Aw, but Saintie, we're a sailing family, you have to—"

"No." And now, Sophia's voice had an edge. "I do not want my child involved with any of Father's enterprises."

God. There it was again — a jab, right in Rebecca's chest. But she could not muster any surprise — she would not want her own children anywhere near the family business. She tried to smile. "But what about a trip across the Channel with his favorite aunt?"

"Perhaps," Sophia allowed, shooting her that look again. "*It might not be a boy.*"

"I think it is a boy."

"It might be a girl, Rebecca."

"Nah, it's a boy."

Before Sophia could reply, there came the sound of footsteps in the hall. A sure and steady stride — unmistakeable. Rebecca leapt out of her chair, grabbed the blanket, and flattened herself to the wall behind the door. She caught a glimpse of Sophia's wide, frightened eyes before the lock turned and the door swung open, trapping her against the wall.

Rebecca could not see their mother, but her anger was palpable, following her into the room like a second shadow. "Your father and I have discussed it, and we have decided that you may attend tomorrow night's festivities."

"The opera?" Sophia's voice was hard, but she could not hide her surprise. "Why such a sudden shift in attitude, Mother? I thought I was to be confined until the wedding."

"You are," said Lady Alwyn, "apart from the most important events. And," she added, with obvious reluctance, "the occasional supervised public appearance with Lord Dashwood." His name was spoken with such venom it was a surprise to Rebecca that Lady Alwyn did not keel over on the spot. "The day after tomorrow, you will promenade with him in the park. His parents will be there, along with his younger brother. When you are with him, Sophia, you will not touch," she went on. "Or speak beyond pleasantries."

"I see." Sophia's voice was cool. "And what of the wedding? I can hardly plan it from within these four walls."

"I will handle the wedding. You should be thankful you are having one at all."

"I am thankful," Sophia replied. "For more than you can imagine."

But this kindness did not seem to touch their mother. Rebecca held her breath, forcing herself to keep as still as possible. One wrong move would instantly reveal her.

"The modiste will be here tomorrow afternoon," Lady Alwyn said. "To fit you for your wedding gown and *trousseau*."

"Lovely," said Sophia, still in that determined, amiable way. "And tonight? Might I take supper with the rest of the family?"

"No." Lady Alwyn's voice was ice. "You lost that privilege when you spread your legs for the first idiot to kiss your hand and call you pretty. I shall have Mrs. Fawn bring you something on a tray." With that, she left the room, closing and locking the door behind her.

Rebecca stayed where she was until their mother's footsteps faded, unable to look away from her sister's face. She had expected to see nothing short of devastation in Sophia's features, but instead they were flat, calm, unaffected. Sophia met her gaze, and for a moment, in spite of her simple dress and unadorned hair, she reminded Rebecca of a figurehead, bold and placid, floating above the turbulent rage of a stormy sea.

Perhaps that was why Rebecca dropped the blanket, crossed the room, and wrapped her arms around her sister, burying her nose in Sophia's shoulder. Sophia smelled like plums and lilacs, and after a moment, she returned the embrace.

"This will pass," Rebecca managed to say, her eyes burning. She squeezed them shut, unable to imagine yet another day without Sophia at the dining table, or a world without her.

"Of course it will," Sophia said, her words muffled by Rebecca's shirt. She turned her head, kissing Rebecca's cheek, a simple maternal gesture that dropped Rebecca's stomach to her feet. "But first, we must get through the wedding."

WINTER 1812-1813

26

A heavy wind curled around Mosswood Heath, rattling the window panes in the south-facing wall. It carried the scent of forest damp and holly, brittle and heavy in the crisp winter air. Katherine listened to its doleful howl, and shivered beneath her thick woolen shawl. But her shiver was one of nerves, not cold.

Beside her, Brandon muttered something under his breath and checked his pocket watch. "They are late."

Katherine did not shift her gaze from the windows. The panes were ancient and provided a warped view of the snow-dusted front drive, but she could tell that there was no sign of a carriage. "There could be traffic on the road."

Brandon snorted. "In Durham?" He looked behind them, up the main staircase. "Where are Mother and Father? I thought we were to make a welcoming committee."

As if on cue, there came a thud from above, and Mr. and Mrs. Knight appeared, hurrying down the stairs. Mrs. Knight, pinning her shawl, frowned at them. "Have they not yet arrived?"

"No," said Brandon, while Katherine sighed. "Kat thinks there might be traffic on the road."

"At this time of day?" said Mr. Knight. "Surely not."

Mrs. Knight looked at the grandfather clock mounted opposite the front door. "If they have not appeared within the half hour, we shall send Lucas and Bran with the pony and trap."

But there was no need. Through the swirled glass, Katherine caught a glimpse of a dark mass coming up the drive. She swallowed past the sudden lump in her throat, the heartbeat roaring in her ears. "They are here."

Time, which crawled before, now passed with infinite speed. Katherine did not hear the chatter of her family, did not notice when Mrs. Knight tugged Lucas in from the drawing room. She only had eyes for the carriage, and all too quickly, it grew in size, larger and larger until it rolled to a halt before the front door. Katherine could see the horses and their steaming breath in the frigid air — she heard rather than saw the carriage door opening, a set of feet approaching. As if by magic, Brooks appeared, stoic in his winter wool, and opened the door.

And in that instant, Katherine ceased breathing.

Rebecca glowed at them from the threshold, her face shining, her eyes gleaming with delight. She met Katherine's gaze with a warmth so deep it was almost tangible, fixing Katherine to the spot upon which she stood — a fresh heat burst in Katherine's gut, face, and feet. She could hardly believe that this was happening, that it was not a dream.

"The Lady Rebecca Alwyn," said Brooks, unamused.

"Rebecca!" Mrs. Knight swept her up in an embrace, kissing her cheek. "How glad we are to see you! Come in, come in!"

"I am so thrilled to be here." Breathless, Rebecca let Lucas and Brandon kiss her hand and bow in greeting. "And cold!"

"You're shivering!" said Lucas. "Brooks, would you escort Lady Rebecca's maid to the kitchens?"

"Certainly." Brooks stepped outside and closed the front door, pushing another gust of chilly air over the family. Rebecca shivered afresh, and Katherine ached to hold her.

But she settled for a curtsy, and a smile. Rebecca returned both, with a teasing look in her eye, as Mrs. Knight draped her own shawl over Rebecca's shoulders. "Upon my word," said Mrs. Knight. "You are dressed for a Mediterranean winter, not a Scottish one!"

"I thought I had an adequate wardrobe," Rebecca said, curling into Mrs. Knight's touch. "But it appears I was quite wrong."

"Come through at once," said Mr. Knight, ushering them all into the drawing room. "You must sit by the fire."

It was nothing short of surreal, seeing Rebecca take a seat on the Mosswood hearth, a brilliant figure amongst the deep wooden paneling and hanging tapestries, features and fixtures that were so familiar to Katherine, and now seemed so alien. Mr. Knight and Lucas draped Rebecca in thick wool blankets the family only reached for on the coldest nights of the year, and Brandon took off her sodden shoes, wrapping her feet in yet another blanket.

Rebecca gave a feeble laugh, and Katherine saw now just how cold she was — the tips of her fingers were pale. "Goodness, what a lot of fuss. I feel quite the damsel in distress."

"Perish the thought, dear." Mrs. Knight poured the tea, and splashed a healthy measure of Scotch into Rebecca's cup. "Everyone is equal under the cold."

"Now." Mr. Knight settled in his usual armchair. "Tell us of your journey, and eat at least a dozen biscuits to get your color up."

Rebecca obliged, and Katherine took a seat upon the nearest sofa. She listened dutifully as Rebecca told them of the roads and the inns — rough, but welcoming — and of how surprised she was by the northern countryside. "It is vast," she said, her gaze finding Katherine's. Katherine, who was watching her mouth, hardly noticed. "And wild."

"It can be," said Mrs. Knight, smiling. "But we shall get you some proper wool, and a fresh skirt for the ceilidh."

Rebecca blinked at her. "Beg pardon?"

"The ceilidh," said Lucas, grinning. "A dance, Rebecca, though rather unlike the diversions you left behind in London."

"The next village over has one every Christmas," said Brandon. "It is high entertainment, I assure you, and we shall teach you the dances beforehand."

Rebecca grinned. "I cannot wait."

Katherine tried not to stare at her, but the action was compulsive, something she could hardly control. Seeing Rebecca for the first time in months was like receiving a glass of water after weeks in the desert. She all but drank Rebecca in, taking in every detail of her features, her hands.

"And how fares your family?" said Mrs. Knight. "When Katherine told us of the circumstances, we could hardly believe our ears."

Rebecca's grin stuttered, as if jilted by the reminder. "They are well," she said. "Sophia has renounced all sisterly affection and cannot stand the sight of me. Apparently, my attempts to look after her are unnecessary as well as stifling."

Mr. Knight twinkled. "Ah, yes. The joys of expecting. I remember it well." He shot Mrs. Knight a cheeky glance.

"And your parents?" said Mrs. Knight, ignoring her husband.

"I believe they are recovering. But I have not heard from them since I left London."

Mrs. Knight let out a sigh of relief. "With any luck, you shall have a letter from them within the next few days."

Rebecca nodded, and Brandon refreshed her cup of tea. "I must offer you my thanks once again, Mr. and Mrs. Knight. You have been quite generous in allowing me to stay here."

"Not at all, dear," said Mrs. Knight. "It is no trouble at all — we could not bear the thought of you all alone in some London hotel. And I'm sure my children will be glad of the company."

"We are indeed." Lucas smiled. "Your presence is a welcome change of pace."

"You flatter me," said Rebecca, looking around at them. "And for the sake of preserving honesty in our friendship, I will admit that when the door opened, I hardly recognized you all."

The Knights chuckled, and Katherine understood what she meant. Dressed in their winter wool and tartan, the Knights looked nothing like they had a few months before in London. The men had grown their beards, and Lucas was still wearing his tall boots from that morning's excursions.

"You are seeing us in our natural element," said Lucas. "The Knights, *al fresco*."

The conversation continued, winding around the difficult topic of Rebecca's family, until the clock in the hall chimed the hour. Mrs. Knight took the opportunity to say, "Lady Rebecca, why don't you have a rest before supper? Rita will make a new outfit ready for you, and you can take the time to unpack your things."

"That would be wonderful, Mrs. Knight."

Rita was sent for, and she escorted Rebecca upstairs. Katherine watched her leave with a twinge in her chest, aching to follow her, to reach for her, to kiss her—

"Poor thing." Mrs. Knight sighed. "Did you see her hands? To think that her mother allowed her to travel with such inadequate clothing—"

"Her mother is recovering from the 'flu," Brandon replied. "I doubt she was terribly concerned with Rebecca's luggage."

"Still, I find it strange that she is so unprepared. Amsterdam's climate is not very different from London's, after all." Mrs. Knight stood up. "Kat and I shall go and see about supper. Lucas, Bran." She turned to them. "See if you can drag your brother out of the hills."

And like that, Lady Rebecca was welcomed to Mosswood Heath.

Supper passed pleasantly enough, and gave Katherine ample time to think. To think, and to remember the world she had behind left in London, a world that felt like another person's life.

Once Sophia's engagement was announced, the season passed at a frightening and break-neck pace. Now, to Katherine, it was little more than a blur — a blur of cut-throat rumors, wedding whispers, and a flurry of other engagements. Rebecca became even busier than usual, conscripted by Lady Alwyn into planning the wedding and playing the dutiful younger sister. She would sneak away very late at night, slipping into Katherine's bedroom for a few hours of simple, decadent pleasure. Once or twice, she even fell asleep in Katherine's bed, and barely managed to escape before Rita's arrival. Over the past few months, when Katherine had lain alone beneath her sheets, she would close her eyes and imagine that stolen time, slack and blissful with Rebecca's body pressed into hers, Rebecca's arm draped over her waist.

Not once did the topic of Sophia's condition arise, not with Rebecca. When giving a reason for the engagement, Rebecca shrugged and stated that the couple did not want to wait any longer, and their parents were eager to see the match through. Katherine never pressed the matter, and never revealed what she knew. But she could not help her gaze from wandering to Sophia's midsection whenever Sophia happened to appear in public, which was a rare occurrence in the lead-up to the wedding. Katherine wondered whether Lady Alwyn was keeping her under a tight watch, perhaps even under lock and key. She would not have been surprised.

The sudden engagement and all its consequences gave Madam Kensington plenty of material, and copies flew across London like the birds of St. Paul's. Within a week, Lady Hearsay, whose readership had already dwindled to pitiful numbers, vanished, and never again reared her head. And the money... The money was close to unbelievable. By the end of the season, Lucas was able to pay off the vast majority of what he owed the Tyndales, and sign a promissory note to guarantee the remainder, provided that he took on no further debt in the meantime. Even now, all these months later, Katherine could hardly believe that she and her brothers had managed to pull off such a maneuver. Stranger still had been the moment when Katherine had rested her quill for the last time that summer, not to pick it up again as Madam Kensington for another eight months.

Sophia's wedding to Lord Dashwood had been the event of the year, with the reception hosted by her older sister, Gertrude, and her new husband, Lord Cawdor, at their London residence. Lord and Lady Alwyn spared no expense, and invited the entire Knight family to the reception. The party was uproarious, full of every proper indulgence, including a cake so light and sweet Brandon nearly wept at the table. And when one of the guests tripped over a fresh crate of new Parisian glass, smashing it to pieces, the celebrations only paused for the briefest moment, as if nothing more relevant than a stray breeze had occurred. Over the course of the evening, Katherine watched Lucas dance with half the young ladies of London, breaking hearts left and right, and wondered if he would ever fall in love. He seemed to be immune to every smile, every shining look, every quip and flirtation. Sometimes, she would see him looking across the room, his gaze lost and unfocused, as if he were searching for something he could not see.

Thomas, however, was the brutal opposite. He danced and played along, but with a look so sour it was a wonder he did not curdle the wine. He spoke in low, truncated sentences, snapped at the slightest provocation, and began spending long stretches of time out of the house. For weeks, Mr. and Mrs. Knight could do little apart from observe him in shock and confusion, until one evening when Thomas failed to appear for supper — Lucas looked at them and said, "Well, is it any wonder? He was utterly besotted with Lady Sophia."

Time, it seemed, did not aid in the healing of Thomas' wounds. Upon their return to Mosswood Heath, he brooded, and disappeared for hours at a time, wandering the land like a shepherd in search of his sheep. His countenance, surly and dark, rarely showed any glimmer of a smile, let alone a laugh. Brandon told Katherine he was giving Thomas until Boxing Day to sort himself out, after which point, a trial by combat was warranted.

Once Sophia was married and off to her new country home, her parents and younger sister left London for Brighton with Gertrude and Lord Cawdor. Katherine could remember the day of their departure all too clearly — Rebecca had slid out of her bed just as dawn kissed the horizon, pressing her mouth to Katherine's shoulder, squeezing her hand with such urgency that tears had caught in the back of Katherine's throat. She had looked up into Rebecca's face, into the eyes that she knew so well, and found herself speechless.

What could they say to one another, with so much left unspoken?

Thus, Katherine had found herself quite alone, and her bed quite cold. Were it not for the persistent distraction of Madam Kensington, and the impish delights of her fellow debutantes, she would have become nothing short of miserable, wracked with a feverish longing so acute she could hardly sleep.

She and Rebecca began writing to one another, sneaking in snippets of flirtation between bland sentences about the weather and the so-called delights of Brighton. Katherine guessed, perhaps correctly, that their trip was related to Lord Alwyn's business matters, and an effort to avoid any lingering rumors about Sophia's condition. Leaving London was a clever decision, perhaps the smartest decision the Alwyns could have made. But this knowledge did little to dampen her frustration, which was encouraged by Rebecca's creative turns of phrase.

I think of you in the night, Rebecca had written one choice evening. *I think of you naked, splashed in moonlight, gleaming and wet from the weight of my mouth. I can taste you, Katherine, even in my dreams.*

Needless to say, it was enough to make Katherine's head spin, and to inspire a steep learning curve with the abilities of her own hand. But with every word, every splash of ink, she found herself falling further and further down the dark, rough passage of uncertainty, with little encouragement or hope in sight.

Realizing that one is quite in love with another person can be startling, even brutal. For Katherine, the experience was only heightened by their distance, and by the constant doubt she felt in all matters pertaining to Rebecca. Leaving London and saying goodbye to Madam Kensington removed all worthy distractions from Katherine's sphere, and she found herself reliving every moment she had shared with Rebecca, reliving and questioning and wondering. Was their... attachment... one of convenience, of pure lust? Did affection, or fondness, or anything resembling love even factor into Rebecca's understanding of their relationship? Or — as Katherine dreaded to imagine — was she little more than a passing amusement to Rebecca, who lived a far more adventurous and indulgent life than Katherine could ever imagine?

But all such concerns faded in the face of the Alwyns' return to London. Rebecca, who had taken a detour en route from Brighton to visit Sophia, was spared the bout of 'flu that overcame her parents, Gertrude, and Lord Cawdor. Unable to return to her family home in London, and unable to remain with Sophia for the course of her confinement, Rebecca had written to Katherine with a plea for help.

As soon as Mrs. Knight heard of Rebecca's circumstances, there was not even a question of what should happen. Rebecca, who had no other relations in England, should not spend Christmas alone when there was a northern family ready to receive her.

And now, finally, seven months after their first encounter in the palace, and five long months after the Alwyns' departure from

London, Katherine had the surreal experience of watching Rebecca, dressed in a woolen skirt, hang a piece of mistletoe in the doorway of the Mosswood drawing room.

"How splendid!" Rebecca grinned at them, hopping out of Lucas' handhold. "Now, am I to kiss you all?"

"If you insist," said Lucas, returning her grin. "After, it would be impolite for us to refuse."

"I suppose I shall have to follow tradition," said Rebecca, mockingly contemplative. "After all, you might finally turn into a prince." With that, she gave Lucas a kiss on the cheek, then Brandon, before rounding on Katherine with a gleam in her eye.

Something caught in Katherine's throat. "Oh, oh don't—"

"You heard your brother, Katherine." Rebecca came towards her, as fierce as an arrow. "It is tradition, after all." She leaned in and kissed Katherine on the cheek, her mouth warm and brief, and it took everything Katherine had not to lean into it, not to weep.

Rebecca stepped away, then winked at her. It was the closest they had been to one another since her arrival, and Katherine had to curl her hand into a fist to stop herself from reaching for Rebecca's waist.

She took a deep, steady breath. Scotch, ash, snow, mistletoe. These scents, the hallmarks of her life at Mosswood, grounded her, and reminded her of the circumstances.

"So, boys." Rebecca rounded on Katherine's brothers. "Give me the tour?"

With Mr. and Mrs. Knight in bed, the house was left to the mercy of their children. Katherine followed as Lucas and Brandon led Rebecca through the dark and cozy house, while the wind groaned outside. She heard little of what they said, and paid little attention to their three extra shadows — Nettle, Briar, and Maple, whose eager panting echoed down the halls.

"You would have met them earlier," said Brandon, after noting the way Rebecca watched the hounds in a wary manner. "But they were out in the stables when you arrived, and Mother insists upon keeping them at bay during supper."

"I can hardly imagine why."

Lucas smiled, pausing beside an ancient tapestry depicting a hunt. They were in the north end of the house, not far from Katherine's own bedroom. "They are as gentle as babes, Rebecca, perhaps even more so. Look." He reached for Maple, who he had raised from a pup, and lifted her by her front paws, ruffling her ears and kissing her muzzle. Maple's tail thumped a merry rhythm against the wall as she panted in Lucas' face, and Rebecca frowned.

"They won't hurt you," said Brandon. "But they might slobber on your hem."

"How many of them are there?"

"About a dozen," Brandon replied. "More if you include the ones that belong to Mr. Jeffords, our estate manager."

Katherine stepped away from the group, and Nettle watched her. "I think the excitement of the evening has rather worn me out. I must bid you all goodnight." She looked directly at Rebecca.

"Likewise," said Rebecca. "But thank you, boys, for such a warm reception."

"Of course," Lucas replied, giving her a nod. "Sleep well."

Briar and Maple trotted off after Lucas and Brandon, but Nettle kept close to Katherine. Rebecca looked at Katherine, her eyes full of too much to say aloud, and followed her down the darkening hall. Once they were well out of earshot, she breathed, "I have waited for this moment all day, Katherine—"

Katherine's stomach leapt into her chest. "I want to show you something."

"Oh?" Rebecca's smile became devious, illuminated solely by the candle Katherine had in hand. "What a delicious offer. Show away."

After forcing herself to take a long breath, Katherine led

Rebecca around the corner, to the room Rebecca was staying in. She said nothing as she went inside, where the banked fire illuminated a small but well-furnished space. The bedding was tangled from Rebecca's earlier nap, providing an enticing sight, but Katherine walked towards the far corner, her candle glimmering over the wooden panels.

"Katherine?" Rebecca closed the door and glanced at Nettle.

"Mosswood Heath is a very old house," Katherine murmured, turning to face her. "It was built to withstand raids and difficult winters. As a result, it has a few surprises tucked under its skirts." She reached for the top edge of the corner panel and pressed hard. There came a muted *thud*, then the panel slid aside, revealing a dark passage roughly half her height.

Rebecca was a well-seasoned traveler and a salt-toughened sailor — she was not easily surprised. Her eyes gleamed as she came towards Katherine, the warm light of the candle flickering over her features.

"Follow me, and mind your head." Katherine stepped into the pitch-black and musty passage, walked a few paces forward, and reached for the well-worn latch. The corresponding panel slid open before her, a fresh beam of dim light spilling into the passage.

Katherine went through the opening and into her own bedroom, putting the candle down on her desk. She watched as Rebecca climbed in after her, her expression full of amazement.

"When my mother wondered where we should put you," said Katherine, the words clogging her throat, "I suggested the room beside mine."

A smile curled in the corner of Rebecca's mouth. "Does anyone know about the passage?"

"Anyone other than me? No, not to my knowledge."

"Why, Katherine." Rebecca sidled up to her, coy as anything. "Do I detect an ulterior motive?"

"Never." Katherine's heart gave a funny jolt, and she could not keep herself from staring at Rebecca's mouth.

And they were alone. Truly alone, for the first time that day. The fire crackled, echoing around the room, heightening the sparse distance between them. Katherine could hear Rebecca's breathing, could see the rise and fall of her chest, could smell the muted scent of her skin. In many ways, it felt like a dream.

Rebecca's gaze dipped to her mouth, and her hand went to Katherine's waist. She leaned in, her lips no more than an inch away, when there came a sudden, petulant whine from the other room.

Katherine closed her eyes, wincing. "Nettle." She pulled away, sighing. "She refuses to come through the passage. I shall have to fetch her."

"I see."

Katherine looked at Rebecca, a fresh tremor in her stomach. "The day has been long, and you should rest."

"Perhaps," Rebecca said, and for a moment, Katherine feared the worst. Then she smiled, squeezing Katherine's hip. "What time do the servants come?"

"Seven. We rise early."

"Very well, then. I will be sure to return to my bed by then."

Katherine blinked at her, her heart swelling. "You cannot mean—"

"Oh, but I do." Rebecca leaned in, brushing a kiss to her cheek, an echo of the moment beneath the mistletoe. "Now that I have you to myself, did you really believe I would surrender so easily? For shame, Katherine." She stepped away, grinning, and tugged on Katherine's hand. "Come. Let's fetch your poor pup."

＃ 27 ＃

Katherine woke early, early enough that her bedroom was still thick with darkness. Her banked fire cast a red glow over everything in sight; Nettle was a slumbering lump on the hearth, curled up on the rug she had used since puppyhood. Katherine watched her dog's gentle breathing for a few moments, then rolled onto her side, careful not to jostle Rebecca.

Rebecca slept like an octopus. She always clung to Katherine, threw her leg over Katherine's hips, and pressed her face into the small of Katherine's neck. Beneath the many layers of bedding, they formed a tidy, heated cocoon, warm enough that a light sweat hazed over Katherine's shoulders.

In the dull light, Katherine's gaze traced the fine, feathery shadow of Rebecca's eyelids, the line of her nose, the swoop of her mouth. She grazed the tip of her finger over the tiny mole beneath Rebecca's left eye, pressed a kiss as light as down to her cheek.

A dream, Katherine thought, a fresh wave of delight tingling through her. *A waking dream*. She gently shifted away, then pulled down the sheet, and put her mouth to Rebecca's chest.

Several delicious minutes passed before Rebecca woke. It happened slowly, so slowly that Katherine felt it build, felt the moment that Rebecca opened her eyes. She let out a stifled gasp, her hands skating over Katherine's shoulders. "Oh— Oh, Katherine—"

Katherine kissed her inner thigh, then licked the seam of her hip. Rebecca stifled a moan, her hands tangling in Katherine's hair, her body hitching to chase Katherine's mouth. A smile crept across Katherine's face — she could not help it, not when her own longing was just as acute — and she nuzzled the cluster of curls between Rebecca's legs, inhaling deeply. A dizzy, fresh heat slid down her throat and pooled between her legs, but Katherine tried to ignore it. She had dreamt of this for months, and would not be delayed, even by her own desire.

Rebecca tasted like salt and rain, bitter and wonderfully pliant beneath Katherine's tongue. Katherine licked over her sex, sucking until Rebecca twitched against her, slow and indulgent and without a stitch of mercy. She licked everywhere except where Rebecca wanted her most, then opened her eyes and met Rebecca's gaze.

Rebecca took a shaky breath.

The edges between them blurred, shifting the moment into something laced with desperation, with a need so potent Katherine could almost taste it. She pushed the flat of her tongue over Rebecca's sex, then slid up her body, fastened her mouth to Rebecca's breast, and tapped once on Rebecca's clit.

Rebecca shook, and it was a testament to centuries-old craftsmanship that the bed did not shake with her. She lay there, panting, her body livid with tension, as Katherine worked her with an agonizing, lurid slowness. Katherine watched her, feeling the hitch in her chest, the coiled heat of her body, and thought that she could die here, most happily, without a single regret.

Pleasure built in Rebecca like a flame roaring to life from

ashes. When it broke, it was with a hushed, quivering suddenness, and with Rebecca's face buried in a pillow.

Katherine stroked her through it, waiting until the twitch in Rebecca's hips subsided. They were both sweaty now — Katherine's nightgown clung to the small of her back, her thighs. And the ache within her was almost too much to bear. Once Rebecca began to stir, tugging the pillow away from her face, Katherine climbed up to straddle her, her nightgown fanning over Rebecca's naked body. Rebecca watched her, slack with surprise, as Katherine ground into her thigh, wet and wanton and utterly without modesty, one hand slipping beneath her hem and the other reaching up to play with her own breast.

She knew that Rebecca loved this. Loved seeing her mussed and riddled with lust, her nightgown barely clinging to her body. She let one of her straps fall, baring her breast, and saw the way Rebecca's eyes widened and darkened.

"Look at you." Rebecca's hands came to her thighs, gently pushing her gown up, exposing Katherine's legs and the efforts of her feverish hand. "You have learned a thing or two during our time apart."

Katherine could not speak, could only let a moan leak out of her throat. Her pleasure crested and churned, low in her gut, seething in response to the weight of Rebecca's touch. She pushed her body onto Rebecca's leg, and the pressure was almost enough, almost—

"I could watch you like this for hours." Rebecca spoke in a low purr, a devilish glint in her eye. One of her hands went to Katherine's breast, a teasing touch that sent a fresh shiver down Katherine's spine. "And the idea of you, tucked up in this room, in this bed, touching yourself—"

Heat, pressing at the base of her spine. "I thought of you," Katherine managed to say, hips stuttering, fingers slipping. "I thought of you every night—"

"And I you," said Rebecca, pinching and holding and looking at her like—

Her pleasure broke in a sudden, fierce rush, ripping through her like a thunderclap. Katherine gasped into it, lurching, and Rebecca caught her, kissed her, eased her down into the sheets. Put her fingers in Katherine's hair, grazed her nails over Katherine's scalp.

For a long time, Katherine simply lay there and breathed, soaking in the delight and the comfort of Rebecca's closeness, of her breath on Katherine's skin. The low crackle of the fire, the oily scent of the wool. She kissed Rebecca's shoulder, then her arm.

"You never told me," Rebecca said, "that you had a dog."

Katherine had to blink a few times, to drag herself back to earth. "Did I not?"

A low chuckle. "No, dear Katherine." Rebecca curled into her. "You mentioned the various menagerie of Mosswood, and that Lucas has a particular fondness for training pups. And I believe there was a horse?"

"Beatrice," said Katherine. "You shall meet her tomorrow."

"But never a dog." Rebecca kissed her. "Not one that sleeps on your hearth."

"Nettle was the runt of her litter, and she took to following me around when she was a pup. She is not particularly affectionate, or desiring much in the way of attention, but she enjoys a long walk. We were all surprised when she outgrew her siblings, and became the leader of the group."

Rebecca hummed. "And ever since...?"

Katherine raised her head to glance over at Nettle, who was now awake and watching them. "Yes. Ever since, she has been my near-constant companion."

"Why not bring her to London?"

"She detests it. And Father prefers to keep the hounds in the country, where they are of greater use."

"You are so secretive, Katherine." Rebecca was teasing, but her words sank like lead in Katherine's stomach. "I feel as if I am spending Christmas with an entirely different person."

Katherine swallowed past the sudden lump in her throat, past her own guilt. "Hardly."

"Whatever shall I discover next?" Rebecca went on. "A hidden fondness for black pudding?" She yawned. "Tell me about the estate."

Katherine kissed her neck. "There is not much to tell. And you shall see it later today. Lucas and Bran quite enjoy taking visitors on a tour."

"Speaking of your brothers. What on earth is the matter with Thomas? He was ever such a sour-puss at supper, and he disappeared right after dessert."

Sighing, Katherine lay back in the pillows. "He has been out of sorts ever since your sister's engagement was announced."

Rebecca stared at her, then sat up. "You cannot mean—?"

"Yes."

"*Thomas?*"

"Yes!"

Rebecca pushed a hand through her curls, fighting back a grin. "But they hardly spent any time together!"

"It was enough, apparently. He was besotted."

Rebecca gave a sudden, uncharacteristic giggle. "Oh dear. Poor lamb."

"You cannot tell him that you know."

"Never. Has he been in a sulk ever since?"

"Yes. Much to our chagrin. If he is still sulking after Christmas, Bran intends to box his ears and sit on him until he gives it up."

"That will be high entertainment indeed." Rebecca glanced at the clock on Katherine's bedside table. "We always seem to be fighting for time, do we not?"

Katherine looked at her, at the delicate curve of her collarbone. A part of her wanted to agree, to tell Rebecca that she would give anything for a day, a week, to themselves, without fear of being caught, of being seen. "I would rather a handful of stolen moments than none at all."

A smile, rueful and yet full of warmth, crept across Rebecca's face. She leaned down and kissed Katherine, sighing against her cheek. "I suppose there is some truth to that. But I should return to my own bed."

She was correct, of course, although that did not prevent a pang of longing from welling in Katherine's stomach. She watched as Rebecca slid out from beneath the sheets and pulled on her nightgown and robe. Rebecca was so beautiful like this, bathed in the light of the fire, wearing a look so indulgent Katherine wanted nothing more than to pull her back into bed.

"See you at breakfast."

"Yes," Katherine said. "Dress warmly."

Rebecca smirked. "Do I have any other option?"

And when she vanished into the hidden passage, the panel sliding shut behind her, Katherine let out a shaky breath, curling into the warmth Rebecca had left behind. She met Nettle's dark and glittering gaze, and thought that, by the end of Rebecca's stay, she would tell Rebecca the whole truth. Of course she would. She had to. Did she not?

A FRESH SNOW HAD DUSTED THE GROUNDS, LEAVING A delicious crunch underfoot and a thrilling bite in the air. Visibility was excellent — Katherine could see every smudge of brush and holly along the forest line, and hear every flap of wings through the brilliant gray sky. As she followed her brothers and Rebecca through the grounds, cutting the same path they had walked since childhood, she could not help but feel a renewed sense of love and wonder for the land around her. It was all so familiar, and yet so breathtaking, so enticing.

Her delight was further bolstered by Rebecca's appreciation of the Knight property, which was effusive and genuine. Snow and ice suited Rebecca — her complexion sang against the bleak landscape, and a charming blush rose in her face. The Knights showed Rebecca the woods, the frozen pond, the barn and all its inhabitants, and, from a distance, the buildings that shaped the family business.

Rebecca sniffed like a bloodhound, raising an eyebrow. "Is that... oranges I smell?"

Brandon grinned. "You know very well that we only ship the marmalade."

"It is a unique business," Rebecca said, leaning on her borrowed walking stick. "How did your family become involved with it?"

"Through one of Father's acquaintances," said Lucas. "Mr. Keiller approached him looking for advice on expanding his market south, and Father suggested a partnership. That was about fifteen years ago. We export to Britain, the Continent, and even America. Business has been good."

"Has it?" Rebecca did not seem convinced. "I know that the import of citrus has been difficult indeed these last few years. Has Mr. Keiller had any trouble with production?"

Brandon and Thomas exchanged a look, Lucas raised an eyebrow, but Katherine alone was not surprised. Of course Rebecca would know such a thing.

"Some," said Lucas. "The wars have been hard for us all."

That was a vast understatement, but Katherine could not fault him for it. There was a reason why she and her brothers had been wearing hand-me-downs for the past couple of years, and why so many of their neighbors had taken on flocks of sheep.

"So the estate itself does not produce?" Rebecca went on,

undeterred. If she was embarrassed, she did not show it. "How many farms does it keep?"

"Well," said Lucas, "none. Father sold the farms back to their owners, under the condition of a partnership with our family."

"Mosswood employs the locals to mill grain and process wool for the whole valley," said Brandon. "And we ship all over England. In return, we receive a discount on the finished goods we purchase for our own household."

Now it was Rebecca's turn to be surprised, though 'shocked' was perhaps the better word.

"And Mosswood is overrun by deer," said Thomas. "Our neighbors form a staff of seasoned hunters. They help us to maintain the population, for the sake of the land and the herds as well as the predilections of southern households."

"We process and sell the meat, and give the locals a discount in return." Lucas smiled at Rebecca. "Our venison has enticed the palates of several prominent English families, including Her Majesty's. We have standing orders across London."

"Like your family," Thomas said to Rebecca, "we are merchants. Though perhaps in a slightly less conventional manner."

Rebecca stared at them all, speechless. When she finally spoke again, it was to say, "Well... how... modern, I suppose."

Now, to Katherine's surprise, Thomas smiled and said, "I could not think of a better way to put it, Lady Rebecca."

"But modernity has its drawbacks." Lucas stepped away, turning his back on the warehouse and sundry out-buildings. "Come. It is time you learned to shoot."

Rebecca's smile dropped, and she went quite pale. "Pardon?"

Within a quarter of an hour, Rebecca had learned the basics, and mastered the safety procedures. Though she was dressed in a heavy wool skirt, and not her trousers, an unmistakable air of piracy wafted over her, encouraged by the rifle she left crooked open on her arm.

"I suppose this is payback," Rebecca said, glancing around at the boys. "For thumping you all so thoroughly at fencing."

"Perish the thought," Lucas said, his tone mild, though he winked.

They were standing in a loose cluster at one end of a stretch of land the Knights affectionately referred to as the firing range. It sat a healthy distance away from the house and the stables, and behind a small hill that buffeted the wind as well as the bulk of the noise. A series of well-loved targets squatted at various intervals through the snow-dusted land. Katherine, Thomas, and Brandon all stood to one side, rifles on their arms, content to let Lucas do the bulk of the teaching. He was the only one with the patience for it.

"How often do you hunt?" Rebecca said as Lucas loaded her rifle for her.

"Depends on the season," Lucas replied. "And on what Mother wants for supper." He looked at Katherine. "Did she ask you for anything today?"

"A few rabbits," Katherine replied, not missing the way Rebecca looked at her askance. "Or pheasants, whichever we see first."

"Excellent." Brandon adjusted his scarf. "I could do with a nice bit of rabbit."

When it came time for Rebecca to shoot, her nerves showed plainly on her face. But Katherine watched her set her jaw, aim, and then take a low, careful breath.

BANG.

Rebecca staggered, falling to the ground. She gaped at Lucas, who was grinning. "God in Heaven!" she shouted. "This thing kicks like an angry mule! And I can't bloody hear."

"Steady on." Lucas helped her to her feet. "You will get the hang of it."

Rebecca looked at her audience. "Did I hit anything?"

"No," said Thomas. And Brandon: "Perhaps a very unlucky passing bird."

"Damn!" Rebecca was still shouting, and Katherine stifled a giggle. "May I try again?"

"Certainly." Lucas swapped their rifles and began the process of reloading hers. He kept one eye on Rebecca as she lifted the rifle, aimed, and fired.

Once the smoke cleared, Brandon gave Rebecca an encouraging look and said, "At least you stayed on your feet that time."

"You menace." Rebecca met Katherine's gaze. "What a lot of fuss, needing to take the trouble of reloading each time."

"It can be an annoyance," Lucas admitted. "We often reload for one another, on a hunt."

"But it helps," Thomas said, "to shoot well enough that you only need one attempt."

"Katherine alone has mastered that," said Brandon. "Except for Lucas, on a lucky day."

"Excuse me," said Thomas, frowning. "I have been practicing very diligently, and I heard no complaints about the ducks I brought to table last week."

"Go on, then." Rebecca was looking at Katherine again. "Show off for me."

All of Katherine's brothers sighed, but Katherine smiled and obliged her. She took Rebecca's position, and waited for the others to move away — Brandon kept nearest to her, a spare rifle in each hand.

And now, the moment.

Katherine lifted her rifle, settling the stock against her shoulder. This was not her personal rifle, but a family one, and she knew it as well as she knew her own arm. She looked down the sights, taking note of the light wind, the dry air, the nearby rattle of the forest, and took a slow breath in, smelling oil and metal and gunpowder.

BANG.

Katherine did not need to hear the distant sound of her shot connecting with the target to know that her lead had found its home. In a flash, she passed the spent rifle to Brandon and took a fresh one. She lifted it, aimed, and fired.

BANG.

And again, with the third rifle.

BANG.

Satisfied, Katherine stepped back. Even from this distance, she could see where she had hit the nearest straw target — dead center twice, and then just beside it.

"Absolutely appalling." Thomas was making his usual expression of mild distaste. "To think that she was blessed with such keen aim, while her brothers were overlooked."

But Katherine only had eyes for Rebecca. Rebecca, who was staring at her with an expression of absolute wonder and shock, her eyes wide and full of—

Katherine blushed and looked away, taking her original rifle back from Brandon. "It will be dark soon. You should return to the house, and give Rebecca time to rest before supper."

"Very well," said Lucas. "Do you require assistance?"

Katherine shook her head. "The rabbits have gotten far too complacent, and will make my work easy indeed."

Lucas passed her the satchel of reloading materials. "Take care not to turn your ankle. The burrows are quite hidden beneath the snow."

And with that, they parted ways. Katherine started off in the direction of the woods, where the burrows began. She only glanced over her shoulder twice, watching as her brothers and Rebecca grew smaller, swallowed by the gentle vastness of the land. And she could have sworn Rebecca was watching her, her gaze as keen and piercing as a knife.

❧ 28 ❧

Katherine could not get all three of her brothers alone that evening — she had to settle for Lucas. After they had finished a rich supper of roasted rabbit and mince pies, she cornered him by the withered piano in the drawing room, where he hovered over their collection of sheet music.

"Lucas." She spoke in a low hiss, with one eye on the rest of the company — Mr. and Mrs. Knight had begun a game of whist with Rebecca and Brandon, while Thomas took up a book. "I must discuss something with you. A matter of some urgency, and delicacy."

"Oh?" He paged through a sonata, then opened the piano's lid, exposing the yellowing keys. "I am hearing shades of Madam Kensington, dear sister."

She almost rolled her eyes — what a knowing guess. "You have hit very close to the point, Lucas." Another glance, just to ensure that they could not be overheard. "I think we should tell Rebecca the truth. About who we are."

His hands paused in their work, and Katherine felt as if she could see the understanding pass through his body. "Why?"

"Perhaps your conscience can carry such a weight, brother, but mine cannot." Katherine licked her lips, ignoring the tremor in her stomach. "Rebecca has become our friend, our dearest friend, and we owe her the same honesty we owe to each other. I can hardly bear to look her in the eye, to laugh with her, to speak with her, knowing that we have behaved in such a duplicitous manner."

"Have we?" Lucas met her gaze, an uncharacteristic shrewdness in his expression. "We never insulted her, or her family, or compromised their status. We owe her no apology, no explanation for a slight on her good character."

Katherine had suspected this rebuttal, and pivoted accordingly. "Rebecca will be one of the most prominent debutantes next year. We would be fools not to use our connection with her to our advantage."

There — a glimmer in his eye. "You think she might be of use?"

"Undoubtedly. Her family will have a level of access we could only dream of, Lucas." She took a steadying breath, feeling a numbness take over her tongue. "Our own status next year will be precarious indeed, given my failure to find a match. We cannot afford to turn down such an opportunity, not if we wish Madam Kensington to continue her present rise to eminence."

"Do not diminish yourself in such a manner," he replied. "But I will concede that Rebecca does live on a rather different plane." For several moments, he was quiet, then spoke again. "Telling her is quite a risk, Kitten."

She stared at him, more than a little surprised. "You would question her loyalty?"

"I question her motives," he murmured. "You speak of owing her our honesty, and I agree. She has been nothing but forthcoming with us, and she has made several overt gambles in the course of our acquaintance. Not in the least by repeatedly turning up to the house in her fencing gear without an escort."

"You see?" Katherine put her hand to his arm, trying not to squeeze it too hard. "Rebecca showed us her true self from the very first moment, and trusted our discretion. Do we not owe her the same courtesy?"

Lucas hummed, noncommittal. "You say she can be trusted, and the evidence I have seen with my own eyes only enforces that conclusion. But I stand by my assertion — I doubt her motivations in forming an acquaintance with us are as clandestine as you assume." He met Katherine's gaze again, inscrutable. "It was all too perfect, Kitten. The way she inserted herself into our family, befriended us, wrote to us in her hour of need."

Katherine could hardly believe what she was hearing. "Lucas, how cynical—"

"I could be wrong," he admitted, holding up a conciliatory hand. "My instincts have led me astray before."

"But what reason— Why on earth would she undertake such a venture? We are a family of no consequence, Lucas, none at all. A young woman like Rebecca would have little to gain from our association, let alone our friendship."

"True." Lucas glanced at the table, watching Rebecca finish a trick. "But Lord Alwyn is a clever and dangerous man. One can only imagine that he sees advantages everywhere he looks, even where they do not yet exist. His cunning is matched only by his ruthlessness, and I imagine he passed on those qualities to his children."

"Lucas, we do not even have a title."

"No," he agreed. "But we have land. And connections. A whole network of operatives in the world of trade, from Scotland to Ireland and even further abroad than that. For a businessman such as Lord Alwyn, in times such as these... those opportunities would be very enticing."

Katherine looked at her brother, her heartbeat like a stab in her throat. Was it possible that he shared her fears about Lord Alwyn? Her assumptions, her conclusions?

Lucas returned her gaze, and Katherine could not be imagining the look of hesitation, of conviction, playing about his expression. What did he know? What could he suspect?

She slowly let out her breath. They had to return to reality, to the realm of fixed knowledge and indisputable fact: the realm of Madam Kensington. "I do not want to tell Rebecca anything without Tom and Bran's approval. Will you speak to them?"

He sighed. "I suppose so, yes."

"Good. I would like to tell her on Boxing Day, first thing in the morning."

"You are not one for wasting time, are you, Kitten?"

"Not unless absolutely necessary." She squeezed his arm again, and had the fleeting observation that he looked quite a bit older, with his hair arching over his brow and his thick beard. "Thank you, Lucas." She left his side and went to join Thomas on the couch, feeling Rebecca's gaze on the side of her face.

Later that evening, Rebecca yawned into Katherine's neck and cuddled closer to her, pressing her icy feet to Katherine's leg. "I never knew Lucas could play the piano."

"He is the most musical of all of us. Bran is quite tone-deaf, and Tom, though a gifted baritone, never had the patience for any instrument apart from his own."

"Tom sings?"

"With gusto. You shall hear him quite clearly in the church tomorrow evening."

"What an eventful Christmas Eve. Service, carols, and a ceilidh."

"And a hunt, in the morning."

After a moment, Rebecca opened an eye, and that familiar wariness crept back into her expression. Katherine watched her in return, wondering how long they would tiptoe around this. "A hunt?" said Rebecca.

Katherine nodded. "We always try for a stag at Christmas. If we succeed, Father has it mounted in time for New Year."

"And you...?"

"Yes. I will be in the hunting party. As will you."

Rebecca did not reply, but continued to watch Katherine, chewing her lip.

"Does it frighten you?" said Katherine, edging out onto the fragile bridge between them. "Seeing me with a gun?"

"Yes," said Rebecca, and an ugly swoop went through Katherine's stomach. "And no."

Well. That was quite possibly one of the most confusing things ever uttered.

"It frightens me because I am unfamiliar with guns," said Rebecca. "I am not like you, Katherine. I did not grow up in a hunting family; I had no reason to learn how to use a firearm. I am... wary of them because I do not trust them. And, even after my lesson, they still seem more dangerous than they are worth." Rebecca reached out, stroking Katherine's cheek with her finger. "But seeing you today... in your element..."

Katherine smiled. "It was only target practice."

"No, you... You are different, Katherine, when you have a rifle in hand."

"Am I?"

"Yes." Rebecca shifted, sitting up and moving closer to Katherine. "Do you remember that night, when I came to see you after the assassination?"

Katherine remembered it all too well. The garden, splashed with moonlight; glow worms and lilies and mud. The bench cold beneath her legs. "You snuck through the back gate."

"And I saw you with your rifle." Rebecca shook her head. "I did not know what to think. I was surprised, and a bit frightened, but it wasn't until I returned home that I realized... you were keeping watch, were you not?"

Katherine swallowed. "I suppose."

"You were keeping watch," Rebecca repeated, "all on your own. You and your rifle against a world of invisible intruders, waiting for the worst to happen. And I thought to myself, she must be the bravest person I have ever met. Certainly braver than me."

An odd, warm feeling pooled in Katherine's chest, beneath her breastbone. She could not think of what to say.

"And today... you were only shooting at targets, but I saw it in you." Rebecca was so close now, close enough that Katherine could feel her breath. "The conviction. The ability. The deadly accuracy, honed to a point so fine as to be imperceptible." Her chest hitched, and a raw heat pooled in her eyes. "You were fearsome. So powerful I could not breathe."

Katherine's mind spun, trying and failing to understand what was happening. Rebecca was not afraid of her, then — it was just the opposite.

"I will admit, Katherine, that I underestimated you upon our first meeting." Rebecca rolled on top of Katherine, straddling her, pressing her down into the bedding. "But I am all too keen to profess my error in judgment. I know now what you are capable of." She leaned in, touching Katherine's nose with her own. "I can see everything you do not show."

The air seemed to have gone out of the room. Katherine looked at her, and felt a surge of emotion so powerful her knees tingled.

"Now tell me something." Rebecca tangled a hand in Katherine's hair, giving it a warning tug. "Why has this ferocity of yours never appeared in bed?"

A startled, unbidden laugh caught in Katherine's throat. "I— I—"

Rebecca bent down, kissing her silly, then straightened up again, reaching to pull off her own nightgown, in spite of the chilly air. Her nipples pebbled at once, and goosebumps spread across her bare belly, her chest. And yet she was stunning, a brilliant picture, half-red in the glow of the banked fire. "We must rectify this at once, come here—"

Breathless, laughing, pulsing beneath the night, Katherine gave in to Rebecca's demands, and did her best to fulfill them.

❧

IN SPITE OF THEIR DELICIOUS EVENING TOGETHER, IT WAS obvious that Rebecca's nerves had not fully abated, though she did an excellent job of hiding them. She watched as Katherine polished and checked her personal rifle, the metal details gleaming in the light of the fire, and asked her questions about its provenance, its abilities. When the clock chimed the hour, they both dressed in thick woolen sets of men's hunting apparel, pinned their hair beneath woolen caps, and buckled their sturdiest boots. It had sleeted during the night, leaving a fresh layer of frost on the land around Mosswood. Tracking would be simple, yet difficult — ice and mud in the dips between the hills, and stiff ground along the hillsides.

Katherine took note of everything as she, Rebecca, the boys, and Mr. Knight made their way to the barn. She took deep, calculating breaths, scanning the forest for any signs of movement, but saw nothing.

Soon, they were joined by a handful of neighbors, all of them dressed in their wool trousers and tall boots. Cups of piping hot tea laced with Scotch were passed around, and all the hunters were soon red-cheeked and grinning, gathered by the nearest open fire. Once the sun had risen enough, the time came to split into groups — Katherine hid a smile when she was partnered with Rebecca and Brandon. She glanced out the open barn doors, looking up into the bleak, pale sky. Visibility was excellent, and the air smelled of snow. Hopefully, it would hold off until later that night. It would be cozy indeed, to curl up with Rebecca by the fire, sore and tipsy from the ceilidh, while snow drifted past the windows.

Katherine pushed such imaginings from her head with a force

so sincere it was almost physical. Now was not the time to be fanciful. Though being at Mosswood seemed to encourage such flights of fancy — Katherine had found herself repeatedly picturing moments alone with Rebecca, in a home familiar and yet unrecognizable. Trading smiles and kisses in the open, lying together on a couch, napping the afternoon away. She did not know what to make of these thoughts; such a future was quite impossible, not in the least because Rebecca would marry soon, and marry a gentleman far outranking any match Katherine might hope to make. And yet she could not help herself. *Tantalizing*, Katherine thought now, watching the way Rebecca smiled around the rim of her teacup.

Mr. Knight clapped his hands together, grinning at his merry band of hunters. "You know the rules, ladies and gentlemen — the killing shot keeps the head!"

The party split into groups and set out in different directions. Katherine led her trio at a measured pace, smiling as she sucked in delicious lungfuls of that cold, clear air. Beneath her feet, the ground crunched; above her head, a bird called. She was in her element, and ready to hunt.

"The herds keep to the woods more in the winter," Brandon was saying to Rebecca. "Which makes them difficult to track. But Katherine has the eyes of a hawk."

"Artemis personified," said Rebecca, and Katherine's ears grew warm.

Over the course of the next hour, Katherine led Brandon and Rebecca deeper into the woods, following the minute but tell-tale signs of a herd. Fur, snagged on branches; clusters of fresh dung, untouched by the frost; divots where hooves had hit a rare patch of muddy, thawed earth. The herd was moving west, and she was not surprised — it was a familiar route, one that would take the deer to a low, wet gully where mushrooms bloomed, even in winter. All around Katherine were the sights and scents of a hibernating forest. In spite of the leafless trees, identical in their shrouds of dark, wet bark, she knew exactly where she was.

And then, she caught sight of a pile of steaming dung. Fresh enough that the herd had to have passed by just minutes before. She stopped, and waited for Brandon and Rebecca to catch up with her — they were chuckling at some shared joke.

"We are within spitting distance of our quarry." Katherine spoke in a low whisper, but her words seemed to echo around the trees. "Try to walk as silently as possible, and avoid any sudden movements." Then, she turned to Rebecca. "Would you like to take the shot?"

Rebecca stared at her, shock melting her smile. "I— I would not dream of it."

Katherine tried to pack a world's worth of unspoken words into her gaze, and said, "I will help you."

"It is only fair," Brandon whispered to Rebecca. "You are our guest."

Rebecca looked at them both, speechless. Then she gave a nod, her chin steady in spite of her unspoken nerves.

"They are just over the next rise." Katherine pointed behind herself, where the gully lay beyond a swell of land. "We shall have the high ground, and therefore the advantage."

Brandon gave a chuckle, his breath smoking in the cold air. "This is where Lucas brought down his first doe."

"With any luck, we shall have the same good fortune today." Katherine met Rebecca's gaze again, and gave her arm a reassuring squeeze. "Come along."

The three of them crept towards their target, and as they drew nearer to the gully, where the land began to fall away in sharp, jagged edges, the sounds of the herd grew louder and louder. Katherine could smell their pelts, their grassy breath, their tangy hooves. A few steps closer and she could see them, does and bucks, old and young. Chewing and snorting, unconcerned with their relative vulnerability. If they noticed their predators, they did not show it.

Unease had surfaced in Rebecca's expression, but she appeared to swallow it, keeping to Katherine's shadow. A yard from the edge of the land, Katherine dropped to her belly, the slight sound drowned by the rumble of the herd. Rebecca copied her, her body pressing up against Katherine's side.

In slow, measured movements, Katherine slid her rifle forward, muzzle pointing down into the gully. Propping herself up on a nearby decaying log, she began the process of aiming and adjusting, then aiming again. Behind them, Brandon sank into a squat, his own rifle ready. He lifted a pinch of dead leaves, then let the detritus fall — they were still upwind.

The sound of Katherine's breathing swelled in her ears, heightened by Rebecca's proximity. She met Rebecca's gaze, then guided her into position behind the rifle. A hand, a touch; Rebecca's ear, close enough to kiss. They were practically embracing.

Katherine forced herself to focus. "We want the one with moss on his antlers. He is older, and unlikely to survive the winter."

Rebecca nodded, a tremor going through her body.

"Breathe out before you fire," Katherine whispered. "And worry not. I am here."

She had her arms draped over Rebecca's, preventing her from moving the rifle. Guiding her, checking the aim from behind her ear. Keeping her steady.

"Wait until that doe moves." Then, in the space between seconds— "Now, fire—"

BANG.

A shockwave, vibrating through Rebecca's body, settling into Katherine's jaw. A flash of smoke, acrid in Katherine's mouth. A splash of crimson, a dozen yards away, then a thud. The sudden fright and fury of the herd, hurtling out of the gully and up the opposite rise, hooves scrabbling at the half-frozen ground. In seconds they were gone, careening through the forest, leaving behind a moaning sack of hide.

Rebecca gasped, then gasped again, heaving for air. Katherine pulled away, watching her, then glanced at their quarry.

The shot had veered, and had not killed on impact. The aging buck stared up at the sky from where he lay among the mushrooms, his eyes bulging.

Katherine sighed, suppressing a blinding wave of emotion, then stood up. "The others will be here soon. Brandon, could you—?"

"Of course." He went to Rebecca's side, putting a tentative hand on her arm.

And Katherine made her way down into the gully, withdrawing her knife.

❧ 29 ❧

Christmas Eve fell with a fresh, bitter snow and a pile of Mr. Salk's infamous toffee. Rebecca, Brandon, and Lucas snorted their way through the carriage ride into the village, trying in vain to unstick their toffee-glued jaws, tears glistening in their eyes.

After the church service and carols, the Knights and their guest walked to the village hall, a cheerful building blazing with light, heat, and voices. As they approached, Katherine saw an unmistakable look of glee flit across Rebecca's face. She was glad for it — the hunt had shaken Rebecca, she knew, perhaps more than Rebecca cared to admit. But none of that unease appeared as Rebecca stepped into the hall, surrounded by the crowd of northerners. She beamed, radiant, and turned a few dozen heads.

Something in Katherine trembled at the sight of their awe. It was a feeling she herself was well acquainted with.

And when Lucas offered Rebecca his arm, grinning like a cat, she could practically see the whispers flitting through the hall. Such rumors had chased the Knight family's heels, tangling around their ankles, ever since London had watched Lucas dance with Rebecca on the night of Sophia's wedding. Katherine could not fault anyone for thinking it — it was a natural conclusion, if one forgave Lucas' inferior social and financial status. But stranger things had happened than a handsome young man marrying into money.

A raw feeling curled in Katherine's stomach, and she did not know if it was jealousy.

"How jolly!" Rebecca said to the Knights, taking in their merry surroundings. Tables of food and drink, garlands of holly, pine, and mistletoe, a small but determined Christmas tree in the far corner. And before them, a wide, scuffed floor with a low platform for the musicians. The air smelled of cinnamon and mince pies, sweat and cigars, Scotch and mulled wine. Wool and leather and perfume.

Katherine basked in it, relishing the taste of winter. Relishing the sight of Rebecca here, in her tartan skirt and her brilliant white blouse, glowing beneath the chandeliers of candles. In a world that was hers and not hers, new and yet old.

Then the music began, Lucas spun Rebecca onto the dance floor, and the evening swelled with promise.

☙❧

CHRISTMAS DAY PASSED IN A BLUR. EVERYONE WOKE LATE, encouraged by their raucous and indulgent night, and Rebecca was surprised to learn that not a single gift would surface until they had all returned from a vigorous, lengthy walk through the Mosswood grounds. When the boys emerged, Thomas was the palest of them all, and two miles into their excursion, he had to excuse himself and bend double behind a shrub. He emerged a few minutes later looking a bit less peaky; Lucas clapped him on the shoulder, and pushed him along.

It was a family tradition to give the servants all of Christmas and Boxing Day off, and the Knights rallied to make themselves a rather splendid supper of roasted venison, parsnips, potatoes, and carrots, rounded off with an excellent (and flammable) bowl of punch. Then, finally, it was time for gifts; they all sat together in the drawing room, bundled and rosy while even more snow fell outside, frosting the windows and lending light to the dense, unforgiving darkness.

The presents they exchanged were small, practical. Katherine received books, stockings, new soles for her favorite boots, and from her brothers, a beautiful stationery set, complete with a fine, freshly-sharpened quill. Unexpected emotion clogged her throat, and given the presence of their parents, she could only smile her thanks.

Later, when they were alone, Rebecca pressed a beautiful ink and watercolor rendition of the Knights' London home into Katherine's hands. Their own blurry figures stood beneath the oak, heads bent together as if sharing a secret. Katherine gaped at her, speechless, then handed her her gift — a small but well-made set of artist's pens, including charcoal and a pot of indigo ink. They stared at one another, then burst into laughter, and laughter gave way to kisses, which gave way to—

And for a moment, Katherine could forget what would happen the next day.

❧

IT HAD TAKEN SOME NEGOTIATING ON LUCAS' PART, AND MORE than a little reluctance from Thomas, but eventually, all the Knight siblings had agreed. Katherine could tell Rebecca the truth about Madam Kensington, and let the pieces of their friendship fall where they may.

The whole thing was a gamble, of course. They had no idea how Rebecca would react, though Brandon was quite convinced that she would take it in stride, after some understandable shock and outrage.

And anger, Katherine had thought, swallowing hard. Her

brothers had no idea what else she was planning to tell Rebecca — her suspicions about Lord Alwyn, and what she knew about Sophia.

Katherine had never in her life willingly done something that might hurt another person, except perhaps for biting and punching her brothers, when necessary. She had never undertaken such a risk, not when the depth of her love outweighed any practical considerations. She had never been poised to break another person's heart, and today, she feared that, for the first time in her life, she would shatter something she could never mend.

Her fear was so caustic, so bitter, Katherine almost choked on it, shook with it. It swallowed her adoration for Rebecca and threatened to pull her beneath a complete and ceaseless tide. Katherine had no idea how she would surface from this afternoon, or if she would emerge a completely different person — someone with the capacity to cause genuine injury, and the conviction to value honesty above every other concern, even that of her own heart.

So, when Rebecca looked up from tying her boots, Katherine did her best not to tremble.

"When does the wrestling match begin?" Rebecca was smiling. "Or has Tom cheered up enough to escape it?"

They were alone in Katherine's bedroom, not long after breakfast. Nettle lay in the corner, watchful, somehow knowing. Before them lay a day of walking, visiting the horses, singing raunchy songs with Lucas at the piano. But that future dissolved as Katherine stood up and steeled her nerves. "Rebecca, I need to speak with you about something."

"Oh?" Rebecca glanced up at her, tied a final knot. "Is Bran plotting some disastrous prank?"

"No." Katherine waited until Rebecca straightened in her seat, her eyes clear and bright. "I need to speak with you about Madam Kensington."

Rebecca's brow furrowed, and she leaned an elbow on the table. "That old hag?"

A jolt, in Katherine's gut. "You dislike her?"

"Of course I dislike her. Everyone does." A pause, like missing a step. "Why?"

There was nothing for it. "Rebecca," said Katherine, and thank God her voice did not tremble— "I am Madam Kensington. Well," she quickly added. "I, and Thomas."

For several moments, Rebecca stared at her. Then an uneasy grin broke across her features. "What a ridiculous thing to say, Katherine."

Katherine had expected this. She went to her desk and unlocked the side drawer, which happened to be the deepest. A thick pile of paper greeted her. Katherine took up a handful of Madam Kensington and one of several bundles of paper bound in thick blue ribbon — her original notes. She walked over to Rebecca and placed these items on the table beside her, a peculiar numbness taking over her mouth. "I would not lie about this, Rebecca. As you may recall, Madam Kensington first appeared in early May, not long after my debut at court."

Rebecca's grin melted as she looked at the papers. Then, she reached for them, her fingers pausing on the lines of Katherine's handwriting.

"It is no secret that my family is struggling," Katherine said, because she had to say all of this, now, as quickly as she could. "We are not like your family, Rebecca, we do not have piles of money at our disposal. The war has been hard on us, very hard, and my father has been struggling to turn a profit. When we arrived in London, matters grew worse. A situation transpired that required us to come into money, and quickly." She swallowed. "Lucas was threatened, as was our father. My brothers and I had to find a way out of it, and we took a gamble. We never expected Madam Kensington to succeed, let alone become a fixture of the London season."

A glance, then, as sharp as flint. Katherine trembled, but kept speaking.

"I was adamant that we never defame or decry any of the debutantes, especially Sophia. Gossip was one thing, yes, but betraying the trust of my peers, my friends, was quite another. Everything was dramatized, sensationalized." Another breath. "I recognize that our venture was a dangerous one, and perhaps a selfish one. But it was a choice we made to protect our brother, and our family. I would make the same choice again in a heartbeat, even under more damnable circumstances."

Silence fell. Rebecca was sifting through Katherine's notes, glancing between them and the published copies of Madam Kensington. Katherine could almost hear the words that she was reading, and see the nights she was reliving. Nights spent at the Knight house, laughing and joking and playing cards with the boys, or slipping out to the garden for a fencing match. Nights spent in Katherine's bed, between her legs, under her hands.

"You were very adept at hiding it." Rebecca cleared her throat, not looking up. "I never suspected anything."

An odd, half-tilted relief spun through Katherine's stomach. "We had to be. Our parents are completely unaware of it, and..." She faltered, then, at the sight of Rebecca's hard, implacable expression. "I wanted to tell you sooner, Rebecca, but we barely knew one another, and—"

A short, brittle laugh that did not contain an ounce of humor. "And you did not want to jeopardize your connection to a very useful source of information."

"No." Katherine tried not to let her voice waver, her stomach churning. "No, Rebecca, I never regarded you as such. But the situation was so delicate, and we could not bear for anyone to know the extent of our family's situation—"

"But you were content to parade the details of my beloved sister's life out in full view of the public." Rebecca looked up then, her eyes flashing. A steely anger had overtaken her expression, leaving it devoid of all warmth. "You were content to profit off of the whims and emotions of others, their loves and their losses, without once exposing yourself to the same kind of scrutiny."

There — outrage. Fresh in the base of Katherine's spine. "The town would gossip regardless, Rebecca. Given your own family's background, you can hardly blame me for trying to take advantage of a ripe market. Especially when my brother's safety was in question."

"Lucas is a grown man, and the eldest son. It was never your responsibility to rescue him, or protect him."

"No," Katherine agreed. "But he would have done the same for me. As would Bran, or Tom. We are all each other has in this world."

Rebecca got to her feet, pacing the short distance between the table and the fireplace. Nettle raised her head to watch, eyes unblinking. "And you were content to spy on our peers? Our friends? To undermine their trust, their loyalty, their faith in your friendship?"

"Of course I was not *content*." Katherine clenched her hands into fists to keep her arms from trembling. "But I was no different from anyone else. We all watched one another, and whispered about one another behind closed doors. Do not feign innocence — do not pretend to be immune from the machinations of our world, when you were all too keen to participate in them."

Rebecca stopped mid-step, staring at her. "What do you mean by such an accusation?"

"Fencing," Katherine said, the word sharp on her tongue. "Do you really think me such a fool?"

Silence, and Rebecca's glittering stare.

"Perhaps you were looking for friendship, Rebecca. Perhaps you were lonely in London, in spite of your family's connections, your sister's status, your well-crewed boat. Perhaps I am nothing but a cynic, and keen to distrust everyone I meet." Katherine stepped forward. "But you inserted yourself into our lives at the first opportunity, and with an eagerness that could be called an agenda." She paused, letting her words settle between them. "Am I wrong?"

For several long, gut-wrenching moments, that horrible silence prevailed, broken only by the crackle of the fire.

Then Rebecca sighed, her shoulders slumping. "No," she said, her voice low. "You are not."

The small prickle of victory that wormed down Katherine's spine was dampened by the fresh-dawning horror of the truth — that Rebecca had had an ulterior motive the entire time, just as Lucas had suspected.

"My mother..." Rebecca bit her lip. "My mother told me to become close with your family. To this day, Katherine, I do not know why, or why such a connection should be of interest to my parents." And her expression, though twisted with emotion, seemed full of honesty. "And— and our acquaintance may have begun like that, Katherine, but I swear to you — I swear that after those first few days, I came back to you because *I* wanted to, not because of my family's demands."

Katherine wanted to believe her; her entire body screamed for a reason not to lose her faith in Rebecca. But she had to see this through. "You truly do not know why they asked you?"

"No," Rebecca said, her voice firm and clear. "Although I have my suspicions."

Just as Katherine had hers. "I suppose I should feel some relief, knowing that my instincts were correct."

"You certainly have a talent for guessing such things, Katherine." Rebecca returned to the table, brushing her hand over the piles of writing. "That much is evident."

Katherine did not dignify that with a reply. "I will confess I was impressed by your interest in my family. And by *your* family's sudden ascendancy."

Rebecca looked up, with a twitch of one brow.

"So, I did some digging. I looked into the history, the business records, of Lord Alwyn, better known as Maximus Johnson."

Rebecca's nostrils flared, but otherwise, her expression did not change.

"But I found little information. Certainly not enough to quench my curiosity in your family's status and wealth. The records I had at my disposal were limited, and incomplete. Following the advice of my father, on the night of the Hartford ball, I snuck into the library."

"I gather you use a loose interpretation of the word 'advice.' Had your father known your true intentions, I doubt he would have aided you in such a manner."

Katherine ignored this as well. "Lord Hartford's records are meticulous, and cover a wide range of markets from our corner of the hemisphere. I was able to see a much more complete history of Lord Alwyn's business, and the shipments he brought in and out of England." Katherine took a shaky breath. "And I was able to draw a few conclusions about his practices."

Another pause tensed between them as the full implication of Katherine's words sunk to the floor. Then Rebecca gave a soft huff and shook her head. "I suppose I should not be surprised. If anyone were to figure it out, it would be you."

"What?" Katherine pressed. She wanted to hear Rebecca say it. To hear the phrase 'my father is a smuggler' spoken aloud. "*What* have I figured out?"

"Oh, I don't believe we need to put it in so many words." Rebecca's voice was light, airy. "Not if we understand one another."

Katherine looked at her, and had to know. "Do you work for him?"

Rebecca nodded.

A stab of fear, just below her ribs. It must have shown on her face, because Rebecca added, "Not frequently. Only when he needs an extra pair of hands. Or a very stealthy ship."

"I see." Katherine's mouth seemed to be full of cotton. She tried to think of what she had to say next, but her mind was filled with images of Rebecca facing down a pistol, or fighting off some faceless threat with a real saber. "I suppose I can assume why your family returned to England, and why Gertrude's marriage was so rushed. With the growing war in America, and a new son-in-law from an old English family, your father saw an opportunity to grow his business."

Rebecca made a soft noise in her throat. "Gertrude willingly agreed to the marriage," she said. "She did nothing under duress. And it was a smart match." Something like amusement filtered into her voice. "It protected her."

Katherine squeezed her eyes shut. Somehow, it was quite terrible, finding all of her predictions coming true. "There is something else," she said. "Something else that I learned at the Hartford ball." She opened her eyes to look at Rebecca. "I never told anyone of my suspicions about your father. And I never told anyone of what else happened that night. I kept your secrets, Rebecca, and I believe — I *know* — that that counts for something."

Rebecca watched her, her expression giving very little away.

"That night, when I went into Lord Hartford's library, I was alone for an hour, undetected." Katherine sucked in a breath. "Two guests snuck away from the party and into the library, and I was forced to hide. As the minutes passed, I realized who they were. Your sister, and Lord Dashwood."

The tiniest flicker, a twitch beneath Rebecca's eye.

"I heard them speaking to one another." Bile rose in Katherine's throat. After months of keeping this secret, revealing it was like a self-inflicted injury. "And I heard your sister tell Lord Dashwood that she was pregnant with his child."

Shock, utter and unrepentant, rippled over Rebecca's features. She gaped at Katherine, her eyes shining.

"I could hardly believe my ears." Katherine's voice was trembling. "I was so frightened for her, and so concerned about how your mother would react to such news. And I knew, Rebecca, beyond a shadow of a doubt, that if I allowed this information to influence anything I wrote as Madam Kensington, I would make more money than I could have ever imagined." One breath, then another. "But I made my decision. I would never do that to you, or to Sophia, not for all the money in the world."

Rebecca's inhale was as sharp and bitter as salt. "I suppose you would like me to congratulate you, for showing the barest modicum of sympathy?"

"No," Katherine bit out. "No. But earlier, you accused me of willingly, even joyfully, profiting off of the lives of others. At the very least, I am entitled to defend myself by presenting evidence demonstrating that I did the precise opposite."

Silence, and it was almost comforting. Katherine and Rebecca looked at one another, the space between them shifting as if it were the sea.

One tear, then another, skated down Rebecca's cheeks. She wiped them away, and her voice did not waver when she said, "Where does this leave us, Katherine? What happens now?"

Ignoring her churning stomach, and the instincts screaming at her to go to Rebecca, to cling to her, Katherine said: "Now that you know the truth, my brothers and I will understand if you wish to sever our friendship." The words felt so hollow, so devoid of depth, that Katherine could hardly believe she was speaking them to the woman she loved. "Granted, they are not aware of what I know. The truth about your father, or about Sophia. And I do not plan to enlighten them at any point in the near future." One breath, then another, until some of the dizzy feeling passed. "However, they would agree with me when I say that it would be in our best interest, and yours, to maintain our connection."

Another sharp inhale. "*Our* connection?"

Katherine winced. "No, not— That is not what I meant." Tears pricked at her eyes. "I meant your connection to my family as a whole. To my brothers, my parents. My damn dogs." She would not cry. "I will understand, Rebecca, if you would prefer to maintain the social friendship between you and I, but to end our... personal attachment."

"Tell me, Katherine — how might I benefit from a friendship with the Knights?"

"It is no secret that your family is far more powerful, far more connected, than my own. Next season, you would be able to offer me and Thomas a level of insight that would otherwise remain inaccessible to us. In return, we would offer you a portion of the profits. It would not be much, but it would be something."

"And why do you think I would be interested in money?"

Katherine could not help it — she smiled. "Because I know that you desire nothing more than to have your own income. Your own path towards independence, without any ties or obligations to your family or whatever husband they choose for you."

Perhaps there was something terrible about knowing someone so well. Rebecca seemed to think so; she shuddered and looked away, crossing her arms over her chest. Nettle watched her, and whined.

But they could not part ways like this. Not without—

"I will do anything, Rebecca," Katherine said. "I will do anything to preserve what we have found in each other these past few months. You have awakened something in me that I never knew was there, and I never want to return to a world without you in my bed." She took a gulp of air, and steeled herself. "But one thing I will not do is beg your forgiveness, just as I do not expect you to beg for mine. I will not beg," she said, "because I do not believe in begging for something I do not need. We understand one another, and that is enough for me. If you would have me, Rebecca, as I am, then I will be here."

Rebecca made a soft, incoherent sound, and still did not look at her. "I need time." She cleared her throat, and when she spoke again, her voice was steady. "I need time to think, Katherine."

Katherine forced herself to nod. It was not an answer, and not a rejection. "I understand."

For a long moment, the only sound in the room was the crackle of the fire, and another whine from Nettle. Then Rebecca moved, crossing the room. Katherine watched her approach, trying not to feel an inch of hope as Rebecca came closer, and closer. She choked on a sob when Rebecca passed by her, opened the door, and left the room.

Katherine was alone.

$\maltese$ 30 $\maltese$

"**W**ell, what do you think?" Mrs. Knight tilted her head to one side. "If we let down the hem, perhaps add another petticoat, it might be quite serviceable."

"Indeed," Katherine murmured. In the distance, she saw a flurry of movement by the woods — a tangle of rabbits, bolting around one another. The deep snow made them quite obvious, thorny brown smudges amidst a sea of dazzling white. A fresh howl of wind echoed around the house, and Katherine shivered, even though she was not cold.

"Katherine." Her mother's annoyance was tangible. "You did not even look at the dress."

Katherine forced her attention away from the window and turned to look at her mother. Mrs. Knight sat among a huge pile of dresses; in her hands was a pretty, if outdated, muslin gown. White fabric, green ivy print. It probably had a stain somewhere on the skirt. Even from across the room, Katherine could tell that the gown was at least three inches too short, as all the hand-me-downs from her cousins were. She nodded. "Yes, dropping the hem will do nicely."

Mrs. Knight tsked, unimpressed, but set the dress aside. "It is a shame you got your height from your father. If only my sisters had managed to marry tall men, they might have ended up with tall daughters, much to your benefit."

Katherine went over to her mother, picking up the nearest gown — a somewhat threatening blue number, with lots of frills along the hem, waist, and neck. "I did not think we would start preparing for the season so soon. It is still months away."

"The early bird catches the worm, so they say." Mrs. Knight tossed the ivy gown into a smaller pile on the nearest armchair. "And, we want to ensure that you turn as many heads as possible, Kat. I fear we did not prepare as well as we might have last year."

A spike of nerves lanced through Katherine's stomach, and she had to swallow past a sudden wave of unease. She and her mother had never discussed the disappointing outcome of the previous season.

So, perhaps it was expected that a tense silence fell. Katherine watched her mother, wondering what to say, then crossed her arms against her chest and steeled herself. "I am sorry, Mother. That I did not... make a match."

Mrs. Knight's surprise was almost comical. "Why, Katherine! I would never expect you to apologize for such a thing!"

Katherine looked at her, somewhat at a loss. "No?"

"No!" Mrs. Knight frowned at her. "Why on earth should you apologize? You did nothing wrong. At least," she added, recovering some of her usual spirit, "nothing that I know of. But I can hardly take any credit or condolence for what might occur out of my sight."

"Oh, I thought..." Relief, welcome though temporary, eased through Katherine's chest. "I thought you were upset about Mr. Ransom. After the way you questioned me at Aunt Linda's—"

"I will admit," said Mrs. Knight, with a sigh, "that I was upset, yes, but more accurately — I was curious, Katherine, and you can hardly blame me. You both seemed to be moving towards a happy match, and it all fell apart so quickly. I couldn't think of what might have spoiled it, and I was anxious to see you so unhappy."

"Unhappy?"

"Yes, Katherine, it was quite obvious that you were upset." Mrs. Knight raised an eyebrow. "Just as you are upset now, and have been for the past fortnight."

"Oh." Katherine's cheeks burned, along with her forehead. She glanced away, her gaze once again seeking the window.

"Yes." A touch smug, Mrs. Knight picked up her next victim — a pale cream-colored frock. "A mother never misses these things, as you will one day discover. You and the boys have hardly spoken a word to Rebecca, outside of the dining room. She avoids the drawing room at all costs, and has taken to exploring the grounds alone." She tsked again. "What was it, then? An argument?"

"I suppose," Katherine murmured, closing her eyes just for a moment, just to banish the echo of Rebecca standing poised in front of the fire, hands in fists at her side, her expression quaking as Katherine revealed truth after truth. To banish the truth of her own bed, which had remained empty, devoid of its usual guest, ever since Boxing Day. She cleared her throat. "Yes, a disagreement. About politics."

"Good Lord." Mrs. Knight gave a light scoff, trading the cream-colored frock for a delicate yellow one. "I cannot think of a more ridiculous reason. Though I suppose all the rules have changed now, for you young people. Time was that politics rarely entered the conversation, and when it did, it was only in the most general of terms. Best to avoid the topic at all costs, for the sake of preserving conversation."

Katherine rolled her eyes and took care not to remind her mother that they lived in very different political climates. For God's sake, most of Mrs. Knight's siblings still referred to America as 'the Colonies.' But Mrs. Knight's diagnosis of the situation at Mosswood Heath was nothing short of accurate —

Rebecca had spoken just a handful of words to the Knight siblings since Boxing Day, and had ceased joining them in the drawing room for their daily diversions. She spent time alone, or with her maid, and had taken to wandering the grounds on long, rambling solitary walks. When the weather kept everyone inside, Rebecca remained in her own room.

And she unraveled Katherine's sanity, while she was at it. Rebecca had said that she needed time to think, and clearly, she had not lied. But never would Katherine have imagined that she would need as long as a fortnight.

Selfish, Katherine told herself, as she had been telling herself all too frequently. It was selfish of her to impose upon Rebecca's emotions, for the sake of bolstering her own wounded heart.

"I am certain that the situation will resolve itself in due course," Mrs. Knight went on. "It would be so horrid to return to London without the assurance of Rebecca's friendship, for you as well as the boys. You all have gotten on so splendidly."

Not for the first time, Katherine wondered if Mrs. Knight believed the rumors swirling about Lucas and Rebecca. "I suppose there is no question, then, of us attending the season this year?"

Mrs. Knight paused for a moment before replying. "No, Kat. We will be attending as planned, regardless of matters here at Mosswood."

The unspoken was all too obvious. The family would play along as expected, fulfilling the silent obligations of their status, until Katherine secured a husband.

A barbed shiver went down Katherine's spine at the idea of marrying a man, the feeling even more repulsive now than it had been seven months before. How could she be expected to kiss a person she did not love, let alone share their bed, their home? And give birth to their *children?*

Perhaps I shall run away, she thought, turning her back on the window. *Perhaps I shall take Nettle and set off to America, where I can find any life I please.*

But then she thought of her brothers' faces, and her resolution withered and died, as it had so many times before.

Mrs. Knight reached into a pile of virtually identical white dresses. "Kat, look at this!" She unearthed a gleaming white gown, far more delicate and finely-crafted than any Katherine had seen yet. "How pretty!" Holding it up to the light, Mrs. Knight smiled. "For the Opening Ball, perhaps?"

"Yes, Mother." Katherine forced a smile onto her face. "What a lovely idea."

"Worry not, Kat." Mrs. Knight's voice was warm with encouragement. "Your second season will be much easier than your first."

"I suppose." And Katherine could see how Mrs. Knight ached for it, for her only daughter to find a husband, to find a happiness and a stability that the family could not offer. In return, Katherine ached to be the daughter her mother so clearly wanted, instead of the daughter she had. She could not imagine hurting another person as she had hurt Rebecca, or letting the truth about herself be the cause for such damage. Secrets were dangerous, she knew, but useful, when kept for the sake of protecting someone you loved.

Katherine widened her smile and reached for her sewing box, which she had hastily wiped free of telltale dust. She sat down across from her mother, in the sea of dresses, and resolved to pretend as well as she could, for as long as she could. "Where shall we begin?"

☙❧

KATHERINE HAD TO GIVE HER BROTHERS SOME CREDIT — THEY handled the ongoing disagreement with Rebecca like true gentlemen, and did not press the issue at all, or try to goad her into speaking with them. In fact, they acted as if nothing were out of the ordinary, convinced that Rebecca would come around, and see things from their perspective.

For many long nights, Katherine had thought them foolish. But as she spent day after day alone, trudging the grounds of Mosswood with no one but Nettle or the occasional brother for company, she could think of no fool greater than herself, for thinking that honesty was worth the gut-wrenching heartache.

By all appearances, Katherine's life was quite the same. She hunted, tracked, played cards and drinking games with her brothers, helped in the kitchens, and, when all else failed, bothered Rita. But Rebecca had changed Katherine's entire world, and everything seemed quite pale and somber without her in it.

When nearly three weeks had passed since Boxing Day, Katherine began to give up all hope of resolution, of having Rebecca in her life again. So perhaps it was fitting that, once she'd surrendered to the inevitable future, there came a knock at her bedroom door.

Katherine opened the door, unable to hide her trepidation.

Rebecca's face was clear, but unsmiling. "Shall we go for a walk?"

"Yes," said Katherine, then: "No." She glanced at the window. "It is about to snow."

"That's fine." Rebecca's voice was steel. She waited for Katherine to put on her boots, shawl, mittens, and overcoat, then led her out of the house and out into the frosty, brutal landscape.

Katherine followed her with her heart pounding in her throat, her face numb with anticipation. It was not lost on her that Rebecca was leading them quite a distance away from the house, through a thin outcropping of trees. Far from where they could be overheard, or watched.

Finally, with her breath steaming silver, Rebecca halted, and turned to face Katherine. Around them, a soft hush of minuscule snowflakes began to fall.

"I shall not mince words," said Rebecca. Her voice was clarion, resonant in the cold air. "Katherine, I forgive you." The corner of her mouth twitched. "I forgive you, though you have not apologized, and though there is nothing to forgive."

A weakness, like fever, pooling in Katherine's knees. "Oh?"

"Yes." Rebecca watched her. "I understand why you kept the secrets that you did, Katherine. I suppose I have to thank you, in some way, for what you did for my sister. For protecting her from her own carelessness. Were our situations reversed, and under similar circumstances, and the same financial pressures, I do not..." Her voice faltered, then strengthened. "I do not know if I would have done the same."

Katherine sucked in a breath. This, here, was Rebecca, raw and flayed to her center.

"And while I do not enjoy the fact of your secret identity, I suppose I can accept it." Rebecca offered a thin smile. "It is strange, to think of you as a gossip-hound. But perhaps that shows me what a poor job I have done of seeing you, of learning you, just as you are."

A broken chuckle fell from Katherine's mouth. "Is that a compliment?"

"Of sorts." Rebecca's smile broadened, beautiful and rich in the falling snow. "And about my family's business..." She gave a rueful sigh. "I truly do not know what to say, apart from congratulating you on your fine investigative skills. But it seems that our parents have saddled us both with complicated, demanding legacies. Neither of us chose our inheritance, Katherine, and we do what we must to survive. I do not and will not judge you for your occupation, if you will not judge me for mine."

Katherine let those words sink in, then nodded.

"When the season comes, I will work with you," Rebecca went on. "And your brothers. I will help Madam Kensington when I can, and support you from afar when I cannot. I make no guarantees, Katherine, and I reserve the right to silence on any matter of my choosing."

"Of course," Katherine whispered, her hands burning. "Of course, Rebecca—"

But this turn of conversation was not surprising. Rebecca was speaking in the terms of a business contract, and would see it through to its conclusion.

"With that said, perhaps it will not surprise you to hear that I plan to continue my social relationship with your family." That smile again, now teasing. "After all, the next few weeks would be awkward indeed, if I continued to sulk."

"We will be glad for it," Katherine said quickly, her heart skipping in her chest, hardly daring to imagine—

"Thank God," Rebecca replied, quirking an eyebrow. "How I have missed the games of Bonaparte and Two-Card Charlie. Mary —" her maid— "is poor company indeed."

"And we have missed you." Heat, pressing in the back of Katherine's throat. "I hope you don't mind my saying that my brothers and I have come to think of you as a fixture here at Mosswood, and it is strange to be without you."

"Of course I do not *mind*, Katherine." Rebecca came towards her, footsteps crunching through the new-fallen snow. She looked like a figure from one of Katherine's favorite fairy tales, or perhaps a myth. A queen from an ancient and wonderful time, well out of Katherine's reach. "I feel more at home here, with you, with your brothers, than I ever have with my own parents." She reached for Katherine's hand, their woolen mittens muffling the touch. "Just as I feel most myself, and most at peace, when I am with you."

Something in Katherine broke, and another piece of her lifted up into the trees, beyond the branches and the snow, into the sky. She shook, a sob building in her throat, but it was not a feeling of sadness; rather, one of relief, of familiarity. Of sanctity.

"I may not know you as well as I should, Katherine," said Rebecca. "But I know you well enough to have conviction in your character. The actions you took, and the decisions you made, came from a desire to protect your family, and to protect your-self." She leaned forward, pressing their burning foreheads together, her breath a whisper on Katherine's cheek. "They were not actions of spite, or malice. Or cruelty. It was not your inten-tion to hurt me, and I could see what it cost you, to believe that you had done so."

Katherine could have wept. Could have screamed. Could have laughed.

"And I want you, Katherine." Her lovely voice broke, and Rebecca squeezed her eyes shut, leaning forward, her touch like a brand. It was a wonder the snow falling around them did not melt into rain. "I want you as you are now, and as you were in London. As you are every day. Just as yourself, with or without the secrets." A wet, shaky chuckle. "Though I would prefer it if the secrets were laid to rest."

"Of course." Katherine hiccuped, squeezing Rebecca's hand as hard as she could.

"And in return, I make you a vow." A tear slipped down Rebec-ca's cheek, and she pressed her lips together to swallow it. "I vow never to take you for what you only seem to be, or to take any part of you for granted. I feel as if I let my own judgment, my own presumptions, my own..." She licked her lips. "Desires... to take the helm, rather than allowing *you* to steer my course. I want to know you, Katherine. I want to know you as well as you know me."

"But you do." Katherine closed her eyes to stem her tears, her other hand snaking around Rebecca's waist to hold her tight. "I am the same person I have always been, Rebecca."

"Indeed." Rebecca's voice was insistent, fierce. "But I feel as if I have seen only one facet of an enormous diamond. And I have a keen and pressing need to see the rest of it."

"A diamond?" Katherine could not help a hysterical giggle. "That is a little too flattering, I think." She kissed Rebecca's cheek, feeling the bite of the cold on her lips. "No more secrets,

Rebecca. That is a remarkably easy promise to make, and one I am all too willing to uphold."

Rebecca pulled away, just enough to look Katherine in the eye. "Then am I correct in saying that we have an understanding? An agreement?"

"Of course," said Katherine. "You will aid my work where you can, and—"

"No, Katherine." Rebecca squeezed her hand. "I mean you and I." Her mouth came closer, hovering a breath away from Katherine's. "Do we have an understanding?"

Katherine swallowed, hard. Counted to three. "I must confess a certain degree of ignorance in these matters. I do not know what you imply with the phrase 'an understanding.' "

A soft, frustrated sigh fell from Rebecca's mouth. "That you are mine. And I am yours. We belong to ourselves, and to each other." Her voice dropped to a whisper. "And that is all."

Katherine closed her eyes for a moment, the cold seeming to swell within her. The air thickened with snow. "Rebecca... we are expected to marry."

Rebecca made a noise in the back of her throat, a noise of derision. "Let us see how the season unfolds, before we make commitments to the ghosts of men."

"Rebecca—"

"No." A fierce, bruising kiss, hard enough to make Katherine's head spin. Rebecca panted against her mouth. "I love you, Katherine. And I do not share well with others."

The earth, tilting on its side. Katherine blinked at her, swimming in an emotion so deep it threatened to overtake her. "I— I love you. Just as well."

Rebecca's mouth trembled, then sought Katherine's. They kissed once, twice, clinging to one another, the snow caking their shoulders, their hair, their eyelashes. Katherine's heart throbbed in tandem with Rebecca's touch, eager and aching.

"Do not think of the season," Rebecca murmured, still in that fierce, determined way. "Do not think of our obligations, of what is expected. Think only of what you want, what we might have together." Another kiss, with a gentle nip to Katherine's bottom lip. "Then imagine what I would do to protect it."

Katherine's knees did wobble then, buckling beneath her. She swayed a little, and Rebecca caught her, a shadow of her rakish grin sliding into place.

"Your teeth are chattering." Rebecca pulled her close, brushed a kiss to Katherine's temple. "Come, let us go inside. We must tell the boys that the embargo has been lifted."

As they made their way back to the house, the snow continued to fall, crusting the land in a fresh, plush blanket. Katherine sucked in deep, cleansing breaths of the sharp, metallic air, drinking in the scent and the taste of winter. It cleared her head a little, but it seemed that nothing, not even the pure, piercing January afternoon, would dampen the effect of hearing that she was loved.

And all along the way, she had Rebecca's hand in hers. Gripping, holding. Clinging and pulling. A lifeline and an anchor.

When they crashed into the house, panting and dripping all over the stone floor, Graves gave them a look that would break glass. "Your brothers are in the drawing room, Miss Katherine." He took their cloaks and mittens. "I shall have Rita bring you a fresh pot of tea and some candied ginger. We can't have you catching cold."

"Thank you, Graves," Katherine managed, but she only had eyes for Rebecca. Rebecca, who smirked and walked straight into the drawing room.

Katherine hesitated, then followed her.

"Goodness me," Rebecca said, considering the scene before her. "Am I interrupting something?"

Katherine's brothers did an excellent job of hiding their surprise at being addressed in such a friendly manner. "No," said Lucas, his hand pausing above the drawing pad. "Not at all."

"You can say that again," said Brandon. He and Thomas were posed in a most unnatural attitude by the fire. There was a fox skin involved, and a sextet. He looked at Rebecca. "It is so dire, being trapped inside. Drives poor Lucas to insanity."

"And arrogance," Thomas gritted out. "He cannot draw so much as a flower, and yet he insists upon posing us as if he were Reynolds himself."

"Oh, come now." Rebecca went over to stand behind Lucas, looking over his shoulder at the drawing. "It is not so terrible."

"You flatter me." Lucas stood up, passing her the pad. "But we all know you are the true artist of the group."

Smiling, Rebecca took the pad and his seat. She reached for the charcoal, and began sketching in quick, fetching movements. "I have been thinking about Madam Kensington these past few days."

A stir in the air. Lucas glanced at his siblings, then quickly closed the drawing room door. "Have you?"

Rebecca hummed. Her movements sped up. "Yes. She runs a most successful enterprise, but I think she needs to personalize her work. Create an emblem, a calling card, for her empire."

"Really?" Lucas was smiling. Thomas and Brandon watched him, and Rebecca, without saying a word. "Such as?"

Rebecca looked up, returning his smile. "Such as this." And with that, she turned the drawing pad around to face him and the rest of the Knight siblings.

Katherine sucked in a breath, gripping the back of the newest chair. She looked, then found Rebecca's gaze. And nearly quivered from the love, the boldness, blazing in her eyes.

It was a quill. A long, elegant quill, with a sweeping line of vanes. Its point honed and sharpened to that of a dagger.

And as Katherine looked at the drawing, at the hands and the face of the woman she loved, she felt as if she were seeing her future, offered to her on a plate.

SPRING 1813

Katherine opened the window in the parlor and took a deep breath, reveling in the warm breeze listing over the garden. The scent of lilies pooled in her face, and she could not withhold a smile, her eyes slipping shut as a tide of memories washed over her. Memories still so vibrant that she felt as if she were living those moments again, as if the previous season had never ended, and Christmas at Mosswood had been but a dream.

But no. Katherine was far from the person she had been the year before. So much had changed within and around her. Sometimes she looked in the mirror, and failed to remember what she had looked like with such long hair.

She took another breath, filling her lungs, making herself a little light-headed. In spite of this, she smiled, almost giddy. Because when she closed her eyes, she saw Rebecca in her stunning gown at the Opening Ball the day before, scowling, her nose upturned. An expression of the utmost distaste and disregard, so completely at odds with the rest of her image as one of the season's most prominent debutantes.

Katherine had loved it. Had hardly been able to contain a

giggle when she saw Rebecca standing behind Lord and Lady Alwyn, receiving guests and looking as though she were being held over a bed of hot coals. And a part of Katherine sympathized — she knew all of the finery and the attention fell well below Rebecca's concern. But in some ways, Rebecca did not realize how lucky she was. To be part of such a prominent family, to have the admiration of the entire peerage. To entertain a whole flock of suitors, to have her pick of any eligible gentleman in the land. To never worry about her family's financial situation, about the practical concerns of marrying well.

But envy did not aid Katherine, and she knew it. She turned away from the window, relishing the sunlight beaming into the dusty parlor, and went to the desk. Fresh ink and her new quill lay waiting for her beside a thin stack of paper, accompanied by a pot of tea and a dish of biscuits.

An hour later, she heard a telltale footfall in the hall. Katherine looked up as the door swung open and Rebecca, wearing a delightful scowl, wandered into the parlor.

She was dressed in her motley trousers and tattered shirt, face hidden beneath her tricorn. "Good afternoon."

Katherine grinned at her. "Is it?" She lay down her quill, eased back in her chair. "I would never have guessed as such, based upon your expression."

"Do not tease me, dearest." Rebecca's voice was flat, devoid of amusement. She perched on the armrest of Katherine's chair. Brushed a kiss to Katherine's hair, slid a hand into her lap. "What a horrible night."

Katherine did laugh, then. "You speak as if you attended a funeral, instead of the Opening Ball."

"Are they not one and the same?"

"Rebecca, all you had to do was greet your guests and dance with a few gentlemen. Not surrender your favorite saber and perhaps a finger or two."

Rebecca hummed. "Did you enjoy yourself? I hardly saw you."

Katherine shrugged. "It was not the most entertaining of evenings. Scandal was thin on the ground. Though I did make a new acquaintance — Miss Rosaline Bailey."

"Bailey," Rebecca repeated, with a touch of a frown. "I don't believe I remember her."

Katherine leaned forward, reaching for that season's first edition of Madam Kensington, printed just the week before under a lovely new emblem — a quill, coming to the point of a knife. She held it out for Rebecca, pointing to the final sentence, which hinted at a rose-scented breeze arriving from the Continent. This information, of course, had come courtesy of the White Fox. "Her father is Sir Ian Bailey, the new Royal Physician. They returned to Britain from France, whence they fled after her mother's death some years ago. His appointment to the royal household caused something of a stir. Sir Ian is rather an unorthodox choice, given his relative youth, his background, and his methods, but it seems that he is connected to the Queen through his late wife."

"Intriguing. And what is Miss Bailey like?"

"Sharp," Katherine replied, sifting through her memories from the previous evening. "Clever. Not a bit amused by our delightful peers."

Rebecca smirked. "Imagine that."

"Miss Brown was quite rude to her. I had to step in, clear the air." And a part of her wished that Miss Bailey had come to find her in the garden, where they could have spoken more freely. Katherine itched to hear stories of France. "You might remember Miss Bailey's close friend and companion, who led her introduction at court. Lady Charlotte Prince."

Recognition, flickering in Rebecca's gaze. "Our Star of the season."

"Indeed. And Miss Bailey was named the Sapphire."

"Lady Prince," Rebecca mused. "A little blonde thing. With

naught but air between her ears, though an undeniably pretty face. As our Queen noticed."

"I have not made her acquaintance. Do you know her?"

"Of her," Rebecca replied. "She and her father are very solitary. And, apparently, a bit dotty."

Katherine snorted. "Then it seems that Miss Bailey is Lady Charlotte's precise opposite. But my God, Rebecca, is she beautiful."

"Is she?" A teasing, glinting edge in Rebecca's voice. Her fingers nudged Katherine's ribs.

Smiling, Katherine brushed a kiss to her cheek, squeezing her hand. "Let me put it this way. When you see Miss Bailey next, you will find it a challenge to maintain eye contact."

"I only have eyes for the woman I love. Unlike some people, apparently."

"You say that now, but her *décolletage* could start a war."

For several long, lovely moments, they sat in the steady birdsong from the garden, breathing in the dueling scents of must and flowers, sunlight and shadows. Katherine looked up at Rebecca's artful profile, thoughtful beneath the brim of her weathered tricorn, and felt an utter, bone-deep peace. With any luck, they would not be interrupted for some time.

"Will you form an acquaintance with them?" Rebecca's gaze was fixed upon the far wall, and Katherine knew that her true thoughts were elsewhere. "Miss Bailey, Lady Charlotte?"

"If they would have me," Katherine replied. "I would be a fool to turn down an opportunity to become close with the Star. Besides, with two such beautiful ladies at the forefront of the season, the gentlemen are sure to be entertaining indeed."

Rebecca hummed low in her throat, and did not reply.

Unlike her eldest brother, Katherine was not a gambler by nature. But now, she would stake her entire earnings from the week before that Rebecca was thinking about her own status. Not being named the Star had been a blow to her ego, and to her family's image, as much as Rebecca was loath to admit it.

Rebecca was beautiful, yes, and carried an unmistakable air of mystery, of elegance, of superiority. But unlike her sister, she did not allow her mother to drape her in the finest dresses, the most precious jewels. Rebecca dressed in stunning, though simple, gowns, and only wore a thin silver necklace. In the court, or in front of the peerage, she rarely smiled, did not charm or flirt, and never made light conversation. She did not pretend to enjoy an enterprise so entirely at odds with her character. She was herself, and that, it seemed, was not enough to make her the Star.

Katherine had a theory that the Queen liked to single out newcomers when bestowing her endorsement, perhaps for the sake of capitalizing upon the intrigue that already existed. It certainly explained her preference for Sophia as well as Charlotte, who was a relative unknown in spite of her father's rank. And Katherine had to give the Queen some credit for complimenting Rosaline as well — Rosaline, who was beautiful, but hardly fit the mold set by Sophia, by Charlotte.

"I am most curious to see who Miss Bailey might match with," said Katherine.

Rebecca gave a soft snort. "Should we not worry about who *we* might match with?"

Katherine brushed a kiss to her warm cheek, wishing that she could pull Rebecca into her lap, perhaps slide a hand beneath her weathered shirt. "There will be time enough for that, once we have legitimate suitors on the horizon."

"Where are your brothers?"

"I have no idea." Katherine frowned, thinking through the conversation from the breakfast table. The Knight family was still on 'country' time — they were rising early, and going to bed early. Much earlier than any of their peers. "I believe they mentioned something about going out of the city, perhaps with a few friends.

Or a boxing match, in some seedy bit of London I prefer not to think about."

Rebecca glanced at her. "You would trust Lucas in such an environment?"

"Yes." Katherine did not think about the tickle in the back of her throat, the tickle that spoke to her continued misgivings. "He is not alone, and between the two of them, Tom and Bran could restrain him, if necessary."

A smile. A small smile, but a smile nonetheless. "It was so amusing to see them last night. Freshly-shaved and wearing their starched suits."

"A shocking sight?"

"Blood-curdling." She squeezed Katherine's hand. "I think I preferred Tom with a beard."

"He was furious that Mother made him shave. He hardly spoke all afternoon."

"Will they join us for the rest of the season? It would be so dull without them."

"It is difficult to say," Katherine replied. "They have quite lost their patience for it. And I imagine Tom is still nursing his broken heart."

Rebecca rolled her eyes. "What a fool. He barely knew Sophia."

"To love is to learn. And Tom is a slow learner."

Rebecca eased to her feet, sighing. "I am exhausted, Katherine, and yet I cannot sit still."

I know the feeling, Katherine thought. Here, standing at the cusp of the season, with the music from the Opening Ball still ringing in her eyes, she felt as if she had not slept in weeks, as if the rumors and watchful eyes and the ruthless, cutting gossip were seeping into her skin, weighing her down. Madam Kensington had only just lifted her head from slumber, fresh and bright-eyed in the dawn of a thousand beginnings. But it was so much more difficult, now, to romanticize any of what was happening around them. One summer, one season, had been a ruthless and exacting education. Katherine knew the true, seething underbelly of her world all too well, and had to spend every moment pretending otherwise.

She stood up, going to Rebecca. "Imagine we were on the boat."

Rebecca turned to frown at her. "Pardon?"

"Imagine we were on the boat," Katherine repeated, draping an arm across Rebecca's shoulders, putting a hand to her waist. "Or standing at the ocean's edge. Salt and water all around us." She began to sway them in place. "Imagine a breeze, drifting over us. Pushing us together."

A smile crept across Rebecca's features. She let out a sigh, tipping her forehead down to Katherine's. "You cannot swim."

"Well," Katherine corrected her. "I cannot swim *well*."

"It rather dampens the excitement of being beside the water, dearest."

"You will teach me, then."

Rebecca pulled away, her eyes soft, their sharp edge dulled somewhat in the soft sunlight. She looked at Katherine. The moment pulled between them, glossy and content, full of promise, full of tragedy. They both knew it could never be, would never be.

"Yes." Rebecca closed her eyes, pressing her cheek to Katherine's. "I shall."

◈

"I SUPPOSE I SHOULD RETURN TO THE FESTIVITIES." MISS Bailey's voice carried a dry humor, but did not mask her palpable reluctance. She glanced over her shoulder, at the merry light and noise of the Denison Ball, and for a moment, seemed like a martyr.

Katherine put on a smile, trying to banish that melodramatic thought. "Yes, I imagine Lady Charlotte is searching for you."

A soft snort. "Not if Cadogan is within spitting distance." Miss Bailey looked at her, her gaze shining in the dappled moonlight. "Thank you, Katherine. For the company, and the refreshment. I do hope to see you again." She curtsied, and returned to the bulk of the party.

Once she was out of earshot, Katherine slumped back against the cool stone pillar, sucking in a lungful of air. She could hardly believe the scope of what she had just witnessed — the Duke of St. Alban's insult had been both flagrant and uncanny, precise and yet exaggerated. For Miss Bailey to have overheard it, and under such circumstances — it was the stuff of melodrama, of Shakespeare. Almost beyond the reach of Madam Kensington.

Katherine pressed her knuckle to her lips, attempting to ground herself. But it did very little good. So she took another breath, and went to find Brandon.

Several hours later, the parlor door closed behind them, and Katherine leaned against the faded wall, her mind churning. Beside her, Brandon stared into space, frowning at an invisible quarry. He hunched over the back of an armchair, his collar tilted, his jacket creased.

"Well?" Lucas glanced at both of them, arching an eyebrow. "Did we enjoy ourselves?"

Neither Katherine nor Brandon replied.

Thomas shot them a knowing look from his seat at the desk. "Something happened."

Katherine glanced at Brandon; she had given him a full report in the carriage. "Yes," she said. "Something quite odd."

Thomas dipped his quill in ink, ready. "Fire away."

Katherine told them everything, from her picnic with Miss Bailey to the Duke's insult, and the shock of Miss Bailey and the Duke entering the ballroom arm-in-arm not two hours later, glowing and twinkling at one another — or as much as the Duke was able to glow and twinkle — as if nothing had ever happened.

"It was so... strange," Katherine finished lamely. Her glass of Scotch sat untouched by her hand; she reached for it now, seeking solace. "Miss Bailey was candid in her dislike of the Duke, and he made his feelings about her quite clear. Why they should form an attachment — and dance together as if they were the only two people on the planet — is beyond my comprehension."

"Perhaps Miss Bailey is desperate for a match," said Lucas.

"No," said Thomas. He had ink on his fingers. "Her father earns a generous income, and her mother came from wealth."

"Did she?" Katherine frowned at him. "I never knew."

"Or the Duke apologized," Lucas went on. "Won Miss Bailey over."

Katherine thought of the expression on Miss Bailey's face when she'd overheard the Duke. She thought of the anger, the hurt. And the undeniable edge beneath it all. Miss Bailey did not seem like one to forgive lightly, or to trust her heart to such a dismissive and arrogant man.

"No." Katherine shook her head, took a sip of Scotch. "There has to be something else."

"You are too suspicious, Kitten." Lucas offered her an easy smile. "But perhaps that is rather an excellent quality, in our line of work."

"At any rate, now you have justification for staying close to Miss Bailey," said Thomas. "If a secret does come out, Madam Kensington should have the scoop."

Katherine rolled her eyes, though she could not fault his logic. As much as she wanted her relationship with Miss Bailey to be for the sake of friendship, ulterior motives were now her calling card. Katherine would be a fool to deny a link to two of the season's most eligible debutantes.

"It is late." Glass in hand, Katherine made her way towards

the door. She was followed only by the shadow of her conscience. "See you in the morning."

❧

KATHERINE WOKE SLOWLY, AS IF SLIPPING INTO A WARM BATH. Before she opened her eyes, she became aware of an arm wrapped around her middle, a chilly nose pressed to her neck. A mouth, brushing over her bare shoulder.

Katherine buried a smile in her pillow. "Good morning."

"Morning." Sighing, Rebecca nuzzled closer. Around them, the early light bathed Katherine's room in a gentle periwinkle, softened by birdsong. It could not have been long past six.

Katherine put a hand to Rebecca's hair, turned to brush a kiss to Rebecca's nose. It was a moot point to ask how Rebecca had snuck in — she now knew half a dozen secret ways into the Knight home, and somehow managed never to be caught by the staff. "What are you doing here?"

"I returned to shore an hour ago and wanted to see you." Rebecca kissed her in return, slow and gentle. "Before this infernal tea party at Kew."

"Oh." What a reminder. "My Aunt Jocelyn insisted that I attend. She is marching me there herself."

Rebecca grimaced. "What is the point? The men won't even be there."

"No," conceded Katherine. "That was my mother's perspective. She far preferred that I attend the opera."

"Ah, of course, the opera. Where lovers are destined to cross paths and pet one another in the darkness."

"*Rebecca.*"

She smirked. "I doubt Miss Bailey will enjoy the tea party."

"No," Katherine agreed. Something like unease rippled through her stomach, and she rolled over to face Rebecca properly. "I have been meaning to tell you. I might have been too honest with Miss Bailey."

Rebecca's eyebrows said enough, but she went ahead: "About?"

"About us. I did not mention you by name, of course," Katherine quickly added. "But she knows that I... well. That I love a woman."

A sharp silence fell. Rebecca broke it in a flat tone: "You trust her that much?"

"I did," Katherine replied. "I do. Besides... She is French. They are rather more open-minded about these things."

Rebecca said nothing. In the soft morning light, she was inscrutable.

"We are safe, Rebecca." Katherine squeezed her hand. "I promise. She has never even seen us together."

"No," said Rebecca, pointedly. "She has not."

Katherine looked at her, stung. "We agreed it was for the best."

A sigh. Rebecca turned to lie on her back, her hand falling to Katherine's waist. "We did."

Katherine could still remember that night. The night they had decided to spend the season at a distance from one another, just to dispel any potential suspicions. Those words, once they were out in the air, had carried the weight of a vow, though Katherine had not known the scope of what she had agreed to. The loneliness. The longing. The deep, dull ache of distance.

Katherine kissed Rebecca's cheek. "Tell me about your callers."

"Not now." Rebecca leaned into her touch. "Let us just lie here for a while. Listen to the sunrise."

Something in Katherine's heart trembled, and she squeezed her eyes shut.

❧ 32 ☙

Madam Kensington's High Society Papers,
No. 26

Rarely, my dear readers, am I ever proven wrong. Did I not promise that an evening at the opera would be full of surprises? Though even I can admit that much of the evening's delicious tension rested on a certain... shall we say, confrontation... that occurred during a very Floral afternoon. A writer such as myself could not possibly comment about the impropriety and admitted violence of certain actions, thrilling and deserved though they might have been. No, like everyone else, I must simply frown, stifle a giggle, and say, "Oh, yes, well... let us hope it does not happen again."

The opera itself was divine, and a winning choice for a season with an unmatched selection of eager Ladies and reluctant Lords — Marriage hangs in the air like a friendly spider, ready to draw us into her web. Even the Queen herself was seen laughing and smiling on more than one occasion, though she was understandably outshone by our favorite Star, whose brilliance glimmered even in the stuffy orchestral air. She certainly seemed to enjoy the evening more than our Sapphire, who appeared to disappear between the acts…

⁂

"Somewhat of a dull report, Thomas." Katherine looked up from that morning's copy of Madam Kensington, meeting his ready glare. "You could not give any further detail?"

"Your dear friend Miss Bailey disappeared during act three, then reappeared after the intermission. What more was I supposed to say? That she grew a pair of wings and fluttered over the Queen's head?"

"I told you you should have gone to the opera," Lucas said to Katherine, smirking over the morning paper. "Especially after the high drama of the afternoon."

Katherine grinned. "I needed time to recover my wits after seeing Miss Brown shrieking like the Devil had surfaced from the pond instead of Miss Bailey." In truth, she had been conscripted for supper at Aunt Jocelyn's, who had demanded all the gossip behind the commotion at Kew.

"I wish I could have seen it." Lucas gave a huge sigh. "Our lovely debutantes, sopping wet and ready to kill one another."

"Behave." Brandon threw a pillow in his face.

"What of the Duke?" Katherine said to Thomas. "Did he exit the theater with Miss Bailey?"

"I do not believe so," Thomas replied, still snippy. "Though I could barely see him from where I was sitting."

"Why do you ask?" said Lucas to Katherine, now putting Brandon in a headlock. "Do you suspect the Duke and Miss Bailey of engaging in something untoward?"

"I do not know." Dropping the pamphlet onto the couch, Katherine shook her head. "I cannot tell if their attachment is as genuine as it seems."

"The odd nature of it does not necessarily discount a true

affection," Lucas pointed out. Brandon, trapped between Luke's elbow and forearm, was turning red. "They could have overcome their mutual dislike by now."

"I agree with Kat," said Thomas. "The Duke is far too head-strong to surrender, let alone change his mind so readily."

"You would be surprised, dear brother," Lucas replied, "what a set of pretty eyes in a pretty face might do to a man's will." He finally let go of Brandon, who wheezed and dropped to the floor like a sack of potatoes.

"Does Cadogan say much, Lucas?" said Katherine, holding out her glass of water to Brandon. "At the Fox?"

Lucas shrugged. "He is as friendly as ever, though now that the Duke is in town, he claims much of Cadogan's attention."

There was an undeniable hint of jealousy in his words, and Katherine bit back a smile. Lucas always had trouble sharing, and until this year, the Duke of St. Alban's had rarely appeared in London, leaving Cadogan, on his occasional visits, at Lucas' disposal. "You dislike the Duke?"

"No," said Lucas, perhaps a touch too quickly. "He is affable enough. He was much more fun when he was at Cambridge. Ever since coming into his estate, he has become so serious and irrita-ble. It is a wonder Miss Bailey goes anywhere near him."

A marvel Katherine had noted all too often. "And does Cadogan make much mention of Lady Prince?"

"A little." Lucas drained his Scotch and watched Brandon clamber to his feet, still wheezing. "He is besotted, like any fool."

Thomas snorted, and Katherine let out a cackle. "Such harsh censure, brother! What has turned your heart so vehemently against the course of love?"

"Merely the fact that it is not a course at all, but rather a whirlpool."

"One day, Lucas," Katherine said. "One day, you will fall in love, and eat your words on a silver platter. Tom and I will see to it."

"I'll help," added Brandon.

"I doubt that," Lucas replied, and Katherine did not miss the look that passed through his eyes. A darkening, a shadow where there had once been a gleam.

"But are Cadogan's intentions genuine?" she pressed. "I do not want to encourage my friend's affections if they are not returned."

"I believe so." Lucas shrugged. "But I am hardly going to ask him, Kitten."

"Well, what can you tell me of his character? Does he drink, does he smoke, does he gamble, does he run amok in the streets?"

Lucas smiled, in a gentle and teasing way. "Only on occasion, and with encouragement."

"Ah." Katherine nodded. "Then I shall advise Charlotte to keep him well away from you."

"Perhaps you should instead encourage Lady Prince to show a fraction of encouragement to poor Cadogan," said Thomas. "Rather than Lord Crawley."

Lucas frowned. "That pompous idiot?"

"Rosaline and I are... working on it." Katherine cleared her throat. "Now. Which of you is escorting me to the Rosier Ball?"

All three of her brothers groaned, and Thomas was the last one to put a hand to his nose.

"Fabulous." Katherine grinned at him. "We shall find you a wife yet, dear Tom."

His glare, to her delight, could have stopped a heart.

❧

KATHERINE HAD LONG SINCE LEARNED NEVER TO FIGHT THE sheer chaos invited by the London season, and Madam Kensington was already reaping its rewards. Lucas' idea to increase their publishing — three or four editions a week, as opposed to two — had been a bit of a risk, but the peerage of London had been all too keen to contribute to the effort. Already, Katherine had lost track of the scandals, the whispers, the never-ending drama of courtship. Without Thomas' help, she would have already succumbed to the season's inexorable tide, disappearing beneath its turgid surface.

During their second week in London, Brandon had begun the long and delicate undertaking of siphoning minuscule parts of their income into the family's account. With sales climbing higher and higher, Madam Kensington could afford it, along with a small but steady stipend for Katherine's own pocket. Lucas, nearing the end of his debt to the Tyndales, had insisted upon it, pressing the coins into her hand with a silent and undeniable force. Katherine, speechless, had looked at her brother and seen a resolve reminiscent of their father. Her protest had withered and died in her throat, meaningless in the face of Lucas' conviction.

She began to wonder, then, with a genuine curiosity, as to what the family, and the business, might look like under his guidance. This prospect, which had once been distant and faint, now seemed reasonable, even proper.

It was only a matter of time before their parents noticed the increase in the household account. Brandon already had an excuse at the ready — that he, following the advice of some of his friends, had made a few clever but prudent investments, and the returns were already beginning to accumulate. This excuse wisely shifted focus away from Lucas, and gave Thomas leeway to bolster Brandon's story.

Rebecca, meanwhile, had proven an excellent source of gossip from the mothers, who appeared to have little restraint around Lady Alwyn. Rebecca reported everything to the Knights with an undeniable relish, and Katherine could not fault her for it — there was redemption in trading gossip, in undermining the nonexistent but pervasive sanctity of the wealthy. If only she had the opportunity to show Rebecca the depth of her gratitude, preferably behind a locked door, in a bed, with a few candles burning. But their resolution to keep one another at a distance —

and Rebecca's overflowing social calendar — made such an indulgence all but impossible.

Katherine had stopped counting the days since she had last
had Rebecca entirely to herself. Doing so only invited grief.

But Rosaline and Charlotte had proven diverting indeed.
Katherine watched their courtships as one would a tennis match,
knowing beyond a shadow of a doubt that the Duke and Cadogan
were utterly besotted, and would bend over backwards for their
ladies at the slightest provocation. At the Rosier Ball, she had
caught the Duke looking at Rosaline with a gaze so full of heat it
was a wonder that Rosaline's dress did not melt off her body.
Rosaline herself seemed almost unaware of the Duke's attention,
however, lending support to Katherine's theory that there was
more to their supposed attachment than met the eye.

And when Miss Brown collapsed in a dead faint in the center
of the Eventide Ball, Katherine did little apart from smirk and
lean in towards Thomas. "An excellent falsehood," she whispered
as the entire room converged on Miss Brown and her prey, the
young Rosier. "I should award her extra points for breaking so
much glass."

"And not a scratch on her." Thomas glanced at her. "How do
you know it to be false?"

"Because a true faint is never so large, or so artful. Miss Brown
practiced that move. I would swear to it in a court of law."

But Thomas' attention was elsewhere. He looked across the
crowd, raising an eyebrow. "Our Sapphire seems flustered."

Katherine followed his gaze, and had to agree. The Duke and
Rosaline were flushed and panting, as if they had just finished
dancing a jig. Cadogan and Charlotte converged on them;
Cadogan clapped the Duke on the shoulder and a large puff of
dust rose into the air.

"What do you make of that?"

Katherine shook her head. "I have no earthly idea."

And she suspected nothing, not even at Lady Ednam's tea

party the next day, where Rosaline seemed a touch distracted, a touch distant. Katherine's instincts only began to prickle the following night, when Lucas and Thomas returned from the White Fox earlier than expected.

"Before you ask," said Thomas, pouring himself a Scotch, "the Duke was not present this evening."

"Oh." Katherine exchanged a look with Rebecca across their game of casino. Brandon sat between them, a somewhat unwilling participant. "That is unlike him, is it not? I thought he preferred not to take supper at home."

Lucas nodded. "Cadogan was alone, though in good spirits." He paused before taking his usual spot on the couch. "You are too paranoid, Kitten."

"Katherine's instincts have not failed yet," Rebecca pointed out. She, like Rosaline, had come away from Lady Ednam's tea party much the tipsier, and a delicate red haze still shone on her cheeks. "Though it might be a fluke."

"It might," Katherine agreed, drumming her fingers on the card table. She could have kicked herself for not pressing Rosaline for information earlier that day, though she had no idea how she might have managed it without raising any suspicion.

In the end, of course, Katherine was right.

❧

THOMAS CLOSED THE PARLOR DOOR, PUSHED HIS WINDSWEPT hair out of his face, and said: "He is gone. The Duke of St. Alban's has left London."

Katherine paused mid-sentence, splattering ink across her knuckle. "How do you know?"

"Rita just told me that his cook failed to show at the market today, and I drove past his house myself. It is quite shut up, without so much as a whisper of life. He either took his staff with him, or left but a few of them behind."

"How odd." Katherine met Brandon's gaze, but he looked as confused as she felt. "What might force him out of the city?"

"Is it not obvious?" said Lucas, looking between them. "A broken heart."

"What?" said Brandon, incredulous.

"You mean that Miss Bailey denied him?" said Thomas.

"No," said Katherine at once, a jolt in her stomach. "No, if the Duke had made such an offer, she would have told me."

"But would Miss Bailey have accepted him?" pressed Thomas.

"Yes." Katherine blinked a few times. "No. I have no idea."

"For being one of the most prominent couples of the season," said Lucas, "they are terribly good at keeping us guessing."

Guess was all that Madam Kensington could do in the end. And as Katherine watched her half-wild theories spin across London, she could not deny a spike of self-loathing. If the Duke's departure did have anything to do with a broken heart, she disliked being the one to claim it.

Though Rosaline seemed entirely unaffected by the whole matter. When the subject of the Duke's absence arose in public, she did not appear surprised, or distressed; rather, she offered the simple and basic refrain: "The Duke has gone to the country on urgent business matters, and will return as soon as he is able."

If Rosaline *was* concealing any personal strife, Katherine had to applaud her acting. But this assumption was proven false — Rosaline soon confided in Katherine and Charlotte about the break-in at the Duke's country estate, and Katherine felt inclined to trust her. Perhaps the Duke would return, in his own time.

So, Katherine forced Madam Kensington's hand to other topics, other couples. She forced herself to write about Rebecca's suitors, though it made her stomach churn and her heart fill with bile. She forced herself to withstand her brothers' jokes on the matter, on the persistent and obvious lack of her own suitors.

And this, perhaps, should have been her warning. That it was all too wonderful, and too terrible, to last.

The letter arrived in the morning post, as if it were any other letter. Mrs. Knight had already departed for Aunt Linda's, and Mr. Knight was dozing over his newspaper. This, it transpired, would be a small mercy.

"Oh." Lucas smiled at the envelope, broke the seal. "It is from the Emperor himself."

"Ah!" Thomas took the rest of the bacon, ignoring Katherine's scowl. "Has he returned from— where was he, again?"

"Hamburg, the poor lamb. August must have hated it, if he has returned this early." Lucas scanned the letter, and his smile broke into a grin. "Oh, how excellent. He is in London, and staying in his new house across the river. He would like to visit, to come to supper, if we would have him. He says—" Lucas' voice faltered, and he glanced at Katherine, his expression sobering. "He says he is particularly looking forward to seeing Katherine."

An astonished silence filled the air, broken only by their father's snore.

For a long, aching moment, words failed Katherine. Her mind spun and fumbled, attempting to reconcile *August Heath* and *supper*.

"He cannot mean," Thomas began—

"I rather think he does." Lucas' voice had become clipped and short; he passed the letter to Katherine, who took it with unfeeling fingers. "August never wastes his words. He would not have mentioned— would not have even *hinted*— if he did not mean—"

"What should we do?" said Brandon, glancing at their father, who had not given a single sign of hearing them. "Should we invite him?"

"We have to," Thomas replied, as Katherine read the letter for herself. True enough, there were the words, in plain, unrelenting ink. August Heath wanted to see her. "Tonight."

"Tonight?" Katherine repeated, finding her voice. "Thomas, surely not—"

"Better than to wait, Kitten," said Lucas, with something like sympathy in his words. He stood up from the table. "I'll have a word with Salk, and get a message to Mother. She will want to see August as well. It has been years, after all." With a final look at his sister, he swept from the room, leaving her to the endless spiral of her own thoughts.

And in that moment, all Katherine wanted was Rebecca. To bury her face in Rebecca's neck, to tremble and scream and carry on like all the heroines in the novels were wont to do. But she couldn't. Rebecca was on the ship, and they would not be able to steal a moment together at Lady Linley's garden party later that afternoon.

The room spun. Katherine realized it was because she had stopped breathing. But whether from outrage, anxiety, or anger, she could hardly tell.

❧

LIKE HIS MUSTACHE, AUGUST HEATH WAS PUNCTUAL, TRIM, AND short. Katherine became painfully aware of this last fact as he bowed in front of her, a sweeping, delicate movement far beyond her own capabilities.

"Miss Knight." His smile was polite, though warm. "How wonderful to see you again."

"You as well," she replied, accepting a dry kiss on her hand. He was at least an inch or two shorter than her, though his curling hair did attempt to make up the difference.

Behind him, Mrs. Knight stood and smiled, beaming brightly enough to light half of London. Katherine tried to ignore this, as well as the reluctant approval on her father's face. *This visit means nothing*, she told herself as they went into the dining room. *It means nothing.*

Over an excellent meal of lamb and roasted vegetables, Mr. Heath recounted his tales from over a year spent on the Continent, traveling between cities and falling monarchies. His father, who owned and operated a very successful business specializing in the trade of furs and pelts, had been using his son as somewhat of a go-between with his suppliers as well as his buyers. It was a strange and fascinating profession, but Katherine had no interest in it, not today.

Perhaps it had been unwise, to confide in Rosaline and Charlotte about Mr. Heath's visit the way she had earlier that day. But Katherine was desperate, and unashamed to admit it. Desperate for reassurance, for support. Any hint of understanding, any scrap of advice. Anything that might spare her the indignity of hearing, let alone accepting, a proposal—

After supper, Mr. and Mrs. Knight left their children and their guest to their own amusements, retiring to the library. Katherine did not miss the sneaky grin her mother shot her before exiting the drawing room, and she swallowed a wave of panic.

But then, thankfully, Brandon brought out a fresh deck of cards, Lucas poured a fresh round of Scotch, and they settled down for an excellent match of whist.

Katherine had forgotten just how well she and Mr. Heath played together, and for a lovely hour or so, it was as if no time had passed since his last visit, and they were still sitting before the fire at Mosswood, winning tricks and laughing with triumph. More than once, she caught Mr. Heath watching her, his expression inscrutable, though tinged with a curiosity, a watchfulness, that she could not readily explain.

He is kind, Katherine reminded herself, as they won yet another trick and Thomas threatened them with disembowelment. *He is kind, and sweet. He would never do anything untoward.*

She was expecting it, when Mr. Heath asked her brothers if he might speak with her alone for a while, but that did not make his request any less startling.

Lucas looked right at Katherine, and said nothing until she gave him a tiny nod. "Certainly," he said, dropping his cards.

Thomas, looking a touch unconvinced, reluctantly did the same. Brandon stood up from the couch, wearing an unconvincing smile.

"We shall wait in the dining room," said Lucas. He took the decanter in hand. "Heath, you still owe me those stories from Rome."

"Yes, of course," said Mr. Heath, and they all understood what Lucas actually meant. He had set an expectation, a deadline of sorts, and if Mr. Heath did not meet it, Lucas had the right to interrupt his time with Katherine. With this final, silent agreement, the Knight boys exited the room.

Katherine noticed that her brothers left the door ajar behind them. She forced down a spike of nerves as Mr. Heath's gaze found hers, as the corner of his mouth lifted.

"Miss Knight," he began, but that would never do.

"There is no need for such formalities, August," she replied. "Not if you are going to say what I suspect you will say."

His brow quirked, but he did not seem surprised. "Fair enough, Katherine." He eased back into his chair. "We are hardly strangers."

"No," she agreed, and a few more memories from Christmas two years prior floated to the surface of her mind. "We are the precise opposite, I would say."

Here, finally, his expression sobered. "Thank you," August said, dipping his voice low, "for your continuing discretion."

"There is no need to thank me," she replied. "I saw nothing, remember?"

"Katherine." God, there was such a weight in his voice. "Your sincerity is flattering, though not necessary. Not now."

She took a trembling breath, squeezing her hands into fists beneath the card table. "How can you make me an offer, August? When I know what I know?"

A wince passed over his delicate features, and she was once again reminded of how ridiculous his eyelashes were. "Because I know the truth as well, Katherine. About your family's finances." When he met her gaze, it was with a remarkable sincerity, rather than pity. "I know that marriage would be the most reasonable, the most prudent, course of action you could take."

A horrible chill had seeped into Katherine's stomach, reaching to her toes. "How?" she demanded. "How could you know such a thing?"

"Because I have a pair of functioning eyes, Katherine." He quickly added, in a softer tone, "And I am aware of the trade situation, the state your family's business is in, thanks to the embargoes. You are not alone, Katherine — hundreds of British businesses are suffering, thanks to these bloody wars."

But this was not good enough. "You can be a kind man, August, but not generous, and certainly not unless you were to gain something in return. Why ask me now?"

Another wince. "Because my father... My father is ill, extremely ill, and he has been hounding me to marry. Forgive me," he said, his words gaining an edge, "but I could not find it within myself to deny a dying man his last wish."

Katherine stared at him in horror. This, at least, explained his sudden return to England. "August," she managed, recalling the dozens of stories he had told of his childhood, of his father— "I am so sorry. I know you are very close with him."

August nodded, a shade of pain passing through his gaze. "I have to try," he said. "For his sake as well as mine. And I thought..." He looked at her. "I thought why not approach a friend, who might need some assistance?"

For a moment, Katherine almost left it alone. She believed him, of course — August was a man who kept his word, who valued honesty above most other considerations, including politeness. But he was a clever man as well. She had to know— "There is more to it, August, isn't there?"

He gave an unsteady laugh, and his gaze darted to the door. "I had forgotten how perceptive you are. Much to my own detriment."

"Give me the whole truth, August," Katherine went on, squeezing her hands into fists again, even as they ached. "I deserve at least that much."

"You do." He nodded, then sucked in an unsteady breath. Anxiety and unease showed on his pretty face, and he said, "Quite inconveniently, I am in love."

Katherine looked at him for a moment, and something within her quivered. "Oh, August—"

"He is under the same pressures as I," August went on. His hand was trembling. "To wed. And he is concerned that our... shared bachelorhood... attracts too much attention. But if one of us were to... to..." His voice cracked, and he let out another laugh, glancing once again at the door.

Understanding, terrible and absolute, washed over Katherine. "I see."

"It is mad," he said. "And selfish. But I cannot bear the thought of losing him, Katherine. Just as I cannot bear the idea of your family's difficulty. You and your brothers have been good to me, Katherine, when so many others have not."

She nodded, her mind whirling. This was hardly the direction she had expected the conversation to take, and she felt as if she had been set adrift on a vast and endless tide.

"Give me a minute to think," she said, and August nodded.

Katherine got up from the table and began to pace the distance between the fireplace and the opposite wall. She kept her eyes on the floor, on her own feet, refusing to acknowledge that this conversation was happening at the same table where she and Rebecca had shared their first kiss.

An idea had taken root in her mind. A wild, mad, crazed idea. And she could not bring herself to discard it, not even at the behest of her own rationality.

I have gambled before, Katherine thought, coming to a halt. *Perhaps I can test my luck again.*

"August," she said, and he looked up at her. "What if I were able to find a wife for him as well? The man you love?"

Surprise flickered across his expression. "I— I should imagine that he might be amenable to it, if there were an understanding—"

"Yes," said Katherine quickly, going over to the desk. "Yes, there would be a most adamant and mutual understanding." She handed him paper, ink, and quill. "Please write down your income, and his." When he raised his brow, she added, "I cannot make any guarantees, but I can best argue your case, as well as his, if I already have the figures before me."

"And what case would that be?" August glanced up at her, busy writing. "What are you planning, Katherine?"

Another ripple of anxiety went through her, but Katherine ignored it. "What if, August, we could each spend our lives with the people we loved, even if we were married to someone else?"

This time, when he looked at her, a new understanding, a new sympathy, a new surprise, grew in the depths of his gaze. "I see."

"I make no promises, however." She bit her lip. "I cannot guarantee that she will accept my proposal."

He nodded, finishing his note with a flourish. "I quite understand. It is a lot to ask, especially of someone you love." A sigh eased out, and he swept a hand through his hair. "I make no guarantees for Lord Oswalt, either. He is cantankerous at the best of times, and very prideful."

"But we have an agreement?" Katherine folded his note in half, and slipped it into her pocket. "Not to speak of this with anyone until we are certain?"

"Of course. I shall tell your brothers that you needed some time to think." August stood up, hesitated, then reached for her hand. Katherine let him take it, realizing that she might as well become accustomed to his touch. "You will send word, once you've spoken to your beloved?"

"Yes. I imagine she will want to meet Lord Oswalt, if we are to... proceed."

"As will he. I look forward to your correspondence." The corner of his mouth lifted. "Thank you, Katherine. Sincerely."

"I might be the one thanking *you*, August." She squeezed his hand with genuine gratitude.

With that, they parted ways. August went to join her brothers, and Katherine made her way upstairs, an undeniable bubble of hope building in her chest.

❧ 33 ❦

"You would have me marry," said Rebecca, "a complete stranger?"

"In an ideal world, no," said Katherine. "If it meant getting to spend the rest of my life with you, yes."

"But it would not *be* the rest of our lives, Katherine." Rebecca's eyes flashed, though her voice remained steady. "It would be whatever time we might cobble together in the midst of our lives as married women. Women who are married to men."

"Men who are like *us*," Katherine hissed, glancing at the door, even though they were completely alone on the ship. It was a habit she could not shake. "Rebecca, they would not want to spend any more time with us than strictly necessary. Under the circumstances, we do not have a better option. Would we have to marry? Yes. Would we have to marry two gentlemen we barely know? Yes, just as we would have done regardless." She raised her voice as Rebecca stood up and began to pace the short space of her cabin. "And would we be able to use those marriages to our social and financial advantage, while protecting our own attachment to one another? Yes!"

"It is evident that you have already made up your mind." A

hard edge crept into Rebecca's voice. "And decided what would be the best choice."

Katherine fought the urge to scream out of pure exasperation. "Rebecca, all I did was see an opportunity that would benefit the both of us, and seize upon it."

"This is not just about me, Katherine." A cutting glance. "This is about your family. Your finances. Your inconsequential prospects."

Katherine sucked in a breath, trying to bury the sting of those words. "You never had to worry about your family's finances, Rebecca, and I would beg you to remember that privilege."

Rebecca glanced at her again, and Katherine saw the apology in her features before she spoke it aloud. "I am sorry. I spoke too harshly. But it..." She shook her head, pushing a hand through her wild hair. "It is a lot to take in."

Katherine nodded. "I completely understand your reluctance, given that neither of us knows Lord Oswalt."

"What have you learned about him?"

"He is a bachelor, as August said. He is two-and-thirty, cunning, handsome, and rather arrogant. Socializing is not his strong suit, but he can be polite when necessary." Katherine swallowed hard. "Lord Oswalt has a reputation for indulgence, tempered only by a somewhat religious sense of self-hatred."

Rebecca let out a scoff, incredulous, and muttered something in Dutch.

"But," Katherine went on, heat in her face. "He is a fair employer, and generous to his staff. His estate oversees three separate charities, and he keeps little in his houses, apart from the bare minimum."

"Is that supposed to compensate for his deficient character, his want of propriety?"

"No. To soften it, perhaps."

Rebecca sighed, and looked at her. In the slanting light of the ship windows, her profile was lush, framed by her wind-tossed curls. Her clothes were filthy, stained by the long hours of work on the ship, and she smelled of wood polish and river mud. Katherine wanted to lick her from top to toe, but those concerns faded as Rebecca asked her, "And you and I would be together? Properly? Alone?"

"Yes. As much as we liked." Katherine tried to smile. "I imagine Lord Oswalt will go out of his way to keep August to himself. I hear he does not share well."

"Delightful." Rebecca rolled her eyes. "Can I meet him, at least?"

Katherine's heart leapt into her throat. "Yes, of course. I need only write to August — he will make all the arrangements."

"Very well." Rebecca crossed the room, and reached for Katherine's hand, an echo of August's own endearing farewell. She kissed it and said, "What of August? Is he a kind man?"

"Yes." The heat of her mouth was distracting; Katherine fought off a shiver. "And, according to Rosaline, we have more than enough money to keep a pleasant household between the two of us."

"I am beginning to think that Miss Bailey could run a bank, if she so wished."

"Or the country."

Rebecca stroked her thumb over the skin she had kissed. "Perhaps it is too fanciful, Katherine. To believe that we might have a life together. A private life."

"Perhaps." Katherine looked her directly in the eye. "But shouldn't we at least try?"

"Yes," said Rebecca, and something darkened in her gaze. She kissed Katherine's hand again, then turned it and licked, sucking Katherine's thumb into her mouth.

Where words failed, it seemed, their bodies spoke all too clearly.

❧❦❧

August sent a worried glance at the clock. "He is normally much more punctual."

Katherine watched Rebecca bite back a scowl and ignored her own tremor of unease. "That is quite all right," said Katherine quickly, with a pointed glance at Rebecca.

"You were candid about the nature of this meeting?" said Rebecca, leaning against the mantelpiece. "He is not under the impression that he is seeing you alone?"

"No," said August, though a fresh blush did rise in his face. "And he indicated that he is most excited to make your acquaintance, Lady Rebecca."

She smiled without humor. "I am certain he is."

It was another tense quarter of an hour before there came the sound of footsteps in the hall, and the drawing room door opened with a *bang*. In strode a tall, broad man with rugged, broad features and a thick, broad scowl.

"Good evening." Lord Oswalt glowered at Katherine and Rebecca, while August hurried to close the door behind him. "Shall we get this over with?"

"Lord Oswalt, might I introduce Miss Katherine Knight," said August, "and Lady Rebecca Alwyn?"

"Charmed." Though Lord Oswalt's tone indicated nothing of the sort. Rather than join the three of them at the table, he went over to the sideboard and helped himself to a glass of wine. "So, which of you is to be mine? Or are we to close our eyes and pick at random?"

"Henry," said August, his tone sharp. He shot a quick, apologetic glance at Katherine and Rebecca; beneath the table, Katherine took Rebecca's hand and squeezed. "These ladies have been very kind and generous thus far. I beg you not to jeopardize our acquaintance."

Lord Oswalt snorted but came to join them, taking a swig of wine. Katherine found herself mesmerized by his features; they were plush, oddly historical, and heavy, almost foreign. He was handsome, yes, but unconventionally so. "Well, how should we proceed?"

"First, we should discuss our expectations," said August. "And if we might be... compatible."

Lord Oswalt smiled without humor. "You have rather the advantage, August, considering that you have known your intended for longer than a space of a few minutes."

"Lady Rebecca and I have reviewed the financial aspects of the match," said Katherine, as Rebecca's grip tightened. "We believe it will be a suitable proposal for both our families."

"Of course it will," said Lord Oswalt. "As well-off as the Alwyns seem, their money is new and wanting a good dose of old English wealth. And you, Miss Knight, will take anything you can get, will you not? The ladies will be the ones benefiting in this situation," he said, ignoring Rebecca's poorly concealed rage. "Not you and I, August."

August had closed his eyes and gone a bit pale. "I beg you, Henry," he said. "To remember your manners."

For the first time that night, Lord Oswalt looked at August, and Katherine watched something in his face soften. She reminded herself that he was prideful and protective, and realized that this prospect was probably just as painful to him as it was to Rebecca.

"I think," she said, her voice low, "we should all acknowledge that this is far from an ideal situation. The four of us are simply trying to make the best with what is available to us, while fulfilling the obligations with which our families and ranks have saddled us."

"Indeed," said August, his eyes still closed.

"With that in mind," Katherine went on, "let us return to the topic of finances." With her free hand, she took out the sheet of Rosaline's calculations, laying it on the table between them. "Lord Oswalt, you and Rebecca come from similar enough backgrounds that the match between you would make good financial sense, and benefit you both. If you wished, you could even keep your finances separate, and still live in the style to which you are accustomed." She took a rallying breath, and felt Rebecca squeeze her hand. "My situation is a little more complicated, but the numbers likewise speak to a beneficial arrangement for me and August, in the long-term. Each couple can determine privately, in the space of their own relationship, what would be the best path forward, but overall, I see no monetary reason why we should not proceed."

Lord Oswalt was frowning at the sheet of calculations. "You've got a very good accountant. Might I have his name?"

"No," said Rebecca, her tone even. "She is far too busy being courted by a Duke."

"Shame." Lord Oswalt pushed aside the numbers and met Rebecca's gaze. "What next?"

Over the course of the next half hour, the four of them hammered out the details of their hypothetical marriages. Here, Katherine was content to let Rebecca and August take the lead — Lord Oswalt offered little, apart from an adamant claim upon August for the majority of the summer. This suited Katherine and Rebecca's demands to be in London for the annual season; after all, Madam Kensington could hardly disappear, and it was far easier for Katherine to see her family in London than to travel all the way north.

And as the conversation continued, not once did any of them mention the question of children. Katherine could not bring herself to voice it, but she wondered if it would surface in the future. Though it was difficult to imagine Lord Oswalt having much concern for anyone apart from himself or August. Try as she might, she could not picture him with a baby.

"Well, ladies?" Lord Oswalt had put down several more glasses of wine, and now he raised an eyebrow, testing them. "What say you? Shall we proceed?"

Katherine caught a glance from Rebecca and quickly said,

"We will take a few days to think it over, and consult with our families."

"Ah, of course." Lord Oswalt smirked at August. "The proverbial tribe of older brothers. You shall have to be on your best behavior, August."

He was not wrong. Lucas had made it very plain to Katherine what would happen if August should offer her anything less than her worth. August managed a smile and said, "They have been nothing but pleasant thus far, and are a testament to the Knight family's well-polished manners."

Both Katherine and Rebecca laughed at that, then stood up from the table. The men copied them. "Gentlemen," said Katherine, gathering their notes, "you have been most helpful. Lord Oswalt, we sincerely appreciate your coming to meet with us today."

"Do you?" Again that eyebrow, and that smirk. "Lady Rebecca does not seem to agree, not that I can fault her for it." He shifted closer to August, looked down into his eyes with a tenderness that made Katherine's heart hiccup with surprise — this was the first sign he had given all evening of their attachment. Perhaps it was the result of the wine. "I have found the only man in Britain who can put up with me."

Katherine and Rebecca left together, taking a cab back to the Knight house — or, rather, a house two streets away from the Knight residence. They sat in relative silence, and Katherine guessed that Rebecca's mind was as full and fraught as her own. Full of questions, of doubts. Of that blind, tentative, ceaseless hope.

Once they were out of the cab, they began to walk. The early evening air pooled around them as they rounded on Katherine's street corner. "Here," Rebecca murmured, brushing her hand against Katherine's. Katherine followed her into the shadows, recognizing the dull, old brick of the Knights' back garden wall, and past their rusting, ancient gate.

"No wonder you never had any trouble," Katherine murmured, as the faint sounds of the street faded away. Even in the dense shade of the trees and hedges, she could see Rebecca's smirk. The rich, wet scents of lilies and mud tangled in the air, and Katherine could not deny the feeling that they were wandering through a fairy land, a place of mystery and magic.

Rebecca drew to a halt near the edge of the lawn, where, less than a year ago, she had pressed Katherine into a tree and driven her to pleasure after pleasure. "Your family is lucky to have land like this."

"We are lucky it survived the Riots," Katherine replied, running a hand over the smooth, delicate bark of the nearest tree. "Most of it burned black and flat. It was years before it grew back, and ever since... My father cannot bear to cut it. We let it run wild."

"I bet your gardener appreciates that."

"Oh, it is an ongoing argument. A tradition. On the summer solstice, they call a truce for one day and go to the pub together."

Rebecca went silent for several moments, and a prickle of apprehension went down Katherine's spine. As she watched, Rebecca looked at the house, with its cheerful, warmly-lit windows, and seemed to make up her mind.

"Katherine." Rebecca's voice was smooth. "We have another option, and I would beg you to give it due consideration."

Katherine's heart thudded in her ears, and her face began to tingle. "What option?"

"The option of going our own way, without the guise of matrimony, without our family's knowledge or approval." Rebecca turned to look at her, and her gaze was full of nothing but sincerity. "I have my own savings, Katherine, as do you. Enough that we might find a new life far away from London, away from the eyes and the ears of everyone who might judge us for what we do, or who we love."

"I have savings," Katherine began, stumbling around the

words, "yes, Rebecca, but not very much. It does not compare to my dowry, or the future earnings from Madam Kensington—"

"Nor does mine. But it is still enough."

"You are talking of running away."

Rebecca's eyebrows lifted. "I would prefer to think of it as eloping."

"You would abandon your family? Your sisters? Your *niece?*"

"I would do anything, if it meant I could have you. Completely and utterly. Without any condition upon our behavior or the time we spent together."

And a part of Katherine understood what she meant. Understood the quiet rage that never dampened, never dulled. The rage and the hurt and the pure desperation to spend the rest of one's life with the person one loved. The desire to never hide, no matter the cost. To chase what other couples had, and what many of them never truly wanted. To chase it, to protect it. To nurture it and let it flourish.

As much as her brothers loved her, Katherine knew they would never understand this part of her. They would abhor it, condemn it. They would call her a fool, perhaps even an aberration. She was their sister, yes, but they saw only what they wanted to see, what she allowed them to see. They saw only one side of her true nature, and never the whole.

Katherine's mind turned to the question that had plagued her ever since she had first kissed Rebecca in the drawing room. Was Katherine's family genuinely her family, if they did not know her to her truest and fullest extent? Were they her family, if they would reject her fundamental nature, while lauding and upholding their own?

"You would prefer anonymity, poverty, and infamy," said Katherine, "to marrying Lord Oswalt, and bedding me in his country manor?"

"Lord Oswalt did leave a few things to be desired. But I will admit, he was not as terrible as I imagined." Rebecca came closer, the shadows shifting over her face. "I would settle to be his wife, if absolutely necessary."

"But you do not believe it to be necessary?"

"No," Rebecca replied. "Not if we are careful, and frugal. And not if we leave at the end of the season, as opposed to the height of it. After we have cashed in on every stitch of gossip."

Unbidden, Katherine's mind shifted to imagining the looks on Rosaline and Charlotte's faces, if they would hear such a truth about their dear friend Katherine. *Gone, vanished in the night, without a trace.* And then she thought of her mother, her father.

She thought of what they would say, if they knew the truth.

Katherine squeezed her eyes shut, then opened them again, white bursts flickering across her vision. She breathed in the humid, mossy air and said, "I will need to ask Rosaline. If we have enough money to survive."

"You trust her with such a task?"

Katherine swallowed past a very dry throat. "She need not know the truth of what I am asking, or its full scope."

"Katherine. That is a very serious risk."

"I have trusted Rosaline thus far, with the most sensitive information possible, and she has proven her loyalty a thousand times over. She does not know your true identity, and giving her this information will not change that. Besides," she added, "the only other person who is any good at sums is Brandon."

Rebecca sighed, but nodded. "Fine." She then gave Katherine the details of her personal income, an amount she had saved over the years; a sum of leftover pocket money, and her cut of the errands and tasks she had performed for her father.

Katherine made a quick note of all of it on a spare scrap of paper, including their estimated earnings from Madam Kensington through the end of the summer. Now that Lucas' debt was repaid, Katherine, Rebecca, and Rita were earning a higher percentage.

And though she could hardly see her own writing in the dense shade of the trees, Katherine could not deny that those messy figures fed her burgeoning hope. She and Rebecca were not accustomed to luxury, to finery — they could live within their means, take work as they found it, build a small, comfortable home together. It was all within reach, and Katherine felt that all she had to do was hold out her hand, and take it.

⚜

KATHERINE STARED DOWN AT THE NOW-FAMILIAR handwriting, at the sum of money Rosaline was referring to as a 'wedding present.'

"I have done some research," Rosaline was saying, as if she had not imploded Katherine's entire world. "This—" she tapped the note— "should be more than enough to purchase a seafront cottage in Cornwall, Devon, or Brighton. Or, even a modest townhome, should you not wish to be so remote. You can use the remaining amount to purchase all incidentals, pay your taxes, and even guarantee your servants' discretion."

Katherine felt all the heat leave her body, then flood back in, as if someone had opened and closed a dam. "Rosaline—"

"And with your combined allowance," Rosaline pressed on, "you and your beloved could be entirely self-sufficient, should you wish to be." She squeezed Katherine's hand. "You would have your own life, your own space. And your husband and Lord Oswalt would have the whole of their estates to themselves. You would not lose anything, Katherine, or anyone, and you would be safe."

For several moments, Katherine just stared at Rosaline, her vision blurring as the future opened before her, so much wider than it had seemed before. "Yes," she managed to choke out. "Oh, Rosaline, you are too kind, I do not deserve—"

"Hush." Rosaline smiled and squeezed her hand again, her

gaze warm and full of reassurance. "Don't you have a letter to write, and a proposal to accept?"

"Yes!" Katherine hastened to wipe away her tears, which were threatening to grow into full-blown weeping. "Oh, yes, I must— I must go at once— Please, give the others my goodbyes, make up some urgent matter—"

Rosaline nodded. "Of course. Now go!"

Katherine hurried across the park, keeping her face dipped and thankful, for once, for her bonnet. When she reached Lucas, who had been waiting for her by the fountain, he looked at her with alarm.

"God in Heaven, Kitten — are you well?"

"I'm very well, Lucas, but must return home at once."

Thankfully, he did not argue, though he looked displeased by her lack of explanation. As they made their way home, Katherine fought to regain her composure, her body a vicious tangle of nerves and hope and joy and fear — fear that Rebecca would reject Rosaline's gift, and everything it might bring.

Now, she had only to wait. And in the meantime, to write.

❦ 34 ❦

Rebecca appeared at the drawing room not long after midnight, when a gentle rainfall had begun to kiss the darkened windows. Katherine stood up at once, gripping her own hands to keep from reaching for her. She did not want to presume, to impose—

"Well?" Rebecca closed the window behind her, shaking off the rain that clung to her tricorn. "What news?"

"Come here," said Katherine, gesturing to the table. "I think it is best if you see the numbers yourself."

Once Rebecca was seated, a cloud descended across her expression. "Rosaline found fault in our plan?"

"Yes. But more importantly—" Katherine pushed Rosaline's note towards Rebecca. "She has offered us a most generous gift."

Rebecca read the note, and her expression changed at once, though she went a bit gray. "What on earth does this mean?"

"If we wed Mr. Heath and Lord Oswalt," said Katherine, her heart beating a tattoo against her ribs, "Rosaline has promised me a wedding gift. She has done some research—" Here, she indicated the lists of property figures— "And determined that, with such a sum of money, we would be able to purchase our own private property, separate from our husbands' estates."

Rebecca stared at her. "*What?*"

"I know it is not what you envisioned." Katherine gulped, trying to steady her nerves. "But if we had our own property, we need not be dependent upon Mr. Heath and Lord Oswalt for much, and we might live together, alone. We would have our own space, Rebecca, our own home, without having to forfeit our families, our reputations."

Still, Rebecca just stared at her, her mouth parted with shock.

"We could find a place that is secluded," Katherine went on. "As isolated as you might like. Somewhere close to the water, perhaps. Anywhere... anywhere you would wish." She looked into Rebecca's eyes, and fought a well of emotion. "I agree with you, Rebecca. I want nothing more than for us to live as we are, and as we please. But I do not think I am ready to forfeit my brothers, or to cast them into infamy." She reached for Rebecca's hand, and clung to it. "I understand that you do not wish to be wed to a man, even if it is just in name. But I beg you to consider the multitude of options we would have, if we would make this one sacrifice. Let me marry Mr. Heath, so that I might have you."

Rebecca took a deep, trembling breath, and blinked at the figures before her. "I— I— It is a lot to take in."

"I know." Katherine squeezed her hand. "If you need time—"

"Yes." Rebecca looked back up at her, her eyes glittering, her expression resolute. "Yes, Katherine. Let's marry the men, and make the most of it."

Elation, bursting like champagne in Katherine's stomach. "Really?"

"Yes." Rebecca leaned in and kissed her, fierce and burning. She cupped the back of Katherine's head, brushed a kiss to her cheek. "It was selfish of me to ask you in the first place, Katherine. Your family, your brothers — they mean more to me, in some ways, than my own family. I did not consider the loss we might incur, and I—" Her voice broke. "I think you and I might be quite happy with what we can make for ourselves."

"We will." A quiver shook Katherine's voice, and she clung to Rebecca, to her future— "We will, Rebecca. And if we *had* to marry two gentlemen..." She managed a weak laugh. "I would say we could have done a lot worse."

"Indeed!" Rebecca chuckled as well, and they kissed again, and again, their faces burning, their hands searching, reaching—

Katherine broke away with a gasp, her face tingling. "We must — we must write to the gentlemen at once, so we may tell our families tomorrow morning—"

Rebecca grinned. "Your mother will explode."

"Don't remind me."

Rebecca reached for Katherine's quill, and the ink. "Let me." Her voice was a purr, and she nosed Katherine's cheek. "Lest Lord Oswalt think me too pleased."

And as she began to write the notes, Katherine watched her, adoring the delicate line of her face, the warm surety of her gaze. "In another lifetime," she said, before she could stop herself, "would you meet me at the altar?"

Rebecca hummed. "In another lifetime, I would have carried you to the altar long ago."

❧

"KATHERINE." MRS. KNIGHT'S EYES GLIMMERED WITH UNSHED tears, and she put one hand to her chest; the other was fixed upon Mr. Knight's knee with surprising strength. "Please tell me you are serious."

"Of course I am serious, Mother!" Katherine could not hold back a laugh. "Why on earth would I jest about such a thing?"

"Oh, how wonderful!" Mrs. Knight clapped her hands together; Mr. Knight frowned. "Oh, I am so thrilled— so *relieved*—"

"Hear that, Kat?" Thomas smirked. "Mother had such faith in your prospects."

"It seems very quick," said Mr. Knight. "Mr. Heath just returned to London — how can you possibly know you wish to marry him?"

"August was very clear in his intentions, Father," said Lucas. "Besides, he is hardly a stranger. He and Kat have known each other for years."

"But not well." Mr. Knight continued to frown at his daughter. Katherine met his scrutiny, fighting the urge to squirm. "How can you have the measure of his character, his merits? His temperament?"

"I know August very well." Lucas spoke with an undeniable authority. "I would not have encouraged the match had I thought him to be anything less than worthy."

Katherine looked at him, a touch surprised. Lucas smiled at her in return, and she felt, again, as if she could hardly recognize him. Gone was the boy who had come home with bruised ribs and a blackened eye; in his place was a gentleman, with a determined and steady gaze.

"We must have him to tea," Mrs. Knight said, practically vibrating in her enthusiasm. "Today, if possible. And we must begin plans for the wedding—"

"You are happy, Kat?" Mr. Knight continued to peer at her, as if looking for some hint, some telltale sign of unease. "With Mr. Heath?"

"Of course." Katherine's smile did not waver. "Thrilled."

"Please tell me we can have new sets of tails for the wedding," said Brandon, looking at his parents. "Mine are hopeless."

"Bran!" Mrs. Knight flashed her son a pointed look. "Congratulate your sister!"

"Oh, yes. Congratulations, Kat."

"This will be an absolute nightmare," said Thomas, "once Aunt Linda finds out."

"I think," said Mr. Knight, "that I ought to have a conversation with Mr. Heath, before we make any suppositions. After all, there are matters that require discussion, before we can take the match as a given."

"Oh, hush, Richard." Mrs. Knight leapt to her feet, manic with glee. "I shall have Graves personally deliver the invitation to Mr. Heath, and ready Mr. Salk for our visitor."

"Edwina," said Mr. Knight, a little pained. "There is no need—"

What then followed was a most delightful chaos. Katherine watched all of it as if from a great distance; her mother was all too happy to take charge. Graves soon returned with Mr. Heath's enthusiastic acceptance of their invitation, and Mrs. Knight all but levitated. Katherine could hear Mr. Salk's enraged protest from the kitchens below, until she was whisked off to be shoved into a different dress, have her hair freshly pinned, and—

"Good Lord." Katherine made eye contact with Rita in the mirror. Rita held it, then rolled her eyes. "Am I an ugly duckling that must be made into a swan?"

Thomas and Brandon, once they saw her again, snorted and laughed. "Be quiet," said Lucas, though he was fighting off a grin. The boys, too, had been shoved into neatly-pressed jackets and trousers. Katherine also suspected that someone had taken a comb to Thomas' hair. "She looks lovely," Lucas went on, pointedly. "Like a true bride-to-be."

His brothers winced. "Ugh!" said Brandon. "What a horrible thing to say!"

"It is a rather depressing thought," said Thomas. "That we are to lose the best shot in the family to something so dull as matrimony."

"And you know that Mother will set her sights on us once Kat is out of the house," said Brandon. "It will be torture, to say the least."

Together, over the course of the afternoon, they watched Mrs.

Knight's storm unfold. Graves, Rita, and Sally all descended upon the drawing room to buff it free of all dust, shadows, and hints of impropriety. Soon after, the dining room was subjected to a similar treatment, and Katherine began to worry that she would not recognize her own home. But perhaps that was rather a small concern, in the face of her father's impending audience with Mr. Heath.

Once he arrived, Mr. Heath was all smiles and politeness. His eyes gleamed with genuine pleasure as he kissed Katherine's hand and bowed to her parents. Mrs. Knight melted, though Mr. Knight was unimpressed. He quickly whisked Mr. Heath upstairs to his office, much to Mrs. Knight's displeasure.

Katherine, her mother, and her brothers were left to wait in the drawing room. "It is a bit ridiculous," said Katherine. "That I am not involved in discussions of my own finances."

"Hush, poppet," said Mrs. Knight, stabbing at her embroidery. "Your father will ensure that matters are handled with the utmost care."

"I must admit," said Thomas, from where he lolled in an armchair, "I did not expect courtship to involve so much damned waiting."

A year seemed to pass before Mr. Heath and Mr. Knight reappeared — Mr. Heath smiling, and Mr. Knight... well. Wearing an expression of reluctant approval.

"Congratulations, Kat," said Mr. Knight, gruffly. "I hope you and Mr. Heath will be very happy with one another."

Katherine heard none of her mother's delight, none of her brothers' grumbling — her stomach swooped, dropped, then lifted, and all she could do was beam at August, triumph rich in every part of her body — it was happening, it was real — she would be married, and would spend her life with Rebecca—

August took her hands, his touch sincere and warm, and leaned in, brushing a kiss to her cheek. It was the smallest, most chaste of touches, but still it felt strange. Katherine forced herself not to fight the blush that rose in its stead. She smiled at August, and felt him squeeze her hands in return.

You see? his touch seemed to say. *We have won.*

⸙

KATHERINE PUSHED THROUGH A SET OF DOUBLE DOORS, HER feet throbbing, and stopped short when she saw the figure standing at the window. "There you are!" She walked over to Rebecca, reaching for her. "God in Heaven, I feel as if I have been searching for an age."

Rebecca smirked, slipping her hands around Katherine's waist. "This house is rather a labyrinth. Had I known, I would have suggested we meet in the garden, to spare us the staircases."

Katherine kissed her cheek, accepted a kiss at her temple in return. "Where is Lord Oswalt?"

"Searching for a decent bottle of wine."

"Your parents must be thrilled."

"They are so blinded by his wealth, he could probably dance nude in their drawing room and they would hardly notice." Rebecca's smirk deepened. "And where is yours?"

"Coming presently. He wanted to bring us a plate of *hors d'oeuvres.*"

"Mr. Heath endears himself to me more and more each day." Rebecca nosed at Katherine's bare collarbone, making her shiver. "I saw him dancing with Rosaline."

"He wanted to thank her personally. For aiding us in the manner that she did."

Rebecca shook her head, as if in surprise. "He is a gentleman through and through."

Katherine lowered her voice. "I, too, wonder at the match between him and Lord Oswalt. Almost daily."

"There must be more to it than what we can see. Perhaps Lord Oswalt is not so terrible as he seems, or Mr. Heath not so lovely.

Or, better yet, perhaps there is nothing more to it, and they love one another as they are." Rebecca's smirk grew. "I wonder which of them takes it up the—"

"*Rebecca.*"

"Don't act as if you have not thought about it yourself."

"Beast." Katherine kissed her cheek. Two floors below them, the Black and White Ball was in full swing; Katherine could hear music, laughter, toasts, the tinkle of cutlery and fine glassware. But she had grown weary of the season — she had patience for little else, now that her future with Rebecca was well within sight. "How fares your mother?"

"Well indeed." Rebecca snorted. "She is happiest when she is planning a wedding. Pity that this will be her last, until her grand-daughter finds a suitor."

"Have your sisters decided whether to come to the wedding?"

"Yes, they will both attend, with their husbands in tow. Apparently, Gertrude finds it quite amusing that all three of us have ended up with Englishmen. She imagined that I would run off with some Ottoman or lost French prince."

Katherine smiled. "I wish I could come to your wedding, so that I might spend more time with Gertrude."

"You shall have plenty of opportunities in the future. I imagine she and her delightful Lord Cawdor will insist upon visiting me and Lord Oswalt."

And a part of Katherine thrilled to hear it, this reminder of the life she and Rebecca had ahead of them.

The preparations for Katherine's wedding were in full force as well. She was all too content to let her mother take the lead, bolstered by the aid of her enthusiastic aunts. Mr. Heath, bless him, had the patience of a saint (unlike Katherine's brothers), and put up with demand after demand, question after question. Katherine grinned at the thought of Lord Oswalt under such a deluge; Rebecca was quite relieved that he had shown no interest in their wedding at all.

A few days prior, Mr. Heath had taken Lucas and Katherine to visit his father, who was house- and bed-bound. The elder Mr. Heath had been yellowed and withered beneath his thick piles of bedding, but there was an undeniable spark in his eye. Katherine had taken his hand and spoken with him about the novels he liked best, and which parks offered the best views in London. Together, they had passed a very peaceful hour, and August had had to clear his throat and excuse himself after his father pressed a kiss to Katherine's hand and pronounced her lovely.

It was a little strange, the friendship Katherine had begun to form with August. But she would not have ruined or traded it for anything.

On the ground floor, the song reached its end, and Katherine was surprised when the music did not start up again. Then, she heard a great crowd moving through the house — raised voices, laughter, and she guessed that the Marchioness Camden was doing what she had promised; taking the guests on a tour of the garden. Katherine could hear conversation, laughter, the thunder of feet, the crash of the front doors — and then a stunning silence, quickly broken by raised voices.

Something was wrong.

She caught Rebecca's gaze, only to find Rebecca frowning at her. "We best see what happened," said Rebecca, then led Katherine out of the room, down the hall, and down the main staircase. As they approached the ground floor, Katherine could see people hurrying to the front of the building, trading furious whispers. "*The Duke—*" she heard. "*The Duke and that woman—*"

Ears burning, Katherine hastened to the foot of the stairs, where she was met by August, plate of *hors d'oeuvres* in his hand. Lucas and Thomas were right behind him, confusion written across their faces.

The guests had packed the front hall. Katherine could see nothing, hear nothing, save for the furious cloud of gasps and whispers. "What on earth happened?" she asked the gentlemen.

"It is the Duke and Miss Bailey," said August, and he nodded at Katherine's shocked expression. "Yes, it seems that the Duke of St. Alban's has returned, and in a most dramatic manner. He and Miss Bailey were caught in... shall we say, a compromising attitude, at the front of the house." He gave a genteel cough, as if to spare Katherine and Rebecca of the implication. "But it seems there is nothing to worry about — they are engaged."

"Engaged?!" Katherine all but shrieked, her body flooding hot and cold. "What?!"

August stared at her, taken aback by her reaction; from behind him, Lucas and Thomas shot her warning looks. "You are surprised? I thought — Katherine, are you not close with Miss Bailey?"

"Very close." Her heart thudded, and she gulped, trying to steady herself. "She has mentioned nothing— *nothing*— Where is Charlotte?"

"Out front," replied August, gesturing to the entrance. "With Miss Bailey."

"I must speak to her at once—"

Katherine plunged into the crowd, her brothers and Rebecca but one foot behind her. She pushed past ladies and gentlemen, caring little who she stepped on, who she elbowed — she had to know the truth, had to find out—

There was no conceivable— The Duke and Rosaline — *engaged?*

What of McGrath? He had seemed very keen on Rosaline, and the same could be said of Rosaline. Was the Duke aware of their flirtation? Was this engagement perhaps a reaction, a determination to stake some sort of claim upon Rosaline?

But all these questions faded as soon as Katherine pushed to the front of the crowd, and saw the front drive. Empty, devoid of either the Duke, Rosaline, Charlotte, or Cadogan.

"Where are they?" she found herself saying, looking around for some familiar face. "They cannot have vanished—"

"They left just a moment ago," a gentleman to her right told her. "It seems that Miss Bailey was injured, and required medical attention."

"Injured?" Katherine repeated, just as Thomas caught up with her. She grabbed him, pulling him to one side. "Apparently, we have missed the greatest scandal of the entire season."

"I know." His voice and his expression were grim. "We shall have to listen diligently for the remainder of the evening."

"I cannot shake the feeling that something is amiss, Thomas." Katherine frowned, her mind whirring as she sifted through her last few conversations with Rosaline. "An injury? A proposal? It all seems very rushed, and strange. Charlotte's engagement to Cadogan was formally announced prior to their first shared appearance in public, and Rosaline's father... No, something is wrong."

But they could not discuss it further; August appeared, Rebecca and Lucas in tow. Katherine shook her head at them, and resigned herself to an evening full of whispers.

❄ 35 ❄

Perhaps Katherine should have expected it, then, when the Duke and Rosaline's engagement seemed to do nothing apart from crumble.

"But their behavior adheres to no discernible logic," Katherine argued, watching Lucas toss one of his mauled pillows into the air. "They love one another — I am certain of it."

"And this is why you had me test Miss Bailey's fidelity earlier?" Lucas shot her a coy smirk. "Safe to say, she passed with flying colors."

"Or," said Thomas, pointedly, "she has a functioning mind between her ears and did not fall prey to your saccharine charm."

"You wound me, brother. I will say — Miss Bailey can handle her drink, and her sword." Lucas caught his pillow, which earlier that day had played the part of Bonaparte's chest, and gave it a thoughtful look. "Perhaps I missed an opportunity, this season."

"And perhaps you should focus less on Miss Bailey's match," said Thomas to Katherine, "and more on your own."

She sniffed. "Mother has the wedding planned to within an inch of its life. As of this afternoon, the dresses have all been pinned and fitted, and little else remains, save for the day itself. What have I to concern myself with?"

"It is so strange," said Brandon, shaking his head, "that you as well as Rebecca are to be wed. And on the same day!"

Katherine did not blush when she said, "Such is the way of the world, Bran. Women are born to be married, and mornings were invented for the sake of the wedding breakfast."

"I am quite thrilled that Mother forced you to agree to a proper send-off," said Lucas, smirking again. "Rather than some stuffy eggs in some stuffy room with some stuffy priest."

What a reminder. Unlike her brothers, Katherine was dreading her wedding reception. Her aunts and cousins would be on full display, and likely on their worst behavior. And all Brandon cared about was her wedding cake, which promised to be one hell of a confection, or possibly the unraveling of Mr. Salk's sanity.

"I do worry that we cannot afford the festivities," Katherine said, glancing around at her brothers. "Even with Aunt Linda's generosity."

"Never you mind," said Lucas, and there was something odd, something soft, in his voice. "Yours is the first wedding in the family."

Thomas snorted. "And likely the last."

"And," said Lucas, ignoring him, "it deserves to be properly celebrated."

Katherine raised her eyebrow. "Is that sentiment I detect?"

"Not even a little."

❧

When the fateful day arrived, the Duke and Rosaline's engagement seemed to be on steadier ground, and Katherine had to summon all of her courage to turn and face her reflection in the mirror.

Mrs. Knight let out a low gasp, dabbing at her eyes. "Oh, Kat. You look so wonderful."

Katherine swallowed, her throat thick with too many emotions to name. One of them — dread — did not show any signs of fading, in spite of her conviction that she had made the right choice. Her whole body throbbed with the desire to be with Rebecca, to be near her — but they would not see one another until the following day, after the wedding festivities had ended.

So, she forced a smile, and the unrecognizable figure in her mirror smiled in return. "Thank you, Mother. You are very kind."

"I am so thrilled for you." Mrs. Knight took Katherine's hand and kissed it, her face shining with genuine joy. "You have found such a wonderful husband, and you will be so happy."

"I hope so, Mother." Katherine studiously avoided Rita's raised eyebrow, and glanced around her bare bedroom. All of her belongings had been packed away, and most of them shipped off to Mr. Heath's new country home. What little remained, along with Katherine's *trousseau*, would accompany her to Brighton, for the honeymoon.

It was strange to see her bedroom so empty. Yet another swoop of emotion rolled through Katherine's stomach, and she tried to swallow it. One could not feel homesick before they had even left home.

Her father, once he saw her, fared little better than Mrs. Knight. Mr. Knight blinked several times, and took an unsteady breath. "Well," he rumbled, offering Katherine his elbow, "well, I suppose this is it."

Katherine smiled at him, pressed a kiss to his cheek. "It is not as if I am going to war, Father. I shall see you at Christmas."

His face twisted, just for a moment, then he cleared his throat and turned towards the front door. "Come along, dear. Straight into the lion's mouth."

The journey between their home and the church was little more than a blur. By the time Katherine made her way to the side chamber, where she was blissfully alone, she had to suck in several lungfuls of air, attempting to ground herself in the reality of the moment.

This was her wedding day. She was getting married.

A knock at the door, then Lucas poked his head in. "Father said you wanted to see me?"

"Yes." Katherine waited for him to enter and close the door behind him, wishing that she could have taken a seat. But no, that would have wrinkled her gown.

His brow furrowed. "Is everything—?"

"Everything is quite well, Lucas." She managed a smile. "I am not about to leg it out of the window. But I am about to ask you for a favor, and that you do not question its provenance."

"Very well," he said, wariness evident in every line of his body. "What is it?"

Katherine took one breath, then another, and handed him a slip of paper. *My last secret note*, she thought, almost derisive, almost melancholy. "If you follow these instructions, you will find a sum of money hidden beneath the floorboards in my bedroom. I want you to take that money, and make enquiries about a property in Devon. A cottage, ideally, not far from the water, perhaps with its own dock. I wish to keep this purchase separate from my husband-to-be's estate," she went on, ignoring Lucas' look of utter surprise, "and Mr. Heath is aware of my intentions. He approves of this measure, even encourages it."

"A cottage," Lucas repeated, unfolding the slip of paper and scanning the instructions. "In Devon?"

She nodded. "Not too far from Mr. Heath's property, if possible. Near or far from a village — I care little about that. But it must be close to the water. I long for the sea air," she quickly added.

"And August..." Lucas looked at her. "August would reside with you?"

"If he pleases. But I wanted to have a space of my own, Lucas, for when he travels. I hate the idea of sitting alone in that country house, and journeying to Mosswood for the space of a week or a fortnight is simply impractical, as much as I—" The words caught in her throat, and her eyes welled with a mixture of joy and sorrow. "As much as I might wish—"

"Oh, Kat." Lucas closed the distance between them and wrapped her up in his arms; Katherine pressed her cheek to his chest. She could hear the steady beat of his heart through the fine fabric of his new tailcoat, and she forced herself to keep breathing, to blink away the tears that threatened to break free.

She could not remember the last time Lucas had embraced her like this. When she was very young, perhaps, or after her first hunt.

"Promise me that you are doing this," he said, his voice low, hushed, "because you want it for yourself. And not for the sake of our family."

Katherine swallowed a sob that was equal parts grief and relief. Thank God, that she had a brother who knew her so well. "Of course, Lucas. Mr. Heath is a wonderful man, and I know I will be very happy with him."

Lucas held her for another moment, then stepped away. Every part of his expression told her that he did not quite believe her, but he nodded, then smiled.

"I shall do everything in my power to ensure that you have your cottage when you return from Brighton." He slipped her note into his breast pocket, then offered her his elbow. "Now, shall I take you to Father before he calls off the entire occasion?"

A laugh bubbled free before Katherine could stop it, and she nodded, squeezing his arm. "Yes, please. At the very least, we need to ensure that Bran and Tom do not fall asleep at the altar."

And with that, Lucas led her out of the chamber and into the vestibule, and into her future.

KATHERINE WOKE THE NEXT MORNING IN A NEW, UNKNOWN bed and looked up at a new, unfamiliar ceiling. She yawned widely, stretched her aching limbs, and marveled that her headache was not worse.

August's London house — where he lived with his father — was a lovely, newer build with plain fixtures and casual trimmings. Katherine admired the simple elegance of it, and the fact that it never seemed to be up to its own tricks. Her personal chambers were of a generous size, and contained new furniture, a large bed, and a view of the minuscule, though quaint, garden.

And, to her delight, a wide, elegant desk sat just beside the windows.

"Its twin resides in the country house," August had said to her with a smile. "Rebecca told me how you love to write, and I could think of no better gift. You can take one of them with you, of course, to your cottage, if you'd like."

Katherine was very fortunate, she knew, to have a husband like August Heath.

Husband. What an odd word — stranger still that it was a word she could use now, in reference to an actual person in her life. Katherine raised her left hand above the sheets, looking at the gold ring sitting on her fourth finger, and felt a swoop in her gut.

It was a ring, yes, but not from August. It was from Rebecca. Just as Rebecca now wore a matching one, and August wore a ring from Lord Oswalt.

The previous night had ended shortly after dawn; Katherine had a vague memory of Lucas pouring her into the carriage, August swaying in after her. Then clinging to August to keep both of them from falling onto the floor in a dead sleep. Some of the details of the reception remained quite distant and fuzzy, but Katherine could recall the music, the dancing, Brandon nearly weeping over the cake, and Thomas besting several of the gentlemen at some sort of drinking game. Her mother holding court, glowing and laughing and radiant, Mr. Knight standing beside her, almost smiling.

For Mrs. Knight, the entire evening had been nothing short of a dream come true. And Katherine could admit that she had enjoyed herself, in spite of the pressure, the attention, the ceaseless noise and celebration.

Except for one moment. That one, fateful moment before the cake had been cut.

But there was nothing she could do about it now. The dominoes had fallen, and Katherine was inclined to let them lie.

It was difficult to worry, in the growing light of a new day. A day full of promise, and the first step in their journey towards Brighton.

August kept a very small staff — he hated being waited on, which was apparently a point of contention with his dear Lord Oswalt. Katherine, who had refused to let Rita leave Mrs. Knight's service, began her morning toilet alone, then dressed herself.

It was one of her new dresses. A plain but pretty muslin in a delicate green that fastened at the front. Katherine smiled at her reflection, carefully pinning her hair back, and felt an undeniable bubble of excitement.

The house was still quiet, awakening slowly in the fresh light of the summer day. Katherine found a simple cold breakfast laid out in the drawing room, along with a fresh pot of tea. She buttered a scone, poured a cup of tea, waited a few minutes, then went back down the hall.

August's chambers were directly across from her own, and when she put her ear to his door, she heard nothing. Smirking, she knocked loudly, and received a groan in response.

"My lord," she called out, putting on a funny voice, "it appears that you have overindulged."

"Katherine, please. Be quiet."

Grinning, she leaned against the wall, taking another bite of her scone. "Our guests will be arriving within the hour. Wouldn't you like to be washed and dressed when they do?"

Incoherent mumbling, but then the encouraging thud of someone getting out of bed.

"I shall see you shortly." Katherine made her way back to the drawing room.

As she ate her fill of pastries and cold ham, she wandered about the room, looking out the windows at the street below. Lambeth was a charming area; she could see the edge of the river, and the street was alive with traffic, merchants, and laborers. This house was quite new, and Rita had told her that Lambeth was rapidly expanding, building to suit the whims of wealthy merchants and industrialists. An elegant little park shone a merry emerald around the corner; Katherine watched a group of children playing in the shade of a generous tree, a spaniel barking at their heels, and felt a strange but sudden sense of peace.

In the corner of the room was a harpsichord. A lovely little instrument, hand-painted with flowers and the occasional nymph. August was a dedicated player, she knew, and had an adept hand for nearly any instrument that crossed his path. The rest of the room was dotted with books, atlases, and little curios from his travels. Everywhere she looked, she saw shades of his character, his interests, and she began to wonder what echoes she might leave on the space.

August surfaced a while later, dressed in a simple shirt, waistcoat, and trousers. He was very pale, a little green around the gills, and moved with all the speed of a snail.

"Good morning." Katherine smirked at him.

"Good morning, Kat." August winced as he made a cup of tea. He shrank away from the sunlight, and sat down at the nearest table.

"Would you like a scone?"

August winced again, hunching over his teacup. "Perhaps... later."

It was almost an hour before there came the sound of the front door, then muted voices. Katherine sat up, excitement jolting through her, and when the butler knocked at the drawing room door, she could hardly contain herself as she said, "Yes?"

The door opened, and Helier, their butler, stepped in. "The Lord and Lady Oswalt, Miss Katherine."

A wide grin broke across Katherine's face, and she nodded.

Helier stepped aside, and there they were.

Lord Oswalt and Rebecca came into the room, looking much the same as August. Rebecca was dressed in elegant yellow silk, Lord Oswalt in a blue suit with a yellow cravat that matched Rebecca's gown. Katherine drank in the sight of Rebecca. It had been but two days since they had last seen each other — they had stolen a delicious hour together the night before their weddings — but it felt like a year.

"Good morning," said August, and received a few mumbled replies.

Rebecca was pale, shaken, and as soon as Helier left, she bent over the back of the sofa and let out a groan. Lord Oswalt, meanwhile, leaned against the wall and took several deep breaths.

Katherine grinned at them. "A good party, was it?" She stood up and went over to Rebecca, putting an arm around her waist.

Rebecca leaned into the touch, sighing. "The party was nothing, dearest, compared to what happened afterwards."

"I still maintain," said Lord Oswalt, his voice deep and ragged, "that I won."

"You did nothing of the sort," said Rebecca, lifting her head to scowl at him. She caught Katherine's eye and said, "When we arrived home last night, Lord Oswalt claimed that he could out-drink any sailor in the British navy."

"Oh." Katherine's eyes widened, and she put a hand to her mouth to stifle a giggle.

"And I, naturally..." Rebecca straightened up, wincing. "Could not let that abide."

August gave a soft snort and began pouring them cups of tea. "It is a wonder that you are awake at all, let alone vertical."

"Must we leave today?" Rebecca said to Katherine. "Can we not put it off for a day, or—"

"A week?" grunted Lord Oswalt, his eyes closed.

"Afraid not," said August grimly. "My time away from the office is quite set in stone."

"In that case," said Lord Oswalt, heaving himself away from the wall. "I shall ring for Helier. We need tonic water, tomato juice, raw eggs, and whiskey."

"God in Heaven, to do what?" said Katherine.

"To drink, my pet." Lord Oswalt shot her a humorless smile, and pushed a button hidden behind the sideboard. "It is our only hope."

"I suppose I will take what I can get," said Rebecca, looking rather green again. She closed her eyes and pressed her forehead to Katherine's cheek. "If I have to sit in a carriage for six hours."

Once the ingredients were ordered, August and Lord Oswalt lingered by the breakfast, and Rebecca leaned away, looking at Katherine. "Did you have a good evening?"

Katherine nodded, rubbing more circles into her back. "We can discuss it later, but I daresay that Madam Kensington will give a very favorable report."

Finally, a smile. "I am sure she will. How does Thomas feel about taking the helm for the remainder of the season?"

"He rolls his eyes and complains, but I think he is quite excited. I left him a few snippets and quotes, if he needs inspiration."

Rebecca snorted. "With the Star and Sapphire getting married on the same day, he will have no shortage of material."

This was as good a time as any. "Speaking of our precious gems," said Katherine, dropping her voice. "I believe that last night, at the reception, they figured out that you were my beloved."

For a long moment, Rebecca just watched her, then frowned. "How did that happen?"

"One of my damned aunts mentioned your wedding to Lord Oswalt. As soon as Rosaline and Charlotte heard his name, they realized the truth."

"And was it obvious?"

Katherine thought back to the way Charlotte had choked on her wine, loud enough to turn heads across the entire room, before Rosaline spirited her away. "Only to me," she said. "They said nothing to anyone, as far as I know."

Another few moments passed, and Katherine felt as though she could see the thoughts turning through Rebecca's head. "I am not worried," she finally said. "I trust them."

Katherine squeezed her hand. "You do?"

Rebecca nodded. "Of course. After all, without them..." She looked at Lord Oswalt and August, who were speaking in hushed tones to one another, their expressions soft in the midday light. "We would not be here."

"No," Katherine agreed, emotions tangling in her throat. She brushed a kiss to Rebecca's cheek, and put an arm around her waist. She could hardly believe that they were here, together, standing at the helm of their new life together. "We owe them more than we can ever repay."

Rebecca smiled at her, small and warm, and Katherine drank it in, feeling as though she would overflow with this moment, with their future.

"Yes," said Rebecca, grinning, arms akimbo, looking out on the wide, empty beach. "This will do quite nicely."

Katherine grinned back at her, wiggling her bare toes into the warm, silky sand. Behind her, the waves crashed into shore, a ceaseless, hushed sound that she was still becoming accustomed to hearing. She could hardly wait for their first night together, to fall asleep with the gentle push and pull of the ocean in the air.

Their weeks in Brighton had been diverting and full of amusement, but a touch strained by the necessity of maintaining the appearance of their marriages. Katherine and Rebecca had had to share many a night with their spouses, but thankfully never the same bed. According to Rebecca, Lord Oswalt had a deep and treacherous snore, and it was a miracle that she had not smothered him with his own pillow.

They had attended a few gatherings and balls in Brighton, of course, necessitated by the newfound status of Lord and Lady Oswalt. Rebecca wore her new title well, and with a tangible pride — she had pleased her parents, and saved herself another season of unbearable courtship. She was fulfilling the role she had been bred for, and a part of Katherine thrilled to watch it play out before her.

And there was something delicious about it, about calling Rebecca 'Lady Oswalt.' Now, Katherine shivered at the thought of a night they'd stolen together in Brighton, when Lady Oswalt had ordered her to her knees and made her wait.

Yes. Safe to say that she quite enjoyed Rebecca's newfound title.

Upon their return, Lucas had met Katherine at August's country home with a ready grin and a wide hug. He'd handed her the deed and the map of her new property — he'd had to purchase it in his own name, but he'd left it separate from the rest of the Knight family accounts. The little cottage was only a few hours away from the country house, sat on the water, and came with its own dock.

"It is a charming place," Lucas had told her. "I think it will suit you very well, dear sister."

Another two days had passed before Rebecca arrived, ready to accompany Katherine to the shore. Lord Oswalt had arrived with her, but left an hour later with August. Together, they would be traveling north for business, and Lord Oswalt under the guise of shopping for a hunting chateau. One glance at the pair of them told Katherine how desperate they were to be alone together, and she could not blame them.

After all, she felt much the same way, especially once she saw Rebecca clad in her new attire. A fresh pair of breeches, and a shirt with her initials embroidered on the pocket.

"A wedding gift from Lord Oswalt," Rebecca had told her before they left. She'd nodded at Katherine's shocked expression and frowned down at her own sleeves. "I am beginning to suspect that he is kinder than he lets on, which is rather disappointing."

The carriage ride to the cottage had been a short one, and once they'd arrived at the small, quiet piece of land on the shore,

Katherine's breath had caught, hardly able to believe that this was happening, that this was her future.

White-washed, stately, and brimming with light, the cottage faced west and had an admirable little back garden. Roughly space for them to grow a few vegetables, keep a flock of chickens, perhaps even plant a tree or two. Katherine had returned from Brighton with a large pile of books — volumes on gardening, housekeeping, cooking. She and Rebecca were determined to be self-sufficient, and thankfully, Katherine's will, along with her rifle, would go a long way in helping them.

But it was difficult to think of such practical matters, here in the delicious sun, with the spray of salt and rosemary in her nose.

"Well?" Rebecca came closer, her smile as brilliant as the sky. "Shall we go down to the water?"

"Certainly, but—" Katherine looked down at herself. "Shouldn't I change, first?"

Something hot swept through Rebecca's gaze, and she stepped closer, her hands going to the front ties of Katherine's dress. "No."

She undid the simple knot, and eased Katherine's gown off her body. Katherine, mute with surprise, could only stand there as Rebecca kissed her cheek and did the same thing to her petticoat. She was left standing in her chemise and her pantalettes. The ocean breeze wafted over her skin; it was not cold, but Katherine shivered, unable to deny the way her body stirred, coming to life.

Rebecca hummed, her gaze dipping over Katherine's figure. Her hand slid up Katherine's belly, along her waist, and cupped her breast. Rebecca's thumb worked in a slow, languid circle, worrying what was already standing at attention, and Katherine could not help the way she shivered anew.

"Later," said Rebecca, low in her throat, "I shall make the most delicious mess of you. But first, dear Katherine, we must begin the inevitable." She stepped away, took Katherine's hand, and drew her towards the ocean.

Neither of them spoke as they stepped into the water. Rebecca grinned; Katherine gasped, surprised by the warmth. She had expected the water to be freezing, but it felt like a cooling bath, and she smiled as they waded further and further in, the sand a delicious squeeze between her toes.

Waves, salt, a delicate spray across her face. Rebecca pulled her further into the water. The waves splashed over their hips, up to their chests. But the water was delicate, easing around Katherine's body, touching every part of her. Seeping into her skin, her mind. A wave crested against her stomach, splashing into her mouth, and she swallowed it, relishing the taste.

She looked at Rebecca, and saw all her joy, all her love, all her adoration, reflected back at her. Everything they were, everything they had said and would ever say, pooled around them, swirling like an ocean of its own. A release, a promise. A sanctity and a home.

Katherine tilted her face up to the sky, her eyes sliding shut, and was free.

ACKNOWLEDGMENTS

Thank you to my beta readers, B., B., and D. If it weren't for you, this story wouldn't exist. I owe you infinitely many cookies.

Endless gratitude to Mya Saracho for bringing Katherine and Rebecca to life.

Thank you to Jennifer Shore, for her steadfast support and advice.

Thank you to everyone who has supported my writing, both published and unpublished, whether it be through kudos, comments, DMs, or mood-boards. I don't have the words to express what it means to me.

Thank you to my family for your unwavering support over the years, and for keeping me fed and watered.

The next installment of this series will feature Lord Martel's love story. Follow me on social media for all the updates on its release.

ABOUT THE AUTHOR

E.B. Neal lives in Cincinnati, Ohio. This is her second book.

You can find more about E.B. Neal at:
www.authorebneal.com

ABOUT THE COVER ARTIST

Mya Saracho creates queered, body positive art under the name
A. LoveUnlaced. They began in various fandoms and now create a
mix of original art and fan art. They live with their spouse and a
gremlin cosplaying as a dog.

You can find more from Mya at:
https://aloveunlaced.carrd.co/